PIRATE MEETING HOUSE

SYNAGOGUE

San Madrigal

BALLAD & DAGGER

AN OUTLAW SAINTS NOVEL

BOOK 1

BY DANIEL JOSÉ OLDER

HYPERION

LOS ANGELES   NEW YORK

First Edition, May 2022
1 3 5 7 9 10 8 6 4 2
FAC-020093-22077
Printed in the United States of America

This book is set in Baskerville MT Pro/Monotype
Designed by Phil Buchanan

Library of Congress Cataloging-in-Publication Data
Names: Older, Daniel José, author.
Title: Ballad & dagger / by Daniel José Older.
Other titles: Ballad and dagger
Description: Los Angeles : Disney/Hyperion, 2022. • Series: Outlaw saints ; book 1 •
"Rick Riordan presents." • Audience: Ages 12–18. • Audience: Grades 7–9. • Summary:
When sixteen-year-old Mateo and Chela discover each other and their powers during
a political battle between neighborhood factions, they set aside their differences to
unravel the mystery behind their sunken homeland and to stop a dangerous political
operative who is trying to harness their gifts to unleash terror on the world.
Identifiers: LCCN 2021051377 • ISBN 9781368070829 (hardcover) •
ISBN 9781368070867 (ebk)
Subjects: CYAC: Magic—Fiction • Ability—Fiction. • Cuban Americans—Fiction. •
Jews—United States—Fiction. • Brooklyn (New York, N.Y.)—Fiction. • Fantasy. •
LCGFT: Fantasy fiction.
Classification: LCC PZ7.1.O45 Bal 2022 • DDC [Fic]—dc23
LC record available at https://lccn.loc.gov/2021051377

Reinforced binding
Follow @ReadRiordan
Visit www.hyperionteens.com

This one is for Tito—¡Bienvenido!

INTRODUCTION

DO YOU REMEMBER SAN MADRIGAL?

Oh, that beautiful island swallowed by the sea . . . the Atlantis of the Caribbean! The irresistible music of the kameros electrified the tropical evenings. The Grandes Fetes swirled with color and joyful chaos: dancing, singing, and drumming; gifts and prayers for the spirits. Platters overflowed with luscious seafood.

Nowhere else in the world had that particularly wonderful mix of humanity: the three "founding" groups of Sefaradim, Santeros, and pirates, and also Indigenous peoples, dispossessed European Jews, and freed West Africans. San Madrigal was a haven from persecution, slavery, and colonial rule. It wasn't perfect, no, but it was fiercely, proudly independent. A tiny jewel of a country!

And then, fifteen years ago, it disappeared beneath the waves, leaving behind only the diaspora community of Little Madrigal in Brooklyn, New York. I still ache with sorrow when I think about such a loss to the world.

Wait, you say.

You check a map. You google "San Madrigal."

Uh, Rick? San Madrigal isn't real. It never existed.

Balderdash! I say. (Because I am the kind of person who says "balderdash.")

Just because a place is fictional doesn't mean it isn't real. San Madrigal is as real as Wakanda or the Shire or Earthsea. Once you read *Ballad & Dagger*, you will see what I mean. Only the best authors can make me feel nostalgic for a place that never existed but *needs* to exist, and Daniel José Older is one of the best.

In *Ballad & Dagger* he gives us not only amazing characters, not only a compelling story, not only beautiful prose, humor, and heart (all of which come standard with every Older novel), he also gives us an entire *culture*—the heritage of a lost island we didn't know we needed until it had sunk beneath the sea. That, my friends, is powerful writing.

Like all San Madrigaleros, our hero, Mateo Matisse, is many things. He's a musician, a healer, a young man in search of his place in the world. He's also going to be your new best friend as he guides you through the wonderful world of Little Madrigal: a community infused with magic, where spirits live side by side with the living, and where the fractious, pirate-inspired democracy of San Madrigal fights to maintain its culture without its island.

But what if San Madrigal could be raised again? What kind of magic would that require? What kind of sacrifices? These are the questions Matteo Matisse will have to wrestle with in *Ballad & Dagger*, and he's going to need all his healing skills, because the fight for the soul of San Madrigal is going to open up some very old wounds.

For many years, I have aspired to work with Daniel José Older. I have read all of his books. I have been in awe of his breathtaking range. I have longed to find the largest soapbox available, stand upon it, and shout into my megaphone: *HEY, EVERYBODY, YOU NEED TO READ THIS GUY!*

I am delighted that I finally get to do this. And while any Daniel José Older novel is worth shouting about, *Ballad & Dagger* is something truly special: the first Rick Riordan Presents novel geared toward young adults. It is also, in my opinion, the most daring, ambitious, and memorable story Older has written yet, and that is saying a lot.

Rick Riordan

PART ONE

I.

With one thing the world begins . . .

A single raft in the broken sea,

Three enemies within:

A child of the book,

An outlaw of the waves,

A son of the stones.

Each thrown from their burning vessels

Amidst cataclysmic warfare,

Cursed to drift forever through a storm.

Until

Light breaks the darkness.

A glowing shroud appears,

Guides them through the early-morning mist.

Three rocky peaks seem to rise from the horizon before them.

Sanctuary.

And so begins a new life, new world, new age.

Life and Death walk hand in hand, creation and destruction.

Each being, each story, each world contains the essence of its opposite
   within.

They forever chase each other, the moon and sun, in eternal balance.

So begins the island, three peaks and a whole world born from the waves,

The journey, the storm.

With one thing, the world begins;

With one thing, the world ends.

—*Divination Manual for San Madrigal*, expanded edition, Baba Mauricio
   Batalán

I.

Con una cosa empieza el mundo . . .

Una balsa sola en el mar roto,

Tres enemigos adentro:

Un hijo del libro,

Un bandido dc las olas,

Un niño de las piedras.

Cada tirado de su propio buque quemando

En guerra cataclísmica,

Malditos a ir a la deriva en la tormenta.

Hasta

Una luz rompe la oscuridad.

Un sudario brillante aparece,

Les guia por las nieblas de la madrugada.

Hasta tres montañas de piedra que parecen crecer desde el horizonte.

Santuario.

Así empieza una vida nueva, un mundo nuevo, una edad nueva.

Vida y Muerte caminan mano en mano, la creación y destrucción.

Cada ser, cada cuento, cada mundo contiene la esencia de su oposito
   adentro.

Siempre se cazan, el sol y la luna, en balanza eterna.

Así comience la isla, tres cimas y un mundo entero nacido por las olas,

El sendero, la tempestad.

Con una cosa el mundo empieza,

Con una cosa se acaba.

—*Manual de adivinación de San Madrigal*, edición ampliada, Baba Mauricio
   Batalán

CHAPTER ONE

"¡PUÑETA!" TÍA LUCIA SNAPS AS I HEAD TO MY ROOM TO GET READY
for tonight. At first, I think it's because I'm just in a towel and dripping
all over her floor. But no, she's reading her shells—divination—and
her swear means they said something she didn't want to know.

Tía Lucia looks up and rolls her eyes. My heart sinks. She's not
coming with me tonight—it's all over her face. And here I am about
to be dressed and ready. "You go 'head, Mateo," she sighs.

"But, Tía . . ."

Tonight is the Grande Fete, the biggest night of the year for us
Galeranos, and my aunt has never missed an opportunity to carry
on, gossip, and dance the night away. Plus, she's one of the three
members of the Cabildo, our leadership council, and it'll be a whole
thing, her not showing up.

But something in those cowrie shells told her she has more
important matters to attend to. She's been divining for longer than
I've been alive, and she doesn't play around when it comes to messages from the spirits. So she shrugs. "Así es." *That's just what it is.*

Thing is: this isn't just a regular fete. Tonight, Councilwoman

Anisette Bisconte will name her successor on the Cabildo, and every-one knows it'll be Tolo Baracasa. At just eighteen, he'd be the youngest member of our leadership trinity, but he seems like he was born for it. Tolo comes from a long line of pirates and inherited the nightclub we gather in, along with all the nefarious dealings that go with it.

Yeah, yeah, politics, whatever. The *real* reason tonight matters—to me, anyway—is that because it's such an important fete, Maestro Grilo Juan Gerval is supposed to be there. It's one of those rare nights he's not off performing at concert halls across the world alongside other icons. And that means he'll hear me play keys. He might even sing! Maybe he'll realize I'm destined to bring our music to the world along with him, and he'll pull me out of high school and away from the local festivities circuit to go hit the road, and I'll just step on into the rest of my music-filled life . . . right?

What's wrong? Aunt Miriam asks Tía Lucia, shattering my fan-tasy in a voice that implies an extinction-level event is at hand (she uses this tone at least forty-five times a day). Dead people are a trip, man. Aunt Miriam has been a spirit almost as long as the sixteen years I've been alive. She must've been a wisp of a woman in life—long and slender, with aggressive cheekbones and a slight smile. Now you can just barely make out those sharp features on her translucent shroud. The harsh glare of our overhead lamps flushes right through her, only glinting slightly off the edges of her spectral form.

She and Tía Lucia and I all live in this tiny apartment off Fulton Street in Little Madrigal, a hidden-away nook at the far end of Brooklyn. It's just a couple hundred of us and a scattering of Dominicans, Puerto Ricans, and Ecuadorians who mostly mind their own business and don't mess much with all the weird politics of the people from the lost island.

You're not going, Lucia? You're already all made up and pretty!

And it's true: a colorful silky scarf conceals Tía Lucia's short bleach-blond curls. Bright purple lipstick shines from her mouth, and she's done up her cheeks with rouge. That aquamarine eyeliner is the finishing touch, and I know she spent at least an hour standing in front of her vast makeup selection, going back and forth about what color to use. She's a small, round woman, my aunt, but when she's armored up in all that regalia and paint, she seems to tower over everyone around her.

"Nada." Tía Lucia wraps up the shells and shoves a cigar in her mouth. "I'm still going, just a little later." She only lights that thing when she's super-stressed out, almost never. Otherwise she just chews on it till it's mulch and replaces it every once in a while. Gross. She turns to me. "You go ahead without me, Mateo."

Suddenly, her eyes narrow, and I realize, a second too late, that I'm still just in a towel, dripping all over her, which means an extinction-level event may now *actually* be at hand—"¿Y MI PISO, COÑO?" Tía Lucia yelps and stands up, and I scatter into my bedroom and close the door before any chancleta torpedoes can fly through it.

My folded T-shirt and jeans from earlier go in the drawer; my wet towel on the rack by the closet. Everything in its place.

I'm pulling on my suit pants—I *hate* suit pants—and fussing with my phone to pull up my get-ready music when I hear a muffled argument on the other side of the door. Aunt Miriam trying to convince Tía Lucia to go, probably, but also . . . is one of them crying?

This is none of my business.

I hit Play and lean my phone against the mirror as the video of Gerval comes to life and his voice rises over whatever's happening in the living room.

It's from a live show a few months ago. They're covering an old Galerano bolero, some murder song—all these old ditties are either about praising God, falling in love, or murdering someone (sometimes all three at once)—and the band has fallen into a fierce vamp while Gerval stands at the edge of the stage and just lets out a howl.

He's only a year or two older than me, but that howl over those jangling chords sounds like an ancient battle cry, and the crowd devours it, breathless, screaming.

On the small screen, Gerval flashes a wily grin.

And of course he's grinning: Gerval went and broke the one rule of San Madrigal's traditional musicians, the kameros: he blew up. We're supposed to be heard and not seen, you see. *Sea espíritu* is what people say to kameros before we go onstage. *Say-ah espee-ree-tu*—be like a spirit, basically, let the light pass through you. It's from an old instruction manual by one of the back-in-the-day masters, a great-great-great-grandpa of mine, in fact, Archibaldo Coraje Medina. He supposedly lost his mind and started playing creepy, nonsensical music late at night in the plaza, but before that, he was one of San Madrigal's number one kama composers. Walking around with a name like Archibaldo is probably stressful, though.

Anyway, what a legacy, right?

But I get it: our work isn't about us, it's about the music. And personally, I'm much happier vanishing into the shadows. Besides my family and my best friend, Tams, I don't really know how to talk to people. Unseen works for me.

But Gerval threw together an album of redone Galerano hits in the little music studio on Fulton, and one went viral and suddenly his face was everywhere we looked, grinning from our TV screens and phones, there onstage with some famous pop star that everyone cared about except us, touring the world.

And since he's been gone, I've been the one playing most of the weddings, bar mitzvahs, funerals, which is cool and all but . . . kind of a dead end, no pun intended.

Tonight, though . . . tonight is my chance to jump on board with Gerval and help bring our music to a wider audience. I don't want to be in the spotlight like him, just one of the guys in the band, there in the shadows, doing what I love.

I pull on my dress shirt, and it sticks to my still-damp skin, but I barely notice because here comes the part I love most: the howl swings up into a kind of siren-wail and the band jumps keys and unleashes a frenzy of tight staccato hits as Gerval works his way back down the scale. You can see him making eye contact with the drummer, bopping his head in time, and then the camera follows his gaze to a bulky, tall figure at the far end of the stage: Trucks. That's Gerval's right-hand man. He's always wearing a helmet with a visor and all kinds of heavy military gear—just walks around cosplaying a riot cop, basically—but I guess when you're an icon like Gerval, it makes sense to have someone like that constantly at your side.

Trucks and Gerval trade a nod, and then the band falls into a series of solos.

I finish buttoning my shirt, shaking my head at the way the whole moment comes together. I'm probably responsible for a good half of the eleven million views this video has on YouTube, but it still amazes me the way they move so smooth through all those changes without a word being spoken. If I had to guess, they probably didn't even rehearse that—they just *know*.

Goals, man. Goals.

Anyway, the thin line of my goatee has just today reached the thin line of my mustache, which makes today basically my bar mitzvah, and it's a fresh October night, the kind that's perfect for entire lives to change forever, so I slide one arm and then the next into my suit jacket, roll my shoulders back to get the whole thing in order, and walk out into the living room.

And the most awkward silence I've ever known.

"What's . . . uh . . . what's up?" I ask into my two aunts' inordinately blank stares.

You're not going to tell him, Lucia? Aunt Miriam demands.

"Tell me what?"

Tía Lucia waves off her deceased wife and me. "Nada. Go on.

Don't forget to salute the santos on your way out." She opens her big fleshy arms for a hug. There's no getting information out of her she doesn't want to give. Whatever's going on, she'll tell me when she's good and ready. I cross the room and lean over. It's like a cloud of Florida Water travels everywhere that woman goes, I swear. The sharp, spicy scent sizzles my nostrils as she wraps around me and then holds me at arm's length and says, "Escucha."

Of all the many words in all the different languages my aunt speaks, that's gotta be her number one favorite. *Escucha*. I could be, as I am now, staring directly at her, at full attention, completely tuned in, all ears, and she will still command me to listen. "I'm listening, Tía."

She squints at me, because we go through this constantly. Then she softens. I notice the slightest tremble in her hands. Too much of that good strong Puerto Rican coffee, maybe. Or maybe it's whatever those shells told her that has her shook, literally. "Be careful tonight, Mateo. A ver no te toquen a ti."

Predictably cryptic. *Make sure they don't pick you*, or *touch you*, or *that it's not your turn*, depending on who you ask and when. Typical tía-type messiness. She loves getting woo-woo after reading her shells. Plus, since I supposedly almost died as a baby, both my tías and my parents get a little extra precious with me sometimes. You can see it in their eyes, the sudden memory of whatever strange illness I had. No matter how much I've worked out, or how much taller I am than all of them (a lot), I just become this tiny, fragile thing again, their baby.

Still, this one sounded more ominous than usual.

"What do you mean, Tía?"

She nods at the bookshelf, where various soup tureens and vases house her spirits. "Dobale, m'ijo." *Doh-bah-ley*—it means *salute*.

And yeah, the whole setup is beautiful, don't get me wrong. She has me wrap them in colorful, silky fabrics every year on the anniversary of her initiation as a Santera (which is coming up, actually), and each is adorned with sacred implements, ceremonial blades, and tacky porcelain animals.

The three original spirits of San Madrigal—the ones that, according to myth, emerged from the ether when our island rose from the sea—glare from paintings on the wall around the altar. There's the island's namesake, Madrigal herself, majestic and radiant over the sea in her shimmering, gold-lined magenta robes. Beside her is Okanla, the Destroyer, a badass warrior woman, her face covered by chains dangling from her elaborate silver headgear, and each hand holding a machete—one large, the other shorter. And then there's Galanika, a stern and ridiculously buff older guy with a scar running down one side of his face and a frown to match it.

I'll be honest: it's been about a year since my parents and I agreed it was time for them to stop taking me along to disaster areas all over the world—in part so I could finish high school in Brooklyn—and I've been with my aunt here in Little Madrigal that whole time, but I'm still not totally used to all this spirit stuff she's got going on. Mom and Dad are doctors, science people. They love data, facts, things that can be proven. We always dipped in and out of the neighborhood throughout my childhood. Usually just long enough for me to take some music lessons and, later, play some events. Then we'd be off again, to some new catastrophe. It sounds exciting, but mostly it meant me studying music in a hotel room while they risked their lives at some run-down clinic.

But Tía Lucia's santos (or orishas, they're also called)—I don't really go in for all that stuff. And I know what you're thinking: Mateo, you literally live with a dead woman. But the dead are one thing, and santos are a whole other. They're like supercharged spirits, got all kinds of powers and complicated backstories and intertwined connections and stuff. It's beyond me.

I just play my music, drink lots of water, and mind my business.

I do go through the motions, though, mostly so I don't get in trouble. But that's all it is: going through the motions.

My hand taps the wicker mat in front of the altar, and I kiss my fingers. It's not a full salute, just enough to appease my tía. I blow an air smooch to my dead aunt, nod once more at my living one, and head for the door.

Sea espíritu, Aunt Miriam calls after me, and I know she's winking because Galeranos can never let something have just one meaning; every possible pun must be mined, and get it? She's a spirit. I just shake my head with a chuckle.

There's a little wooden doohickey on the wall, and I tap that, too—yes, it's called a mezuzah, not a doohickey—and kiss my hand. Then I do a little two-step in front of the small stone head with cowrie-shell eyes that's glaring up at me from the floor—he's Elegguá, the santo who makes mischief at the crossroads. And finally, that's it! I'm done! I'm practically out . . .

. . . until I almost trip over a tiny, furry lump sleeping on the doormat. After running the gauntlet of tías and spirits and sacred doohickies, there's one final boss who must be defeated in order to escape the Medina house. *Fwezeeeeeeeeblorppp!* comes the only warning I get, and that would be Farts the Chihuahua. Well, his name is Dash, but no one calls him that. We call him his favorite thing to do. "Later, Farts," I say as I step over him, close the door, then pause in the dim exterior hallway to catch my breath.

Through the thin door, I hear the *flick flick* and then *fizz* of Tía Lucia's lighter.

———◆———

That musty fall smell fills the crisp air—but it's still just hoodie weather, not too cold—and everybody's out and about.

In these moments, sometimes I think I have taken *sea espíritu* a little too much to heart. This place, it's my home and not my home. I grew up coming and going, endlessly in and out, and those hotel rooms in Karachi, Djibouti, Caracas—the stale air, the ugly carpet patterns and mirror frames, the dullness and aggressively neutral decor—that was home, too. *The man at home in every house is never home,* one of our old ballads says, and man, I swear it was written about me. *Always Home, Never Home: the Mateo Matisse Story.*

Usually, learning all the intricacies of our songs, that was how I found home. Even if I wasn't here physically, I could play the melodies and chords on my little keyboard, and each memory, fantasy, and idea would rise within me, a thread I could pull to find my way back.

And now I am back, and all I want to do is disappear. Because I know my culture, my music, my history, my people . . . but do they know me? Hardly. To almost everyone besides Tams and my tía, I'm just that weird music kid, the one who was gone a lot, the one who doesn't talk. Stuck somewhere in between, neither here nor there. A ghost.

The train rumbles overhead, and its clanks and growls and squeaks join the chatter of ladies waiting to get their hair done outside the peluquería, which gives way to an old drunk guy humming to himself as cars whoosh past, and a bodega owner yelling about how fresh his mangos are.

It's so alive, my little corner of Brooklyn, and while I wish Tía Lucia had come along tonight, being alone for the walk gives me a moment to do my favorite thing: listen. This isn't what my aunt means when she says *escucha.* She's talking about doing whatever she tells me, being careful or whatever. This is a different kind of listening—listening to the world. It's what every kamero, every musician, really, has to learn. That's what the old maestros teach.

Everyone's getting ready; the whole neighborhood jitters and banters with the excitement of the night ahead. You can hear it in the squeals of kids in the park running around the much-graffitied statue of some colonizer, and you can smell it in the mix of freshly baked bread, perfume, and coffee. A little farther down, Tortuga Mariscos, the best seafood spot this side of Atlantic Ave., must be making a special enormous platter for tonight, because you can smell that spicy goodness from blocks away.

Little Elegguás peer out from every storefront, and I know there's a mezuzah fastened on the inner slat of each doorframe.

Neighbors chatter and debate, pray and guffaw. I let their voices slide into the mash-up of sound and add it to the growing tapestry of song inside me.

We're a messy, upside-down people, the San Madrigaleros. We each hold a hundred contradictions, but we wear them proudly. Our genesis sounds more like a bad joke than the actual founding of a nation: One stormy night centuries ago, a pirate, a rabbi, and a Santero escaped some battle together and watched in awe as the island of San Madrigal arose from the Caribbean Sea. This ridiculous trinity settled on it, and soon more escapees and outlaws showed up—they brought their hopes and fears, gods and demons. They made new ones. They fell in love and fought wars, and managed to stay out of the vengeful, gluttonous glare of empire for ages. Then, fifteen years ago, that island sank beneath the waves during a hurricane, and we migrated here, where we've been in a spiritual crisis and state of constant yearning ever since.

No one really knew about San Madrigal when it existed. It was the stuff of legends, sailors' delirium, and the dreams of pirates and revolutionaries—a hideaway. But not one that many people found or even believed in. So when it was gone, there was no one to notice except the people who lived there. My people.

But at least most of them have memories to cling to.

Me, I have nothing; don't remember my birthplace. And because

I was gone from Little Madrigal for so much of my childhood, mine feels like a double diaspora, my own personal haunting.

And now a whole new form of diaspora is opening up, as the first generation born here in the States comes of age. They have real documents, unlike their parents, who had to rely on Si Baracasa's extensive false paperwork hookups. The kids born after the sinking of San Madrigal have never even *seen* the island we all called home, and they never will, because it's gone forever.

Yet it's all around us still.

San Madrigal sings and saunters and simmers through these Brooklyn streets. I can feel that place rattling and clacking all around me as I cross Fulton and head toward Tolo's club. A tinny old-timey shanty streams out of Barbudo's Barbershop, and the clack of the clave tack-tacks along beneath it in a series of off-kilter exclamation points while the accordions wail out the harmonies. A rumba sounds from a rooftop nearby, the breezy lows and highs of those congas, voices blending with acoustic guitars and a hoarse wail over the muddled traffic.

I take it all in as I stroll, and a melody forms, just like it always does. Some kind of rising, falling blend of these different worlds that smashed together so long ago, made us what we are, and led us to this weird exile world a thousand miles away.

The melody is just getting going when I stop in my tracks and everything seems to snap into silence around me.

Tolo's club is just ahead, across the next street. It's all decked out in Christmas lights and tacky pirate-themed decorations, and the words SAN MADRIGAL GRANDE FETE TONIGHT!! proclaim what's happening across a bright marquee. Tonight's a big deal for all of us, and for Tolo Baracasa more than anyone. The guy's been waiting his whole life to take over his rightful role as pirate leader.

As lit up as the event hall is, though, it's the figure standing in the alley behind it who stops me cold. He's tall and bulky, and the orange streetlights glint off the face shield of his helmet.

Trucks. Which means Gerval is somewhere nearby.

Look, I'm not good at the whole talking-to-people thing—just give me a keyboard, you know? But I'm *especially* not good at talking to people I look up to. Usually, all the words I've planned out and practiced mysteriously evaporate the second I open my mouth, so I just end up making gurgley noises instead.

And then puking. Ha-ha, just kidding. Usually.

Point is, if I could get the awkward talking-to-Gerval part out of the way before the performance, I'd actually enjoy the night instead of stressing out, and I'd play better, and then I'd definitely get hired as his new pianist and tour the world!

So I take one step into the street and open my mouth to say *Hey* (or, more realistically, just to gurgle), when something moves through the shadows toward Trucks. It's so fast, I just catch a flicker against the darkness as the slight form launches into the air.

"Oh, ah, um . . ." I say, my eyes wide, and Trucks looks up at me, then spins suddenly, swings one burly arm out, and smashes the figure hurtling at him.

Who appears to be a girl about my age.

I can't make out her face as she grunts and lands in the shadows. It all happens so fast, and Trucks's bulky frame blocks my view.

I'm not sure whether to run toward them or away; none of this makes sense.

She's already leaped back up to her feet as he swings again, this time with one of those extendable batons that dudes like Trucks buy online to feel more like cops.

The girl slides nimbly out of the way and then—*bap, bap!*—I hear the sharp thunks of fists finding their mark, and Trucks stumbles back a step, arms flailing.

It all seems to slow as a rare, trembly music opens up inside me.

Songs just come when they feel like it—there's no logic to it. This music, the music of their fight, is like nothing I've ever heard: shrill and melodic, with a splatter of snare hits beneath and a thunderous bellow throughout.

She's on him in seconds, climbing his body like a tree. Then Trucks lets out a guttural kind of burp that's cut off suddenly and becomes more of a whistle. He drops to his knees and keels forward, cracking his face shield on the pavement.

He's dead. He's definitely dead.

She stands over him, panting, a blade in one hand. As she looks down at what she's done, her slim shoulders rise and fall. Her thick red hair is pulled back in two afropuffs, and her face is a few shades darker than mine. Above her round glasses, her brow is creased with fury.

I know her.

That's Chela Hidalgo.

I grew up with Chela. She's Rabbi Hidalgo's daughter, and Tolo Baracasa's cousin. We don't know each other that well 'cause she's super quiet and minds her business even more than I do.

Well, I thought she did, anyway.

She just murdered a man. Right in front of my eyes.

And then, because I'm the biggest schmo in the universe and because, let's be honest, I'm in shock, I go, "Ahm . . . urg?"

I don't even know what that's supposed to mean. It's just a useless sound I let escape from my useless mouth, which is hanging open uselessly.

Now we're staring at each other, ten feet apart with a dead body between us. She's still out of breath, but her expression is firm, not surprised. It says *I will kill again if I have to.* And mine probably says about what I'm thinking: *OHMYGODOHMYGODOHMYGOD WHAT DID I JUST SEE WHAT THE OHMYGOD HELP.*

She takes one step toward me, her eyes narrowing, and then a strange blue light erupts in the air like a slo-mo lightning flash, and suddenly standing between us is a shimmering form in a hooded robe looking like Death himself.

Both Chela and I take a step back, our mouths open, our faces lit with that blue glow. I can't see under the hood.

I'm not sure who to be more afraid of.

And I don't have time to decide, because with a flash and fizzle, the figure vanishes. I wouldn't believe it really happened except Chela clearly saw it, too.

Very slowly, very deliberately, she looks at me. Then she turns and walks away, vanishing like a phantom into the shadows of the alley.

As soon as she's gone, I lean over and puke my guts out.

CHAPTER TWO

I'M STILL WIPING SNOT AND PUKE OFF MY FACE WHEN A BLACK SUV
with tinted windows rolls up between me and Trucks's body.

The shimmering form is gone. So is Chela.

It's just me and the dead guy. And then the door on the far side
opens and I hear the clomping of boots. A few seconds later, the
SUV screeches off and the body is gone. And then it's just me.

A man just died. I saw him die.

I've seen dead bodies before—plenty, thanks to playing music
for all those funerals. But that's a whole other thing from watching
someone go from person to corpse in the span of a few seconds.
Another wave of nausea rises in me, but there's nothing left in me
to hurl. I don't know if Trucks had a family, people who would miss
him. . . . I barely know anything about the guy except that he's been
hanging around Gerval like a bodyguard ever since Gerval got big.

A man just died, and a girl I know killed him. Right there across
the street.

The way his body went loose as his life left . . . it keeps hammer-
ing through me.

For a few more moments, I just stand there, trying to catch my breath, failing miserably.

Let me tell you something about us Galeranos: we don't call the cops. It's just not done. That's what happens when an island is full of pirates and people escaping either slavery or the Inquisition—a healthy distrust of authority figures settles in. It's canon, and that's carried on to our diaspora here in Brooklyn unabated. Plus, we're mostly one shade of brown or another. So, it's only when an NYPD cruiser glides quietly past that I realize calling 9-1-1 is technically what you're supposed to do when you witness a murder.

Two pairs of eyes glare out at me from the front seat as the squad car rolls by. I stand perfectly still, but I'm sweating from my puke party and breathing all heavy. Also, I'm tall for my age and just brown enough to makes cops unsure which box to profile you into (and non-cops ask all kinds of probey questions about where you're from).

Those glares make me feel like I did something wrong even though I definitely didn't.

Well, maybe I aided and abetted? Or something? I have no idea. I just know I'm terrified and confused, and also, *why are there cops cruising around Little Madrigal right now?* They tend to stay out of our way, especially on the night of the Grande Fete. That was the whispered understanding Si Baracasa brokered with some on-the-take brass at the local precinct, back when he was running these streets, scaring away well-to-do college students to make room for a migration he assumed would be coming anytime. And when our diaspora went from a trickle to a flood (probably much more dramatically than Si could've imagined), Anisette Bisconte solidified that loose working arrangement into a firm understanding with the NYPD: no guns in Little Madrigal means no cops in Little Madrigal. We can stab and beat one another into bloody pulps, but as long as no shots ring out, the cops will keep clear of this whole district.

Yet some just drove past.

Doesn't matter.

I mean, it does. But right now, it can't.

There's nothing for me to do, no move to make, no one left to help. I could tell someone inside the club, but, like, tell them what? *A girl I know ninja-assassined Trucks and then a shimmering guy showed up and then an SUV snatched Trucks's corpse oh and I puked?* There's no girl, no body, no SUV, no license plate memorized, got no idea who was driving. It's just me and my puke.

Plus, and this is really the thing: I have no idea who's on what side of what. I follow local politics even less than I keep up with Tía Lucia's spiritual-lore talk. For all I know, I could be telling the people who ordered the hit about me witnessing it.

Anyway, I have a gig to play.

Thank God.

When everything else fails, there's still music. So, after I stand there just blinking a few more times, once my breath has caught and my heartbeat simmers down, I shake it off as best I can and take one step forward, then another.

Across the street and up the block.

Under the shining marquee, through the crowd of families waiting to get inside.

Past Big Moses Arroyo the bouncer, who shoots me a solemn nod that I return halfway.

Down a narrow, dimly lit corridor.

Out into the main event hall, where the final string lights are being hung and tablecloths are sliding into place as waiters from Tortuga Mariscos set up chafing dishes and burners.

In the middle of it all, as large and languid as an iguana in a sauna, is Tolo Baracasa, wearing his usual wide guayabera shirt and well-creased slacks. He glares at a tall, thin figure in jeans and a T-shirt: Maestro Grilo Juan Gerval.

Gerval's smile takes up his whole face, and his hair is pulled back into a ponytail. He stands with one pointy-toed shoe sticking out and a hand on his hip, like some kind of elaborate flamenco-dancing swordsman.

I had so many words ready for this moment, said them so many times in my head. I knew all the while none of them would come out in the right order, because Mateo, but now that I've just witnessed Gerval's buddy get murdered, I have even less idea of what I'm supposed to say.

Anyway, it seems like Tolo and Gerval might be getting into it over something. Word is they used to be tight in high school, before they both dropped out. Then one got famous and the other . . . Well, the other runs the pirate syndicate out of this club.

It's impressive, really. Tolo just turned eighteen; he's built like a refrigerator, and while pretty much everyone loves him, there's not a soul alive who'd want to be on the receiving end of his death stare. Any and all underworld shenanigans that happen in Little Madrigal go through him, and he's about to add the political weight of the Cabildo to that, once Anisette Bisconte passes on her position as pirate rep and we formalize it with a vote.

But the maestro seems utterly unfazed, his smile turned up to ten.

I wonder if Gerval knows that his bodyguard just got stabbed up by Tolo's cousin. I also wonder what it must have felt like for Trucks, standing there minding his own business, to suddenly end up sucked into the eternal void and—

"Earth to Mateooo!" Something soft bounces off the back of my neck. I whirl around to find my best friend, Tams, staring up at me with a mischievous grin, ready to let fly another dinner roll. "We setting up, or are you staring off into space like a five-star goober in a ten-dollar suit?"

See, this is how you know everyone loves Tams. She says

ridiculous stuff like that—makes no sense!—and nobody ever has any slick comebacks. If I ever tried to let the phrase *five-star goober* come out of my mouth—which, first of all, what does that even mean?—I'd be mocked to within an inch of my life.

But I don't care, to be honest, because even on a normal day—one that doesn't involve homicide—Tams is the only person outside my family who I somehow know how to talk to. Maybe it's her own special magic, but I know that when I talk, she's not judging me, not gauging who I am or where I've been. She's listening. And when we don't know how to say something to one another, we play. The music has always felt true when I play with Tams. Just about every Galerano kid knows most of these weird old ditties by heart—I had to learn them by head, since I was studying them in hotel rooms, far away from all the wild street parties. But Tams somehow did both: she grew up hearing them all around her, and then went ahead and studied the complicated charts and theory behind the songs. She's the only person I know who's as nerdy as I am, and rebuilding our friendship after I'd been gone for months at a time never felt like work, it just felt true.

I swallow back another roiling simmer of panic. Trucks keeps collapsing over and over again in my mind. But I have to be present. I shove it all away, best I can, and say, "I do look pretty good." Then I try a little two-step (the same one I do in front of Elegguá) to really bring home the point that everything is fine even though it's absolutely not. Dressing up isn't really my thing, but it's the Grande Fete. My hair is cropped close and I'm wearing some leather bracelets to accentuate my (one and only) suit, and hey! Hey, hey!

Tams rolls her eyes. "All right, calm down, buddy. The bar is low for tall dudes. You opt for something better than a T-shirt, and everyone is in awe. Well, I'm not impressed."

I finish my jig with a spin, almost trip but catch myself, and close out with two extra-corny finger blasts. "Hey, hey!"

"For the record, ten dollars is not a lot to pay for a suit, buddy."

She's in all white as usual, the brightness contrasting perfectly with her dark skin, but this time it looks like a specially tailored suit. Elaborate textured patterns seem to dance along the sleeves and pants, and her shoes . . . "Is that snakeskin?" I gape.

She bows, answering my two-step with one of her own. "Gator, baby. Don't tell the vegans."

"I don't think you have to worry about that here. But . . . you didn't notice!" I make a show of looking disappointed.

"Notice what?"

Jazz hands around my chin don't help.

She squints at me. "You got a haircut?"

I give up and just point aggressively. "The mustache! The beard? They have touched! Eh? Eh?"

She squints harder. "Are we sure the word *beard* is appropriate here?"

"Bah!" I throw my arms in the air.

"'Whispers of possible growth follicles on the lower jaw area,' perhaps?"

"Forget it!"

"Chinsinuations, if you will."

"*Never mind*, I said!" But I'm laughing as we head toward the band corner. "How we looking?"

Tams nods over to the fully set-up kit, complete with a regular jazz snare and toms, kick pedal for the bass drum, congas, maracas, and an extra-large tambourine. "Looking like the percussionist always has to get here an hour early while the pianist strolls in five minutes before hit time, acting the fool."

Tolo is walking away, his big bald head shaking slowly back and forth, and Gerval is on his phone. I'm not sure if I should tell the maestro what happened to Trucks or not, but I can't now anyway, so

I follow Tams to our corner of the performance area and slide into my seat at the old wooden piano.

This is my favorite place in the world—the only place where things make sense. Here, I can work out the world and its terrors, turn them into something malleable. Here, I am unseen, *espíritu*, like a good kamero should be. I can hide.

There's a crisp certainty to these keys, these notes. No matter how terrible I'm feeling, a C minor chord is still a C minor chord. No amount of loneliness or homesickness or fear can change that. Even witnessing a murder can't change that. People like to get gooey about music, but the truth is, there's a simple mathematics to all this beauty. It's just pieces fitting together, notes piling on top of each other, shimmering alongside other notes, becoming chords. Chords rise and fall, harmonies jangle, dissonance escalates, and our emotions follow. Tension builds, then it shatters. It's right there on the page, hiding in those notes. See? Certainty. A certainty I can vanish into when everything else is vague, terrifying, covered in shadow.

And it is, so I do.

My fingers dance along the first couple notes of a chord. Something settles within me. I drop my head back and glimpse scattered stars through the huge skylight that makes up most of the ceiling of Tolo's club.

When I was a kid, I'd wait till my parents were asleep in the hotel room, plug headphones into the little starter keyboard my dad got me, and just go to town, playing whatever I wanted, making up riffs and melodies, chords. They gave me a book of scales for my ninth birthday, and I had it memorized within a month.

During our brief stints at home, they'd send me around to the different music masters in Little Madrigal. And then everything really started clicking: all those winding, overlapping Sefaradi melodies, that mix of joy and sorrow, calling out to God, aching for a lost homeland; the singular hilarious tragedy of the shanty, so many voices on top of each other rattling along beneath the relentless stomp forward; the call-and-response praise songs for each spirit over the rumbling batá drums.

It never felt like I was learning something new, just finding out the names of harmonies I'd made friends with long before.

And it felt like home. If I couldn't be in the place itself, the one thing I could do was hear it, over and over; I could feel it sliding out of my fingertips, across those keys, right back into my ears.

On the wall behind me, a mural shows the three archetypal founders in a battered raft. A pirate, a rabbi, and a Santero gaze up in awe at a beautiful woman made out of light who floats above the ocean: San Madrigal. A banner across the top reads NUNCA VENCIDO, NUNCA CONQUISTADO—*Never defeated, never conquered*—our motto, which, you know, sounds nice. And it's true, San Madrigal was one of the only Caribbean islands to have made it out of the colonial era and into the neocolonial one without ever falling to European rule. Of course, that's mostly because the place was so tiny and hard to find that no one bothered conquering us—it's strategically useless, really. It was a myth, and then it was gone.

And we never had slavery, a point the elders will bring up again and again when arguing with other island folk. But really, the bar is so low; like, wow, none of our founders owned another human! Congrats! No one should get gold stars for the bare minimum, if you ask me.

And sometimes I wonder . . .

Tams, now at her kit, catches my eye. "You okay?"

I nod, shake my head, shrug.

Onstage, this kid from school, Vedo Bisconte, is warming up the crowd with another dry *We are all pirates, we are all Sefaradim, we are all Santeros*–type spoken-word joint.

It.

Is.

Abysmal.

At least he looks appropriately awkward about it—his light brown, freckled face is burning with embarrassment, and those big puppy eyes keep blinking. And here's the thing about all that *nunca conquistado* stuff with us. Somehow, we still managed to end up with the lightest-skinned folks wielding all the economic power. Vedo, for example, is from the wealthiest, most politically connected Galerana family. His mom, Anisette, is a city councilwoman and the pirate rep on the Cabildo. His dad's a businessman of some unclear but probably corrupt type. And on and on. You can't tell me that's coincidence. (They also pretty much raised Gerval after some tragedy with his parents, but that's a whole other story.)

The Hidalgo-Baracasas are one of the only darker-skinned families to come anywhere near real wealth—but as far as I've heard, they had to fight for generations to get there.

And because the pirates are in charge of the banking, no one really knows where the money comes from. But they're pirates, so the understanding is that they've robbed the rich and corrupt, and that works well enough for most people.

Tams and I have stayed up for hours trying to figure out the intricacies of how race and power worked on the island, but it's all hazy, because folks are so caught up in that One Big Familia myth and don't talk about it much. It all comes back to this, though: so much of the colorism problem around the world goes back to the colonial powers bringing slavery and all its false justifications and hierarchies everywhere they went. Then how do a people who have supposedly escaped the shadow of empire still manage to cling to some of the worst power structures inherent to it?

My parents and I are all right in the muddled middle somewhere, like most Galeranos, a little this, a little that. They both went to medical school off-island, which brought them its own strange outsider status, and then they kept traveling the world, never quite settling in any one place. And me? I'm still figuring it all out, but mostly I'm just staying here in the shadows, heard and not seen.

"Did something happen outside?" Tams asks me as Anisette clacks onto the stage in her high heels, hugs her son, and takes the mic from him.

Yes, indeed. "That guy, Trucks . . ." How to even say it? My voice trails off with an "Umm . . ."

"The dude who wishes he was a cop so bad it hurts to look at him?" She cranes her neck around. "Where is he? Usually, Gerval doesn't leave home without him."

"See, that's the thing—"

"Ahoy, mi gente!" Anisette Bisconte croons, half singing, half speaking over the loudspeakers as Vedo retreats to his table, shoulders slumped. "And shalom! Before the announcement, we will do the customary prayer for the dead. Please rise, and Hakham Hidalgo will get us started with a brief passage from the Talmud!" Most people just call him rabbi, but Anisette winks when she says the more traditional Sefaradi term for a religious leader—*hakham*—probably trying to score points with the elders.

Rabbi Hidalgo lumbers to the mic, looking dead serious. Then flashes a sudden, disarmingly gentle smile and waves at everyone. Then he gets somber again. "Be as bold as a leopard," he recites, "and light as the eagle, and swift as the deer to do the will of your Father in Heaven."

That's the cue.

Tams knows exactly what to do when her dad, Baba Maximo, begins listing name after name and Baba Johnny bangs a heavy, ribbon-covered stick on the ground. She comes in with a thundering roll on the tom in time with the slow-pounding dirge, and I drop a chord full of all the dissonance and shimmer I can muster, just right for the Muertos. Reading off the names of the dead is usually

Tía Lucía's part of the ceremony, and it feels a little weird not to hear her familiar voice calling them out. I don't like that she still hasn't shown up. It's not like her, and this night is already too much.

But in this moment, the moment of music, I come alive. No matter what else is going on—even murder—somehow those notes, they protect me, become me, and everything else falls away.

Rabbi Hidalgo begins the mourner's kaddish: "Yitgadal v'yitkadash . . ." All the while, Baba Maximo rattles off muerto after muerto, and I lead Tams into a bluesy vamp. I spot Chela in the crowd behind the rabbi. She's solemn-faced, head nodding to the rhythm. How can she just . . . be here acting normal after what she's done? I imagine myself leaping up, running across the room to confront her, telling the world she's a murderer.

Instead, I just keep playing as the list of names goes on and on.

And here comes the part that always creeps me out: one by one, the slightly glowing translucent forms of the ancestors appear all around us.

Most Muertos aren't like Aunt Miriam. I've always assumed she's superpowered on account of Tía Lucía being a badass spiritualist. All that talking and flitting around the apartment Miriam does, mostly visible? That's rare. Usually the dead just kinda hang there creepily translucent, unable to talk or move very much. Some wear Santero whites or regalia from various Turkish and Spanish and West African traditions or torn sailor's outfits. Others have on suits and ties, or T-shirts and hoodies, or ball gowns.

I catch myself glancing around for a specter in body armor.

The whole thing, it's always . . . unnerving. But especially tonight, and not just because of what I saw earlier. Something's different. I can't put my finger on it at first, but then I realize: the Muertos normally show up with their heads bowed, eyes closed in quiet reverence for the ceremony.

Now, though, all those hazy shrouds are glancing around with urgent, worried glares. Something is happening. It's like they hear a distant rumble but can't figure out where it's coming from. And it's getting louder and louder.

My fingers find each chord as I trundle up and down the keyboard, keeping it sparse so everyone can hear each name, keeping it a little off-kilter, a little jangly, a little weird. The San Madrigal way. I wonder if Gerval is paying attention.

The song winds down, and the ancestors are fading, still glancing around fearfully even as they vanish. A concerned murmur erupts across the hall.

Tams and I ham it up with the music, all shimmering cymbals and elaborate major chords rising in intensity as Anisette takes the stage. "Alafia and shalom!" As is our way, San Madrigalera greetings take a while—lotta bases to cover. People settle down, and various segments of the room respond in kind; the Santeros cross their arms over their chests and dip into slight bows.

"I come with some exciting news tonight!" she says, bopping her head in time with our vamp. *Sea espíritu.* No one looks at us, light moves through us. Our music is all we are. "Some news that will change the very fabric of our lives!"

Tams hits the cymbals again, totally over-the-top.

"For centuries, we have been a people of the shadows! Hidden from the world! *Sea espíritu,* the great maestro Archibaldo Coraje Medina taught, and maybe, just maybe, we all collectively took that advice just a little too seriously!"

Uh . . . this is awkward. No one seems to know what to make of this speech, or what the pivot will be, but clearly, it's coming.

"And tonight I'm here to tell you that it's finally time for San Madrigal, our culture, our people, to step out into the spotlight and be seen by the world!"

Yo! That is not the kind of thing you shout into a room full of pirates! People yell out in confusion, anger. But . . . surprisingly, others cheer, so that shows you what I know. The result is an absolute cataclysm on my ears—just pure dissonance. I signal Tams, and we play louder to try and drown it all out.

Gerval is really the only example of a Galerano getting anywhere near a spotlight, and he's caught a small amount of hell for it from certain more traditional folks. Others adore him regardless—or maybe because of it—but either way, he's the closest we've ever come to being on a map. Literally. But tonight he seems to have taken my old ancestor's words to heart and melted into the shadows; I don't see the guy anywhere.

Tolo, though, is one of the pissed ones. How is this transition of power supposed to work with two opposing sides in play? Guess we'll find out!

"Which is why . . ." Anisette yells into the chaos, nearly peaking out the sound system. "Which is why . . . I have decided to temporarily delay my planned transition off the Cabildo!"

Guess we won't find out.

More chaos. More yelling.

"For the past fifteen years," Anisette continues, "we have lived in mourning. Bereft of the very land we call home, we are a people in exile! A lost diaspora from a lost island!"

People keep cursing each other out and carrying on, right up until Anisette clicks a little remote and an image appears on the wall behind me. Everyone gasps and shuts up real quick.

"But no more!"

I can't see the image. I'm too busy trying to keep this majestic epic waltz going.

"No more!" she says again, that big grin plastered across her face.

People are standing, blinking, gaping. Finally, I just ramp up the song to a dramatic pause and twist myself around.

And then I understand. The slide is a picture of the ocean, the dazzling Caribbean blue beneath a wide-open sky. Three rocky embankments cresting up from beneath the waves.

It can't be.

The tips of San Madrigal's three peaks. Even with barely a memory of the island, I'd recognize them anywhere: they're plastered all over everything.

"Together, we are going to raise our home!" Anisette yells over the rising tide of confusion and excitement. "As you can see, we've already begun!"

"Impossible!" someone yells, but what does such a word mean to people from a sunken pirate island with strange gods and bewildering ceremonies? A people who escaped inquisitions and slavery even while the rest of the world suffered and shattered?

"The work has only just started," Anisette insists, motioning at everyone to be quiet. "As everyone knows, in order to finish raising the island, to fulfill the prophecy, we will need the three initiated, fully awakened children of the original spirits of San Madrigal to reveal themselves!"

Everyone knows that? Man . . . the number of things *everyone knows* about my culture that I find out for the first time at some random moment like this . . . it just deepens that uncomfortable nagging feeling that I don't really belong, no matter how many songs I have memorized or events I've performed.

And so I play harder, let the music envelop me, hoping it will help (it doesn't). The voice that says I don't belong gets louder, tries to yell over each note, the clamor of the crowd.

When Anisette says *children*, it isn't literal; they do these elaborate ceremonies to consecrate people as priests of a certain deity, basically. My aunt's spirit is Shango, the thunder santo, so she's a child of Shango. It means they have a whole connection and she's kind of his emissary in the people world, I guess you could say. Tams talks about her guardian spirit, Ochossi, like he's some kind of magical uncle/best friend. It's pretty awesome, really, I'm just always very aware of seeing it from the outside.

But . . . as far as I know, no one's been initiated to the priesthoods of the Madrigal, or Okanla, or Galanika in ages. And the *fully awakened* part is lost on me—some deep-cut spirit stuff, I'm sure.

"Only then—" Anisette continues, but someone interrupts her with a shout: "¡Basura!" *Trash.*

"No se puede," another person insists. *It can't be done.*

"What most of you don't know," Anisette yells over the rabble, "is that all three children of the original santos are here in this room with us!"

Wild guffaws all around. Angry voices rise, arguing and cursing each other out.

I hate seeing my own people squabble like this, even when I feel a hundred miles away. It's like I'm being torn to pieces along with them. Turmoil erupts everywhere, inside and out, but that's what music is for. That C minor chord is still a C minor chord, so I hit it with all I've got and riff up and down the scale. Tams follows along, leaning into the snare hits.

"Well," Anisette says, managing to quiet the boil into a simmer again, "there's the one we all know about, of course!"

Every head in the room seems to turn at once. At first, I think they're looking at Tams. They must be confused, I think.

But when I turn to her to ask what's going on, she's looking directly at me. And so, I realize, is everybody else.

CHAPTER THREE

ME. THEY MEANT ME. I'M THE—WHATEVER IT IS . . . SON OF SOME saint I don't care about.

I made it around the corner. My feet stop just after the curb, my butt lands hard on the pavement. My face finds my hands, and I just sit there, heaving. Not crying, not puking. Just rocking as these wild, unfathomable gasps heave through me, send my shoulders up and down, and nothing, nothing makes sense.

I remember standing up, feeling all those eyes on me. I feel them still, like they left sweltering burns across my body. Because I know what everyone was whispering, thinking, laughing about: *This kid who's never around shows up and finds out in front of* everyone, *the whole community, that he's been initiated.*

How did I not know?

What does it even mean?

It doesn't matter. Not to me. What matters is I have been seen, a thousand times over; all at once, very suddenly, with no warning, the intrusive, penetrating glare of everyone I know landed on me. I am un-vanished, and I can never disappear again. Never be heard and not seen, never sea espíritu like I'm supposed to.

My name is on their tongues; they're chewing up and spitting out my story, a story *I don't even know*, like it's another tasty morsel of gossip for the mill. And it is, it is. *The kid we barely know and still know better than he knows himself.* That's all I am.

I stood, bristled, burned with shame, embarrassment, confusion. The bright red exit sign seemed to stare back at me from across the room like a beacon. I muttered something to Tams about how she should just keep playing, not to follow me, and then I put one foot in front of the other, blocked out all the blistering whispers as best I could, and got gone fast.

And now I'm here, heaving, on the very curb where . . . I look up. Yep. Somehow, I managed to land in the exact spot where this night first went left. Trucks lay right behind where I'm now sitting, and I stood there, just across the street, and Chela . . .

I put my head back down as another heave trembles through me, then another.

And then a hand lands softly on my back, right between my shoulder blades. It's a light touch, calming. Tams, I think at first, because she's the only person who would run out of the club to check on me. But it's too small to be her hand.

I look up and only barely manage not to leap away.

Chela's sitting next me, her knees up at her chest, one arm stretched across my back. "I'm not going to kill you," she whispers.

I'm not so sure about that, and my face is probably splattered with doubt, because Chela unleashes the slightest of smiles and says, "I promise."

And I guess if she wanted to, she had plenty of opportunity to do it when I was sitting there with my neck out. Still . . . "Wha . . . what . . . then?" The heaving has simmered to an occasional tremor, but I still can't make words come out very clearly.

"You didn't know, did you?" It's not cruel when Chela says it. In fact, I'm pretty sure there's sympathy there. Not pity, just . . . she can tell it hurts. I'm not sure how she managed that, because every time I've said those words to myself in the past ten minutes, it's come out like a damning accusation of an unpardonable sin.

I shake my head, blinking. "I don't even . . . I didn't even . . ." Where's a piano when I need one? Even when the world is *not* horrible, expressing things is just about impossible for me. And now here I am trying to explain impossible emotions to an admittedly comforting murderer. Murderess. Whatever, she killed somebody.

"Galanika," she says. It's not even answering my unasked question—I haven't gotten to the part in my processing where I've calmed down enough to wonder which spirit I was initiated to.

"The buff old dude with the jacked-up eye?" I ask, finally finding words.

She nods, that slight smile returning. "Healer."

"How did you—" I stop myself when she looks down, because that's all I need to confirm my deepest fears. "Because everybody knows."

Feels like the floor is falling out from under me again. I mean, I had figured they all knew. It was clear from their reaction. But still . . . her confirmation somehow makes it even worse. Maybe I'd been holding out hope that there was some other explanation, that it was all a mistake.

I scowl. "Except for me."

Somewhere, way in the murky depths of my memory, there's a conversation about this. The name Galanika. Lots of crying. But it's barely there and makes no sense, doesn't pair with any other memory or feel grounded in the reality I know. It's just a shard.

"That . . . figure . . . the spirit . . ." Chela says. "What we saw in the alley."

She did see it too. "Was that Galanika?"

"I think so."

A moment of silence slides by, but my mind is on fire with all the things that this means. I'm an initiated child of Galanika, the first in ages. I must've been made when I was tiny, probably back on San Madrigal.

Everyone knows all this, and I'm here guessing.

"Listen," Chela says, suddenly sounding exceptionally about-the-business, "what happened earlier tonight . . ."

You mean when you murdered somebody? I almost say, but I manage to stop myself. She may have just killed a man, but she also just came and made sure I was okay even though we barely know each other. And now she's the one who looks some kind of shattered, head drooped, breath coming in quick, sad bursts, eyes squeezed shut.

Is it weird that I want to comfort her when she's the one who did the killing?

Yes. But I do it anyway. Don't ask me to explain.

My hand lands on her back, the same spot hers had been on mine. Her shoulders rise and fall as she gathers herself. "I . . ." she starts. Then she scowls, tries again. "It's more complicated than what it looked like."

"It looked pretty complicated, actually."

She barks a gritty laugh, then shakes her head. "I don't know how to explain it to you." Chela looks me full in the face; the street-lights send an orange sheen across her brown skin, her eyes glisten with the fury of everything she's going through, all that just happened. The night seems to slow around us. The faraway rumble of the city goes quiet; all that's left is her voice: "But I want to try."

I would like that very much, I think but don't say.

Please, I think but don't say.

Because there is calm even in her turmoil, like we're both sitting within the eye of her terrible storm, both our storms, and somehow we're safe here.

"Mateo?" Another voice ruptures the moment, and I'm already standing by the time Tía Lucia has finished her question. "¿Pero qué tú haces aquí afuera?"

"Why didn't you tell me?" I demand, launching across the street toward her. "Why didn't you . . . ?" The words get stuck again in that forever traffic jam in my throat, and I just stand there blubbering for a moment.

"What is this about, m'ijo?"

"I . . . That's what . . ." I glance back. Chela is already gone. The empty spot where she once stood is the empty spot where Trucks once lay.

Tonight has been too much, and somehow I feel like it's only just getting started.

"When were you going to tell me?" I demand, glaring down at Tía Lucia's defiant face.

"Tell you *what?*" Tía Lucia growls back. "Mateo, ¿qué—"

"That I was initiated!" I yell. "Without my permission! Into a tradition I barely understand and didn't have a say in! Because I was just . . . a baby!"

Tía Lucia's eyes go soft, her whole face unclenches. "Oh, Mateo . . ."

"Don't!" I insist. "Don't *Oh, Mateo* me!"

"Pero—"

"I had to find out from *Anisette*! In front of *everyone*! I'm sixteen! Were you waiting for me to hit voting age? To be a senior citizen? *Then* would it have been a good time for me to know what happened to me?"

"Mateo," Tía Lucia says, firmly now. "Tranquilo."

"I *am* tranquilo," I growl extremely untranquilly. Then I take it down a notch or two. "Considering the circumstances."

Tía Lucia pounces. "Oh, ¿sí? And what are the circumstances, mi corazón? Dime, por favor."

"Well . . ." My voice trails off because she's right: I have no idea what happened or why, and those, I guess, are the circumstances. "I don't know. And that's *exactly* the p—"

"Point," Tía Lucia finishes for me. "No sabes. But I have tried—"

"Problem! I was going to say *problem!*" Two can play the interrupting game. "The *problem* is I don't know. I didn't know that I'm—what? Initiated? Without my permission? A child of some spirit I don't know and don't care about?" I'm trying not to yell—people are finally minding their own business, or at least pretending to. But the words coming out of me keep getting louder and louder. "Did my parents know?"

"Of course! I wouldn't have—"

"Well, when were you all going to tell me?"

"It's that, I tried," Tía says quietly.

That takes some wind out of my righteous sails. "Huh?"

"The first time was when you were four or five, I think. Then again when you were eight."

Uh-oh.

"I think the last time I brought it up you were ten or eleven. You just didn't want to hear it. Cut me off as soon you realized what I was talking about. Finally, your parents told me to give up, so I did," says Tía Lucia. "Of course, they weren't happy about it happening in the first place, but they understood it had to be done."

"I don't . . . I don't understand."

"The initiation was done to save your life, Mateo. The letters that fell for you were explícito—you were going to die. Initiating you as the first son of Galanika in generations . . . it was the only way to save you." Tía Lucia smiles sadly, her eyes meeting mine. "You are a healer, Mateo. Es tu destino."

I shake my head. "I'm a musician. A kamero. *That's* my destiny.

Mom and Dad are healers. People getting hurt makes me puke." I try not to think about Trucks, but the image of him falling, forever falling, returns. And somehow, I was being comforted by his killer. I shake my head. One thing at a time. "I just want to play music."

"Things are happening very fast." Tía Lucia's expression sharpens. "You can't afford to get stuck in your own head anymore. You have a role to play in this world, Mateo. En esta comunidad. There is nothing more dangerous than a power denied, left to fester. It's gone on long enough. You are a healer, and you must heal."

"I don't . . . I don't *want* to learn to heal, Tía." I'm sure I sound like a little kid. I feel like one. Suddenly, all I want to be is off in some boring hotel room, studying music, far, far away.

Tía Lucia takes my hand in hers and she's smiling, but her eyes are sad, full of a hundred secrets, and all I can think about is a destiny that was forced on me, and all those glares and wandering thoughts back in the club. "Escucha," she says lovingly.

I pull my hand away. "Tía, stop! Stop telling me to listen! I don't want to listen!"

Tía Lucia steps back like I slapped her.

"*You* listen!" I say. "This . . . it's not me. You don't get to decide *my* destiny. I don't want this."

I think she's going to scream at me, curse me out. Instead, she just watches me sadly as I turn away.

And that's much, much worse. I feel like all my insides are crumbling. I'd been expecting her to bite back. We'd argue until we were tired of it and then calm down and figure out some way to make up and keep going. This is different. I just feel empty.

What have I done?

There's a yell from inside the club, the sound of breaking glass. More yells.

Someone stumbles backward through the front doors—it's Arco "El Gorro" Kordal; he's a year above me in school. He lets out a stream of curses, backstepping as he goes, both arms raised, and then Big Moses comes barreling out and plows directly into him. Both tumble into the street with grunts and curses. Before they can rise, a whole flood of people burst out of Tolo's club, fists finding faces, feet skidding and stumbling across the pavement.

At the far end of the intersection, I see the cops from earlier. They glance at each other, then just turn and walk away, shaking their heads.

CHAPTER FOUR

HERE'S SOMETHING IT'S *NOT* GONNA SAY ON MY GRAVESTONE:

HERE LIETH

MATEO MATISSE MEDINA

HE WANTED TO SEE WHAT HAPPENED

Whatever's going on here? It's got nothing to do with me. I'm out.

At least, I *would* be out, if Tía Lucia wasn't standing right at the edge of the fighting, shaking her head.

I know I just got into it with her, but that doesn't mean I want to see her get hurt.

"Tía," I call over the sounds of scuffle. "Come on! Get away from—"

"Así nos caemos," she says just as I approach. *This is how we fall.* "But I will calm them. They will listen to me." Then she steps into the fray.

Tía thinks she's invincible! This is ridiculous. Sure, she could defeat Satan with that chancla swipe of hers, but this is a teeming street fight! She's being ridiculous, and somewhere, deep down, she surely knows it.

But ridiculous or not, I can't let her get hurt.

I take a deep breath, try to ignore the aching imprint all those eyes left on me—and follow. Bodies tumble and thrash all around me. My hand reaches out to grab her little arm, and someone collapses right between us, yelling and flailing as he falls. Two more people crash on top of the first. And then, very suddenly, what started as a bunch of shoves and a few sloppy punches explodes into something much, much worse.

Yes, weapons come out. That's the most obvious part—as if some silent understanding passed instantly between friend and foe alike, hands scramble into pockets, flip open leather sheaths concealed beneath pant legs, snap extendable batons into position. But there's something worse, or maybe *that* is the secret that leaped from one head to the next—a shift in energy, the difference between a puddle and a whirlpool. . . . I don't know what's caused it, but the fighting seems to catch fire; the hits—once just sloppy, drunken swats—now find flesh and bone and break them with wet, nauseating cracks and thuds.

I try to find my way through it all, dodging swipes and shoves, stepping aside as bodies rumble past. But I don't know where Tía Lucia went, or how to get us out of here even if I could find her. The fighting has taken over the world; everything beyond it seems foggy, impossibly far away.

"Tía!" I yell uselessly.

In the middle of it all, Tolo stomps back and forth, whacking folks who roll up on him and trying to calm others. I don't see Tams or Tía or even Chela, who seems made for moments like these.

Someone rams into my side—by mistake, I think—and I stumble out of the way, barely stopping myself from hitting the pavement.

Even as I straighten, my foot suddenly slides out from under me and I almost go into free fall.

Blood, I realize, once I manage to regain my balance.

Someone's bleeding.

"Tía?"

Someone's bleeding and no one cares, and maybe that's the moment—the third time tonight? I've lost track—when I feel myself breaking inside. It could be Tía Lucia; it could be any one of our other neighbors and loved ones. But the fighting rages on around me, and I'm about to start shoving people myself, just to get out of there—for all I know, my aunt already made it to safety—when a crackly voice blasts out of a loudspeaker: "This is the New York City Police Department! Everyone is to evacuate the premises immediately!"

That gets people's attention, but probably not in the way the cops expected.

Those words haven't been heard in Little Madrigal, well . . . *ever*, probably. This neighborhood was mid-gentrification eighteen years ago when Si Baracasa staged some elaborate public executions right in the middle of Fulton Street (no one actually died—supposedly) and scared away all the hipsters. He'd won the battle for Brooklyn—our little corner of it, anyway—without a live round fired, taking a page from the Blackbeard book of scaring the crap out of people so bad you don't even have to fight them. Si was the epitome of the pirate trifecta: showboat, warrior, and businessman. He bought up all that suddenly empty and rapidly devaluing real estate, and Little Madrigal was born. By the time the island sank and the rest of us showed up, Si had already set up his own little criminal empire and laid the foundation for a working arrangement with the cops, the same one Anisette would later codify, that kept them far away from these streets and our business.

Until now . . .

"Anyone who doesn't leave will be arrested for trespassing!" the voice continues, and already the people who were just smashing each other to pulp have suddenly worked out their differences and turned all their ire on the cops.

"We can't trespass on our own streets!" Tolo Baracasa yells amidst thunderous hoorahs. "*You're* trespassing!"

Nothing unites Galeranos like bucking authority. Even in our worst moments, we can agree on that much.

"Please evacuate!" the loudspeaker croons, sounding a little more conciliatory now.

The crowd of brawlers moves as one. They shove past me toward the quickly retreating line of police.

And just like that, the intersection around me empties as the yelling, pushing mass tumbles away through the streets.

Well, not all of it.

Around me, the injured writhe and moan, and there, just a few feet away, lies Tía Lucia.

No.

The whole night seems to collapse around her unmoving body.

I drop to my knees by her side, barely aware that I even crossed the distance to reach her.

This is . . . Somehow this all feels like my fault.

The last thing I did was pull away from her. The last thing I said was *I don't want this.*

Something tiny crystallizes inside me. Terror, heartache, regret—they're all competing voices having a screaming match within. But there's something else there, too: a quiet certainty, deep down beneath it all.

You are a healer, Mateo. You must heal.

Maybe, just maybe . . . there's something I can do.

Suddenly, it doesn't matter that all this magic and Tía's spirits in pots have always seemed like over-the-top woo-woo to me. All that matters is that I might be able to help her. I'm all there is right now. Everyone else is off fighting the cops or lying low to keep from getting arrested. There's no 9-1-1 for us. Calling an ambulance means the cops will come, too, so we make do in other ways the best we can. And if she's right, if I carry the magical essence of some ancient healing santo, if I have . . . powers . . . then I'm all she's got.

I hate this. I hate all of it.

I have no choice.

Okay, Mateo. I glance down at her body. Dirt and street grime are splattered like gashes across her white dress. There's a nasty bruise on her forehead, but no bleeding. What did I learn in that CPR class my parents forced me to take a few years ago? See if she's breathing! Right. Her chest rises slowly as I watch, once, then again.

So she's alive.

Tía Lucia is alive. I want to cry just realizing that much, but I have to keep it together.

Gently, gently, I touch my fingers to her head. Maybe something will make sense. Maybe a bright light will issue forth and she'll pop up to her feet and laugh like nothing happened, stroll away.

No dice.

She's alive but still knocked out.

"Tía . . ." I try shaking her a little. "Can you hear me?" Nothing works. Not words, not touch. I'm not a healer. I'm just a kid. A mess.

"Mateo!" Tams's voice cuts through the chaos inside me. When I look up, there are tears in my eyes and she's running across the street. "What happened to Tía Lucia?"

"I don't know! I'm . . . I'm trying to . . . help?"

Tams looks as confused as I feel. "You don't . . ." *Even know how your powers work* is the rest of that phrase, I'm sure. *You didn't even know you had them until ten minutes ago.* Tams doesn't have to finish it. I've been saying it to myself this whole time. But she's nicer to me than I am to myself, so instead she gets down to the practical. "How?"

"I don't know, but . . . I have to try!"

She squats on the other side of Tía Lucia and squints at her like she's trying to solve one of those impossible trigonometry problems Ms. Fernandez gives to keep us busy when she wants some quiet time. "Probably a concussion," Tams reports a few moments later.

How is she so calm? And how does she know that? Doesn't matter. "What do we do about it?"

"Did you try using your . . . ?" She waves her hands around to indicate *woo-woo*.

"I . . . Tía made it sound like I'd just know how, but I don't. 'You're a healer,' she said, 'so heal.' What does that even mean?"

"Try again," Tams says. "Whatever it is, it's in you."

I shake my head but bite back a retort. Seeing Tía Lucia's mostly still body feels like an explosion that rocks through me every couple seconds. All I want to do is run away. Instead, I take a breath and slide my hands along the side of her face to her forehead.

"Close your eyes, Mateo," Tams instructs.

I do, because why not? And immediately the world seems calmer. I don't know if my best friend actually knows what she's doing or she's just really good at faking it till she makes it, but either way, it's good to be around someone so chill in a crisis.

A swirl of dots behind my eyelids resolves into a pattern. It dances across my fingertips, shimmers back and forth at light speed along my arms and through my chest. What is it? In my mind, I reach out, grasping for meaning, for a sense of how to move. It feels like I'm slipping down a mountainside as my whole being, all the tiny lights within me, scrambles for . . .

There . . .

Purchase.

Just a whisper. It's not a voice; it's a sensation—the feeling of a free fall interrupted. Sanctuary, however brief and tenuous. A tiny way forward.

I must've gasped a little, because Tams asks if I'm okay. The moment is so crisp, so fragile. I just nod, ever so slightly, eyes still closed. I don't want to lose whatever tiny thread I've found, my only glimpse of what this power entails, a way to save Tía Lucia.

There's a flow to the swirl of lights now. It seems to resolve itself into a pattern around me, something like a song. I can do patterns. Music is patterns: setting them up, getting them solidified and clear, and then . . .

There!

. . . breaking them.

Something is off in the flow of lights in Tía Lucia's brain. It's just slight, a little tangle in the flow, but it's all connected—of course it's all connected—and already, the regular swirl of movement is self-correcting. I know—I don't know how, but deep within me, I do know all I have to do is help it out a bit.

Within myself, I reach. Within Tía's swirling mind, I reach.

Somewhere, something clicks, slides into place.

When I open my eyes, Tía Lucia is blinking up into them like I'm the sun and she's waking up from a terrific night of partying.

"¿Qué . . . ?" she groans. "¿Qué pasó?"

"I . . . think I . . . I think I healed you?"

She rubs her face. That bruise has already faded to a yellow-ish blotch. Tams and I help her sit up. "I remember the fighting. The yelling. I was trying to get them to stop. Why were they fighting . . . ?" She swats the question away. "Bah. No importa." Looks at me, eyes suddenly sharp, lucid. "Mateo, you did it!"

"I did." I half laugh. All that panic swirling through me has nowhere to go now that Tía Lucia's okay, so it turns into a weird giddiness, like I just drank ten cups of her incredible café. I want to sit here and hold her and celebrate, but there are more injured people around us, and I . . . apparently, I *am* a healer.

"We'll talk back at home," Tía says, standing and dusting herself off. She must've seen me glance around. "I'll clean up in the club and get one of the fellas to walk me home. Go do what you were born to."

I still don't know how I feel about all that, but fear wiped away my anger, and now I'm mostly just confused. She hugs me, those warm arms squeezing all the uncertainty away, if only just for a moment, and lays her head on my chest. "Gracias, Mateo," she whispers, and then waddles away.

I watch her go. I almost lost her. I also almost cursed her out just before almost losing her.

Ugh. I've always been my parents' son through and through: a wanderer, drawn to things that make sense. Staying with Tía just felt like a temporary stop, just like everywhere else I've ever stayed. The Home Everywhere/No Home problem: my whole existence in a nutshell.

Now . . . in just a few hours, everything has changed. My tía knows things about me, my past; she understands this power I carry.

I almost lost her.

I don't understand it all, but she's right—we can deal with that later. Right now, Bernal Balcón is writhing on the ground nearby, clutching his arm.

I'm about to approach him when I notice Tams's wide stare on something behind me. "Uhhhh . . ." she says, her voice a dark cloud.

Chela's standing there in the hazy streetlamp glow, a shiny blade in her hand. The same one I saw her murder someone with earlier. It's short and forms an elegant curve away from the beaded handle. Her big red hair is pulled back into a single pouf now, and she's wearing all black again. She's not moving, looks relaxed even, but there's no question she's ready to kill.

"Ahrr . . ." I say, once again like a doofus. Is it me she's here to kill? Maybe that whole being-nice-to-me thing earlier was an act so she could get close. I was an eyewitness, after all. That's what you do, isn't it? And why can't I find it in me to just say nothing instead of making random grunts?

For a moment, she and I just stare at each other, like we did a few hours ago, except a little calmer now. I hear Tams stand up behind me, ready to throw down, even though neither of us is armed and Chela is obviously trained in some kind of stabby-death murder style.

Chela raises her eyebrows, maybe smiling ever so slightly? Then she turns around, and I realize there are people gathered at the far end of the street. I recognize some of them—Tomasino Pap, Arco "El Gorro" Kordal, Smernal Colón. . . . Proud pirate types, most of them, but not part of Tolo's crew.

I'm not sure what they're here for, but they didn't come simply to gawk at the carnage.

Everybody's just standing there staring.

Whatever their issue is, Chela Hidalgo's very presence keeps them at bay.

When Beral Balcón groans, I turn, very slowly, and lower myself back down to find that tiny click of connection once again.

———◆———

I can't say whether or not it works exactly, this power in me. Or whatever it is.

When it's all over, I've squatted beside all four of the injured and muttered to myself while I waved my hands, closed my eyes, sweated, got dizzy, spoke meaningless reassurances. I only puked once, hey, hey! (That was probably only because there was nothing left to puke, though. I might've dry heaved three or four times.)

No one was too messed up, thank the seas.

Tams stuck around, checking in with each person as they managed to get to their feet and hobble off to safety. (Wherever safety is—who knows anymore?)

The pirate guys kept their distance, and Chela stayed stock-still all the while, blade out.

And now, as I do the final made-up hand placing and hopeful healing with the last guy—Vedo, the kid with the bad poem—he lets out a gurgley moan. I'm about to ask if he's okay when he goes, "She's so gorgeous."

I roll my eyes and get back to his bruised forearm. Everyone is always bugging me to introduce them to Tams. I get it—she's strikingly beautiful, with cheekbones you could do surgery with, and a fashion sense five years ahead of anyone's time. Plus, she's the only person at school as tall as I am, but she carries it better, like she was born for height. Even more so when she's next to my unnecessarily gangly ass.

But when I look up and follow Vedo's gaze, it's not Tams he's gawking at—it's Chela.

And I mean, she does look kind of radiant there in the street with the blue glow from the club's marquee turning her into some kind of celestial being. A murdering celestial being, I remind myself.

I've never thought that much about her. She hardly speaks, just stays out of the way, mostly. I did play her bat mitzvah, though, three years back, when I was just getting started at this performing thing. Chela had everything memorized perfectly and spoke the words of the Torah like she was having a casual conversation, not with the usual breathy, belabored arrhythmia most kids garble out.

Now that I think about it, she absolutely killed it on the dance floor at the after-party, and I remember being kind of amazed, because she'd never seemed to care about music or, well, anything much.

She'd moved with the same fluidity and abandon to whatever pop song was blaring on the speakers back then as she had tonight, in the run-up to her kill.

I shudder, condense all those thoughts into a mumbled "Yeah," and realize Vedo and I are both staring at her. Chela realizes it, too, apparently, because she turns ever so slightly and catches my eyes— or maybe Vedo's, who's to say. Then she looks back at the goons at the end of the street.

"Just gorgeous," Vedo says again. Then he gets up and wanders away without so much as a thank-you. There hasn't been an actual initiated healer for generations, as far as I know, so I'm not sure why Vedo is taking all this so calmly, but I guess he's in shock. Or too in love to care.

Doesn't matter. I'm done. I don't know what I am, or what I did, but it's over now. I wipe off my suit—it's filthy from street grime and a little spot of (dry heave) blood. And when I look up, Chela's gone. The street is empty except for Tams, who's calling to let her parents know she's okay.

Then a shimmer catches my eye near the club entrance. I already know what—who—it is before I glance over.

That hooded spirit from before. He's watching me, a bright enigma in the shadowy night.

I get up from my squat. Everybody seems to be watching me these days.

Tams's still deep in her phone, and I walk slowly toward the apparition, my whole body a single, thundering pulse. I'm a few feet away when he raises both hands, and I almost leap back, my heart ready to blast out my throat.

But he just places them on his cowl and pulls it back, revealing a stern bearded face over broad shoulders. A single scar runs down the left cheek, over his empty eye and down to his jawline.

I'm low-key impressed that my voice doesn't shake when I say his name: "Galanika."

The spirit stares at me for another moment, and then he's gone.

"What?" Tams says behind me.

"Galanika," I say again, still staring at the dark emptiness where one of the three spirits of San Madrigal just stood.

"Uh-huh, sure," says Tams. "I told my folks I'm crashing with you tonight, because obviously we got a lot to talk about. You ready to get out of here?"

Am I ever.

CHAPTER FIVE

As we walk home, my whole body feels like it's made out of soggy cardboard. Probably just tired, but every step is a chore. Worse than that, though: the streets are quiet. Terrifyingly so. We stroll down Fulton, past the empty stares of dark storefronts and some torn police tape whipping in the October wind. No one else is out.

Tonight's street brawl, how real it got, has already brought a new kind of shadow down on us. Plus, Councilwoman Bisconte's no guns/no cops agreement had done a pretty good job of keeping the police out of Little Madrigal all these years, so their sudden intrusion adds another level of tension.

And on this, of all nights.

Here's the thing about pirates: you really don't know that much about them, whoever you are. Sure, you rode an amusement park ride. You read a book. Congrats. But most of the common junk Joe Regular thinks he knows about pirates is based on, like, a couple random dudes in a very specific moment of history, right? There have always been pirates, though, and there always will be. It's like saying you're an expert on plumbers because you played *Super Mario Brothers.*

There isn't a common pirate culture, but pirates across the world have had to cultivate certain traits by nature of the job. It's so many extremes, or, in Madrigal terms, opposites coexisting. To survive, they had to live either entirely under the radar or be so known and feared that no one would bother messing with them. They couldn't trust authorities, but sometimes had to collaborate with those same authorities to get by. When death lurks over the crest of every wave, you either live in constant terror or live life to the fullest. Or, more than likely, some combination of both.

Either way, the pirates of San Madrigal threw together various folktales, superstitions, love songs, survival codes, and recipes that they'd picked up along the way, and they forged themselves a loose kind of culture. And really, how different is that from any other culture? And because we're just talking about a few hundred people on a rock in the middle of nowhere, that culture seeped into everything. There are Galeranos who cling tight to that pirate identity, the lineage, the lingo—but the core gist of that pirate life reached everyone, Santero, Sefaradi, agnostic, whatever. In San Madrigal, it's as universal as the three spirits.

And the Grande Fete is the epicenter of that. Supposedly, it goes all the way back to the first tumultuous year on the island— celebration of life mandated by the dead, according to some. It's credited with saving us from invasion and plague in various eras, for various reasons. It's core to who we are.

And all that aside, the Grande Fete is when you're supposed to stay up till sunrise, playing music, eating amazing seafood, creating brand-new juiciness for the little viejitas to chatter about from their windows the next morning.

Instead, it's just this shuddering quiet.

Tams feels it, too, but, in typical Tams style, she wards off the creepy quiet by refusing to honor it. "Tell me everything," she demands with a conspiratorial wink, and I obey because that's what we do. She gasps and snickers at all the right moments, and I see her lighting up when I tell her about what it felt like to heal.

The only thing I hold back on is probably the least important part of the night, and Tams already knows about it anyway: that I don't fit in, that I feel like I'm always looking through a window at my own neighborhood, my own life, even. I don't say how much it hurt to suddenly be the center of attention, the name on everyone's lips, because what words would I even use? The only thing that could express that level of emotion is music.

When I'm done with the saga of the night, we've both stopped walking and we take a couple moments of just going "Whoa . . ." because a man died, and my tía almost did, too, and an island is rising, apparently, and absolutely nothing makes sense.

Then Tams launches into an explanation of her own initiation. Santeros spend a whole year wearing white. Tams describes it like she entered into a sacred pact with a guardian angel orisha, Ochossi—and I gotta admit, I feel a pang of jealousy. It's like she has her own personal mystical friend looking out for her.

We were ten when Tams initiated. I wasn't at the ceremony, but I remember her telling me about it then, a little. I didn't really get it, just that she was wearing white a lot, and I kinda resented the fact that she had a bunch of stuff to do and couldn't come over to play as often when I was in town. And then it was just a thing that she and Tía Lucia had in common, and that was cool, but Tams and I never talked much about it.

"Ochossi guided me to play the drums," she says now as we round a corner onto a dark residential street and pass under an old oak tree. "Your aunt told me at my ceremony, at the divination, that I was destined to play drums, but I already knew. It was just confirmation."

"Wow," I say. It sounds so nice to have a destiny calmly mapped during a ceremony instead of finding out about it in the middle of a riot. "You've never told me about that." I don't mean it to sound accusing, but I guess a glint of my jealousy leaks out, because Tams stops walking and turns a devastating glare on me.

"You never asked," she says. "Believe me, I've tried."

"What?" This is news, but I guess that's the point.

She throws up her hands, already over this whole convo. "Mateo, your eyes glaze over whenever I talk about my spirit stuff. I just gave up. Like . . . years ago, man."

"I . . ." I want to argue, but I know she's right. My face scrunches up. "I . . . I'm sorry. For real sorry. That's messed up. It's really important to you."

She nods, one eyebrow raised, mouth twisted to one side. "You were too busy trying to be Maestro Gerval's little clone."

I take a step back. "That's not—"

"It's not true?"

"I mean, it's . . ." The words don't come out because whether or not it's true is beside the point. Her comment hurt! Which I guess was the point.

Tams shoots me her *waiting impatiently for a response* look.

"Music is . . ." *My only connection,* I want to say, but connection to what? The world, it feels like sometimes. But really, it's not the whole world, just *this* one—the one that's shattering all around us. "I don't know how to *be* when I'm here. Like, how to exist. All I can think about is what I'm doing wrong and how obvious that must be to everyone around. And especially after what happened tonight . . ." I hate how my voice goes up a notch or two when I'm defensive, and I hate even more that Tams totally knows that about me. She'll realize she's got me on the ropes.

I try to bring it back to normal. "And Gerval is like . . . the epitome of that. He gets us, he *is* us, but he isn't stuck here. And that's the thing: I don't want to *be* the guy. But seeing how he is showed me a way that I can be, if that makes sense. And I just want him to see what I've got, and then take me along with him all over the planet."

Tams realizes I've hit a dead end in my thoughts, and she knows I tried my best. She keeps it moving. "I get that. And I feel it, too, sometimes. Not the same thing, obviously, but you know . . . this whole game folks are always playing about how we're all in it together, it gets old, when we all know it's a lie. Especially when crap like tonight pops off."

"Exactly." I get what she's talking about. The entire weird riddle of our colorism and economics problems—it's not just an interesting cultural puzzle. It's people's lives, feelings, struggles. She's exceptionally good at fitting in everywhere she goes, sure, but it's nowhere near as easy as she makes it look. I know about the micro- and macro-aggressions, the creepy ways that colorism, legacies of an empire we were never conquered by, still seep into our language and lives.

"And look, what you said a second ago about my initiation? You don't have to apologize. It's cool." She smiles with no malice. "Well, that's not really true, but now you're gonna make it up to me." A wicked glint flashes in her eyes. "Because my house has a bembé coming up two nights from now, and you can come along!"

"Cool!" I say, and manage not to make it sound too much like a question. Bembés are like big parties the Santero community throws for a spirit, usually to mark a new initiation. There's singing, drumming, dancing, and delicious food both for people and spirits.

I've played music at a few but never gone to one just to go. Which I guess is part of the problem. I blocked out my own initiation, and in doing so I put up a wall about something important to my best friend. But the idea of just showing up at a bembé, like, as a participant—it never sat right with me. Those are for people who really believe, people who throw their whole lives into being a Santero and that intimate, complex connection to their guardian spirit. It's never said—technically, everybody's welcome—but those are mostly for initiates. Except it turns out I am one and have been all along.

"And anyway," Tams says, probably reading my mind, "now you're a woo-woo spirit person, too!" She skips off, snickering. "Now we *gotta* talk about it! Ha!"

"Tams! Wait up!"

———◆———

By the time we get to my front door, my body still feels soggy and my thoughts have wandered all the way back to the beginning of the night, that horrible moment when Trucks collapsed beneath Chela's attack, the fury in her eyes. . . .

"What is it?" Tams asks.

I blink. "I wasn't glazing over, I swear!"

She laughs. "I would've punched you if that's what I thought was happening. You just look really sad."

We're standing on the stoop, gazing out at the street. We've spent so many nights right here, talking about the world and music (mostly music). I don't know if I've ever felt this lost and confused, though.

"I saw someone die tonight," I say. "I think? And in just a few hours, the world got a hundred times bigger and scarier than I knew it to be. And I already knew it was huge and terrifying."

Tams nods. "Real."

"Or maybe it's that the big, terrifying world got very close to home all of a sudden. Either way, I . . . I feel like I missed out on something important leading up to this. Something in my own life that's part of me, but I . . . never knew it. You have all these amazing stories of initiating and learning about your spirits, and I'm just—"

"Yeah," Tams says, eyeing the door. "If only you had someone in your immediate family you could ask about this stuff."

"Yeah," I exhale. We're heading up the stairs, and I'm running out of breath; every move feels like an epic quest. "And I almost lost her earlier. At least, it sure felt like I almost did."

"So." Tía Lucia gazes up from the little divining table when we walk in. She doesn't look any worse for wear. "I spoke to some folks while I was cleaning up at the club." She's showered now and has on a puffy pink bathrobe. She even went ahead and reapplied her makeup, even though she's clearly in for the night. Typical Tía extra-ness. "You buried the lede." She holds a lighter up to the cigar in her mouth and lights it.

"I don't even know . . ." I start to say, but then bright colors cloud my vision and then there's just nothing.

CHAPTER SIX

"Okay, okay, up you go," Tía Lucia is saying as the world comes swinging back into focus.

I'm at the altar, and she and Tams are holding me up. I don't think I passed out completely, but I have no idea what happened.

"You okay?" Tams asks.

I blink. "I think so?"

"He's all right," Tía Lucia says, pulling something off one of the shelves where her santos sit. "Just needs to cleanse."

My eyes focus on a long, shiny . . . blade? "Uh!"

"It's fine," Tía laughs. "I won't chop anything off as long as you hold still."

It's a machete. It's definitely a machete. I lean on Tams as my aunt brushes the flat part along my arms and legs and then flicks it at one of her pots. Already, my head feels clearer, but I don't know if that's because of the . . . the cleansing, I guess? Or just because I'm coming around.

"What're you doing?"

"You healed a lot of people tonight, Mateo. Including me,

gracias. Pero that can take its toll, hmm? You pick up people's crap when you heal them. Their energy, their injuries, their problems."

"That's why I felt like mushy cardboard all the way home?" I mutter.

"Sounds about right." She swipes the blade over me one more time, very carefully, and then helps me to a seat. "You'll learn to adjust to it, and sometimes you won't even notice it. Pero it can be jarring at first. I'll teach you how to clean off yourself next time."

Next time. I barely survived this one.

"Now, as I was saying: you buried the lede!"

"Uh, before you go on, Iya Lucia," Tams says, using the traditional Santero title of respect for an elder priestess, "may I salute?"

Of course Tams knows exactly how to defuse my aunt when Lucia's in one of her extra-gangster moods. The method, which I can never quite get the hang of, is to ignore the dramatics and go about your business. Tams lies down in front of the altar and mutters a quiet prayer. She does this every time she comes over—I've gotten used to it. Just one more thing I relegated to the back of my mind. Tía Lucia touches Tams's back and offers up a small blessing. Tams stands, and they embrace on one side, then the other.

"How are you, Iya Lucia?" Tams asks.

The whole place smells like bodega cigars, so the answer is *not well.* My aunt doesn't try to pretend everything's all right, she just waves and directs her glare back at me.

"What lede?" I demand. Honestly, I'm just happy she's alive, so a little attitude from her isn't much of a thing, not after the night it's been.

Anisette says she's raising the island? Aunt Miriam asks, floating in. *All the spirits are chattering.*

"That useless cow," Tía Lucia mutters. "First of all, don't believe one single word Anisette says. Not one." She punctuates it with a severe pursing of her bright red lips. Both eyebrows go straight up. "¿Oíste?"

"Yes, I heard you," I say, sighing. "But, Tía, she showed pictures of the peaks."

"¿Y qué?" Tía slams the table. "Photoshop doesn't exist?"

"Why are you so upset? And why are you actually smoking those things? You never smoke them."

She smirks, shaking her head. "Let's let Lucia worry about Lucia's business, and Mateo worry about Mateo's business, hmm?"

Lucia, Aunt Miriam says with a slight warning in her faraway voice. There's something going on with them—something they're not telling me—and it started with that reading earlier tonight. But I know better than to try getting anything out of my aunts.

"What's my business?" I actually do want to know what she's going on about.

Tía Lucia motions for me and Tams to join her at the little table. My aunt suddenly looks very pleased with herself. "Te despertaste, Mateo," she says, leaning forward with a wry smile once we've settled into the folding chairs.

"I woke up? What do you mean?"

"'Initiated, fully awakened children of the original spirits,'" Tams says, quoting what we'd heard back at the club. "I was wondering what Anisette meant by that."

If even Tams doesn't know, that means it's a concept outside the normal Santería stuff. The Santeros seamlessly wove the three original spirits of San Madrigal into their pantheon; stories about them interacting with the other santos go all the way back through the history of the island. But the pirates took them on, too—plugged them right into that weird, cultish mix of superstitions and saints that they practice. I've never totally understood how the Sefaradim work them into their beliefs, but Madrigal, Okanla, and Galanika pop up throughout the Galerano prayer books and Jewish fable books. I guess the three spirits are like me, in a way, at home everywhere and nowhere at the same time. Or maybe they're just at home everywhere, like Tams.

"An initiate of one of the original spirits," Tía Lucia says with a sagely drag on her cigar, "cannot fully step into their role, their destiny, until they are awakened. To do this, they must *use* their powers. Usually"—she winks at me—"just one time will do it."

"So, I . . . You're saying I awoke my powers tonight, by healing you?"

Tía Lucia nods.

Thank you for that, by the way, Aunt Miriam calls from the far corner, where she's hovering, doing some ghostly stuff, who knows what. . . . *Even if some people want to jump right back into business as usual as if nothing happened, I appreciate what you did.*

"Yo también," Tía Lucia insists. "Pero I also know what it means about what happens next."

Both Tams and I stare at her, because you can't just drop something like that and not elaborate.

Tía Lucia shrugs the Galerano shrug in response—a kind of halfway mambo, one shoulder up, then the other—and tilts her head to one side with a wide frown. "If what Anisette says *is* true—and that is quite an enormous *if*—then many people are about to come knocking at your door, Mateo."

I drag a hand down my face. That is just about the worst possible thing you could tell me. More eyes, more chatter, more bochinche, more beef. "What, I'm going to be like the local doctor now? Everyone showing up to get their blisters and earaches cured and then getting mad at me when a cure doesn't take?"

Tía chuckles, blowing out a mess of smoke. "Heh, no, no, much worse, mi amor. Anisette was right about one thing, and I know that because she was quoting me. Sí, the isla *can* be raised, although I never imagined it would happen in my lifetime. And sí, to do it fully, it requires una ceremonia involving three initiated, awakened children of the original santos of Madrigal. That's why you were made, Mateo. Bueno, that and to save your life, but esa es otra historia."

"Wait," I say, because that's something I'd like to hear, but she barrels right through.

"Fifteen years ago, the shells predicted absolute destruction of our world. The only salvación was in initiating one child to each of the three isla spirits." She shakes her head, a sudden sadness enveloping everything. "We tried. Believe me, we tried. Ay, mi madre . . . We searched and searched for who those initiates should be—you have to check with divination, you know, and . . . you were the only one who took. And then, when I initiated you . . ." She looks away, scowls.

"What?" I ask. "What happened?"

"Ah, Mateo. That was the day la isla went down. We barely made it out of the ceremony alive."

Suddenly, I'm standing and I don't remember getting up. My whole body is ice-cold. "Did I . . . did my ceremony . . . do that? Did the ceremony destroy the island?"

It sounds bonkers, I know, but if San Madrigal can be raised from the depths of the sea with a ceremony, why couldn't a ceremony be what sank it? Nothing is impossible, not anymore.

Tía Lucia waves away the notion. "Tranquilo. No. Absolutely not. Calm down. Sit."

Tams puts her hand on my shoulder as I lower back into the chair. I'm not totally convinced, but I know Tía wouldn't lie to me, not about this.

"Point is," she goes on, "Anisette seems to believe—or wants *us* to believe she believes—that somehow someone initiated two other people, one to Okanla the Destroyer and one to Madrigal the Creator, without me knowing. Seems dubious, sí. Pero if she's right, and she gathers up esa gente along with you, pues . . ." Tía's smile turns grim, her teeth clenched, jaw tight. "Our lore speaks about catástrofes, you know, even about la isla sinking. And it says whoever raises la isla controls the spirits of la isla, becomes a kind of mystical master of all that magia. It's . . . We don't totally know what it means, but it's a lot of power." She scrunches up her face like she just smelled old milk. "More power than that tonta should have, I know that much. There'll be luxury hotels all up and down the three peaks before you can say *But we were supposed to stay hidden.* . . . Trust me on that."

"Yikes," Tams says.

I don't know what I'm supposed to do with all this. I can barely wrap my head around it, but Tía seems to think it has something to do with my destiny, the way she's talking. "So I stay away from Anisette? I can do that."

"It's not that simple, querido. Todo el mundo will be trying to figure out how to do this, now that it's possible, now that the rising has begun. They will be looking for the otra initiated children, and they will be doing whatever they can to bring you over to their side."

"What are these sides?" I demand as panic swirls and rises within me.

Tía throws up a hand. "That remains to be seen."

"I'm not on any sides. I don't want to be on any sides."

"Bueno. They will try to endear you to them, and if all else fails, to convince you by force to do what they want."

"No," I say, shaking my head, but I don't even know what I'm rejecting. The whole thing. "What do they want?"

"Power," Tía Lucia says with a smirk. "Same as everyone else."

I know that face she's making, where the gravity of her tumbling sentences leads. "There's something else," I say.

"I know you don't want to be on any sides, and I understand, especially because the players haven't even revealed themselves yet. But you don't get to sit this one out, Mateo."

Damn, she knows me well. "What am I supposed to do?"

"Find the other two initiated children, the priests of Okanla and Madrigal. Without them, nothing else can be done. Maybe Anisette is bluffing—it's not beyond her, believe me. Pero we must be certain. The risks are too great. If la isla is to rise, it must be us who do it."

I gape at her, a million questions swirling through me. Only one comes out, but it's the only one that really matters. *"How?"*

"Wish I could tell you, I really do," Tía says with genuine regret. "All I can say is, get close to everyone but trust no one." She directs a sharp glare into my eyes. *"No one.* ¿Entiendes, Mateo Matisse Medina?"

"Not the full government name," Tams whispers in quiet horror.

All I can do is nod.

"Start," Tía Lucia says, lighting another cigar, "with Chela."

"Chela *Hidalgo*?" Tams and I both sputter at once.

She wiggles her eyebrows. "That girl's up to something."

"Besides murdering people?"

"Find out, Mateo. Find out what she knows, what she's about. The Sefaradim don't allow initiations, and I can't imagine the head rabbi of Madrigal letting his only daughter be part of some secret ceremony. So I doubt she's who we're looking for. But she definitely knows something. If nothing else, it's a way to talk to her cousin, Tolo, and Tolo knows *everything.* And he'll know even more when he becomes pirate king. There are supposed to be all kinds of secrets passed from one leader of the pirates to the next, and Anisette was close to his mamá, Mimi, before she went down with la isla."

"Messy," Tams says.

Tía Lucia laughs. "The past never goes away, jóvenes. What happened then matters now. Chela knows some things we don't."

"And?" I say.

Her smile vanishes. "Find out what she knows. Pero escu—" She catches herself midway through her favorite word.

For a second, I'm pretty sure we're both thinking about that moment earlier tonight when I pulled away from her.

Right before I almost lost her for good.

"I'm sor—" I start.

But she interrupts me: "No, no, por favor. It's okay. You were right, out there. I don't get to choose your destiny. I have no right."

Now I'm really listening.

"But sometimes we are called to things, to roles, and they're not always easy."

I make a noncommittal grunt, because I guess I know what she means, but I'm not sure what to do with it.

"When I say, *escucha*, Mateo, I don't just mean to listen to me."

"You don't?"

"I mean to listen to the world. Listen more deeply. To stop and listen. For real listen, not just hope you hear."

"What's the difference?"

"Listening is active, it's something you *do*. You have to decide to do it. But you get so caught up in your head, Mateo. You just end up getting in your own way. I mean listen *deeper*. Go deeper. Because at first, all you will hear is your own fear."

Okay, she has a point there. Basically, that's why I try to stop listening when it comes to most things non-music-related, because I'm tired of hearing all the worst-possible scenarios. "Go on," I say, scrunching up my face.

"Fear is a lie." She says it with so much certainty, like it's the most obvious thing in the world.

"How do you know all my nightmares won't come true?"

"That's not what I said. I don't mean there aren't bad things in the world, that bad things won't happen."

"So?"

She smiles. "I mean it's a lie by omission. When you're afraid, that's all you know, all you hear. There is *always* more to the story. The good and bad *always* live in the same space. But fear takes up all the oxygen. This is why you must listen, you must go deeper."

I'm not sure I get it, but I'm not sure I ever will. "Okay."

"Pero ahora, eschúchame."

"You just said—"

"Don't trust Chela Hidalgo, m'ijo."

I throw up my hands. "I thought I wasn't supposed to be afraid!"

"Oh, you should definitely be afraid," Tía Lucia chuckles. "Just don't be *only* afraid! Don't be so afraid you can't hear anything else!"

"This is ridiculous!"

"And don't trust anyone."

"Except me," Tams puts in.

"Look, Tía," I say, "why don't *you* look into all th—"

Tía Lucia's having none of it. "You know very well I can't go snooping around for answers. I'm the head Santera of Madrigal. I'm part of the Cabildo. No one's gonna tell me nothing. And anyway, you may find being an awakened son of Galanika comes with certain benefits. You're a local celebrity now! Live it up."

"Ugh," I say.

"And use it." Tía Lucia nods, barely skips a beat. "Y acuérdate: the good lives inside the bad, which lives inside the good."

I am fully over these mystic riddles. "I don't see how that's supposed to help."

She stands, nodding at me and then Tams. "Go to bed, Mateo. You have school in the morning, and it's already past one a.m."

"But . . ."

"And I have baking to do! We can talk more tomorrow."

"Baking?" Tams gawks. "Now?"

"Late at night is the best time to bake," Tía Lucia says, like it's the most obvious thing in the world. "Buenas noches, kids."

I let Tams take my bed. Every muscle in me groans for rest, but instead of lying on the couch, I sit, for the first time in as long as I can remember, in front of the altar. Too many thoughts are brambled in my head, too many questions. They all seem to congeal and pulse around the memory of Chela sliding her knife into Trucks, his body collapsing, and the way my breath left me in that moment. How can I talk to her? Why does it have to be me? What am I supposed to do with this ongoing memory of a murder cycling through my brain?

That's fear. That's what Tía was talking about. It takes over the world.

Escucha.

What else is there?

Truth is, a tiny trill of excitement has been buzzing beneath all the other thoughts and worries. I felt it spark up when Tía Lucia gave me the mission—just a whisper compared to all the yelling doubts, but still . . . it's there. It's been there. It's real.

Go deeper.

I would never seek out Chela Hidalgo's friendship on my own. It's not that I don't want to be friends—she seemed pretty cool before she turned out to be so stabby. It's more this: Why would I knowingly put myself in a situation where I could mess up some really obvious detail about growing up in Little Madrigal? Tams doesn't care about that stuff, and she knows who I am beyond all that, so it's easy with her. But Chela, Tolo, all the others at school—I'm fine just being the aloof kid.

Except, if I go deeper, I'm not fine with it.

This is why going deeper sucks.

But also, that thrill is still there. Because Tía's mission means I have a reason to toss myself headfirst into the most terrifying social situation imaginable—my own people. And maybe that's something I've always wanted to do, anyway, almost as much as I've been afraid to. Maybe Tía's mission is just the excuse I've needed to do what I should've done a long time ago.

Or maybe I'm kidding myself. Trying to get information is the last way anyone should try to make friends. Disaster hides down every route.

When I go even deeper than that, there's just an emptiness that I don't know what to do with. It's where I imagine all those brilliant, spirit-connected people in my life find solace, find the companionship of their guardian angels.

Maybe here at Tía's altar, this sacred space, there will be a spark, a secret voice, a melody . . . *something* that will make some sense of all this. But no—it's just soup tureens and fancy fabrics. Galanika's scarred face stares stonily back at me from his picture.

There are no answers here, just a silence as grave and unforgiving as the empty streets outside.

PART
TWO

II.

Return to me, my love,

Through stars and burning cities,

Knives flashing,

Calamity the only song you remember.

Your eyes on my skin, enemies cascade around you, then crumble.

Destruction your name,

Tongue made of fire.

A thousand swords, your wings.

When you arrive, we rise,

And the world begins anew.

Return to me, my love.

—*Prayer to the Outlaw Saints*, Juanita Casca Balcón

II.

Vuélveme, mi amor,

Por estrellas y ciudades ardientes,

Kamas brillando,

Desastre la única canción que te recuerdas.

Tu ojos pegados a mi piel, enemigos caen por todos lados, y tumban.

Destrucción tu nombre,

Lengua de fuego.

Mil espadas, tus alas.

Cuando llegues, subiremos,

Y el mundo se empieza de nuevo.

Vuélveme, mi amor.

—*Oración a los santos bandoleros*, Juanita Casca Balcón

CHAPTER SEVEN

"I think you have a crush on Chela Hidalgo."

I blink awake to see Tams standing over the couch looking smug. It's, like, dawn or something, and I hate everyone. Okay, I don't hate Tams, but everyone else. No one should be awake at this hour, but especially not after . . . whatever last night was. The only good thing is that the sweet, tangy smell of freshly baked pasteles has taken over the house—evidence of Tía Lucia's late-night kitchen party. They're probably cooling on the table under a paper towel. Which means one will be in my tummy soon.

I sit up, rub my eyes, scoff. "You mean Chela Murderface McDeathMurder Hidalgo? Not my type."

Tams raises her eyebrows to affirm that she knows more about me than I do. Then she walks into the kitchen, shaking her head. "I'm putting the coffee on. We gotta head out soon, sleepyhead."

"Why are you so chipper?" I demand as the kitchen door closes behind her.

Tía Lucia once said that the public school system was biased for not giving us the day off after the Grande Fete. At the time, I probably rolled my eyes because okay, sure. But today, I'd give my right leg for another couple hours of sleep. Thing is, most years we stay up even later and actually get to party, but the excitement of the wild night—and all that music!—carries over into the next day and gets you through class. Then you go home and knock out for, like, twenty hours and—*ka-zam!*—all good.

This, though? I feel like I got hit by a truck, and every time I remember another shard of the night, the truck pulls a U-ey and hits me again.

Tía Lucia lying there in the street . . . *THUD!!*

The whole community at one another's throats . . . *WHUMP!!*

The three peaks of San Madrigal rising from the sea, Chela's ceremonial blade entering Trucks . . . It's all just too much.

"Coffee's ready," Tams calls, which means I've been sitting here and staring into my own memories like a goober for ten minutes. She opens the kitchen door to entice me in and then pointedly breaks off a piece of flaky baked deliciousness.

"Pastelesss," I mumble-hiss.

Not until you're dressed and ready to go, Aunt Miriam chides from the doorway of her bedroom.

Tams quickly shoves the rest of the pastel in her mouth, and I scowl at her.

You have specific instructions! Aunt Miriam continues. *And don't be too loud—your tía needs her sleep.*

Please. Tía Lucia has been known to sleep through anything, so that's weird, but whatever. Aunt Miriam is consistently over-the-top. And anyway, pasteles.

I stand, stretch, shake off the sleep. "At least I'm not in love with twins," I grumble at Tams as I shuffle past on the way to the bathroom.

"You had all this time to generate a comeback, and *that's* the best you could do?" She grabs another pastel (there are, like, twenty—Tía

Lucia went to town, apparently) and tears off a chunk, holding it just in front of me.

I snatch it before she can whisk it away. "Is it false?"

She shrugs. "I'm a drummer. We like who we like, and we love chaos above all else. And anyway, both Maybelline and Maza are gorgeous. Empirical fact. Not my fault, nor my problem."

Okay, she's right about that. The Alameda twins are both supernaturally, stunningly, supermodel-level beautiful. But still—Tams has flirted with each of them in different classes. "It will be if both of them fall in love with you," I say, walking into the bathroom.

"Still better than falling for Murder Girl!" Tams calls as I close the door.

———◆———

Galerano adults love to brag about how the three main cultures of our island never broke into open warfare against one another.

And that's true. However . . .

Like all things that people crow about, especially when it comes to their own backgrounds, this claim conceals an awkward reality about San Madrigal: the centuries-old path from when it all began to today is soaked in blood. Sure, the Sefaradim and pirates and Santeros never took to the battlefield as singular armies, but that's only because they were too busy dealing with internal strife, joining forces with outsiders to crush their rivals, planning or recovering from gruesome assassinations, or marrying off their children for tactical alliances—all that horrible stuff. Our history contains plenty of shoot-outs, coups, and one notable bar fight in 1899 that escalated into a citywide brawl and only ended when most of the island was in literal, not metaphorical, flames.

On the other hand, our Sunday-school classes are excellent about covering the horrors of every stage of colonialism and conquest. From the early conquistadors right up through the international conglomerates like the Dutch East India Company, and, later, the United Fruit Company (or La Frutera, as it was known) that sowed destruction throughout the Caribbean and Latin America, and straight to today's many rebranded versions of empire. In the classes I did get to attend, and in the handouts they sent me to study while I was away, they talked about it all, often in gruesome detail.

Point is, it's been a mess. And, as I'm sure you can tell, the mess continues to this day. And in our current mess, as with all messes, the echoes of messes past get louder and louder with each new level of messiness.

In summary: mess.

So, I'm honestly grateful to have something more trivial to fuss with Tams over on the way to school. Talking about crushes takes my mind off how bad everything is probably about to get.

"You *are* almost never wrong," I acknowledge as we cross the street and dodge a passing flock of pigeons. "I'll give you that."

"Facts, facts—please proceed."

"And maybe I was too busy trying not to die to notice, but I honestly don't know what you're talking about with me and Chela!" I break into my best impression of our English teacher, Dr. Kobrick, all hunched over and wizened, and squeak, "Can you cite an example from the text, eh?"

We're almost to school, and the rising sun throws the long, flickering shadows of an elevated train onto a brick apartment building. My whole body still throbs with tiredness and nothing makes any sense at all, but three pasteles and some of Tams's unapologetically ferocious coffee have done wonders for my mood.

"I just know things," she says with annoying nonchalance.

Best friends, man. What's even the point?

"Bigger question is," Tams continues, "like her or not, your aunt gave you specific instructions to get close to her and find out what she knows. So how you planning to pull *that* off?"

I gulp. That *is* the bigger question, and I have no idea how to answer it. "Just use my natural whimsical charm?" I offer and then immediately trip over the curb and almost eat pavement.

Tams rubs her eyes. "Tragic."

———◆———

We're standing in front of the school building, a colossal cement cube that takes up a whole city block not far from Tolo's club. The architects must've thought, *How can I combine the essence of* drab *with the notion of* unfriendly *in the form of a building and make it scream* I don't care about your life? Then boom: my school.

All the voices from last night, all the stares, rear up inside me again as we approach. School is hard enough on a normal day. This is where it's most obvious that I've been gone for all the important parts of growing up Galerano. Everyone seems to have a whole secret language of hand signs, emojis, inside jokes, and references to things that happened online years ago, and I understand none of it. Seriously, you thought there was lore from before San Madrigal sank? Historians are going to be swamped for years trying to untangle the wild world of our Brooklyn diaspora secrets and codes.

They are, but I, sadly, am not. There's only so much my brain can hold, and I think I filled it all with musical notes, cadences, chord changes, technique. That's not a boast; sometimes I wish I hadn't and that I could somehow figure out how to just vibe with everyone like Tams does. But I doubt that's in my cards.

"You gonna do your thing?" Tams asks.

My thing. I have to smile. It's become such a part of our walking-to-school routine, she rarely asks anymore, but I think after our talk last night, we both feel a little more like checking in about stuff. "You want to do it with me?"

She nods. "Sure."

And we stand there, the regular traffic of kids flowing by, and take five deep, slow breaths together. It's something my dad does before surgery, and when I told him I get nervous about school, he said to try it. "Ten breaths are too many," he said over the grainy, delayed Skype call. He was laughing while he said it, but I could tell I'd worried him just by bringing it up, my nervousness. "But three won't really get you what you need. Five, though—perfect. People think meditation means you have to take hours and hours of sitting still and not thinking. And, I mean, cool, but for us, that's not gonna happen anytime soon. Meditation is literally one breath. One! If you do it intentionally. Can do wonders! Imagine how far five can take you!" Then he leaned in conspiratorially to the camera, like he was sharing a big secret. "It's just science, of course. The deep breathing slows your heart rate and increases blood flow to your brain, so it calms you down some. Don't tell my sister I said that, though."

I rolled my eyes. "I don't think Tía's a big meditation person, Dad."

"Well, you know how she gets when I chalk up everything to science."

The ongoing family debate: science or spirit. Normally, I'm team science, nodding along as my mom and dad get intricate about anatomy and physiology. Tía Lucia usually just rolls her eyes and shakes her head with a knowing chuckle, like she can't be bothered.

But after last night . . . I don't know. Everything I thought I was sure of is crashing down around me.

"Good?" Tams asks, five deep breaths of me overthinking my family later. At least I got better blood flow or whatever.

"Not *good*, necessarily," I report. "But definitely better. You?"

She tilts her head noncommittally. "Not bad."

I squint at her. "You want to talk about it?"

She laughs, shoving me away. "Ha! I really don't have anything to tell you, but I promise when I do, I will."

"The way I see it," Tams whispers to me as Mr. Varheesy rambles on about . . . something civics-related that would be interesting if it weren't being discussed by someone with the personality of soggy cardboard, "you guys are like the ultimate San Madrigal power couple."

"First of all," I snarl back at her, "we're *not* a couple yet!"

Tams raises her eyebrows just as I realize my mistake.

"Wait! I didn't mean *yet* as in—"

"You said what you said, Mateo. It's okay that you have a crush. I, for one, am happy for you both. Just don't let it get in the way of your mission."

"Ah, which brings us to the, ah, legislative branch," Varheesy drones. "Mmm, indeed, indeed." I'm pretty sure he can trace his roots back to the first Dutch invaders of what became New York, if he wasn't there himself.

"I do *not* have a crush on her!" I hiss.

Vedo's freckly face appears between us. "Have a crush on who?"

"I have a crush on you minding your business," Tams says like she's been waiting her whole life to drop that line.

"Cute, but seriously who?"

"No one!" Tams and I both growl.

"Ah, is there a problem back there?" Mr. Varheesy is glaring at us over his glasses, bushy eyebrows all furrowed.

"All good," I say.

Tams looks thoughtful. "Wasn't today a video day, Mr. Varheesy? I think you said you were going to show us *The English Patient* again."

"Ah, yes, yes." Varheesy scratches his extremely dyed blond mustache and spins back to the whiteboard. "Indeed! Let me set up the TV."

With Tams's distraction tactic in full motion, we continue our conversation. Or we would've been able to. Instead, Vedo prods, "Is it Chela?" his face still between us.

I pinch the top of my nose, like people in movies do when they're stressed. It hurts and does not relieve stress. Why do people do that?

"Why?" Tams counters. "Do *you* have a crush on Chela?"

"I . . ." Vedo turns red.

"Sure looked like it last night," I say.

He retreats quickly. "I just said she's fine! And she is!"

"You're not wrong," Tams says, then twists around to glare at him. "But it's also clear *you* have a crush on her, too!"

"Right!" I say. "Wait, no, not *too*!"

<hr>

If anyone ever tells you it's time to do burpees, run. Run like your life depends on it, because it does.

The only, I repeat *only*, reason someone wants you to do burpees is to murder you, because that's all the push-ups of death coupled with leaps are good for.

It's fourth period, which means gym class, which means Ms. Bonsignore is trying to murder us again. Death by burpee. The slowest, most grueling way to go.

I'm coming up from my third one, soaked in sweat and seeing triple, when Tams decides to revisit our earlier conversation.

"Point is . . ." She pauses to pant, jumps up, and then goes back down for another push-up. "Whew, man!"

"See? That's what you . . ." I pause to pant, jump up, and then collapse into a writhing heap. "That's what you get . . . for . . . trolling me . . . during torture hour. . . ."

"Less talking, more dying slow, horrific deaths!" Bonsignore barks. And that's why, even though she's always trying to kill us, everyone loves her. She's honest, at least. "And don't think I'm unaware that the fete ended early last night for you Galeranos!" That's the other thing: she's one of us, our only teacher from San Madrigal, and we love her as much as we're terrified of her. "Because news flash: I was there! So you have no excuse, scallywags." Obviously, she's a little too enthusiastic about her pirate heritage. All the non-Galerano kids just roll their eyes and keep it moving.

"What are we trolling Mateo about?" Maza asks with a glint in their eye. They're barely even winded, athletic ass. Ugh.

I struggle to my feet. "We're . . . *not!*"

"Oh, we are . . ." Tams pants, mid-push-up. "But the best-friend code prohibits me from . . . revealing his . . . dark secrets. . . ." She pops back up and winks at Maza over my head.

Maza winks back, then executes an impressive burpee. "I respect that! But we could make up some new stuff to troll him over, potentially, yes?"

This is weird, you see. It's not that the twins ignore me—that would imply that I exist. But I'm barely there—espíritu—and I don't take it personally that they never talk to me. (Okay, a little, but not from them.) No one besides Tams talks to me, not really, so it's not one person's fault or another. What I'm saying is I don't hold a grudge, but I do find it very odd that suddenly it's like everyone is in on some joke that I'm supposed to be in on, too. But I'm not.

Tía said people would be looking to use me. Maybe this is that.

I like Maza, though, from far away. They have a shock of bright blue hair that dangles in a smooth dollop over their face, and the rest of their head is always shaved smooth. They move through the world with a dancer's grace and are usually busy inventing some complicated new app on their phone.

I don't want to think of them as an opportunist, even if they never acknowledged I existed until today.

"Two more!" Bonsignore announces. She's always chuckling a

little bit, no matter what she says. "Then we're pairing up for the obstacle course of doom!"

I hate it here.

"I'll have—whew!—to check the code." Tams pretends to think for a half second. "Yep, that works."

Vedo leans over, dripping sweat on everybody. "He likes Chela Hidalgo."

That's it! I've had it! I scramble to my feet, soaked and gasping, and yell, "FOR THE LAST TIME! I DO NOT LIKE CHELA HIDALGO!!"

Everyone stops mid-burpee and stares at me, including, of course, Chela Hidalgo.

"That's great," Bonsignore says, still, as always, chuckling. "You can tell her all about it, since you're partners for the obstacle course of doom."

CHAPTER EIGHT

BRING ME THE PERSON WHO INVENTED OBSTACLE COURSES SO THAT I may punch that person in the neck.

A regular little jump-over-the-sandbox-and-then-turn-around-three-times routine would be bad enough, but clearly Bonsignore has been watching too many of those daytime TV All-American Athletic Barbarian Demon Warrior shows. She's transformed the gym into a multilevel boot-camp-style death trap full of impossible heights, random truck tires, and even what looks like . . . an Edgar Allan Poe pit-and-pendulum type situation. Aggressively ominous.

My thing is: Why work so hard to make the worst part of school even worse? Nothing like that toxic combination of body odor, non-sensical physical exertion, and pure malevolent chaos to take all the regular Mateo eeks and aches and ratchet them up 200 percent.

I already told you I'm long and unnecessarily awkward. Gym shorts only accentuate that. I feel like a pile of sticks that someone velcroed some rocks to and said, *Let there be life*. Doesn't help that people keep sneaking peeks at me out of the corner of their eyes. It's like a million little pocket addendums to that horrible moment last night when the entire world was staring my way.

Yes! I want to yell. *It's me! The guy you barely saw in elementary school except when he was playing music at special events. The guy who doesn't get the jokes and doesn't know how to move, the same one who just found out he has a connection to a spirit that he didn't even know about but everyone else did. Hello! Nice to meet you!*

Of course, I can also add another qualifier to that little bio: the guy who just announced that he doesn't like Chela Hidalgo to a full gymnasium, including Chela Hidalgo.

Chela Hidalgo, who has both killed a man and comforted me in my darkest moment, all within the span of a few hours.

Chela Hidalgo, who I'm supposed to get close to and find out info from but *not*, under any circumstances, trust.

Chela Hidalgo, whose big eyes are full of secrets—secrets she seemed eager to tell me last night.

Chela Hidalgo, who stands beside me right now, aiming those big eyes anywhere but at me.

I can feel the icy chill coming off her like a thousand air conditioners on high.

It's pure hate.

And I can't even be mad. I just proclaimed that I don't like her to the entire class, and she was just minding her (murderface) business.

We're in line, side by side, about three pairs away from the starting line, when I finally turn to her and say, "Look, what I meant was—"

She cuts me off with a simple hand swipe, still not looking my way. "Save it."

"But I—"

Now she turns and looks up at me with an inscrutable stare. It's just blank. Which is terrifying.

I wait a few moments, and now we're two pairs away. "It's not that I don't like you. . . . Heh, I mean, I don't even know you, really! What's not to like?" *Besides homicide, of course, but let's not talk about that right now.* "I was just saying that I don't *like* like you, you know? I mean, I'm not even saying that, either, because I don't know that, either! I mean like a crush, though, right? Because . . ." I stop because I'm definitely making it worse. And anyway, she hasn't responded.

Bonsignore blows the whistle, and the next pair goes.

I take a deep breath. "What I'm trying to say is, I'm sorry!" It sounds more exasperated than apologetic, but it is true. "I didn't mean to announce to the whole class that I don't like you."

She looks up at me again, thoughtfully this time, then says, "But what do you really want to say?"

"Say? I . . . huh? That. I did." Barely even sentences. I long for a piano in front of me to make sense of things with, but music class is still three periods away.

Bonsignore's whistle shrills out again. We're next.

"Ask me what you want to ask me."

"I . . . I just . . ." *Why did you murder that dude?* "I mean . . ."

Another whistle. That's us. Chela rolls her eyes and hurtles forward, bouncing easily through the array of tires like she's floating over them. I clear half with one long step and the rest with another.

"I saw that, Mateo Matisse Medina!" Bonsignore calls out from her lifeguard chair. No pool in sight, but she's gotta sit two stories up just so she can reign from on high. "Don't think being tall will get you out of every problem life throws at you!"

Never crossed my mind, honestly, but I don't have the time or breath in me to get snappy. Chela's already clambering up the mountain-climbing wall like she was born with wings. Didn't even bother putting the safety rope on.

I jog to the wall, grab the closest handhold, and heave myself up, already at the same level as Chela. She snorts out a breath, but that might just be because she's winded. I know I am.

"What I want to say is—*whew!*—I don't really have any idea what's . . . what's going on. . . . Seems like the whole world changed last night in ways that everyone understands except—*hooo!*—except me!"

We pull ourselves up to the top level, and I lean over, hands on my knees, trying not to sweat and pant on her. Chela just looks at me, her shoulders rising and falling a little faster than usual, but otherwise fine. "Like what?" she says quietly.

I'm so startled by her question I just keep panting for a moment.

"Let's go, let's go, let's go!!" Bonsignore yells from her throne. "Time is moving forward, but you lot are not!"

I groan. Thoughts, questions, and weird memories of last night all run chaotic laps around my head, bumping into one another, cursing one another out. A whole mess.

"The clock keeps ticking, but y'all ain't kicking!"

"Like that someone's trying to raise the island," I try.

"Yep." That's clearly not what Chela was getting at. Too obvious, and I know it. Then she turns and leaps into the air, grabbing the first monkey bar and swinging to the next with an aerialist's grace.

"The seconds continue to pass," Bonsignore yells, "unlike your lazy a—"

"Okay!" I growl, and throw my whole long self at the bars.

"Don't interrupt me when I'm cursing you out!"

"I'm on a mission," I say to Chela. I'm right next to her, moving along just two or three bars at a time so I don't shoot ahead.

She glances over, one eyebrow peaked. "Oh?"

Don't trust Chela Hidalgo. Is this one of those things I'm not supposed to talk about? It was unclear to me for so long that it doesn't even feel like my secret to tell.

But it's about me, so it *is* mine.

And how else am I supposed to get her to trust me if not by revealing long-lost truths about my childhood?

That's how people get close to one another, right? Normal people?

We reach the far end of the monkey bars, and Chela looks at me again with that quirked eyebrow. Bonsignore's busy yelling at some other poor fool, and everyone else is trying not to die at one part of the obstacle course or another. So, for a moment, it feels oddly like it's just us, even in this loud gym full of yelling and panting and squeaking sneakers and shrill whistles. Somehow, an immense feeling of calm comes over me. So, quietly, almost in a whisper, I say, "I'm trying to find out who the other initiated children of the island spirits are."

Both of Chela's eyebrows go up now, and her face seems to open. She studies me unabashedly, as if there's light radiating from some secret source within me and she's determined to find it.

It takes only seconds, but it feels like years. Not in a bad way. Definitely weird, though. I feel *seen*.

Then she says, "Well, you just found one of them."

"Wait . . . WHAT? What did you say?"

"Hmm." She shrugs an acknowledgment that's neither here nor there, then grabs the thick rope and Tarzan-swings out over the mats.

Did I say too much? Ruin everything? Who knows? She catches the next rope and reaches the far ledge. Then she turns to look at me, still holding the rope.

I grab the first one easily and swing out. When I get close enough to the platform that I can see a sheen of sweat on her shoulders and forehead, I reach out for her to pass me the other rope.

She doesn't.

"Urk," I grunt, hurling myself at the landing and barely grasping its ledge.

Chela looks down at me like I'm a bug she might step on. She's not smiling, but her eyes are twinkling. "Six o'clock tonight at the betahayim," she says as I grunt and pant, heaving myself up.

I'm halfway onto the platform, struggling. "Betahayim Cemetery?"

When I get to full height, she's glaring up at me like she's about to land a slick comeback. Instead, her eyes go wide at something behind me, then narrow into the stare that I recognize from last night, the one that means death for whoever it's aimed at.

I turn and catch the faintest glimmer of someone tall and burly making their way toward us. Who is that? They're huge. . . .

I look back at Chela to find her eyes still firmly set in murder position, but now there's the slightest smile glinting across her face. She glances up at me. "Oops."

"What do you mean, *Ooo*OOF!" Before I can finish, Chela shoulder-checks me off the platform.

CHAPTER NINE

"How exactly did you end up like this?" Tams asks, gazing down at me. Maybelline stands beside her, arms akimbo, and Maza's there, too, shaking their head.

"Chela . . . pushed me . . ." I groan from the mat, where I'm still lying on my back.

Chela Hidalgo, who, we can now add, is also one of the three initiated children of the original saints of San Madrigal.

Just like me.

Assuming she's telling the truth.

And, I realize as I lie here trying to catch my breath, I really hope she is. Because then it wouldn't just be me. There'd be someone else in this weird predicament. And if we set aside the murder thing for a moment, which I realize is a big if, Chela seems like someone I could talk to. Once I figure out a way around the not-being-supposed-to-trust-her thing, anyway.

Where is she now? Did she go after that stranger? She sure looked ready to kill again.

"Well, that answers that question," Maza says.

"What question?" There's no sign of either Chela or the hulking person anymore, at least as far as I can see from down here. When I landed, the whole class had crowded around, mostly curious, Bonsignore shaking her head like *I'd* messed up somehow. Then she'd shooed everyone off to get changed, because the period was almost over, anyway.

Maybelline hands her twin a dollar. "Does Chela Hidalgo like *you?*"

"Urg" is the approximate noise that comes out of me.

Maza accepts the money with a magnanimous bow. "Clearly, the answer is an unequivocal yes."

"Unless . . ." Maybelline snatches it back. "You didn't say anything untoward to her, did you, Mateo?"

"What? I would nev—"

"Nah," Maza says. "He doesn't seem like the type. Are you, Mateo?"

"No!"

"Half the time it's the ones who don't *seem* like the type that are the worst," Tams points out. "But Mateo's actually for real not the type."

Maza does a little mambo. "Which means she shoved him unprovoked. Which means"—they pluck the dollar away from Maybelline again—"this belongs to me."

"I feel like people in Shakespeare plays get murdered for making bets like this," I grumble.

"Well, at least we know who will be doing the murdering," Maybelline chuckles.

Tams and I trade a wide-eyed look. *Do they know about what Chela did?*

"What?" Maybelline says. "She just shoved him off a platform."

"Ah, true, true," Tams concedes, like it was all just an inside joke.

"A love shove," Maza adds.

Annoying.

"Are we helping me up, or are we just standing around enjoying my plight?"

"Mostly the second option," Tams says, "but I guess now that we've done that, we could do the first thing." She and Maza grab my hands and heave me up.

"You all right?" Maybelline asks when she's done laughing.

"I guess so. Where'd Chela go?"

"See that?" Tams gloats unnecessarily. *"Amor!"*

"No, it's not that. She was . . . There was a . . ." I look around. Tams I trust like she's my own family. As for the twins, they've just been part of the mass of people I'm pretty sure either don't like me or don't really care that I exist, right up until today, basically.

"What?" Maza asks, face serious.

Trust no one. "Nothing," I say. "I don't know."

"Well, we going to next period or what?" Maybelline says, not catching the *We'll talk later* look Tams shoots me.

"Yeah," I say, grateful for the distraction.

Then the overheads flicker and go out.

It's not totally dark—the fluorescents from the hallway spill in, cast an eerie shine against the edges of Bonsignore's torture devices and the metal bleachers beyond them. But that means it's not a school-wide power outage, just this room.

"Um . . ." Maza says. "What's going on?"

The four of us backstep close together toward the door.

"I—I don't know," I say. But this can't be unrelated to whoever it was that caught Chela's attention.

Something moves at the far end of the room—a form dashing behind the bleachers. I barely make them out before they're gone—a tall figure, maybe the same one from before? No idea.

"Y'all saw that?" Maza gasps.

"Oh hell no," Maybelline says, backing away faster.

There's a glint of ethereal light, and the figure steps out from the bleachers. Same one I caught a glimpse of before Chela shoved me. Now that I can look more carefully, it's clear this isn't a person, and it's not like the shimmering visage of Galanika I saw last night. This is a muted, almost-gray glow. . . .

Another figure emerges, and another.

It's the glow of Muertos, the dead. But they shouldn't be out and about, away from any ceremony, and they *definitely* shouldn't be at J.H.S. 765 during third period.

Don't be scared of the Muertos, Tía Lucia always says. And she would know—she's been in love with one for ten years. *Just ask them what they want and set clear boundaries, hmm? Just like with a living person.*

I gather myself, swallow back a scream, and step forward.

"Mateo!" Maybelline hisses. "What the—"

"We can't just run away," I whisper back. It's not that I'm courageous. It's that I know my brain, and if I run now, I'll spend the rest of the day/my life waiting for them to show up again and kill me or whatever, so I might as well get it out of the way now.

"What do you want?" I ask the shadowy figures. My voice doesn't sound too shaky, at least. Just a little.

There are three of them now, and they're all tall and raggedy in a way the Muertos at the Grande Fete weren't. They shamble toward me with a hunched-over, uneven gait. Their heads reach too far upward in an elongated curve and inhumanly huge teeth fill those open mouths. Loose flaps of rotting skin dangle off their arms, which seem crudely long and end in claws.

These phantoms . . . they're not human. They never were.

"Mateo," Tams warns. She's stepped up just behind me, and I feel her hand slide around my arm, ready to yank me away.

Nearby, Maza takes a deep breath. "If you wanna stay and fight, we got your back."

Maza Alameda has my back. That's not a statement I'd ever thought would be true. I wish I could revel in it, but there's a horrific phantom creature heading our way.

And I don't want a fight. I don't have any idea how to fight the dead. I just want to know what's going on.

"Tell me," I say again, a demand this time, "what you want."

Gotta be firm con los Muertos, Tía Lucia always cautions, *or they'll run all over you.*

I tried, but run all over us is *exactly* what it looks like these guys are about to do. The one in front increases its sloppy stomp to something like a charge. The others follow suit, and that's when I yell, "Okay, run!"

Don't have to say it twice. Maybelline and Maza are already almost to the door when Tams and I launch into our long-legged sprints to get the hell out of there. I feel a horrible icy tingling along my spine as I run, but I don't know if it's fear or the actual chilling touch of one of those things.

It doesn't shred me open, so that's something. We reach the doorway and burst out into the regular old school corridor, empty now that third period is fully in swing, but thankfully full of light and away from the dead creatures.

We keep going down the hall in a rapid blitz of body parts and panting and finally stop at the far end, out of breath and still freaked out.

"What . . . in the . . . How?" Maza gasps.

Maybelline throws her back against some lockers. "I thought . . . I thought we were toast."

"Are they following?" Tams asks.

The double doors leading to the gym gape wide open like an entrance to the Underworld, only darkness beyond. But no phantoms emerge. I shake my head, still breathless.

"You know something about this," Maybelline says.

I nod.

Maza eyes Tams. "Both of you."

"I think it's connected to what happened last night at the fete," I say. "My tía said raising San Madrigal is giving someone powers. . . ."

Maybelline looks warily back and forth between us. "There's more."

So much more. Everyone seems to know more about my own life than I do? Galanika keeps appearing out of nowhere? Chela killed a dude? Also, she's like me somehow. But I don't know how ready I am to talk about it all.

"Does this have anything to do with all that mess last night?" Maybelline tries when I just stand there for a few moments, staring internally at all the different ways I'm not supposed to answer that question.

I wonder if she's genuinely concerned or trying to get info out of me just like I'm supposed to be trying to get info from everyone else.

Easiest lie is a half-truth. "Chela wants to meet up tonight at the cemetery. . . ." I cringe, awaiting the inevitable onslaught of cringey jabs. Instead, everyone stares at the gym doors again. "What is it?"

"You heard that?" Maybelline asks. "Like a click?"

I didn't, but Maza and Tams must've—Tams looks ready to fight. For a second, we just stand there.

Then I hear it—a *clack*, then a scraping noise.

"Go! Go! Go!" Tams yells like we're in a bad action movie, and we're all bursting down the stairs and out the door into a fresh October afternoon, gray skies above.

"What the hell was that?" Maza demands as we catch our breath, all with a wary eye on the corridor behind us.

"I don't know," I say. "Do we . . . do we tell someone?"

Tams shakes her head. "Tell who what? That some ghost demons chased us?"

She has a point, but I don't like any of this. "It must've been what Chela went after when she bodychecked me off the platform," I tell them. "Maybe she went after them but they got away?" Or were they chasing her? Or were they chasing *me*?

"And it's not like any of us are equipped to deal with something like that," Maybelline points out. "Let's be gone, sib."

"We finally agree on something," Maza says. "See you guys tonight?"

I cock an eyebrow at her. "Tonight? I don't think Chela wants me to bri—"

Maybelline saves me from awkwarding myself deeper into a hole. "No one's trying to mess up your creepy goth date, Kid Romeo."

"It's not a da—"

"They're talking about the redo," Tams says. "Anisette called for the community to come out for an open-air redo of last night, presumably because she got the hint that it wasn't cool to just hold on to power. Said she's heard the community's complaints and is ready to officially pass on the reins or whatever."

Maybelline rolls her eyes. "I honestly don't know what the big deal is. She's been good for the neighborhood, and, like, it really is high time that the world knows who we are! We're great! People should know about us!"

"That didn't work out so well for other islands trying to stay out of the way of huge empires," Maza points out.

"Haiti and Cuba were conquered literally centuries ago," Maybelline snaps back.

"And how are things going for them these days?" Maza demands.

"Ah, anyway," Tams says, stepping between them. "It's at the intersection outside Tolo's club at seven. It's gonna be a mess. As you can already tell."

A redo of last night seems like the absolute worst possible thing ever, but I guess the community has to gather to sort out whatever it was that happened.

"Ain't you on the listserve?" Maza asks, already calm and chipper again.

I shrug. "I mean, yeah, but . . . I never check my email really."

"I actually invented an app that sorts your email for you and only pulls out the important sentences of each one," they say, somehow sounding slick and not like a super dork. "I'm, ah, still working out some of the kinks, though."

"Literally," Maybelline adds smugly. "You should see some of the *important sentences* that make it through their spam filter."

The twins say their see-ya-laters and head off, bickering about IP addresses and domain names and colonialism. And then it's just me and Tams and the autumn breeze whispering through the orange and red leaves above.

"*What* is happening?" she demands, like I'm supposed to know.

I give the Galerano shrug. "I dunno, but now, with those . . . whatever they were running around, we *gotta* find out."

"Well . . ." Tams says with raised eyebrows, and I know that whatever comes next is gonna be in poor taste. I CAN SMELL IT A MILE AWAY.

"Here we go," I mutter.

"At least where y'all are meeting it won't be hard for her to dispose of the body?"

"Tams!"

"What?" She does her own version of the Galerano shrug, and I can't lie, it's better than mine. "I wouldn't joke about it if I thought she was really gonna kill you!"

"If she does, I will haunt you for the rest of your life to remind you that the last thing you said to me was a corny joke about my death!"

"Yeah, well, it's a risk I'm willing to— Is that Gerval?" She's looking past me, to the edge of the schoolyard.

At Maestro Gerval.

He's waving.

At me.

CHAPTER TEN

MAESTRO GRILO JUAN GERVAL BECKONS ME CLOSER, HIS LONG black hair swinging back and forth on both sides of his face as he sways in the afternoon sun.

"Mateo Matisse," he says brightly, overpronouncing it.

My heart bleats in my ears; my palms are sweaty; my head spins. The world-renowned kamero—the only kamero anyone outside of Little San Madrigal has ever heard of—knows my name and is calling me over. And now he's heard me play. (Sure, just a little, but still . . .)

This is a moment I've been waiting for my whole life, and now that it's here, I have no idea how to feel or what to do about it.

It's not like under normal circumstances I'd be all easygoing about it, obviously. But now I have to balance my own nervousness against the need to find out everything I can and make sense of this mess. Plus, I saw his buddy Trucks get murdered last night, and I don't know if he knows or what exactly it means or anything else, really.

So, of course, I Mateo the whole thing up by waving goofily and garbling out, "Ahai, Mestroa!"

Gerval doesn't notice, though. "Lots going on these days in Little Madrigal. How are you holding up?"

Well, we just got jumped by some phantom creatures, I almost blurt out, but I catch myself. Don't know who to trust. Well, I do: no one.

"What is it?" he asks because I have no poker face and can't even keep a secret when I'm absolutely silent.

I laugh and then frown. "It's just . . ."

"Did something else happen?" His face creases with worry, and his dark, shining eyes look right into mine.

"Yeah, but . . ."

The great maestro of Madrigal steps back, shakes his head once with a smile, then bursts out laughing.

"What?" I demand, halfway laughing, too. "What's funny?"

"No, it's just . . ." He sighs, gathers himself. "Someone told you not to trust anyone, huh?"

"I mean—"

"Let me guess: your aunt Lucia?"

"Well—"

"It was Anisette for me. Adults, man." Gerval gives me an exaggerated eye roll. "Am I right?" He starts walking down the street, away from the school, and after a moment, I realize he's expecting me to fall in step with him.

"It's cool," he goes on. "Whatever it is, I'm sure—"

"There were creatures in the school!" *What the hell, Mateo?*

He stops, gapes at me. *"What?"*

Well, it's out now. "Weird ghosty shadowy creatures."

"Whoa! Did they . . . ?" He shoots me a quick, concerned up and down. "Did they hurt you?"

"No, we . . . I'm okay. We ran outta there. It was just weird. I don't know what's going on."

We start walking, and a moment passes. Then I say, "Do you?"

"Man . . ." Gerval sighs, eyebrows raised. "Where to even begin?"

"Wait, where are we going?" I ask, because Gerval is walking with purpose, and we've crossed Fulton now and are moving along through the quiet residential backstreets of Little Madrigal.

"Oh yeah." His laugh comes out with a gawky rasp; it reminds me he's only a year or two older than I am. Just a kid, really. "Thought you might want to play some music with me."

———◆———

We round a corner and walk across a small street to Sandoval Park. It's one of those little out-of-the-way spots with a playground, a tiny community garden, and a very modest amphitheater for the kids to do little plays in. Except today there's a grand piano there, just casually sitting on that run-down stage like it's the most normal thing in the world.

"Wha—" I gasp, stopping in my tracks.

Gerval nods knowingly. "Wicked, right?"

"How?" It's Gerval who has to keep up with me now because I'm practically floating across the park to the stage.

"Put it like this," he says, a thin, self-satisfied chuckle still lacing each word, "your aunt is right: don't trust anyone. I don't. Not even Anisette. And she basically raised me. But she's still a politician and an adult, and neither can be trusted."

The rumor is that Gerval's parents died in a murder-suicide shortly after he was born. I don't know how true it is, but that shadowy, tragic past certainly added to the mythos of who he was once he got famous. He bounced around with a few different families, including the Baracasas, but I guess he spent the most time with Anisette. Anyway, none of what he said explains why there's a piano in Sandoval Park, which we are now standing reverently in front of, so I nudge him to go on.

I can't believe I just nudged Gerval.

"Point is, even people you don't fully trust can be a means to an end. Anisette may have lots of ulterior motives and some shady dealings, but it's Madrigal! Who among us doesn't, you know?"

He's got a point there.

"I'll be honest, she's been freaking me out a little bit lately. I dunno. She insisted I come home for all this political stuff that I really do my best to stay out of. She's been getting all worked up about old history. Feel like this island-raising thing is really taking her over. Like, it'll be good for her to pass on the mantle finally and get out from under it."

"Wow," I say, partly because I can't believe he's just casually confiding in me like this.

"Yeah, I . . ." He makes a face, scratches his hair. "I decided to crash at the music studio while I'm here. It's like, I'm not a kid anymore, you know? But Anisette can't help but baby me, and with everything going on . . . it's just better."

"Sounds like a lot," I say.

"Anyway," Gerval continues, brightening, "I wanted to do an open-air concert. You know, give people a little something to enjoy."

"Hey, Maestro." On the other side of the piano, a guy stands up and brushes himself off. That would be Arco "El Gorro" Kordal, an enthusiastically piratey pirate if ever there was one. He's the guy who got shoved out of the club last night, just as things were getting hot. "The PA is pretty much set up, so just grab the mic and go to town whenever you're ready." He nods at me. "'Sup, Mateo."

I wave and say hey, but all I can think about is that beautiful Steinway waiting for me in the sun, the way her keys will sing to me as I press them, the secrets they'll reveal. . . .

"What are you waiting for?" Gerval asks, his smile on a thousand.

I sit.

Take a breath.

It's a bright afternoon—one of those October days that randomly feels like summer even though tomorrow will probably be freezing.

Old Maestro Organzo used to tell me, "Mateo, the first thing you do when you sit at a piano is play a single note," in that old rickety voice of his. "Just one note." Sounds a lot like Tía Lucia's shells, now that I think about it. He'd drill that into me during my private lessons, and usually, I still do it. "Every song begins with a single note." He'd hold up one finger, then dance it through the air as if all those chords and changes were blossoming around it. "That note is its beating heart. It beats all the way through, and then . . ." This is where he would tilt his shaky old hand downward and let it plummet. "Then it slides back to the one, once again, and that same note ends it." He'd chuckle, "Resolution, hmm?"

Gerval usually sings in A minor, so I place my finger on the middle A key and then slowly press down.

Dunnnnn.

I let it fade into the sounds of chirping birds and passing cars, kids playing nearby.

Then I hit the whole chord—A in the bass, C and E higher up, and G just for some flavor, why not? The harmonizing notes shimmer out, ominous and resplendent, and man, this piano is magnificent.

"Mmm," Gerval hums into the mic, nodding approvingly.

I hadn't even realized he was already poised to dive in.

I'm about to jam out with my hero.

"Oh!" I say aloud because the next thought comes in so fast it startles me. "Hold up!"

A crowd is already gathering, and Gerval is too busy working it to notice me pull up the recording app on my phone and hit the bright red button. Probably for the best—I'm not sure how he'd feel about me doing it. But I absolutely have to capture this moment, because who knows . . . Who knows? This might be my only chance.

"*Se vaaaaaa, se va, se vaaaa,*" Gerval croons in a rich, vibrant rasp. It's not an actual song, just a Galerano-style improvisation, a brand-new bolero in the age-old key of our lost island, and I know exactly what to do with it. My fingers find the bass notes and spill out a rugged tumbao. Up top, the chords blast out, dancing between the beat, modulating back and forth, playful.

"¡Eso es!" Gerval yells, catching what I've dropped. He swings one arm over his head, whipping the crowd into a frenzy to the beat as synchronized claps erupt in time all around me.

Madrigal.

Every song has its beating heart, but our people are a song unto themselves, and our beating heart is this: not just music, but the swirl of smiles, yells, the simple, unmistakable understanding that passes between each person here about what's happening—a thing beyond language.

"*Se va y volverá, mi amor,*" Gerval sings, and then on the next line he glances meaningfully at the still-growing crowd so they know this will be their part. "*¿Pero cuándo volverá?*" He yells, "¡Asi!" and sings the line again. This time it sounds like the whole world joins in: "*¿Cuándo volverá?*" followed by a double clap. And again and again, on and on to infinity as people start clanging the clave rhythm against the playground structures and stomping their feet in time.

"*¿Cuándo volverá?*"

When will she return? the song asks, the world asks, over and over, and sure, could be about some beautiful girl, but today, we all know what those gathered voices yearn for, and it's not a person.

"*¿Cuándo volverá?*"

I'm rollicking along beneath them, sweating, and Gerval unleashes his mean staccato scat over the thundering chorus— mostly nonsense, but it's trilingual nonsense and that's the Galerano sweet spot, so everyone loves it.

"*¿Cuándo volverá?*"

When indeed, when indeed . . . We all turn our lovelorn, heart-broken voices to the heavens and wonder . . .

"*¿Cuándo volverá?*"

I feel the song barreling toward its close even before Gerval signals me. It's in the tiny, undefinable movements of it, the way certain notes last longer, each harmony becomes a sigh. Gerval glances back, nods, and raises his fist, and we all let out one final round and hold that last *aaaaaaaah* for waaaay too long as I run up and down the keys maniacally and then slam it all home on that last, galumphing chord, the beating heart of it all, back to that single note: the one.

Cheers explode, and I can feel them move through me along with my fevered pulse. It lights me up, like all this might be a dream. It lights me up, and I feel parts of me awaken that I didn't know existed, tiny cells and synapses bursting with energy, fire.

"Ahhhh, that's what I'm talking about!" Gerval says, running over to me and leaning against the piano to catch his breath. He glances at me, and I must be staring off into the infinity of space and time like an absolute goober, because he goes, "Whoa, you okay?"

I nod. "Hooo yeah. Very much so."

"Good! Because we gotta do that again sometime!"

Everyone has already started slowly heading back to the regular world, going about their business, because that's how we do it: absolutely unparalleled sacred musical experience, and then ho-hum, gotta go pick up the laundry, ya know.

"Yes," I manage. "I would really very much." And honestly, it doesn't even matter that I can barely form sentences, because now Gerval has seen that my hands can do the talking. He passes me his phone, and I put in my number, hand it back.

"It's just . . ." He shakes his head, suddenly somber.

"What?"

"Nothing. That was beautiful. It . . . It's been a wild week. My man Trucks vanishing, you know . . ."

Vanishing? That's one way to put it. I guess that means he doesn't know what really happened.

I'm trying to figure out whether to say anything, and how, when Gerval clears his throat and says, "And . . ." He looks around, like the words he needs might be hovering nearby. "I've learned a lot about San Madrigal these past couple days. It's opened my eyes, the things I've discovered. Really . . . weird stuff."

"I mean, our whole history is weird. . . ."

"No." He tilts his head, eyes still skyward. "Not that kind of weird. Things about our history that no one knows. Well, almost no one. There's so much more to it than they ever told us—a secret history—and . . . I'm just now seeing it all. And not just our history—our present tense, too. This. Right here and now. It's . . ." He trails off.

"Who's been telling you this stuff?" I ask. "Anisette?"

"Yeah, her, others. Been reading up on it, too."

"Where?"

"Some . . . books she . . ." He seems to catch himself. Smiles widely, but there's sadness there. "Never mind. I can't . . . I can't talk about it. Doesn't matter."

"Sounds like it matters a lot."

"I need to be able to trust you, Mateo. Can I?"

I don't know. I don't even know which words to use to say I don't know, because I'm not sure if I should say it.

He sighs. "Well, whatever happens . . . I'll do my best to protect you. Protect all of us."

"Uh, thanks," I say, because . . . what do you say to that? "You mean from those shadow creatures? Do you know anything about them?"

"I'm . . . I'm trying to find out more." He shoots me a sharp look. "Can you bring Chela to talk to me?"

"What?"

"Chela Hidalgo. You know her."

I know her, and now I know something about her almost no one else does. And that makes Gerval wanting to talk to her even more interesting.

Also, I'm going to be late meeting her if I don't take off soon, I realize. And then she'll probably murder me.

"We need her on our side," Gerval says when I stand. He's backing away, eyes fixed on mine.

I don't even know what side I'm on, let alone what *our side* is supposed to mean.

"Can you bring her to talk to me?" he asks again.

"I'm not sure." It's the truth! "I don't think anyone can get Chela to do anything."

"You can't tell her it's me—she won't come. But we need her on our side, Mateo. I mean it."

"Okay." The most noncommittal word I know.

"Soon, Mateo. It must be soon."

"When's soon?"

"Tonight." He turns, starts fussing with the equipment, and yells, "I'll text you," over his shoulder.

"Okay," I say again. And then I remember—my phone has been recording this whole time. I snatch it off the piano, press Stop, and head off.

CHAPTER ELEVEN

THE BETAHAYIM CEMETERY IS NESTLED IN A ROCKY EMBANKMENT behind our local synagogue, and both places were originally used by Catholics, so the decor is all Gothic and creepy. Moss covers the decaying brick pillars on either side of the rusty gate, and winged gargoyles snarl from each. And perched on top of one of those stone creatures is Chela Hidalgo, looking right at home.

Behind the synagogue's towering spires, the early-evening sky is torn with crimson streaks across a pale flush of magenta that eases into the growing darkness above.

"I have a lot of questions for you," I say. I'm out of breath, and I don't know why. Well, pick a reason, really. The memory of those *things* in the gym hasn't left me, a relentless haunting. And now Gerval has me keeping secrets from Chela, and my aunt told me not to trust anybody.

"That's fair," Chela allows. "I got some for you, too."

"I mean . . ." I wasn't expecting that. She acts like she knows everything. And I blatantly know absolutely nothing. Well, I know about music. But that's it. My hands land on my hips and I try to find a comfortable way to stand without looking like some clown yelling at a girl on a gargoyle. (I fail.) "Okay."

"You first."

"Fine," I say, because where does one even start in a situation like this? Who has ever *been* in a situation like this? "You said you were initiated when you were a kid, too?"

"Yes."

"To one of the original santos of San Madrigal?"

She nods, giving away nothing.

"Which one?"

She scrunches up her face. "Come on, man. There's a lot going on, and we don't have much time. I know you saw what I did last night." She sweeps her arm toward the shadowy cemetery. "And this is where I asked you to meet."

"Okanla," I say. "The Destroyer."

Legends say that the Okanla Society was a cult of warriors and assassins. They had various tiers and different skills—some were sneaky, others brazen—but they all excelled at murder. All our santos had worshipers charging into battle (it's been a bloody run for us, like I said), but Okanlas were the ones you would keep in reserve until you really needed to turn the tide—the berserkers and calamity bringers.

Chela nods, then slides down easily from her perch and lands at the gates a few feet from me. "Coming?" She turns and heads into the gloom.

If she was going to kill me, she already would've done so. Sure, it's getting dark and she's inviting me into a creepy cemetery, but what am I supposed to do, stand outside and yell over the fence?

I'm just walking in after her when a flicker of movement catches my eye. The gargoyle she was just sitting on—a gnarled, irritable-looking creature . . . I could've sworn it moved as I passed. Ever so slightly?

I stand there staring at it for a moment. Considering everything else that's going on, it'd be right on brand. But the thing remains perfectly still.

"You know what's funny about you?" I say, catching up with Chela on the cobblestone path. "I just realized I've always thought of you as a goth chick, but you literally have never worn anything goth-like in all the years I've known you."

She cracks the tiniest hint of a smile. "It's 'cause I'm a real one. Don't gotta advertise it."

"That and your sunny disposition."

Her grin disappears, and for a second, I wonder if she'll materialize a knife out of thin air. Instead, she stops walking and squints up at me. "Anyway, you haven't seen me in my club fit."

"Oh!" It never occurred to me that Chela Hidalgo might go out clubbing, but why not?

"And you . . . Galanika."

I know it's more a formality, her saying it, like some part of an ancient ritual. But what does it mean to be an initiate of the great Healer? I barely know, can barely claim it. Yet, somehow, it's true. And over the past twenty-four hours, the truth of it has been gradually washing over me, bit by bit. I don't really understand it, but that doesn't mean it's not who I am.

"You already know that. You told me," I point out. "Anyway, come on, man," I say in a rough approximation of her cool-breeze voice. "There's a lot going on, and we don't have much time."

She keeps walking, the edge of her mouth hinting at a grin again. "Look, what happened last night . . . It isn't what you . . ." Her voice trails off. She's either gonna talk about killing Trucks or not, but me pushing won't help, so I just let the silence slide past.

Finally, she seems to think better of it, pushes past. "I'll level with you, Mateo. There's a lot I don't know, either. A whole lot of mess is breaking out everywhere, and these old folks don't want to say word one about it. The only person who will be straight up with me is my cousin Tolo. He and Big Moses trained me in fighting and that whole crew has my back, so that's why I go hard for them. But Tolo's knowledge is limited, too."

She lets that settle in. It's weird to think of that gangster as anyone's cousin, even though I've always known he's hers. I wonder what he knows and how he's involved.

My unspoken question must be hanging in the air all around me. Chela says, "His dad, my tío Si, was the one who had me initiated into the society of Okanla. I'm the only one, as far as anyone knows. My dad . . ." Her lips curl up, teeth clenched. "The family split over it."

"They didn't agree on—?"

"Si didn't ask first. It was all done in secret. So I guess I can see why my parents would be mad. But there's plenty they refuse to talk about, like what all this means. Anyway, I'm trying to figure out whatever I can, and I'm sure you are, too."

These are more words than I've ever heard Chela Hidalgo speak in all the time I've known her. I nod for her to keep going.

"I'm just saying . . ." She circles her hands around each other. Killing hands. *Don't trust her,* Tía Lucia warns in the back of my mind. But I have to find out whatever I can, right? I just have to play it close, play it safe. Stay alert, that's all.

"We're both in this, some way or another," Chela continues. "We should work together."

Does working together include telling her that Gerval wants me to bring her to him? He said she'd never come if she knew. If I tell her, it's me trusting her too much; if I don't, I'm trusting him too much.

There are no right answers.

Around us, the cemetery seems like part of some faraway world. It forms a wide, walled-in half circle around the front and side of the synagogue and winds around to the back. Little lanterns blink to life in the twilight, and I realize they have solar panels on them. This place looks decrepit and chaotic at first, but the grass is cut, the live oak overhead well taken care of. There's no trash, no wilted flowers on the graves. "You did all this?" I ask, waving my hand in a vague arc around us.

She smiles for real now, and it's pure pride. "Someone had to."

"Anyway, yeah," I say, taking her in cautiously. "Together. We're in this together." I'm not sure what that means exactly, but it feels true. And if nothing else, it'll be a way for me to get more information, like Tía Lucia said.

Chela perks up even more. It's a sight to behold. "Great!" She fast-walks back down the little path toward the gate. "We can get started now!"

"Wait, what do you mean 'get started'? I thought you just meant—"

"The redo of last night! It's about to begin!"

I wish people would stop calling it that. Last night was the worst night of my life for, like, ten different reasons.

But Chela's already taken off. "I'll explain more on the way!"

I head after her. Everything is happening too fast. "You're just going to drag me out here to Betahayim Cemetery and—"

"Do you know what *Betahayim* means?" I freeze as the deep baritone rumbles out. I know that voice well—Chela's dad, Rabbi Hidalgo. Usually, it's a comforting sound, like the thickness and breadth of each sonorous tone lets you know how big the man's heart is, his endless capacity to care for so many people in our community.

But after what Chela just told me, I don't know what to think anymore. Up ahead, she turns to me slowly, and I can sense her eyes rolling. When I look, Rabbi Hidalgo stands on the side portico of the synagogue next to his wife, Aviva, a normally cheerful, slender woman who doesn't speak much but smiles a lot. "Hey, Rabbi,"

I say, with a little wave. "Hey, Mrs. Hidalgo. And, ah, no? I just figured Betahayim was some dead guy that they named the place after."

Rabbi Hidalgo smirks, but it's not cruel. You can see a twinkle in his eyes beneath all that bunched-up flesh, like his whole dark face is one big smile behind his big, bushy beard. "Aha, ahh, manseviko, that would be a remarkable coincidence indeed." *Young man,* manseviko means, with that *-iko* giving an added twist of fatherly affection. He walks down the little stone stairwell and joins us on the path. Mrs. Hidalgo stays perfectly still, her eyes glued to her husband. "But no, the answer holds great mystery and wonder, in fact. Perhaps even one that is relevant to you."

"Jaime," Mrs. Hidalgo warns from behind him. "Be careful."

"*Betahayim* means *cemetery,*" Chela says with a groan. "It's not the name of the cemetery—it just *is* the cemetery. And we're all sick of these riddles, Dad. This is no time for that."

I hold up both hands, because *what?!* "Wait, wait, wait."

Chela puts her face in her hands and groans.

"You mean to tell me," I demand, "that all this time I've been saying *the Cemetery Cemetery*? And everyone just let me?"

Rabbi Hidalgo smiles even wider, arms apart like he's come to the end of a great sermon. "Should've paid attention in Ladino class, manseviko."

Look, every San Madrigalero kid has to go to three hours of Sunday school every week. We learn Spanish and Hebrew *and* Ladino, which is a combination of the two plus some Turkish and other things. It's not modern Spanish, it's like ye-olde-pyrate-type Spanish that they spoke back in the days when folks first washed up on the shores of San Madrigal. Plus, we study Lucumí, the Cubanized version of Yoruba that Santeros speak. I'm just saying, it's a *lot*. And since I was only around some of the time and my parents are sticklers for me keeping up with lessons, I had to do half that learning from books and crappy 8-bit language-learning games.

"How does that—"

"Every word means many things," he says, leaning all the way into super-extra rabbi mode now. "The meaning we know—or some of us, anyway"—he winks at me, and it's so corny and avuncular I can't even be mad that he's clearly shading my entire existence— "and also the hidden meanings from the many layers of history and mythology it carries with it."

"That's deep, Dad," Chela says. "But we need answers now, not poems."

Rabbi Hidalgo looks down, shoulders hunched, his entire body a sagging question mark. "I know, fijika mia, I know. I wish I could . . ." He shakes his head, and for a moment, I think he might burst into tears, which would be . . . intense. Instead, he perks up again and nods at me. "Next time, you come in the house, hmm, Mateo?" He means the synagogue, which also serves as the Hidalgos' home. "Aviva makes a tremendous baklava."

Mrs. Hidalgo, still on the portico, finds a smile for me, but it's a tight one, her lips pressed firmly together. "And send our love to your tía, please. Now, Jaime . . ."

The rabbi nods, sadness descending on him like a shroud. "Chela, you're not going—"

"I'm not doing this with you again, Dad," she says flatly. Then she softens it with: "I promise I'll be careful."

And she turns and slips through the cemetery like a ghost into the night.

CHAPTER TWELVE

"Hey!" I call, catching up with Chela. She's hasn't slowed her pace since leaving the cemetery—the *betahayim*, as it turns out. She hooked a right onto Cypress and has been flitting along at a half jog past bodegas and beauty salons for three blocks while I tall-walk along in her wake. "What . . . What happened back there?"

She whirls on me so suddenly that I trip over myself trying not to crash into her. "What happened is what's been happening since last night, and since . . . forever!"

"Which is?"

There's pure fire in her eyes. "Lies and obfuscation! Pretty poems and broken promises. I have *had* it!"

"Last night . . ." I say, trying to be the calm rock she can storm around, an anchor.

But the words—the question, really—send the same look of sadness over her that the rabbi just had. The fire blinks out in an instant.

"I'm sorry," I say quickly. "You don't have to—"

"No, it's okay. Just come on." She falls back into a smooth

saunter, moving like a slo-mo splash of water through the October night. "It's easier to talk about it while we walk."

You know when you put on a great song and it starts out with just a little strut, the deep drop of the bass and a round or two through the chords, piano jangling away, just simple? That's what it's like every time I stroll through these streets. I can't help it. These buildings, all those elaborate storefronts with tacky sea vistas painted on them, or images of santos or pirate ships, the famous three peaks—they're the bass line, the tumbao. That constant rumble. *Whoooom!* And then I've passed them and more appear on the next block, Simpatico's Peluqería, La Altereria de Pedro Chavetz—*whoh-whoom!*—Chacho's Kosher Bakery—*whoom!*

Outside each place, and all along the street around us, neighbors chatter at each other, voices rising and falling amid traffic and the ambient jumble of city sounds. Last night it was a bubbling excitement, about to overflow. Today it's more nervousness, uncertainty about what's ahead. But the regular chitchat persists—it's unstoppable. That's the piano part, scattered but ongoing, a whole world of banter and bochinche, now harmonious, now dissonant, resolving and breaking apart and resolving again. Gossip and barter and the churn of my people in all our messiness and glory.

And now, by my side, there is Chela.

Her voice is the single horn call that rises above the ramble and boom of the rest. Then it becomes a melody, and a whole story unfolds as each note emerges from the last, becomes the next, relates to others and the larger world around it.

Chela tells her story, and I do my best to pay attention, I do. And I catch it, what she's saying, for real. But also, all I hear is music.

"I can't explain everything, Mateo. And I know I'm probably going to sound like I've lost it, but then again we both saw Galanika last night. He was there for you."

Pause.

She studies me as we walk. The world, Brooklyn, Little Madrigal, swim forever forward. *Whoom!* The Biblioteka Club. *Whoom!* La Chankleta Divina. *Whoom!* Botanika Madrigalera. The shimmy and shuffle of old men arguing over a chessboard, kids swarming past on the way home from school.

He was, my nod says. *I may not understand it all, but I know you're not making it up. I know it's real, too.*

"I don't see Okanla," says Chela, "but I feel her. I know she's in me; she moves through me. I've always known. I was only ten when Tío Si took me aside and explained what had happened, but it felt like someone was finally saying out loud a fairy tale that I'd already known my whole life. It felt like the truth. Because it was. It is."

Pause. Little Madrigal swooshes around us, and somehow San Madrigal, the lost island, glides along the warm October breeze, too. It's all over this place, these people.

"I know how to destroy things, Mateo." Pause. "People." Pause. "It's in me. Part of me. I can see it happen like a spirit version of myself is running forward in time, ahead of me, showing me each cut and where it goes, where to slide my knife, when to cut, where to put my fingers. How much pressure to apply and when to let go, walk away; when to run. But I don't do it randomly."

The city. The block. The buildings. Four hundred years of wars and revolutions, trade, and culture and lovemaking. Music. All around us.

"I know how because my body knows. It's like dance, the way your body knows how to tell the story, find the beat, without ever being taught sometimes. I never had to learn how to do what I do— it's a language I was born with. Or . . . I guess it was born into me when I initiated." Pause. She stops walking, and the world stops, too. "Do you know what that feels like, Mateo?" Her whisper is a tiny prayer that I do.

I nod. Quietly say, "Yes." Then I shake my head. "I mean, for what I do, of course. And I'm not a great dancer. But it's music for me. I know I'm supposed to be a healer—I *am* a healer, I guess. But it doesn't make sense to me. Not like music does. Nothing makes sense to me like music does."

There's silence now, but not the horrible earth-shattering kind—it's the kind that's heavy with what just happened and all that lies ahead. Like the moment when a solo reaches its peak and the other players just hang back and let it soar, and then even that stops and silently the beat still pulses inside us so when all that sound blows back in we feel it coming. We can almost hear the echo of it before it happens, and we let it wrap around us like the ocean.

The music comes in again on her sad, simple smile. "It's all still new for you," she says, not unkindly. Then she wiggles her eyebrows. "Who knows what'll happen next."

I want to ask about Trucks, about what Tolo knows and what the beef is between him and Gerval, but I refuse to do anything to shatter this moment.

And anyway, what comes next looms up very suddenly, as we round the corner onto Fulton and a whole world of chaos opens around us.

CHAPTER THIRTEEN

If there was music for this moment, it would be drums, all drums.

You know those solos when the whole band stops and the drummer just goes ham on their kit? *Bagahh bagahhhhh brrrrrrrap brap bap SHASHAA!* And folks are watching with their eyes wide, now standing, not even realizing they stood up, because the sheer force of that rumble and crash *shoved* them to their feet, and then it swings their asses into motion as the chaos and clatter resolves back to the steady swing of the song?

That.

Except here on the streets, there's no resolution in sight, no steady beat underneath—just sheer chaos and that gut-in-your-throat feeling of being about to tilt over the edge of something and plummet.

The whole neighborhood is out, crowded in that now-infamous intersection in front of Tolo's club where everything went bonkers last night. Santeros in their whites with beaded necklaces and bracelets. Sefaradim, some in kaftans with fezzes or silken head scarves.

Pirates all over the place, some looking scraggily and audacious, others dressed to the nines, cool/calm/collected.

The rapid-fire bang of the snare blasts through me as I take it all in, the shimmer of cymbals. No rhythm, just vibes. Bad ones.

My people are divided—that much I can see. Arguments have broken out, shouting matches with fistfights dangling in the air, waiting to happen. Escalation comes so easily: a yell becomes a shove becomes a tackle becomes a full-on beat-down. I've seen it so many times. Been in it once or twice. The air is prickly, about to snap.

"Whoa," I say. "This is bad already."

Chela shakes her head, brow creased. "Yeah . . ."

"In some ways, it's been this bad for a while, hasn't it? I just haven't been paying attention."

She nods.

"It's all just breaking out into the open now. Why do people care so much about the island rising again? It barely seems possible, just a dream."

"It's still home," Chela says. "They—we—never let go of the island, even after it sank. We're still tied to it. If a dream is what's keeping you alive, you cling to it as tight as you can. No matter how ridiculous it may seem."

"What if the dream is what's killing you?" It sure looks like that's what's happening as we make our way through the angry faces in the bristling crowd.

Chela scowls and shrugs. "If you take poison for long enough, it'll save your life."

I get the feeling that's only halfway a metaphor for her.

Up ahead, Davos the hairstylist and one of the guitarists I used to play events with, Ursula Ka, are cursing each other out in three languages.

"And Trucks?" I finally say, the question that's been sitting on my tongue, growing sour for hours. It feels like kicking the bass drum, a low growl beneath this sharp cacophony.

Chela gets up in my face so fast I barely see her move. Her eyes glint with that same threat—no, promise—of violence that sparkled in them last night after I interrupted her midway through an assassination. "Listen to me, Mateo Matisse. Don't you *ever* speak a word of that to my cousin. Is that clear?"

I nod, blinking.

"Tolo has no idea I did that, and it has to stay that way. No one knows except you, Mateo. And that's how it's gonna stay. And anyway"—she gets down from her tiptoes and starts walking normally like she didn't just threaten me—"that was my first time ever doing that." She exhales. "Taking a life. I hate that I had to, but I had to."

I stay quiet. This is her moment.

But inside I have a million questions. Most of all: Does what happened last night mean she awakened her powers of destruction, just like I did with healing?

"I don't even like sneaking up on people like that, I really don't," she continues, smoothly dodging some middle-aged pirate guy as he stumbles past and two more people hurl themselves after him. "I'm more of a direct-approach-type person. But it had to be done, and it had to be done clean. They were planning a move on my cousin."

"You mean— Who's 'they'?"

Chela shakes her head, frustrated at herself. "I don't know," she admits. "And now I might not be able to find out. I'd been keeping an eye on Trucks because he doesn't make sense—dude just showed up a couple years ago, was Anisette's bodyguard before he was in Gerval's crew, and yeah, she kinda raised Gerval, but the whole thing is just weird. Who is Trucks?" She pauses, realizing again, maybe, the everlastingness of what she's done. "*Was.* We never saw his face under his helmet, didn't know his family. But I've learned . . . It's hard to explain." Her eyes meet mine. "Maybe only you can understand, Mateo. If you haven't felt this yet, maybe you will someday, but it's like there's a truth I know in my soul even if I can't explain why. It's Okanla. I feel her. I feel her knowledge—wisdom, maybe—within me sometimes."

"Yes," I say quietly, because that's exactly what healing was like: a knowledge that I didn't totally understand. A knowledge beyond understanding. Like my hands knew what to do before I did. And the only way it worked was when I let go and trusted them.

She takes in my serious face, and I think I see her soften, ever so slightly. "There was something wrong with that guy, Mateo. Something very wrong. Every alarm in me was going off when I saw him earlier in the day yesterday. Like a primordial warning of danger rising from the deep."

"So, what'd you do?"

A little mischievous grin crosses her face, and I can't lie, it's wildly enticing. "I stole his phone."

"What?"

She shrugs, Galerano-style. "Wasn't hard. Point is, I was right. Sure enough, the latest message was a photo of Tolo and a single word: *Tonight.*"

"Whoa! Who—"

"Just another burner phone, from what I could tell. But between that and what every instinct in me was screaming, I knew what I had to do. I wasn't about to wait until it was too late, I know that. Why? So I could sit around for the rest of my life and go, *Damn, if only I'd listened to my gut, my cousin would still be alive?* No thanks, buddy."

"Damn," I say, nodding because she's making some points. If I'd heard this story before everything that happened to me last night,

I might've been way more skeptical. But the truth is, I get it now. I don't know if I would've done the same thing, but I'm pretty sure that if I hadn't, I would've regretted it.

"Anyway," Chela says, "when Si had me initiated to Okanla, he was just following what your aunt's divination said. But pirates don't do stuff in public, and they seemed to think none of it should ever get out, especially to my dad. Of course, he found out, anyway. But the family still kept it quiet. And when Tolo trained me, it wasn't so I could become one of his hired guns. He's always taught me not to use my skills for anything like that. Not for revenge. And not for my own enrichment."

"I mean, technically, this wasn't for your—"

"And *no* preemptive strikes."

"Oh."

"Yeah. I mean, Tolo's not above doing them himself. He just doesn't want me following in his footsteps. Especially because my dad and his fell out over the fear of that exact thing happening, basically."

We stop in a relatively calm area, where folks are mostly just debating and showing each other annoying memes on their phones (like that'll convince anybody of anything, but okay). I see Maza and Maybelline bickering with each other like old people—I guess they're on opposite sides of this issue—and there's Vedo and some other kid from school, whispering quietly.

"Tolo is trying to stop the island from rising!" someone wails.

"That's not true," a voice snaps. "You literally just made that up!"

"And anyway, isn't *this* our homeland? I was born here!"

"Don't bring that crap over here, bro. You know it's not that simple."

"Do you want the whole world to know who we are? There'll be theme parks on the three peaks and more tourists than Galeranos!"

Chela pulls some scrunchies out of her pocket and starts

bunching her hair into puffs. Which may or may not mean someone else is about to get got. "Anyway," she says, "I did what I had to do to protect my people, Mateo. And I'll do it again if I have to." From the expression on her face, it looks like she won't have long to wait. "And so will you."

"I . . ."

"Anyway, I'm not convinced Trucks was even actually—"

"Ahoy, shalom, and welcome, mi gente!" Anisette's voice booms out over a megaphone, cutting Chela off. "Things got a little out of hand last night, it's true! But it's a new day for Madrigal! For our community, for the island! Soon we will see our homeland rise again!"

"Actually *what?*" I whisper at Chela, because come on! You can't just start a sentence like that and not finish it.

"Enough with the niceties!" a voice calls out from the crowd. "What the hell is going on?"

"¡Los Muertos están trastornados!" an old woman yells. *The dead are a damn mess*, basically. Then she adds, "¡*Nuestros* Muertos!" *Our* dead, to emphasize the point. (But, like, who else's dead would be all jacked up over this, honestly?)

"I saw Muertos in the lavandería esa mañana!" Beatrice La Verjez calls out.

"Hey, spirits need their clothes washed, too!" some pirate yells back, and people laugh, but a few others cuss him out trilingually.

"There were spirits in gym today!" Maza yells. "They attacked us!"

This sends a ripple of panic across the crowd. "En la escuela?" "Attacking the children?" people mutter and gasp. "Pero puñeta . . ."

"Okay, yes, yes," Anisette acknowledges with a squeak. "But today's business will help resolve all that! That's why we're gathered here!"

"Mateo!" Tams whisper-shouts as she makes her way through

the crowd toward us. The two of us hug, and then she says hey to Chela, who actually smiles at her. They exchange a friendly elbow bump as Tolo moves through the crowd toward the stage.

This is supposed to be his moment. But so was last night, and we all saw how that went.

Tolo's mom, Mimi, was the only known casualty when the island went down. She'd been on the Cabildo at the time, and her husband, Si, was already here and busy setting up his criminal empire. So Mimi's best friend, Anisette, took the role. And it was always understood that she was just holding the spot for Tolo, and she'd pass it on to him when he came of age. The one thing that's always been true about the pirates' Cabildo seat is that whoever sits in it appoints their successor. There may be some disagreement and fighting, but in the end, that's the pick that always wins out.

So, what was supposed to happen last night—the official announcement of her endorsing Tolo, and then the vote to confirm it (pirates always gotta vote)—was largely ceremonial. At least, it would've been if it had actually happened.

Now, as he stands a few feet from the makeshift stage, Tolo keeps his face inscrutable. Impossible to say what's on his mind, but if I had to guess: murder. A few of his heavies hover close by—Safiya the Butcher and Big Moses, but mostly Tolo is surrounded by Galeranos of all ages, all creeds. He looks somehow both very much like a gangster and very much like a leader, which I guess is about right for us. Over by the stage, Gerval has his eyes on Tolo, his whole body tight, glare intense.

"As we move to fulfill the prophecy," Anisette continues, "and unite our three communities to finish raising the island, as we bring together the three initiated children of our original santos, we need very special leadership to see us through these times!"

There's another pivot coming—I can feel it a mile away. I'm not the only one. A dark murmur ripples through the crowd around me.

"And that's why," Anisette says, "I've chosen Maestro Grilo Juan Gerval to replace me as pirate leader on the Cabildo."

What?!

A riotous uproar explodes all across the intersection. No one seems to know what to think or do.

"I've had it!" Tolo's deep voice thunders as he barges through the crowd. I've never seen him mad before, let alone enraged. The man is like a slumbering volcano—his wrath usually unspoken but unmistakable.

Before Tolo can reach the stage, someone shoves someone else and a glass bottle breaks. The violence ricochets through the street as people tumble and yell and run.

Beside me, Chela glares at the councilwoman with a face made of pure murder.

People start to peel off to opposite sides of the intersection: either Anisette's or Tolo's. There's yelling and jeering back and forth, a raucous duet of cymbals and snares, neither side waiting for the other to finish, and the mood of impending violence fills the air again, like a breath that's been held too long.

"This is bad," Tams says. "I don't fully get it, but it's all bad."

"Word," I mutter, trying to keep track of whatever it is that's about to happen. It feels like it's coming from all around us.

I nudge Chela. "Hey," I whisper, just as angry yells and screams start rising from the rear of the crowd. "You never finished what you were saying. You're not convinced that Trucks was actually what?"

The crowd howls as one and splits like the Red Sea, revealing what all the fuss was about: a crew of five absurdly tall figures in full body armor and face shields stand perfectly still in the crosswalk. A whole battalion of Trucks.

"Human," Chela says, and she leaps into action.

CHAPTER FOURTEEN

Now there's no music, just silence, and it's the worst kind of silence. Not the kind between beats or before a measure starts. It holds no promise of music, no hint of tension, even. It just stretches on and on, blank. Sure, people are yelling, shoes and body parts slap the pavement, fists and clubs meet flesh as fighting erupts all around me. But these towering soldiers—they empty the air around them of rhythm, melody, movement. For all that clatter and crush exploding on either side, an infinite vacuum seems to cover the street, like a black hole has been born in our midst.

The armored figures step forward as one, slashing with their clubs like swords. I see one crack across an old guy's head, and the man clatters to the ground like an empty suit. It's bad enough that these . . . whatever they are move in unison, but then, as if on cue, they each spring forward in different directions, plowing through the crowd and swinging every which way.

Terror rips through me. I'm frozen in place.

But this is the moment everyone has been telling me was coming since last night. This is where I'm supposed to be. Whatever strange powers come with being an initiate into the secret healing society of Galanika, they are meant to be used during this rupture, this shattering.

I know it, but I wish I didn't.

I'm not ready.

I don't know how to heal, not really. I barely know how to move.

"Come on!" Tams yells, yanking me through the crowd toward the edge of the chaos, toward safety. And the need to be safe throbs through me, a constant panic that wells up and up and up.

Louder still, though, is this other voice, this voice I'm coming to hate, the one that understands I have a role to play. It's in Tía's words from last night, and Chela's from tonight, but most of all, it's Galanika. I didn't ask for his powers to move through me, I didn't cry out for hands that heal, but I have them anyway. And now there's no pretending I don't.

"No," I say, stopping in my tracks. My shaky voice doesn't inspire much confidence, I know. But it doesn't matter. I have to try. So many people are already sprawled across the blacktop in bloody piles. "You don't have to stay." Tams looks at me like I just told her I have a second head. "But I do."

"If you stay, we stay," Maza says, appearing behind Tams.

Tams lights up some, but she still throws a scowl at me. "Mateo is a healer," she says. "He's going to . . ." She shakes her head at me, but I can tell she's proud, too. "He's going to try to help these people. We gotta keep him covered."

"So it's true!" Maza says. "I didn't know if he'd stepped into it! Okay, cool, cool, let's do this!" They grimace, eyes tight on the people streaming all around us, and get into position on the other side of me like a bodyguard.

"And for the record," Tams says, glancing around, "I was gonna say that, too—if you stay we stay. Just FYI."

I chuckle, and it feels good to laugh even though terror still rips through me like a bolt of electricity. "I know you were, Tams."

We move toward the crosswalk where the Trucks-like figures first appeared. They've moved on through the crowd now, leaving none close to us, and people are starting to fight back—mostly Tolo's crew, from what I can tell. I watch Tolo himself barrel into one of the soldiers and both of them go clattering to the side. Then the crowd closes in around them.

Chela is nowhere to be seen, but then again, I can't see much.

Up ahead, the old man who was bludgeoned lies still, blood trickling from his open mouth, his chest rising and falling in occasional gasps, his skin paled to a grayish dusty hue. Bad.

"We got you," Tams says to me. "Do your thing."

My thing.

I wish.

My hands are already shaking, and bile leaps up into my throat, filling my mouth with that spiky acid taste, threatening to spill out into the street.

I won't crash and burn. I won't puke. I won't blow this.

There's so much noise around me, but inside is only silence. Which is the worst.

I crouch beside the man—it's old Edgardo Pio, I realize; he used to run the shoe store—and place my trembling hands on his chest.

No, on his head. That's where the injury is, right?

Maybe?

Nothing makes sense. My whole mind is a scattered disaster, and so is the world around me.

And nothing's happening. What did Tams say last night that got things working? *Close your eyes.* Right.

I do.

And I immediately know why I was drawn to his torso first. That's where the problem is, the real problem. Yes, Edgardo got smashed on the head, but it's his heart that's giving out. I feel the fluttering, feeble pulse as soon as I touch him—it's like a tiny frantic bird trying to escape his rib cage. Which means his blood is barely moving through him. That's why he's gray. It's all there, at my fingertips. I can see it, feel it, the quickening catastrophe within.

The strain of all this chaos and then being hit must've caused a heart attack.

But . . . what can I do about it?

This is bigger than anything I dealt with last night. This man is dying; he's dying in my arms. I feel no clinch, no purchase— just the quickening, the fading, the sand of his life slipping away from my grasp.

"All good?" Maza calls from nearby.

I exhale. Don't answer. Nothing is good. What am I supposed to say?

"You gotta let him concentrate," Tams chides.

"Oh, my bad. Keep going, dude."

People are screaming in pain nearby, up ahead, all around. The sounds of fighting grow louder and recede again. I reach for that sense of gripping something, that power, and . . . nothing.

Crap.

My mouth still tastes like bile, and wave after relentless wave of nausea rolls through me.

Crap, crap, crap.

What if I can't figure this out again, if those powers were wasted on me? What if I just— "Watch out!" Tams yells, and my eyes blink open to see a huge soldier guy plowing through the crowd toward us, club raised to strike.

Both Tams and Maza step in front of me, side by side, squared up to take whatever blow comes, but instead, a flash of something zooms out of the crowd and crashes smack into the soldier.

Chela.

Her blade glints in the streetlights as she pulls it back and then shoves it into the opening beneath the guy's face shield, the same place where she got Trucks.

"Holy—" Maza boggles.

"Whoa, whoa, whoa!" Tams yells.

Chela stays in a kneel, whispering something under her breath as the figure beneath her writhes and then goes still.

No blood.

I glance up at her, and she's watching me, panting, just like last night, but this time there's no rage in her eyes. She steps forward, and Tams and Maza move out of her way, staring in some kind of awe. "Keep watch," she says to them, crouching down in front of me. Then: "Thank you."

Tams and Maza turn back to the crowd, which is now thinning around us. Then all I see is Chela, her breath back to normal, her eyes calm, almost sleepy.

"It's n-not . . ." I stammer, feeling every inch as pathetic as I sound. "It's not working. It worked last night, kind of? But I can't . . ." I throw up my hands.

"You're not listening," Chela says.

I shake my head, scowl. "There's nothing to hear. It's all blank. Just silence."

"Not the world," she says. "Not what's around us. You're not listening to *yourself*. The healing is inside you."

I blink at her.

"Just like the music."

I feel like one of my eyes might be twitching. Because even though I don't fully *understand* what she just said, I *know* it's true. I *feel* its truth all through me. My whole body tingles with it.

"Got it?" she says, rising. And then, without waiting for my answer: "Good. Gotta go."

Then she's gone.

And all I see are Tams's and Maza's smirking faces, both glancing over their shoulders.

"I don't wanna hear it!" I snap, and then I look back down at Edgardo Pio, still unconscious, still dying. A tiny melody slips from my lips.

It's just a single phrase, simple: *Badabeeee badooo ba-bahhhh*, but it feels like each note is inscribed in gold as it leaves me, like the world is different because of that phrase. New. And it is, because Chela was right: it's inside me, the music, the healing. They're one.

I sing the melody again, and my focus stays on the sounds as they slip like a shimmering thread through the air and skim along Edgardo's wrinkled arms. Then I hum the riff once more, a little faster this time, with blue notes thrown in, some verve, and the song dives below the surface of his skin.

For a moment, darkness overwhelms me. I am both crouching beside Edgardo Pio on a crowded cross street in Little Madrigal and ranging through the inner workings of him, sliding through cellular networks and across synapses. I am light, I am sound. I am neither, both, something else entirely. The breath of healing sweeps across each burning filament and cataclysm like a night wind, changing everything I touch, becoming everything I approach, expanding, filling, lighting, lifting.

"Holy crap," I whisper, somewhere far away from myself, and Edgardo Pio's eyes open.

The melody cycles through me again; it lengthens, contracts, and then explodes. I *feel* each tiny sliver of it spin outward through the interstitial spaces of his inner workings, take root. That flutter resolves into a double tap: *thuh-THUNK*. And then another. Blood pours through his veins like a river flowing free after a drought, floods through his tissues, which brighten, strengthen, fortify.

I *feel* Edgardo Pio's heart heal. Crinkled gray tissue expands, refreshes, glows vibrant crimson again. Chambers that had jiggled uselessly now thump out an even, steady beat. The world inside him awakens.

We help each other stand, the old man and I. My breath is short, either because I can't believe what just happened or because I was working so hard, I'm not sure which.

When I look around, Tams and Maza are staring at me with wide eyes.

"I . . . I'm a healer," I say. "It really *is* inside me."

"Excellent," Tams says, " 'cause we just got backup."

A wide circle of people surrounds us, facing outward. They're burly and look ready to fight. Tolo's crew.

CHAPTER FIFTEEN

"WELL, WELL, WELL." MY TÍA'S WRY VOICE CUTS THROUGH THE strange darkness of healing as I finish up with the last wounded person, Idi Benyamin. Idi's a librarian; she'd gotten sprayed with some kind of chemical amid all the tussling. She blinks away the last few tears, her eyes cleared up, and looks at me with wonder, shaking her head.

"Gracias, Mateo," Idi says, touching a light brown hand to my forehead and bowing slightly. Then she's gone and Tía Lucia walks toward me out of the protective circle Tolo's crew had formed.

"Ah, let me begin by saying—" she starts, but colorful spots have clouded my vision and the world curves into a spin around me. "Ah, ah, ah." Tía crosses the space between us, faster than I would've thought possible, and catches me as I start to drift toward the pavement. "Easy, easy," she whispers. "I got you."

And somehow, she does, she does. Even though she's a fraction of my height and three times my age, Tía Lucia manages to hold me up, support me. I'm enveloped by that familiar cloud of Florida

Water cologne she always wears, and for some reason, this time it brings me straight back to my childhood. It must've been one of those brief stints we spent staying at her apartment between trips; I was probably three or four. I'd slipped on the just-mopped kitchen tile and split my lip open, and Tía Lucia had swept in like a great fragrant eagle, scooping me up and cooing gentle lullabies to me as I sobbed. "Cúrate, Mateocito," she had whispered. *Cure yourself.* "Try it."

That's all I remember. And I haven't thought about it since it happened, but it definitely happened. She's always been there, cheering me on toward this truth of who I am, long before I understood it.

Suddenly, I'm on the verge of tears. She's pulling me into a wildly lopsided hug, rubbing her hands in calming circles over my back.

"I thought you said it would get easier to deal with the injuries," I mutter once I've managed to hold back the sobs. "This time the heaviness came on so much faster."

"You did more healing, and you did it faster, mi amor. You're getting ahead of yourself."

She's right. These injuries were all more severe, and once Chela helped unlock the secret within me, it all seemed to flow, and quickly.

"When you don't have time to clean off," Tía Lucia tells me, slowly disentangling from the hug, "the trick is to find places within yourself to store the hurt." She narrows her eyes, waving one finger up at me. "Pero escúchame, Mateo. That's only a temporary measure. You cannot leave other people's crap rotting inside you forever and ever, ¿lo entiendes?"

I nod, still getting my balance back. Already, though, I understand what she means. It's like how she explained her altars once—that they're a way of giving spirits a place to be so they won't just roam around everywhere. The illnesses and injuries I've taken on, especially that heart attack, are wandering in a thick cloud through me. I do as Tía suggested and imagine them sectioning themselves off and organizing into tidy little clusters, folding away in corners and pockets of my inner self.

I don't know if that's really how it's done or just a placebo, but it's working. I feel stronger, clearer-headed.

"Are you okay?" Tams pants, catching up to us with Maza by her side.

"Grrrk," I mumble. "Think so?"

"He will be," Tía Lucia reports with a chuckle. "You two head to Tolo's club. I'll send him there when we're done."

Done? Done with what?

Doesn't matter. I'm getting my strength back and can mostly walk on my own now, even if it feels like there are cinder blocks strapped to my arms and legs and cotton candy in my brain. I give Tams and Maza a thumbs-up and stumble along beside my aunt.

"Where we going?" We've cut down some side streets and are making our way down a quiet walkway toward . . .

"The canal," Tía says. "Look, m'ijo, I know you've been through a lot in the past day."

"Uh-huh."

"And I shoved you headfirst into the deep end of the pool. . . ."

We reach the concrete edge of a narrow canal. She nods, pulls out a cigar, and lights it. "But there's no choice, I'm afraid. Anisette is up to something. I saw what happened tonight. I don't know who those guys were or what Gerval's role in all this is, pero . . . pues, eso es el problema: no lo se. And unfortunately, you're probably the only person who can find out."

"Why me, Tía?"

"Everyone trusts you, Mateo. They know you just enough to think they know you, but al mismo tiempo, not at all."

"Sea espíritu," I mutter. There but not there, heard not seen. Sometimes it feels like a curse.

She raises her eyebrows, watching the dark water stream by.

"Sure, eso. I know the world came at you fast, but I knew you'd be ready for it, Mateo. And you were."

"I *wasn't* ready!" It comes out louder than I meant it to, but I guess I'm pissed. "I barely figured it out! You could've died last night, Tía!"

"You *are* ready," she says. "And I didn't. That's the point. You were ready. You just didn't feel ready. Those are different things. I'm not trying to be funny. I *know* you're ready."

"I wish *I* knew it."

"You will. Bueno, pues, let's clean. You feel it, all that muck?"

I nod, because it's been steadily fading but it's still there, like the world is a swamp around me.

"As I said, you will feel it less the more you heal, as your body and soul learn how to manage it. There are also natural ways we get rid of it without meaning to. Puking, for instance!" She chortles to himself, but whoa—it puts my whole puking thing in a totally different light. "Pero, it's better to cleanse yourself on purpose. That's what I'm here to show you. Ahora, dime: How did you figure out how to really use your powers?"

"I . . . It was when Chela said it was inside me just like the music is. And I let the song come out while I did it."

She nods thoughtfully. "Mmm, muy bien." Then she gets up in my face a little. "Pero—"

"Don't trust Chela Hidalgo, I know."

The fact that Chela is one of the people I'm looking for . . . it sits heavy in my mouth. This doesn't seem like the right time to tell Tía. Part of me feels like it would be a betrayal somehow. Everything is a betrayal, it seems. That's the way of things.

"She's right, though," Tía says. "Just like there are songs for healing others, there is a song for cleansing yourself, see? So first place your hands on your heart, hmm?"

I do it, feeling kinda sappy, I gotta admit.

"Ahora . . ." She chuckles a little, meeting my eyes.

"Escucha," we both say together.

"Yeah, yeah, yeah," I grumble, but I'm laughing, and so is she.

"But seriously, this is what I mean, Mateo. Escucha. Escucha al mundo." *Listen to the world.* "A tu propio corazón." *To your own heart.* "A tu espíritu." *Your spirit.* "Tu canción." *Your song.*

I close my eyes. Let the hum of the city rise around me as those color splotches bubble across the sudden darkness.

I tune inward, the way I reached within those injured people, but this time on myself. Shadows envelop my consciousness. I hear . . . nothing.

"Go deeper," Tía's voice says from what seems like a million miles away.

I do, shutting out the sounds of traffic and machinery, shutting out the world until I just feel like I'm falling, falling, forever falling into an impossible void.

And then a hand yanks me forward, hard. "Guh!" I shout, gasping for air.

"Tranquilo, tranquilo," Tía says, rubbing my back.

"What the hell happened?"

"You'll get there, it's okay." She's smiling up at me; she looks . . . proud. I didn't expect that, and I definitely didn't expect the surge of emotion it sends through me. I don't know what I did, but whatever it was, it's got Tía Lucia glowing in a way I've never seen before. I did that. I just wish I knew how. It almost makes up for having seen her laid out and unconscious last night. "Next time," she says with a sly chuckle. "Next time, you'll go even deeper, hmm?"

"Deeper?" I gape. "Feel like I almost drowned this time!"

"Bueno," she says with a wry smile. "That means you're listening. But even without the song, you can still go through the motions of the cleaning, hmm? It'll still work, just not as well. Now do like you've got something nasty on your hands and you gotta shake it off into the canal, eh?"

She shows me, and I do as she says. I feel the weight lighten as I shake, the clouds leave my brain, the world returns to itself. Energy flows within me, then out. The surface of the dark water doesn't change, of course, but I can imagine all that hurt, the broken bones and bleeding organs, sliding away downstream and mixing with the endless waters of the world.

"In the Cuban Santero tradition, they cleanse with coins sometimes, or candy. Machetes, like we did last night. It can get more complicated, too. The most important thing is that you use intention."

"What do you mean?"

"La intención es todo. Everything else is just tools and toys, eh? ¿Qué es lo que quieres hacer? You want to cleanse. You do what you're called to do, and with the intentionality of cleansing in your heart, you will do the right work. This is how these powers function. You intended to heal when you crouched over those injured people. Y entonces your spirit found a way. Música was the method."

"I . . . I think I understand."

Tía Lucia nods toward the street. "Now, go find your friends, Mateo. There is still much to be done."

CHAPTER SIXTEEN

Tolo's club is full of people—old and young, pirate, Santero, Sefaradim, and whatever. He opened up the bar and someone started cooking in the back, so everyone's sitting around, chatting, trying to unwind and process everything that happened when I walk in.

And then they see me, and everyone goes dead quiet.

Welcome, once again, to my worst nightmare: other people's eyes. Lots of them, all pointed my way. I guess it's a little better than last night because I'm ready for it. And at least now I *know* what they're staring at me about.

Still.

My skin feels like it's on fire, and my stomach does several somersaults.

"Uh . . ." I say, because that's what I'm good at: saying *uh*. "Hey, everyone."

Then I realize there's something different about their expressions this time: awe. Some of them are people I healed earlier. The rest must have heard about what happened. What I did. They're looking at me like I'm some kind of hero, but I'm not. I didn't ask to be a healer, didn't choose it. It chose me. I just did what I was told. "The Healer," they mutter, and "It's true," like they can see it on me, like Galanika himself is just hovering around my head. But he's not, and I'm barely a healer at all, I'm just a kid. And it's all too much.

I almost break down into tears of relief when Tams pops up and hugs me. "You were amazing!" she says, and my heart sinks again. Was I? I don't know. Why are all my thoughts turning against me? I'm just glad we're all still alive.

I look her over. "Are you okay?"

She nods, and by the glint in her eye and that overlarge smile, I gather she's more than just okay.

I tilt my forehead down and one eyebrow up. "Oh, word? It's like that?"

She twists her mouth to one side. "I mean . . ."

"Mateo!" someone calls. Chela. Now both my eyebrows go up, and it's Tams's turn to forehead-tilt at me. "Can you come to the back office for a sec—"

"Yes!" I yell before she can finish.

"Tolo wants to talk to us."

"Okay!" I call, jabbing Tams with my elbow so she stops laughing.

"Whew!" Tams wheezes. "The speed with which you said, *Yes, Chela, I would love to go to the sexy back office and make out with you!*"

"I explicitly did *not* say that!"

"And the speed with which she put that possibility to rest. Whew, I say!"

"The prior conversation is extremely not over," I warn Tams. "Anyway, come with me."

She shoots me her dubious face. "Really?"

"*You* had my back out there, Tams. You were by my side the whole time. Whatever he has to say to me he can say to you, too, shoot."

"You know who else had your back the whole time?" She does a little shimmy, and I roll my eyes.

"Yes, bring Maza, too, but hurry up."

"Good, because we both had simultaneous revelations about how incredibly hot Tolo Baracasa is tonight, and we'd like a chance to confirm up close and personal."

"You are . . . really something."

I make my way through the many stares, the faces wide open with wonder, the weirdness I feel inside about it all. Special powers are cool, sure, but me managing to reach the far end of the room without tripping over anything or just curling up in a little ball on the floor—that's real magic, man.

Tams and Maza fall in behind me, and we walk past Big Moses Arroyo, the bouncer (who tonight seems more like a bodyguard), down a narrow hallway and through a huge iron door.

Old leather-bound books line the walls of Tolo Baracasa's office. An oriental rug is stretched across the floor leading up to his huge desk, which looks like it's made from a giant piece of driftwood. Framed on the display area behind the desk, forming a kind of symbolic backdrop to Tolo himself, is an old-school map of San Madrigal, complete with elaborate etchings of those three famous peaks, sea serpents rising from the waves, and various creatures in the wilderness area and even on the rugged streets. I could stare at it for hours, but right now there are more pressing things at hand, like Tolo Baracasa's huge frowning face staring directly at me.

"Ah, hi," I say with a weird little wave.

"Mateo Matisse Medina." Even at the near whisper he speaks in now, Tolo's voice fills the room with its rich and resonant timbre, the pull of a bow across double-bass strings. He cracks a slight smile when he talks, not unlike his cousin. "Your parents still off saving the world in . . . Where are they again?"

"The Congo," I say, impressed that he knows anything about them. Then again, I guess it's his job to know everything about everyone in this community, huh.

"Mmm, but you're not with them this time." He nods at Tams and Maza and then sets his gaze back on me. "Bet they'll be thrilled to come home and find out their little man has taken after them, no?"

I wonder. Like, I can see why someone would think that, but don't forget: Jorge and Sandra Medina are people of numbers, facts, and data. I gather they weren't that thrilled about my initiation in the first place, but they probably accepted it as a necessity. And then they were, I'm sure, happy to whisk me off to their extremely non-magical data-driven world of medications and morbidity rates, hypodermic needles and hotel rooms. I haven't Skyped with them since I found out, and I honestly don't know how to tell them about everything that's been going on. It feels a little bit like a rejection of everything they're about, if I'm honest.

Probably all that thinking and overthinking has me shifting uncomfortably, because Tolo narrows his eyes and then sighs. "Look, we all saw what you did out there tonight." He glances at Chela, whose face is as inscrutable as always. As *almost* always. "I . . . I asked my cousin, and she said I had to talk to you about it." He shakes his head, amused and defeated, and then does the Galerano shrug-mambo. "So . . . here we are. I know what I saw, what the people are saying. But I prefer to go right to the source when I want to know something about a person. Is it true, you've awakened to your powers as a healer?"

"I . . ." Words don't come, no surprise. It feels wrong to claim something I barely understand, just found out about twenty-four hours ago. But then again, I've already seen it work, *felt* it work over and over since then. And Galanika was there, staring at me with those shimmering, translucent eyes. I didn't make it up. Chela saw him, too. "I have," I finally spit out.

To his credit, Tolo shows surprising patience and grace as I squirm. He doesn't make a fuss or roll his eyes, just waits and watches. Then he nods, says a curt but not unkind "Good," and steeples his fingers. "Please sit, all of you. I'll try to be as clear with you as possible."

I exhale. I don't know if he realizes what a blessing it is to deal with someone straight-talking and close to our age after all these riddlesome adults. "Thank you." I take a spot in one of the chairs facing his desk, Tams and Maza flanking me.

He leans forward, smiling slightly. "Do y'all know what I do, exactly?"

Tams doesn't miss a beat. "You want the real answer, or the polite one?"

It's a gamble, man, but Tolo immediately slams one thick hand on his desk and busts out laughing. Whew. "I like her," he says. "But please, do not be polite with me. Not now, not ever. I'm a pirate, man, come on."

"Well," Maza says, "word on the street is you came up as a smuggler under your dad and that's how you made your fortune, and now you run his old crew."

He nods, appraising the info thoughtfully. "And what do they say I smuggle?"

Tams shrugs. "We always figured it was the usual stuff—guns and drugs and whatnot."

Tolo flicks the notion away with a shrug and a swipe of his palm. "I mean, sure, in the beginning. But that gets boring pretty quick, you know."

We don't, but it's not a question.

"I heard," Maza says, "you have crews all over the world hunting ancient treasures and then selling them off on the black market."

He nods, serious now. "Mm, that's part of it, yes. Some people invest in stocks; we invest in . . . long-lost treasures, as you say. But for these past fifteen years, ever since the day of the catastrophe . . ." He raises his eyebrows, eyes far away, voice trailing to nothing. Then he shakes it off. "The real treasure my father and now I have been hunting is lore."

I think we all blink at him at the same time.

"Folktales, stories, songs, spells . . . A lot of cultures make up who we are. Not just the Santeros, Sefaradim, and pirates they always talk about. Taínos and Arawaks came through to trade, some started families. Plus, all kinds of folks trying to get away from the law or the various empires all over the Caribbean. For a while, we had crews going out to take down slave ships, and many newly freed people would stay, so cultures from different parts of West Africa. Plus, Jews would regularly pop up, escaping one pogrom or another in different parts of Europe."

"Wow . . ." I say. I knew other cultures were mixed in; I'd just never thought about the extent of it.

"And all brought traditions with them, their myths and monsters, and those became part of who we are. Our own mythology is gigantic, spans centuries. And somewhere in there, in all those sacred teachings and trickster stories and barroom waltzes and murder ballads and lullabies and love songs, there's an answer. There's a reason our homeland sank, and if there's a reason it sank, there's a way to bring it back. I think we're close. But there's a lot we still don't know. One thing we know is that we need to find that third initiated child, the one made to San Madrigal herself."

Well, at least that makes it pretty certain it's not him. Someone to cross off my list.

"You and Chela were initiated at the same time. Until your powers awoke, though, it didn't matter. For a long time, we weren't even sure that the ceremony had taken with Chela. Now we know. Everyone saw her in action tonight. She is an initiate of Okanla, you of Galanika . . . but we have yet to find the child of San Madrigal herself. . . . If there is one." He grunts the sigh of a very vexed man. "We're working on it. But in the meantime, I need to know—*we* need to know—that we can count on you. That when the time comes, when we figure out what needs to be done, we can turn to you."

I don't even know what I'm agreeing to. I barely understand who's up against whom or why. I'm sure my face says all this, because Tolo puts up his big hand and flashes a wily grin. "I know, I know. It's a big ask. That's fair. Just understand, Gerval will be asking the same of you, and probably more. If he hasn't already." He squints at me; I just stare back. "Yeah, well, I know you probably look up to Gerval, being that you're both musicians and all. And I get it. But you've seen the plan he's part of, and look at the havoc it's wreaked."

"Bash Tolo," a gruff voice says from behind us, using Tolo's formal title. It's Moses Arroyo, wearing a grim frown. He glances from us to the boss, trying to figure out if he can speak freely or not.

"Go 'head," Tolo says.

"The last of our guys are back. No more casualties, but . . . the rest got away."

"Hrmf," Tolo snorts.

"Something else."

"Hmm?"

"Anisette's calling for a quorum vote."

A quorum vote? I think as Tolo says it just as incredulously. No one's done one of those since . . . The last time was about ten years ago, I think; two rival groups were on the brink of a turf war, something like that. They both ended up getting dissolved, and at least three people got shot during the vote itself. But the results are binding. No one breaks ranks once a quorum vote has been called—it's decisive, the last word on the matter.

"She says let the people of San Madrigal decide what to do," Moses adds with open disdain. "She's already got folks out there blaming you for tonight's violence and calling for peace."

"This lady," Tolo snarls. It was bound to happen, anyway, to formalize the new Cabildo member, but I guess with everything going on, people had figured it could wait. "What's the word on Gerval's support?"

"From what we can tell, as it stands, it'll be close. Too close. The QV is set for the day after tomorrow, nine thirty at night. Here, of course."

Tonight, Gerval had said. That's when he had wanted me to bring Chela by. Did Gerval know then what was going to happen? He had said she would never come if I told her it was to meet him. . . . I glance over at her; she's watching her cousin intently, waiting. I had almost forgotten. Anything I do is a betrayal to someone.

Tolo lets out a low grumble. "Get our people out there tomorrow. Door to door. Let folks know what's at stake. Groups of at least three, in case there's more trouble."

"Vale."

The door closes, and Tolo rubs his face.

"What *is* at stake?" Tams asks.

He stands and looks at all of us, studying each with those dark eyes. "Let me show you something."

We follow him and Chela through a door I had assumed was a closet. We head down a dim stairwell into the basement, and then I stop dead in my tracks.

"Oh hell no," Tams and I both say at the same time.

There, chained to a wall in the far corner, both arms stretched back and secured even as he strains and writhes with all his might, is one of the super-tall, armored guys.

CHAPTER SEVENTEEN

"WHAT . . . ? HOW?" I STUTTER.

The rest got away, the bouncer had said.

"How do you think?" He nods at Chela with pride. "Our little burakadóra brought him in." Ha. It means *one who punctures holes in things*. Sounds about right for a nickname, yes. "We need to know what we're dealing with."

It's so strange that I barely know either of them but I still hold one precious secret that Chela keeps from her cousin: she committed murder to save his life last night. I have to tuck it far away in my subconscious so it doesn't explode out of me suddenly. "Wha . . . what *are* we dealing with?" I ask.

"We figured we'd wait for you before going any further," Chela says. "You deserve to see this, too."

"And in case anyone gets hurt," Tolo says with a wily grin.

"Great," I say.

"Okay, well . . ." At least he looks just as awkward as I feel. He glances at Chela. "You brought him here. You want to do the honors?"

She doesn't have to be asked twice. A blade extended in one hand, she reaches up with the other and pulls open the face guard.

I don't think anyone was ready for what is underneath. A shimmering set of razor-sharp teeth the size of a person's head glints back at us. Then the mouth opens, and a horrific shriek comes out that feels like it's opening me up from the inside. That thing isn't human—it never was. But I'm pretty sure it's one of the creatures that attacked us in the gym earlier.

It bucks one more time, and then its hideous mouth lurches forward, like the helmet is puking it out. What emerges through the opening is like a stream of liquid hell. For a second, we all just stare in horror as the empty suit collapses and the ichorous beast lands in a pinkish barf puddle on the floor. Chela is the first to react, swinging her blade in a fierce arc toward it, but the thing has already flashed back into its usual form, a tall, human-shaped creature that seems to be made out of some viscous fluid encased in an expandable skin sack. Long, rigid tendrils rise from its hunched head, which is mostly just a mouth filled with all those gigantic teeth—the only fully solid part of it. And now the empty suit is the only thing chained up.

It catches Chela's blade hand at the wrist and then hurls her backward, smashing her into the wall. I hear her head crack against it, and she slumps to the ground.

"Seal the door!" Tolo yells before I get a chance to reach Chela. Machetes come out all around me. "Get down!"

Seal the door? With us on this side of it? *Someone grab Chela and everybody runnn* is the command I would've given, but I guess that's why Tolo's the big crime boss and I'm just some piano player. He lunges at the creature as a tall woman I hadn't even realized was behind me slams the door shut. The monster lurches forward and pins Chela with one claw while it wraps another one around her head. And then, even as Tolo hacks and slashes away at it, the thing begins to solidify. It starts at the arm that's touching Chela. . . .

What just seconds ago looked like a water balloon now fills with muscle; a scaly, cracked, ridged carapace grows in a creaking sprawl over the monster's entire body.

The tall woman who was by the door runs over, machete out, and starts in on it, too, but it doesn't look like she's accomplishing much. She's Safiya the Butcher, I realize, one of Tolo's bodyguards. Tams and Maza and I all rush around it, trying to pull the thing off Chela, my fingers sliding over its slippery, grime-covered exoskeleton.

Chela moans but doesn't move; beside her leg lies the blade she'd been holding at the ready. The same ornate blade with the beaded handle that killed Trucks.

I'm not convinced Trucks was even actually human, she'd said just a few hours ago.

This is what she meant.

The creature, still screeching and crackling as it solidifies more and more with each passing second, must have the same idea I do. When I reach between its legs for Chela's weapon, a three-fingered claw clamps around my wrist. I'm just inches from the blade, but it's still too far away. The monster turns to appraise me with a snarl. Beyond its dripping maw, I see Chela's eyes open wide and take in the nightmare around her. Then they lock with mine.

She shoves her leg to the side just enough to push the blade closer to me, then pulls back and kicks the creature full in the face as it turns to her.

The second it rears in shock is all I need to snatch up the dagger and then shove it as hard as I can through the crinkling carapace around the creature's neck and out the other side. Chela's eyes go wide again as the tip of her knife bursts through its gaping mouth. The creature squeals and collapses to the side as Chela scrambles up and I step back, gasping.

It huffs, screeches, then lies still.

They say I'm a healer, but I've just taken a life. Sure, it was a vile creature intent on murdering everyone around, but still . . . that sudden silence echoes through me. I've never even gone fishing before. It all happened so fast.

When I manage to look up, Chela is standing, shaking off whatever shock she was in, and everyone is closing in around both of us, doing all the extra things people do when they're worried about someone but don't know how to help.

"You all right?" Tams asks, reaching out to me.

A nasty welt wraps around my wrist where the creature grabbed it, and I'm shook up, my hands still trembly, but otherwise . . . I seem to be okay. I nod, try to make it look true.

"I'm all right—seriously!" Chela says, stepping away from her cousin and his bodyguard. "Just need a second. I . . . I know I was out, but . . . it . . ."

Her eyes meet mine as I pass her the dagger, handle first. "Thank you. This is . . . it's sacred. The kama they presented me at my . . . at *our* initiation all those years ago." She sheaths it.

Kama. Dagger. I wonder how something that causes destruction can also give a name to a whole style of music. It makes a little more sense after tonight, though. Chela wields her weapon like an instrument.

"Seems like it's the only thing that could do any real damage to that thing," I say.

"Because it was a bambarúto," Tolo says, glaring down at the corpse as black blood seeps across the stone floor around it.

"A what, now?" I ask, and we all gather around.

"A creature from the old days on the island," Safiya says, scrunching up her nose. "One that used to walk the streets at night, terrorizing the people."

"So it's all . . . These creatures are . . ." I gesture wildly at the map on the wall with its monsters and the books of folktales lining Tolo's shelves. "It's all real?"

I know, I know: ghosts, so why not everything else? It's still hard to process. Monsters are a whole 'nother thing from ghosts. Trust me.

Tolo nods gravely.

"That's what we saw in the gym!" Maza says, and she's right. They were farther away and barely visible, but those huge jaws and the tall stalks coming off their heads . . . no question. "That's what chased us. But there were four of them."

"And they were . . . They were ghostlier, weren't they?" I say.

"Yes," Tams confirms. "Totally spectral. This one is . . . not."

"It got stronger when it touched Chela," I say. "Even before that, though, it was more solid than what we saw at school."

"It was feeding." Tolo shakes his head. "But . . ."

Chela grimaces. "They're getting stronger."

"What is going on?" I demand. "We need answers."

The gangster sighs. "So do I, kid."

"We'll find out what we need to," Chela says, jaw set with determination. "Meanwhile, Mateo, why don't you walk me home."

CHAPTER EIGHTEEN

IT'S SO LATE. THE NIGHT HAS FLOWN PAST, WITH ALL ITS TERRORS and excitement. By the time we say our goodbyes and head out of the club, the sky's still dark but the morning birds have started their chattering.

For a while, Chela and I just walk side by side down the empty streets, past shuttered storefronts and darkened windows.

La madrugada, that part of night so late it's almost morning, has its own song. It's a quiet one, barely there, like a river flowing somewhere nearby, just a sprinkling of notes through the air, glistening and shining in the darkness.

Soon it will be dawn.

"You okay?" she asks after a while.

"Me?" I guffaw. "You almost had your head bashed in and your entire soul devoured!"

She shrugs one shoulder up, then the other, a mini Galerano shrug. "Hopefully not the *entire* thing!"

I roll my eyes, laughing, and put my hands in my pockets.

"No, for real, though. I feel okay," Chela says. "My head aches, but I don't think I have a concussion or anything."

I want to ask if I can check her out, but it feels . . . it feels cheesy somehow. Like a line.

Then Chela says, "Would you, uh, do you think you could make sure for me?"

"Aho!" I say, in an attempt not to yell *yes!* too quickly.

She blurts out a hasty explanation. "It's just it doesn't add up, you know? It *did* feed off me, the bambarúto"—the way she just aced that pronunciation makes me think she must've talked about these things before with her cousin—"and it doesn't actually make sense that I feel as okay as I do and—"

"Yes," I say, when I finally realize that's why she's rambling. "Of course."

We face each other in front of the rickety betahayim gate.

This place should be creepy, especially with everything going on, but somehow it's not. Those solar lights she put up illuminate tiny constellations around the tombs, and anyway, here I am with the queen of the cemetery herself, the little burakadóra, the Destroyer's chosen daughter. There's probably nowhere safer to be than next to her—as long as we're on the same side.

"Wait." She steadies herself with a hand on either one of my shoulders, then rises on her tiptoes, shoving one open eye at my chin.

"Um, why did you just turn into a close-talking human version of the monocle emoji?"

"Did your goatee finally come full circle?"

I'm so surprised, I grab her shoulders, too, and yell, "Yes! How did you—" I stop because we're very, very close together right now and it's a whole lot. "How did you know?"

She squints at me. "How did I know about something I'm looking right at?"

"You know . . ." I say. I should probably take my hands down now, but I'd much rather not. And she's still all up in my personal space in the best way possible. "How did you no*tice*, I mean?"

"Oh—" She drops back down. "I guess it just seems obvious."

"Right, gotcha," I say, in a way that is neither sarcastic nor convincing. I must change the subject quickly or I will die. "I've never done just a routine physical for someone. Only horrific emergencies so far."

"I could arrange one if that would help you get in the zone," she snickers. "That's my specialty."

"Hush," I say. "And close your eyes." Then I add, because her face is sliding into murder position, "Please." She does.

I don't know if it matters, but I still barely understand what I'm doing, and I don't want her watching me fumble through this. Again.

I shake the jitters out of my hands, wipe them on my T-shirt in case they're sweaty, and then place one on either side of her forehead.

"Ow," she says.

I pull back fast. "Oh my God! I'm so sorry!"

She keeps her eyes closed but lets a wicked grin cross her face. "Kidding!"

"Chela!"

"Okay! Okay! Sorry!" She gets serious again, squeezing her eyes closed even tighter. "I'mma stop messing around, I swear." Then: "Put your hands back."

Can't win with this girl. I crack my neck a few times, then place my hands back in position.

Next I close my eyes.

Have you ever heard La Musika de Antes? You probably haven't. Almost no one has. It's a Galerana women's choir from God knows when—the dawn of recording devices, that's for sure, because the only reason we even know they exist are some scratchy, barely audible songs on an ancient record that Tía Lucia played me once. Their name literally means *The Music of Before*, as in, before time started, clearly.

Anyway, it's three old women and two young ones on the cover, and their voices sound like the forming of a new galaxy, the way they rise and fall and expand around each other. You can catch some of the beginnings of kama music in there, of all the song styles that became big in San Madrigal—the way the chords move, the urgent rasp in that one voice that rises above the rest in a desperate tremolo, the sudden silences.

But as much as those roots are there, hiding, it's also like nothing else in the world. I'd never heard anything else like it.

At least, not until I put my hands to Chela Hidalgo's head and closed my eyes.

It starts as one voice that I feel inside me, inside her, reverberating through my hands, the sweetest earthquake. It's got that Galerano rasp, that ferocity, and it soars. I'm filled with it, can almost taste it, and then other voices join in—a low and a high on either side, a deep, deep drone beneath it all. They reach farther and farther through the darkness, carve open new spaces and expand, until water pours through into the void and gushes around a vine that becomes a single gigantic tree, the whole universe contained within.

Don't let go, I tell myself, because the world has become so dizzyingly huge and seems encompassed in a tiny space around me at the same time. And I don't want it to stop, don't want this moment to end, whatever it is, whatever it means.

Don't let go.

So I don't, and the tree grows, as does the world around it, and a searing light opens across the waters, sends billowing orange reflections up from each small wave.

The sun rises.

"Don't let go," Chela whispers.

Was it her saying it the whole time?

"I won't," I say as the sun swings violently behind the tree and the moon becomes the sky and a gentle darkness settles in. There is peace here. The same peacefulness as in the cemetery. Sanctuary.

I wonder if this is what it felt like to place feet on the shore of an island after so many days and nights at sea. After giving yourself up for dead. And then, suddenly, safety.

Freedom.

A new universe unfolding around you.

We open our eyes at the same time. Smile. She saw what I saw. I don't kill the moment with a corny joke. I don't try to pretend nothing happened. I just look at her, and she looks at me.

Then she takes my hands in hers and raises them to her mouth. She gently kisses one, then the other. "Thank you," she says. "I'm glad you are who you are, Mateo Matisse." She smiles up at me again and then walks through the gates into the darkness of the cemetery.

I watch her climb the steps onto the portico behind the synagogue, wave at me once, and go inside.

Then I turn and head home.

———◆———

I think I have a crush on Chela Hidalgo.

PART
THREE

III.

Silent, invisible, I mend them,

Ablaze with light, you guide them.

With sliver and stitch, hemorrhage becomes trickle,

Each tear now a scar, each scar a story.

Stories grow wings, on lips and strings,

Set the night on fire,

Then find your way home.

—*The Lost Pirate Prayer*

CHAPTER NINETEEN

Man, pirates love voting.

Let me rephrase that: pirates love to talk about how much they love voting—*yada, yada, the outlaws of the high seas were one of the first democracies, blah, blah*. Meanwhile, the people they considered cargo didn't get a vote, and the Iroquois had already been doing democracy for centuries.

But it's a whole thing. So it carried over to our little island world. They pretty quickly set up a governing triumvirate called the Cabildo, with one member voted in from each community. But like I said, the pirates in particular always somehow managed to get the lighter and richer ones into those positions of power and keep them there for generations and generations.

Funny how that works (it's really not).

Anyway, the only exception to the pirates-love-voting thing is war. During battle, the high commander's word is law, no matter what, and any questioning of it is punishable by death. And look, I get it: no one wants to be mid-charge with bullets and cannonades exploding around them and suddenly stop and have a referendum on whether to outflank the enemy on the left or right. Cool.

But what happens when you live in a state of constant battle? Yeah, the last full-scale *war* war was the (boringly named) Madrigal War, more than two hundred years ago, and that ended with some lengthy accord, but the street fights raged on. Or, rage on, I should say, because here we are, on the brink of battle once more.

All that said, the only thing pirates love more than voting is bragging about how much they love voting. So I'm not surprised when all anyone can talk about in homeroom the next morning is the vote tomorrow night. Even the regular ol' non-Galerano kids are paying attention and chiming in. People who had seemed not to give a damn about anything but sports yesterday suddenly have a political science degree and strong opinions about everything from Gerval's second album to criminal justice theory to procedural nuances. It's basically the internet but with body odor and spittle.

The only non-voting word you hear rising through the clutter of voices is *bambarúto*, and it's said in urgent whispers. I wonder if Tolo had his people spread the word about those soldier guys. Either way, people are terrified of them, that much is clear.

One good thing: at least everyone has found a topic more interesting to pick apart than me. No one turns to look when I walk in, no one mutters anything, no questioning eyes stick to me.

Good.

Back to being gone, like I should be.

Maybelline and Maza stand by the door, arguing, and they don't seem like they're just kidding around. All that easy sass has given way to a frustrated back-and-forth. "We just want our island back!" Maybelline yells, exasperated, as Maza counts points on their fingers: "We don't really know what Anisette's got planned, we don't even know if it's possible, and we still don't know who or what those guys were last night!"

Those guys. I make my way through the classroom, skirting around arguments that wax toward fistfights. Tolo's rumor mill notwithstanding, it seems that Maza hasn't told their sister about what happened in his office yesterday. I don't even know how someone would go about describing the thing that emerged from the armor. It's probably for the best. Those huge teeth still glint at me from my memories—it's all I saw when I was trying to sleep last night.

"Bambarúto," someone listening to their conversation whispers, like saying the name will ward away the monster. The whisper carries around the classroom like a shivering echo.

Even Dr. Kobrick is in on the debates, although I can't tell what side he's on. He probably smugly enjoys being all enigmatical and neutral or whatever. He's not a Galerano, but he stays read up on everything so he can be sure to speak with authority on it. A couple students have gathered around his desk, and someone is diagramming the island on the whiteboard. Chaos, man. Chaos.

Chela and Tams are huddled in the far corner of the room, conspiring.

For a brief moment, jealousy flashes through me. You gotta understand: people of all genders, sexual preferences, nationalities, etc. are into Tams. Her fan club has no restrictions or limitations, and she's somehow charming enough that even when it doesn't work out, which is 99 percent of the time, they still manage to be cool with her and wish her well and all that—and not even in a creepy passive-aggressive way.

Which, don't get me wrong, is super cool.

But, you know, being the friend of the hottest, coolest person in the world, every once in a while, it catches up to me.

Chela looks up from what I now realize is a piece of notebook paper they've been studying and smiles at Tams with a warmth she rarely shows. And in that moment, I know it's all over. I was a fool to get myself all excited about someone. It's piano keys and music notes from here on out, that's it!

Then Chela sees me and lights up, beckoning me over excitedly, and Tams turns, tilts her chin with a glint in her eye, and honestly, what was I thinking? Besides all that other stuff, Tams is my best friend in the world, and she has never done *any*thing that would ever compromise that. More likely than not, she was talking about how cool I am. Ugh.

Never let me have thoughts again, please. They only confuse things. I hereby fire my mind.

"We're plotting," Chela says with a devilish grin as I slide up a chair.

"So I see. Voter fraud? Celebrity endorsements? What we got?" I lean into their huddle, which puts me closer to Chela's face than I realized I would be, but also closer to Tams's, so maybe that's less awkward? Who knows. Chela doesn't seem to mind, though.

"Better." Tams wiggles her eyebrows. "Sweet, sweet chaos."

"Passing out cheesy flyers? Buttons? A radio spot!"

Chela rubs her temples in mock confusion. "We said *better*, man! What's wrong with you?"

We're all laughing when Chela whispers, "I overheard my dad saying he was going to meet with Gerval today."

Tams and I exchange raised eyebrows.

"What? We have a landline still. When it rings, I pick it up. And listen. Serves them right for being so old-fashioned."

"So what? We go interrupt the meeting?" I ask. "Barge in and demand to find out what the hell is going on?" Somehow that doesn't seem like the best plan.

"No, Rambo," Tams says. "We go listen."

"They're meeting in the park," Chela informs us. "We could try to get a recording of their conversation, if we hide out in the right spot."

"I feel like the hiding-in-the-bushes thing is gonna be harder than we may think," I point out.

"That's why we should go with my idea," Tams says, wiggling her eyebrows. "A disinformation campaign."

"A *what*?" I gawk.

"Someone on Anisette's side is definitely lying," Tams says. "Probably all of them. They're politicians."

"But Gerval didn't seem to know—"

"We don't *know* what Gerval does or doesn't know," Chela points out.

Tams does a little mambo in her seat. "So, we might as well make it up!"

"Why don't we just find out?" I say. "Gerval's staying at the music studio on Fulton. We could just go ask—"

"Wait," Chela says, "when did you find this out?"

"He told me," I say, cringing inside. All of this is wrong. Too many secrets—I'm getting lost in them. "We played music in the park after school."

Chela studies me for a moment, face blank. "And?"

"And I'm trying to find out who the child of San Madrigal is, just like everyone else."

"Is he?" Tams asks.

"I don't think so," I say. "If he is, I don't think he knows it. But he's definitely invested in trying to find out what's going on."

"I bet he is," Chela says. "Especially now that he's lined up to be on the Cabildo. I wonder if he knew what was coming. . . ."

"Well . . ." As the next words leave my mouth, I realize I'm opening up a whole world of mess by putting this forward, but . . . it's also true. "Only one way to find out."

They both blink at me.

"Gerval said something yesterday that I keep thinking about," I tell them. "He's been reading up on San Madrigal history. Sounded like Anisette's giving him books. What I'm saying is . . ." I pause, aware again of how completely ridiculous this is, and they're probably going to laugh at me for even suggesting it. I can't even believe I am. But what the hell. "What time is your dad meeting him?"

"Ten," Chela says. "In half an hour."

"Mateo Matisse." Tams is squinting at me. "Are you suggesting criminal trespass?"

I scrunch up my face. "Yes?" Then nod. "Yes. Yes, I am."

Now Tams and Chela trade a glance, both of their faces lit up with excitement. "That's what I'm talking about," Chela says.

"Can I invite Maza?" Tams asks. "You know, covert operations and sneaking around are excellent opportunities for flirting."

They are? I didn't know that, and I'm probably just sitting there gaping about it when Chela goes, "Oh, absolutely!" with more enthusiasm than I expected.

"Excellent." Tams waves at Maza across the room and does another small chair mambo.

I check the time: 9:37. Take a deep breath. This is really happening. Glance at Tams and Chela, Maza, who's just walking up. "Well," I say, "guess today's a half school day, huh? We ready?"

———◆———

School isn't the only place where people are arguing. Out in the streets of Little Madrigal, all the viejitos are cursing at each other and carrying on across chessboards and cups of coffee. Iya Tamika is outside her botanika debating Fayin, the shoe seller; Simpatico and Pedro have opened their shops early for the sole purpose of lambasting each other, far as I can tell.

People just love to fuss, is what it is. Everybody wants to have an opinion, and it better be a strong one. It's like all the everyday-type gossip notched up to a thousand, because suddenly it's not just a regular election anymore: it's about home. And everything is more real when it's about home, even if home is an island that's a whole fifteen years underwater, just memories and whatever bits and pieces anyone could salvage amid the collapse.

But the impossible faraway hope of those three peaks somehow coming back—turns out no one ever let go of it. Doesn't matter that it is a fantasy, a dream. San Madrigal was always a dream, even when it existed. Ever since it appeared through the mist to those three enemies, lost at sea—or whatever it is that really happened that night—the place has been an enigma. The answer to so many prayers, made manifest in rocky cliffs and crumbling sea-stained facades.

For so long, San Madrigal meant freedom to anyone who needed to get away from the ever-watchful eyes of empire. For the weary exile, the refugee, the persecuted, the outlaw—those cobblestone streets, the tolling bells, the three peaks, all formed a loving embrace.

And then it was just gone.

So I get it. But it's still wild to see everyone so worked up.

Anisette Bisconte says it's time to go public, tell the world who we are. It makes some sense, then, that she picked the one kinda famous Galerano to step into leadership, and not the gangster from a long line of gangsters. And I halfway get where she's coming from: we've always been hidden away, yes, but we've also moved with the times. Out of necessity, we adjusted, did what we had to do. We've never been static. When the island fell, we found our way somewhere else, and our culture became what it is: Still underground, sure, but who would've dreamed we'd have a whole Galerano presence on the American streets?

Anisette claims it's a matter of survival, that our dream isn't sustainable unless we tell the world about our island, invite hotels and tourists and conferences.

I'm not an economist, but it sounds gross.

Sea espíritu, my long-dead ancestor Maestro Archibaldo told the kameros. Maybe he meant the island, too. Heard and not seen. Now, because of Gerval, we've been heard. Maybe that's enough.

"How do you guys wanna play this?" Chela asks as we stroll down the main thoroughfare like we're just some normal kids playing normal hooky.

"Well," Tams says, glancing back with a sly smile, "we figure Tolo's under a lot of stress right now, and maybe some romance would cheer him up, ya know?" She winks at Maza as Chela gags. "And why not double the fun?"

"Ughh!" Chela groans, grabbing my arm and bending over to fake puke. "I meant this secret mission! Not—ugh! Please never speak of your plans to seduce my cousin again! Barf, barf!"

"I mean, he's hot!" Maza says, laughing.

Chela waves them away. "This is my life story. I have a hot gangster cousin, and no one will ever let me forget it."

"Now you know what it's like being best friends with this one," I say, pointing at Tams and rolling my eyes. "Gotta manage the fan club."

"Oh, a fan club, is it?" Maza punches Tams playfully on the shoulder. "Do tell!"

Tams shoots me a *Shut it* glare, then smiles at Chela. "Anyway, what's the plan, Chela? You're the expert!"

She scoffs. "Nice diversion. And I'm good at fighting. Sneaking is not my game."

"Well," I say, "I was thinking we'd do the ol' distraction-in-the-front, sneak-in-the-back thing. There's definitely a loading dock out back that's usually open."

Tams smirks back at me. "Do I want to know how you have all this information?"

Truth is: I've been wanting to go into this music studio for . . . well, forever. It's a landmark. So maybe I've walked around it a couple times, late at night on the way home from a gig, imagining what it must feel like to just casually stroll in and start playing music where the legends do. Might've also downloaded all the images I could find of it off the internet and studied them so my fantasies could be as accurate as possible. I could say all that. Instead, I just say, "No," and leave it there.

"Well, good news about your plan," Maza says, pointing across the street to where a huge crowd has gathered outside Gerval's studio. "Looks like we won't need a distraction for the front." It's all types of folks, including a good number of senior citizens, most of whom probably never thought they'd see their island home again and now figure whatever Gerval is offering is their last chance at it. People are milling around, chatting, clearly hoping for some direction. A crowd awaiting their leader.

"Yeesh," Tams says. "That's a lotta people."

The studio itself is a simple one-story storefront on the corner of the block. There's a sign on top that says OLD MADRIGAL MUSIC FACTORY, but otherwise the whole operation is pretty modest and nondescript.

This is where Gerval cuts all his albums. It's gonna be a historical landmark one day.

But in all the times I dreamed of going inside, I *definitely* never imagined it would be while sneaking in to steal information from the guy I thought was my hero.

"So . . . around back," Chela says. "You ready?"

"Not at all," I say with a nervous laugh. Then I nod. "Let's do it."

CHAPTER TWENTY

ANXIETY RISES WITHIN ME AS WE WALK TOWARD THE OPEN GARAGE door around back. Nothing is the way it's supposed to be. I should be in the front, beside Gerval, chatting nonchalantly about our next album and where we'll go on tour. No angry crowds, no mad island-raising plots, no . . . Well, I would still want Chela there, too.

"Okay," I say, "you already know not to ask me how I know this. But there's an office off to the side, down a hallway, and there's the studio itself. Guessing he could be keeping important stuff in either or both places."

"So we split up," Tams says, picking up where Chela left off. "Maza and I will find the office—"

"What, so we can flirt more privately?" Maza demands.

Tams nods sagely, as if she's checking a complicated math equation. "Mm, exactly that, yes, yes."

"Fantastic," Maza proclaims. I can't even tell if they're kidding or serious, but either way I'm impressed. Even with all this front-row experience in watching my best friend work her magic, I still have no idea how the whole flirting thing works. These two flow through it like it's breathing.

Chela just smirks, then gets back to business. "Then Mateo and I will take the studio."

I prepare my cringe for the moment when someone inevitably points out what a wild double date this is. Instead, Chela says, "I'm sure he'll be right at home with all that music stuff," which is so true and innocent compared to what I was expecting that I end up swallowing saliva down the wrong pipe and choking on it.

Because I'm amazing.

When I'm done coughing and Tams has made sure I'm okay enough for her to roll her eyes at me, we step over some trash, make sure no one's around, then walk on in like we're supposed to be there, cool as could be.

"What are we looking for?" Maza asks as we head quietly down a super-average carpeted corridor with one blinking fluorescent light and some shoddily framed posters of San Madrigal in the seventies.

"We either want some indication of what Gerval's election strategy is . . ." Chela says. "Notes, memos, charts, whatever—"

"A laptop?" Tams suggests, always tech-and-gadget-minded.

"Or a book," I say, remembering Gerval's cryptic mumblings from yesterday.

"Definitely could be a book," Chela says. "Anything that would tell us about what he and Anisette are up to with this raising-the-island talk. The kinda stuff my cousin would get excited about."

"Like us, hopefully," Maza says, nudging Tams. She waves a quick apology when Chela growls. "No, no, my bad! I'm kidding! We got you. Old stuff, right? Like those antiquey leather-bound tomes he has in his office. Crinkly coffee-stained maps and whatnot."

"Exactly," Chela says, still with a touch of wrath in her voice. "You'll know it when you see it."

We've stopped in front of one of those thick soundproof doors, which means we're at the studio, so everyone gives one another a smooth secret-agent nod and chin tilt, and then Tams and Maza head off to find the office.

"So . . ." Chela says, glancing up at me. "You all right?"

"M-me?" I sputter. Then immediately give up the charade. "Absolutely not."

She opens the door slowly, peeks in, and motions me to follow. "Do you want to talk about it?"

I appreciate how she's made it clear she cares but also hasn't stopped moving. It makes me feel like she knows I'll keep it together, even though I'm nervous about all this. And if she thinks so, who am I to prove her wrong? I follow her into what turns out to be a small anteroom with two big windowed doors.

And I do—do want to talk about it—but instead I'm rendered momentarily speechless. One of the doors leads to the wider, padded studio area, complete with a drum kit, grand piano, a bunch of high-end mics and amps, the works. Heaven, basically. It's all quality gear, but also plain and straightforward, and that's the thing: no fancy extra-ness, no corny effects. Just music. Everything in me wants to go in there and just mess around like a little kid, play and play to my heart's content in the very studio, on the very equipment, that my hero makes his magic with.

Chela tracks the emotions on my face and then tugs my hand one time.

The other door leads down a narrow hall to a walled-off area at the far end of the studio with a huge window in front: the sound booth. This is where the engineers sit during a session, and that's where any paperwork would be lying around, most likely.

I know: stay focused.

I nod, then tear my eyes away from the studio and follow Chela to the sound booth. It helps that she hasn't let go of my hand.

There's plenty of paperwork in here, but it's mostly boring tech notes.

We split the pile in two and are each shuffling through our half when Chela drops to the floor so fast it's like she got hit by some invisible arrow.

I glance up, see a door swinging open in the studio, and I'm already on my way down when Chela pulls me so hard I collapse the rest of the way, barely catching myself before I hit the ground. We scatter under the soundboard, both panting, and crouch facing each other amid the tangled cords and blinking lights.

"Damn, you're fast," I whisper.

"I'll withhold my assessment of your speediness," she says with a grumble.

"I'm grateful."

"Did you see who it was while you were descending in slow motion toward the floor?"

I scowl at her. "I did not." Then I slide partway out and eye the switches and buttons above us. "But I bet we can hear them."

There—the button to feed the studio mics into the sound room monitors. I stay in a crouch, click it on, and then slide back under the desk with Chela as the room around us fills with a familiar voice.

"Ahahaha!" yells Gerval, with a gargly holler that might alarm a normal person but that I recognize as vocal warm-ups. *"Yada! Yada! Yadaaaaaa!"*

This wasn't part of the plan! *Why is Gerval here?* What if he catches me? How do I possibly explain being under a desk in his studio with Chela of all people?

Everything is terrible.

Now that it's gone to hell already, I'm pretty sure that, when I hatched this awful plan, in the back of my mind I thought I could have it both ways. Gerval would be gone; he'd never even know we were here. That *I* was here. We'd get the information we needed.

My tía would be happy. Chela and Tolo would be happy. And if, for some reason, we had to take something with us, Gerval would be upset, maybe, but he wouldn't be able to pin it on us.

Well . . . this is what they mean when they say you can't please everyone. And when you try, usually the opposite happens.

"Well played, music boy," Chela whispers, appraising me with new respect. "But how are we getting out of here?"

I accept her compliment magnanimously and then shake my head. I'm too busy feeling doomed to formulate an alternative to my brilliant plan.

"Can he hear us?" she whispers over the whoops and hollers of Gerval's vocal cords strengthening.

"Nah. It's all soundproof unless I hit the comm button."

"So, since we're stuck here, do you want to talk about why you're so wound up?"

I shrug. "It's Gerval, man. He's always been my hero, you know? And now . . . now I don't know what to think. And here I am under his desk, and—"

"Honestly," Chela says, "I never really got the hype about him. I mean, sure, he's famous and all that, but I tried to listen to his albums and they never sound like . . . How do I say it? The way the music is supposed to sound. The way I'm used to hearing it, you know?"

I do know—it's because kama, the music of San Madrigal, in all its many forms, is a living thing. It's meant to be heard in dim bars or wafting off rooftops, with a bunch of people crowded around and yelling the chorus and clapping impossible polyrhythms like it's second nature. And yeah, of course it doesn't sound like that when it's recorded in a sterile, soundproof studio like this. Sure, something's lost. But new sounds can emerge when there's time and silence at the musicians' disposal. New possibilities. I guess I love both, is what it is. I'm about to try and explain as much when Chela says, "And anyway, I make it a rule never to trust people who are the 'one and only.'"

"What do you mean?"

Over the monitors, Gerval's still warbling through his warm-ups. *"Muhreeeeeeeee! Muhraaaaah! Ah!"*

"I mean our hood is full of amazing musicians!" says Chela. "But only *one* dude has broken out into the larger world? That doesn't seem strange to you? He didn't decide to lift anyone else onto that big platform of his?"

"I mean . . ."

"Like *you*, Mateo? This is your first time in this place, isn't it? I've heard you play. You're amazing."

"You—"

"You played my bat mitzvah, man. I'll never forget that. There was one song you did—"

"'Anenu,'" I blurt out. Because of course she's talking about that. It's not a song you would normally play at bat mitzvahs, but hers fell during the High Holidays, when "Anenu" is chanted. I've always loved that song—it's so sad and happy at the same time, a prayer that could just as easily be a bawdy whiskey dance if you switched up the lyrics, and it seems to stumble along to its own ferocious momentum. So, I added some blue-note flourishes and got extra emo with it, you know, went to town, and when I looked up, everyone was staring at me, wide-eyed, and I thought I'd messed up at first—you never know—but then they all burst into cheers and applause like in a bad rom-com, and whew! I still remember the sense of relief I felt.

She nods, smiling at the shared memory. "You turned it into something different. It felt special that day, like you did it just for me. My dad was so impressed that you knew to play it. Said it meant you'd really gone above and beyond."

I mean, it's all right there on Wikipedia, but I guess the point is that I went looking in the first place. Anyway, it makes me feel warm inside that she still remembers something I did three years ago.

Suddenly, neither of us seems to be able to look at the other one, because I'm not sure what would happen if we did. And then, just like that, a chord sounds on the piano, startling both of us from whatever fantasy we were having. We trade a confused glance. Did someone else walk in? I've never known Gerval to play piano, but we didn't hear the door open again.

It's a sad chord, doubled octaves and a third in the middle, and then the octaves walk a crooked scale downward to the next chord, as the thirds dip in and out of warped harmonies along the way: a down-tempo mambo, very San Madrigal, and even more so when Gerval's rich voice stretches over it all with the first line. *"Avriiiiiiix,"* he croons, and I can't believe I hadn't recognized the song. Even zhuzhed up, I should know this one. *"Avrix mi Galanika . . ."* It's an old Ladino praisesong, about my guardian santo, of course. At least, I always assumed it was, because it says his name, but I've never paid much attention to the lyrics, honestly. I'm usually too caught up in harmonies and rhythms to bother much with words.

A strange tremble moves through me, a series of small, silently crashing waves, but I don't have words for what it is.

Suddenly, I'm not sure I have words at all.

"Okay," Chela admits just as the waves converge and rise, "this is beautiful. See—he should do more stuff like this on his albums." Then she joins him, very softly, on the next line: *"Que viene amanecer. . . ." Daybreak approaches.*

I've lost the thread of what she's saying, because the rising wave has become a light, a beam so big my body can't contain it.

The light hasn't exploded outward yet, apparently, because Chela doesn't seem to notice anything's happening. "It's all so over-produced, you know? And— Mateo?"

The world is just a blur of flickering colors and lights, and so much sound. That song, those tumbling notes on the piano, they prickle through me, open canyons deep inside. I rise—I'm sure I'm rising—and soon I will simply become light. Somewhere in a distant part of my mind, a voice screams to be careful, we're supposed to be hiding, we can't be seen . . . but to the rest of me, which is the whole universe, those trivial things hardly matter.

I am light. Light is unafraid, unbothered, untouchable.

And then a face crests my blurry vision like a rising sun: Chela.

"Mateo." Her voice is molasses, seeping through the music, covering the world. *"Mateo, man, come back."*

With a shrill *clank*, a door opens in the studio, and the music ends. My whole body trembles as I start to return to it. It's like I'd been floating on a bed of air and then suddenly it's gone and now all that's left to do is plummet.

"Ah, there you are." Gerval's voice is loud through the sound booth speakers, but somehow also a million miles away.

I don't plummet because I am wrapped in Chela. She has crawled over to where I'm still huddled beneath the board and covered me with her body as my trembling slows. I never floated upward, I don't think. But I also have no idea what just happened.

"Are you okay?" she whispers, her lips just beside my ear, her breath on my cheek.

I try to nod, but everything is still shaking, so I don't know if it works. And I don't really know if I am okay.

"Man, what is *happening*?" a familiar and panicked voice says from the studio. "Who were those guys breaking heads last night? And why the urgent text? I was in school. I thought you were meeting with the rabbi."

Chela, holding me tightly still, looks suspiciously at the darkness around us. "Is that . . . Vedo?"

It is. It definitely is.

"I was," Gerval says glumly. "Seems he had second thoughts about our arrangement."

Chela's eyes go wide, then very, very narrow. Her grip tightens unconsciously around my arm. Rabbi Hidalgo has—*had*, from the sound of it—an arrangement with Gerval. Suddenly, I feel like I'm the one who should be comforting *her*, but my body is still coming down from . . . whatever that was.

"And I don't know about those armored guys," Gerval continues. "Ask your mom about that. She's the one who put Trucks on me as a security detail."

"Does this have anything to do with those books she gave you?"

Gerval snaps back so fast, I imagine Vedo flinching. "She told you about the books?"

"Sure." Vedo sounds undaunted. "She tells me everything. I mean, I haven't read 'em, but I assume they're some important supersecret Cabildo business, since you're next in line, right?"

"Yeah, well, not if we don't get the votes. More importantly, why haven't you brought Chela to talk to me?"

"I don't know how," Vedo admits.

Chela lets out a low growl, and I imagine her itching for her blade. Gerval asked me almost the same thing yesterday. Why is he so intent on talking to her?

"What do you mean?" Gerval presses.

"I've tried to talk to her," says Vedo. "It's just . . . she won't even give me the time of day—barely knows I exist. And you know she's tight with her cousin. But also, Maestro . . ."

There's a pause, and it feels like a tense one. Inside me, the last sparkling waves of light wink out and my head finally starts to feel clear again.

"What's gonna happen to her?" Vedo asks.

"I don't know," Gerval admits, and he sounds genuinely sad.

"I'm doing everything I can to figure it out, Vedo. But there's only so much I can do without her being here. I need to know more."

Another pause; it seems to stretch on and on.

Pointedly, Gerval asks, "I need to be able to count on you, Vedo. Can I?"

It's a small thing, really, but those words—they were exactly the ones he said to me yesterday. I don't know if it's jealousy I feel, or just a strange, grating off-ness, but I'm also still too dazed to feel much of anything.

Vedo answers quickly. "Of course, Maestro, it's just—"

Whatever he was trying to say is obliterated by a shock of bright flashing lights and screaming tones. Chela and I trade a look. Fire alarm.

"What now?" I hear Gerval growl between the blasts of noise. In seconds, they're gone.

"Come on." Chela helps me stand. My legs seem to work. "You okay? Do you know what happened?"

I shake my head, blinking away the color splotches. "No idea. But we can figure it out once we get the hell out of here."

CHAPTER TWENTY-ONE

"Y'ALL PULLED THE FIRE ALARM?" I ASK AS WE HURRY ACROSS THE street toward where Tams and Maza stand on the far corner, looking some kind of radiant with their triumphant smiles.

Maza scoffs. "*Pshh*, no! That's for amateurs. We set stuff on fire!"

"*What?*"

"It was just a trash can!" Tams shrugs. "Once we got what we'd come for, we figured you guys were probably hemmed in somewhere. Thought a distraction might help."

"It did," I say. "Thanks."

Chela starts to say something, then seems to think better of it. She hasn't said a word since we left the studio, although mostly it's because we were just trying to duck out without being seen. Still, she looks withdrawn and sullen, especially compared to how easygoing she seemed earlier. If I had to guess, I'd say she's frustrated we didn't get to hear more of the Gerval-and-Vedo convo.

"What's wrong?" Tams asks. "How'd your search go?"

How to explain? *Gerval played a song and a giant wave of light crashed inside me, and he's trying to get Vedo to bring him Chela for the ceremony, and, oh, he also wants me to bring her to him, too, and it all sounds very, very bad?*

Chela saves me the trouble. "Not much. Vedo's in league with Gerval somehow; that's about all we found out."

Tams glances at me, clearly not buying it, but then Chela asks how it went for them and Maza lights up. "We scored, y'all! *Scored!*" They reach into their courier bag—"'Find some of those ye-olde-type tomes Tolo loves so much,' you said"—and pull out three ancient books covered in worn leather, two large and thick, the other much smaller. "And that's exactly what we did."

Chela brightens some. "Whoa. Nice work." She takes the smaller one and starts skimming through it.

"Turns out Gerval has a little side room he sleeps in," Tams says, "adjacent to the office. And these three beauties were right there on the bedside table. You know, some peaceful sleepytime reading, I'm sure."

"I wonder if these are the books Vedo mentioned that his mom passed on to Gerval," I say, eyeing the ornate calligraphy on those worn pages.

"She did what, now?" Maza says. "That sounds shady."

Chela hasn't taken her eyes off the book she's holding. "We're gonna . . . Let me . . . Let me take this to Tolo."

"Wait, alone?" Tams asks, incredulous.

Chela nods. "Yes, I . . . I just need to . . ." She frowns. Shakes her head.

All I want to do is talk to her about everything that just happened, make it make sense somehow, but it's like she's drifting further and further away by the second.

"Let me come," I say. "I'll go with you." I make pointed eye contact with Tams. "Then we'll catch up with you guys after."

Tams makes even more pointed eye contact back to me as Chela starts to head off. "You okay?" she asks quietly.

I tilt my head to either side, shake it. "I have no idea."

She squints at me, then puts the huge tome in my hands. "We're talking later, buddy. You and me. At the bembé."

"The . . . bembé!" I catch myself just in time. "Yes! And I'm sure we'll have *plenty* to discuss," I say, reaching for some kind of light in all this mess.

"There's a bembé tonight?" Maza butts in. "No one told me!"

Tams gives them a sly look. "We're only at stage two or three of our epic flirtation, Maza." She pushes her glasses up the bridge of her nose while making an exaggerated nerd face. "By my calculations, we have at least three more stages before we reach *sharing our intimate religious traditions*."

Maza feigns being crestfallen, but you can tell they don't really mind. "Oh, wow, my bad."

That moment would've had me stumbling over my words for hours and thinking about how badly I'd bungled it for years; I don't know how Tams does it.

I laugh, partially out of relief, and head off after Chela. "See you there, Tams! Later, Maza!"

"Wear your whites!" Tams calls. "And don't be late!"

———◆———

The streets of Little Madrigal still bristle with election-eve gossip and whispers of *bambarúto*, and all the way through them, two thoughts fight for space inside my mind:

1) What the hell happened back at the studio? And . . .

2) If I tell Chela about Gerval asking me to bring her to him, too, am I betraying him, or Tía Lucia, or no one? If I don't, am I betraying her? Does it matter? I don't know!

My brain starts to short-circuit as lose-lose scenarios play out in an aggravating death loop. And jumping ship to deal with thought number one doesn't do me much good. I have no idea what happened. Gerval was singing, then Chela was, too, and then light erupted through me and I could barely move.

Galanika, I'm sure. It was his praisesong. And even if I didn't see him this time, he *had* to have been there. Inside me, I guess? Nothing makes sense.

Fortunately, Chela is off in her own world, nose buried in that small, ancient book, so she probably doesn't notice me driving myself bonkers with questions I have no answer to. And she definitely doesn't notice the car zooming toward her as she steps into the street without looking up.

"Chela!" I yell, grabbing her arm and pulling her back toward me. Her blade comes out so fast I don't even know where she pulled it from. I barely have time to stumble backward a few steps, trip over my feet, and land on my ass as she lunges toward me and the car slams its brakes, screeching to a halt right where she'd been standing.

She blinks, frozen in mid windup for a stab.

"¡Puñeta!" the driver yells. "¿Qué carajo estás pensando, muchacha?" Then she glimpses the dagger, mutters, "Ah, bueno pues," rolls up the window quick, and is on her way with a rev of the engine.

Thanks, lady.

Now it's just me and Chela on the street, but I'm on the ground, staring up at her. "You can't just grab people like that!" she blurts out. "I could've . . . I almost . . ."

"Cool. Next time I'll just let the car hit you," I snap, standing up and brushing myself off.

Chela scowls, I think more at herself than me. "No, it's just—" She slowly vanishes the knife into some hidden holster. "Thank you," she finally manages.

I take a step closer. "What's going on, Chela? You're . . . What's in that book?"

She shakes her head, eyes closed. "I don't know yet. I'm still trying to figure it out, but . . . I don't like what Gerval and Vedo were saying. I don't totally understand it, but it feels like they know something about me that I don't even know. Or maybe I've always known but haven't known how to make sense of it." She shakes her head, looking anywhere but at me. "I'm not even making sense to myself."

"Well, let's get to Tolo's," I say, trying to force things to be okay, to create an answer to this mess through sheer willpower. "See if he can help us figure it out."

But who am I kidding? There is no *us*. Whatever happened in that convo, whatever truth is being revealed in those timeworn pages, it's pushing Chela deeper into her unreachable shell.

Tía Lucia was right, of course. *Trust no one.* So I won't. But in the meantime, I'll find out as much info as I can.

CHAPTER TWENTY-TWO

WHATEVER'S GOING ON WITH CHELA, TOLO AND HIS BODYGUARD Safiya are too lit up by the gifts we've brought them to notice.

"Incredible," Tolo mutters in that deep, raspy voice of his.

"How have we never seen these books?" Safiya says, looking over his shoulder. "Or even heard of them?"

Tolo nods at the smaller tome that Chela still has cradled in her arms. "¿Y la otra?"

"A notebook of some kind," she says, sullen. "I'm still trying to decipher it."

Safiya narrows her eyes. "Where did you guys say you got these again?"

Chela looks at me, but I have no idea what that look is supposed to mean. "Gerval's studio," I say.

"You . . . what, broke in?" Tolo demands. The man's wrath is like an oncoming hurricane—you can feel it in your gut miles before it hits. He never has to raise his voice, the danger just inhabits the air all around him, seethes off him in cruel, effortless waves.

"No," Chela says. "We just walked in. Everyone was out front rallying for the vote tomorrow night."

Tolo shakes his head, smirking ever so slightly. "You just assigning yourself missions now, cuz? Trying to be like me, huh?"

Chela stares him down. "We needed more info, so we got it. You're welcome." She retreats to a leather chair in the far corner of his office and falls back into her book.

Tolo sends an exasperated look my way. "How do you solve a problem like la Chela, am I right, Mateo?"

"Um, pretty sure she just helped get us that much closer to figuring out who the initiated child of Madrigal is," I point out.

Tolo isn't listening. "That's the song we used to sing when she was a kid and got into trouble." He chuckles to himself, shaking that big bald head of his, and then places the book on his desk.

Safiya joins him. They open the first tome and then look directly at me. "Well, well, well," Tolo says. "Seems we're gonna need the help of your superpower, buddy."

"Not more healing stuff," I sigh, walking over.

"Heh, nope. The other one." He holds up the book with both hands, and I almost yelp. "Extreme music dorkiness."

It's all partitur paper. Little elegant notes splatter across staff lines. "Whoa! Gimme!" I say, making grabby motions.

With just a glance, I can tell this much: it's a chaotic symphony I'm holding. A whole Galerano mess, splayed out in various colors, I notice, flipping through the pages. Then I look at the top line, where the composer's name is written: *Archibaldo Medina*.

The "madman" of Madrigal. Mr. *Sea Espíritu* himself.

The gasp I let out is so loud even Chela looks up. "You okay?" she asks.

"Yeah, it's just . . . my ancestor wrote this."

"Oh, wow."

"The legend is that he lost his mind and started playing just pure nonsense. But . . . I didn't think his music was written down anywhere. Guess I just figured he was improvising. I don't think anyone knew about this."

"Well, your boy Gerval did," Tolo says. "Probably Anisette, too." He opens the second tome. "This one looks to be a ledger of some kind. Numbers and dates and cargo, I think."

"That's all yours." I plop into a chair across the room from Chela's and dive into my own work.

Immediately, what I can tell you is that there are so many weird things to sort through I have to make a list.

Weird Thing 1: The title of the piece is "La Clave"—that's the rhythm, usually played on two hollow sticks of the same name, that underlies a whole lot of Cuban music. That sweet *tak tak . . . tak . . . tak tak* you hear threading in and out of the pulse on mambos and boleros and guanguancos? That's the clave. Thing is, there's no clave to be found in this piece. Like, maybe someone's supposed to be playing it the whole time, but usually the other instruments will reflect it somehow—echo it, or play in and out of it. You can *feel* the clave in a song that's written with it in mind, even when no one's playing the actual rhythm. This ain't that. It's just not there.

Weird Thing 2: Okay, so there's no sharps or flats in the key signature, which isn't that weird unto itself—means it's either in C major or A minor or one of those creepy modes that old monks used a bunch (wouldn't be surprised if that were the case, given the material). But the notes themselves don't give any indication of a key. There's no *one tonic note* that begins it all, that we keep coming back to, that we finally land back on when it all comes crashing down. In fact, it doesn't come crashing down at all, it just kind of wanders and strays. It's just chaos, at least at a glance.

Weird Thing 3: What's with all these different colors? Each . . . song, I guess, is written in a different-colored ink, and that's just . . . It's different. What's the point?

Weird Thing 4: Each song has two staffs for piano music and one for what I'm guessing is supposed to be a voice melody. That's normal enough. It's even marked *piano* and *voz* respectively. But there are no lyrics to go along with it, which you'd expect for a voice part, unless the singers are just supposed to hum or go *oooh*. I'm just saying: weird.

Final Weird Thing (for now, anyway): At the very end, someone seems to have added a couple pages more recently. On what looks like printer paper, with different handwriting.

"You know what's especially strange?" Safiya says after we've all been at it for a while in silence.

"Literally everything," I say, exasperated.

"Right. But also the fact that we've never seen one single mention of the existence of these books, you know?"

"I mean, yours could just be some shopkeeper's account log," I point out.

Safiya is unconvinced. "It's definitely bigger than that. These dates span centuries."

"And look," Tolo says, "San Madrigal historical docs—everything from banal government ledgers to war poetry—are nothing if not self-referential. Believe me, when you read enough of them, you'll see. Across all three main cultures, across all variety of forms and styles, everything mentions everything else. Nothing stands alone. Whether it's a cookbook referencing a collection of folktales from a century earlier or a Santero's ceremony log that diverges into some Sefaradi bestiary—it's like there was one large meta-mind behind it all, creating a huge web of knowledge and history and myth."

"Exactly." Safiya shakes her head. "But this book . . . This is off the radar."

"When do the dates start?" I ask, unfolding myself and walking over to the desk. I'm all dead ends on the music stuff right now anyway; think I need to let it marinate some. Chela has barely stirred this whole time, just sits curled like a beautiful gargoyle around that strange little notebook.

Tolo carefully flips through the pages back to the beginning. "First date is August twenty-sixth, 1810."

"Not long after the end of the Madrigal War," Safiya says, squinting at the numbers.

She runs her finger along the side column. Seemingly random letters begin each row: *R, V, A, AM.* "That's what's got us kind of stumped. Otherwise, it's pretty clear this is a trade ledger book, and from the look of it, it's major trade. The numbers are big."

"Russia, Virginia, Antarctica, America?" I try.

"I was thinking the *AM* might be connected to the music thing," Safiya says. "A minor?"

I turn it around in my brain. "It could almost work. . . . A minor doesn't have any sharps or flats, and neither does the music. But . . . most of this is in Spanish. They use solfège—do, re, mi, and all that—not letters like music in English."

Tolo grunts his frustration.

"Still," I say, "it's possible. . . ."

The inside of the ledger's front cover looks weirdly bulky. I examine the outer edge and find a small flap there. "Wait . . . Is this . . . ?" The flap opens when I slide my thumb under it, and I stick my fingers in. "It's an envelope!"

Tolo and Safiya both grin at me like little kids for a half second before gesturing wildly at me to hurry up and get whatever's inside.

I pull out a single leaf of paper with fancy antique writing scrawled across it. Fortunately, my Spanish is still pretty good, so I translate out loud as I read.

———◆———

"'Our Dear Fellow Traveler—

"'You are reading this because you have been selected to join the noble and sacred lineage of the San Madrigal Pirate Republic. You will be a member of the Galerano Triumvirate representing the pirate community. You were selected because we deemed you worthy. We believe in your abilities, discretion, and prowess.'"

———◆———

"This book was supposed to come to me," Tolo growls.

"Gerval said Vedo's mom gave it to him," I say.

Safiya cocks an eyebrow at me. "You *talked* to him?"

"Us hearing him say something," Chela points out quietly from her spot, "doesn't mean he said it to us."

I *did* talk to him, though, and now I keep thinking about what he said in the park, about all the weird things he'd been learning about Madrigal, both from Anisette, and I think he said others, too. . . .

"Clearly, you and I have a lot to talk about, little cousin," Tolo says sharply. "Don't think the sulking-in-the-corner routine is going to get you out of it."

Chela goes back to reading, and so do I.

———◆———

"'The secrets contained in this book are known only to a tiny select society of thinkers that you have now joined. Indeed, it is of the utmost necessity that no one else find out about them. Their revelation would bring an end to everything we hold sacred and dear.'"

———◆———

"Whoever these guys are," Tolo says, "I already hate them."

"That's probably why Gerval ended up with the book," Safiya points out.

Tolo grins that long lizard grin of his. "Heh, well, it's ours now. Go on, kid."

———◆———

" 'A war has ended, and we enter into a new era of San Madrigal history, one that will be marked by cooperation and peace. But make no mistake—our war is never over, not until Our Lord has risen.' "

———◆———

"Yikes," I say, because yikes. The worst part about this is that only one of the original three spirits of San Madrigal is male: mine. So, unless they're talking about a spirit from some other tradition, I might be the last member of a very creepy-sounding secret cult of creepos.

———◆———

" 'And when He does Rise, it will only be because of the diligent, patient work of His servants. That is the noble calling to which you now belong, fellow traveler, leader of pirates.

" 'Perhaps you will be the one chosen to lead in that time, and if you are so blessed, there will be many elements to pull together for the Rising to take place. Some are contained in the pages of this ledger. Others are in the accompanying sacred text that our priests have compiled. Both will be given to you upon your ascension to the Cabildo.

" 'But the most important element of all is simply this: blood will be answered with blood. Our island cries out for balance. With its very origin, there was a destruction, and so will there be destruction in the rebirth of its most powerful Lord, who Himself is embodied by the island, the three noble peaks, the teeming populace! The island is His tomb, and if ever the island itself falls, it will be a sign that His Rising has begun.

"'You will take part in this Rising.

"'There are many pieces, but as the old Santero saying attests: with one thing the world begins; with one thing the world ends.

"'The one who destroyed and entrapped our Lord must fall in order for the island to rise, and Our Lord to rise with it. . . .'"

—◆—

I stop.

"Well?" Tolo demands. "That's the missing piece, the thing Gerval's looking for. What's it say?"

"That's it," I say. "That's the end of the letter."

Safiya throws up her hands. "Well, who the hell is 'the one who destroyed'?"

I hadn't even realized Chela was by the door. There are tears in her eyes, and her voice is barely a whisper when she says, "Me."

Then she's gone.

CHAPTER TWENTY-THREE

I start after Chela, but Tolo's soft, raspy voice reaches me before I make it to the hallway, and it brooks no argument: "Let her go."

I stop, knowing he's right—she left because she wants to be alone, not as some stunt to get attention. Then I spin around. "What are we supposed to do? What did she mean?"

Tolo shakes his head. "I don't know, man, but when Chela storms out, you let her go. Them's the rules. She'll figure out what she needs to on her own, and when she's ready, she'll come back with what she's got. Meanwhile, we have our own work cut out for us."

"But what if . . . ?" I shake my head as billions of horrible possibilities dance through it.

"All that energy you spending thinking up what-ifs," Safiya says, already getting back to work, "you could put toward making sense of this mess. Come look."

I do, still trying to rid myself of various imagined tragedies and interpretations of what she meant by that one word, *me*.

"What this appears to be," Tolo says with a little extra growl in his low voice, "is a San Madrigal trade ledger detailing an entire hidden economy that we've never known about."

My eyes go wide. "How?"

"That's what I'd like to know. And also *who*?"

"Who the trade was with?"

He nods. "Who the trade was with, and who was doing it. Because, based on the items alone, there's no way this *wasn't* with slaver nations. Look: *Algodón*, that's cotton. *Azúcar*, sugar. Here's *café*, which you already know."

Then I read a few columns ahead and look up to see Tolo's fallen face. "No . . ." I whisper. With one word—*esclavos*—the whole mythology of who we are feels like it's been blown to smithereens.

"Unless our ancestors were robbing the ships," Safiya says, "or buying from people who were and then freeing everyone . . ."

"San Madrigal was dealing with empire." It comes out of me with a sad sigh. "And part of the slave trade." If that's true, well . . . I guess every story really does contain its own opposite, like the saying goes. Here we all thought we were this big bandit island, off the maps, nunca conquistada . . .

"Problem is," Tolo says, "without knowing what these abbreviations mean, we're just assuming things. It's pretty clear, but I don't know if it's gonna be clear enough to make sense to a bunch of people who don't want to believe how truly jacked-up their own homeland has been all along."

We all stare at the ledger some more, and then I go back to my partitur because those numbers are making my head spin.

Hours slide past without much movement. Eventually, I say my goodbyes and head off. I have a bembé to get ready for. Where people will be staring and gossiping, and I'll feel like an outsider. Should be tons of fun.

Outside Tolo's club, I put on my headphones and pull up a recording on my phone—my park session with Gerval. Need to see if what he said then revealed anything about the books. I jump around through the music and chatter as I walk down Fulton. "*. . . about our history that no one knows,*" his voice says in my ear. Yeah, that's it. "*Well, almost no one. There's so much more to it than they ever told us—a secret history—and . . . I'm just now seeing it all. And not just our history—our present tense, too. This. Right here and now. It's . . .*"

"*Who's been telling you this stuff?*" I hear myself asking "*Anisette?*"

"*Yeah, her, others. Been reading up on it, too.*"

"*Where?*"

"*Some . . . books she . . .*"

Gerval knows what we've seen today. He might not know more than we do, but even what's right there on the surface is enough to . . . enough to count for something! I don't know what, but something. The more I think about it, the more it looks like the maestro is on the inside of this, through and through. Whatever *this* is. And I guess he was almost up-front about that. He seemed to be saying he was trying to protect us from it somehow, from Anisette. . . .

Nothing makes sense.

Fifteen minutes later, I close the apartment door behind me and lean against it, drop my head back with a *clunk*, then let out the longest, saddest sigh I've ever sighed.

I'm home and confused, and surrounded by the familiar smells of Tía Lucia's recently baked pasteles (*again?*), that weird fruity cleaning solution she loves, and . . .

Ppffffooooottt!!

And Farts.

He's staring up at me with those gigantic eyes, looking even more on edge than usual, panting.

"What is it, Farts?" I ask, sounding like I'm about to go find Timmy trapped in the river. I didn't actually expect him to answer, but he immediately whirls around and trots to Tía Lucia's room, where the flickering TV lights up the darkness.

"¿Tía?" I call, poking my head in. "¿Estás bien?"

There's movement on the bed, then she props herself up on her elbows and squints at me, making an unintelligible jumble of sounds.

"Are you just waking up? Tía, it's like three in the afternoon. . . . What's going on?"

"¿Qué pasó? ¿Ya votaron?"

"No, the vote's tomorrow night. I'm heading to a bembé."

She slides off the bed, already throwing covers and clothes around, riled. "¿Un bembé? ¡Ay, coño—verdad! Iya Lisa está hacienda la Yemonjacita esa, carajo."

She stops midway through pulling on a pair of white pantyhose. "Ah." Tilts her head to one side, then the other. Then perks up. "Bueno. Voy contigo."

"Word?" Tía has been up so late these last few nights, I thought she might sit this one out. Especially considering she completely forgot about it. A lot on her mind, I guess.

She shoots me an arch look over her shoulder. "Word. Now go iron your whites, m'ijo. I'm not showing up with some schlumpy-looking malcriado, ¿oíste?"

———◆———

Half an hour later, I'm showered and shaved (leaving the now-acknowledged full goatee alone, mind you, just removing a little scruff here and there) with my well-ironed white pants and guayabera on and waiting at the door next to Farts, who farts.

"Man!" I take a few steps to the side. "I just put cologne on! Now you gonna—"

"¡Vamános!" Tía Lucia calls, shooting out of her bedroom like a bright white-and-brown torpedo with Aunt Miriam floating in her wake.

Oh, you look so handsome! Miriam coos, sliding translucent fingers over my cheeks and squeezing. *Have fun, you two!*

Tía Lucia is already out the door and halfway down the hall. "Come on! We're going to be late!"

Thank you, Aunt Miriam says quietly just as I'm turning to go.

"Huh?"

No, it's that— This is what she needed, Mateo. This will help.

"What do you mean? Help what?"

"¡MATEO MATISSE MEDINA!" The voice booms down the hall, which means it's truly time to make moves.

"Tell me when we get home," I say to Miriam, and close the door behind me, almost tripping over Farts as I go.

———◆———

On the way, I don't have a chance to ask Tía Lucia what Miriam was talking about. We bundle into the taxi, and beneath a rumbling bachata beat, she gets into a heated debate with the driver about the vote tomorrow. Then we pull up to a nondescript brownstone in Bushwick with the sound of congas blaring out of its windows.

Tams is outside talking to Iya Lisa, a middle-aged woman with arresting eyes and a wide smile. "Is that Lucia?" Iya Lisa hollers, peering through the taxi window. She flicks away the cigar she'd been smoking and puts both hands on her hips. "Sis! You back?"

"Yeah, yeah, yeah," Tía Lucia says, waving off the attention while she scooches out of the cab. "No me jodas la vida."

Iya Lisa wraps her in a big hug and kisses her cheek, leaving maroon splotches behind. "Look at you! Hey, Mateo! This kid gets taller every time I see him, I swear!"

"Hey, Iya Lisa."

She crosses her arms over her chest, taps each shoulder to mine, and then embraces me—the Santero greeting—before grabbing Tía Lucia by the arm and escorting her inside. "Come on, Lulu. We got *so* much to talk about!"

"You made it!" Tams's smile for me is huge. She's got on those elegant whites and a headwrap to boot, plus all her beaded necklaces and a bunch of jangling bracelets. We both cross arms, tap shoulders, and hug, and man, even before I've stepped inside the brownstone, it's good to be somewhere else, in a whole different world, away from the lies and secret wars and sunken islands. "Now!" Tams blocks my way in. "Tell me what the hell happened today!"

I just shake my head. "Don't even know where to begin."

We sit side by side on the stoop as the shadows grow long around us and Brooklyn strolls by.

Chela's thing seems personal somehow, private. Plus, I can barely wrap my head around what happened: she got lost in a book and then declared herself the missing ingredient that some secret cult needs to raise the island? Okay, bro. So I start with my own stuff, describe as best I can the whole weird feeling I had at the studio.

"Sounds like possession," Tams says matter-of-factly, and I appreciate how chill she is about it. "You were initiated to Galanika. For us, that means the spirit you're initiated to can mount you."

"I thought it was maybe something like that, but . . . it's all still so weird to me. Has it ever happened to you?"

"Just once," Tams says. "And I think that was only partially. It was kind of beautiful, kind of terrifying."

"Sounds about right."

"But usually it happens at a ceremony—I'm sure you'll see someone with a spirit on them when we go inside." She stands. "Your thing happening out in the world, and just from someone singing and playing the piano . . . that's definitely weird."

I stand, too. "Thought as much."

"I gotta get back in there on drums, and you should meet the brand-new priest and pay your respects."

I'd forgotten that bembés are usually thrown to mark an occasion—someone's initiation more often than not. Turns out this one's for a little kid whose ceremony was yesterday. When we walk in, I spot her underneath a beautiful throne made of blue fabrics and sparkling fish figurines. She's about seven and dressed in a turquoise gown. A silver crown sits on her head, and they've painted blue streaks and swirls on her brown face. She looks every bit the daughter of the ocean spirit, Yemonja.

As I make my way through the crowd of sweaty, smiling Santeros, all dressed in white, I wonder what my own ceremony was like. Who was there? Did I get dressed up like Galanika, too, with a scar painted on my tiny face and a fake gray beard? Did the same warmth and sense of community fill the room, or was it hushed, secret, dangerous?

The drums rattle along around us, filling the place. I step forward, touch the mat beneath the throne of fabric, and kiss my hand, a sign of respect. The little girl does the same, her face breaking out in a big toothy smile.

Iya Lisa is perched beside the throne, looking on like a proud mom, which I guess she is: she acted as godparent to the new initiate. And I know she's a priest of Yemonja, too, making the connection even deeper. "This is Mateo Matisse," she tells the little girl. "He's initiated to Galanika, not Yemonja like us, but we like him all right, anyway." She shoots me a mischievous smile, and I drop down to salute the way my aunt taught me.

Then the drums kick up a furious rhythm, and I hear Tams jump in on cowbell—I'd know that particular clanking swagger anywhere—and everyone who was aimlessly milling about on the dance floor instantly falls into a smooth kind of two-step, moving as one.

The singer stands up and belts out the first phrases of a prayer to Elegguá, the gatekeeper, the small cowrie-shell-eyed spirit of the crossroads. Johnny Afrá immediately steps to the front of the dancers, dipping, pausing, spinning, then falling back into that little old man dance that no one else can quite figure out. Everyone cheers—the guy's like a local celebrity here—and he cracks a wily smile, then jumps back twice, landing on one foot, spins again, and leans all the way back like he's about to limbo.

"Oh, here we go," Tía Lucia groans, stepping up beside me in the crowd. She's smiling, though. She loves this stuff, even if she feigns being vexed.

"Is he getting possessed?" I ask.

"Eh." She shrugs. "Who can ever tell with that one?"

I know what she means. It's been a while since I've been to a San Madrigal bembé—they don't need piano, just percussion—but whenever I've seen people pass spirits, it's been dramatic, a big production; they writhe and twist, and their steps become absolutely otherworldly—either impossibly fast, or they hold perfectly still for a full minute while the other dancers flow around them, and then they seem to explode with the energy, becoming a whole other entity right before our eyes. Of course, no one's been initiated to Galanika in ages, so I've never gotten to see what it looks like when he mounts someone.

Johnny Afrá, who I haven't seen since the ceremony during the Grande Fete, is spinning in a wild dance with an older woman I don't know, and I can almost see the waves of energy vibrating outward from them. Still dapper to the bone, he's all in white now, but it's a full three-piece suit and a Stetson hat with a single red loro feather in the brim. Instead of his usual cane, he carries the sacred beaded garabato walking stick. Judging from that sweet little old man mambo he's doing, though, the cane is purely ornamental. The ancient Santero looks like he could keep going for hours.

"Now everybody gonna pop off," Tía Lucia says, and sure enough, Baba Johnny's dancing partner twirls into the crowd with a series of tiny convulsions, stomps, and twists that mean a santo must be moving through her. A tall man with sweat glistening over his bare chest catches her and then almost flies backward, blinking a thousand times a second, face contorted.

"Spirit pulls spirit," Tía Lucia says as Johnny Afrá makes his way toward us.

"You're not worried you'll pass Shango?" I ask her.

She swats away the question. "You know I almost never do that!"

I salute. Even if he's not Elegguá, Baba Johnny's an elder, and I've been raised to show respect. I wonder, as I lower myself to the ground, if Galanika will take me over. "Are you . . . Are you Elegguá, or Baba Johnny?" I ask when I rise and embrace him, trying to make sense of his strange, faraway gaze.

The old man shakes his head, laughing. "What's the difference, eh?"

Which is exactly the type of answer you'd expect a trickster spirit to give, but also exactly the answer you'd expect from Johnny Afrá. And I guess that's the point, huh?

He takes me by the shoulders, and his ancient eyes meet mine. "Your problem is one of faith."

"It is?"

"Faith in yourself, hmm?"

Sounds vague, but what do I know? "I guess?"

"If it requires proof, it's not faith. You keep looking for proof of something you already know. One thing. It's very simple, just one thing."

Nothing is simple! I want to scream. Instead, I stammer, "I—I . . ."

"And anyway"—he shrugs, right in time to the rolling thunder of those congas—"la mentira mata al mentiroso."

The lie kills the liar. An old Santero proverb.

"Huh?" I demand. "I'm not lying!"

Baba Johnny cracks a wide smile. "Well, good. Then you're safe, huh?"

"But—"

"Did you tell him?" he asks my aunt as she goes down to salute him. She doesn't answer.

"Tell me what?" I demand.

"Well, there's my answer." Johnny Afrá looks back at me. "When it happens, you cannot fight it."

"When *what* happens?" I say.

"You can't stop it. But there are other things you *can* stop. Don't get distracted, hmm? There will be time for that to come, but first we have to get there."

"What are you talking about?" I don't like any of this. I hate it, in fact. "Tía, what's he talking about?"

"There's no other way, is there?" she asks him, ignoring me.

Johnny Afrá shakes his head sadly. "I'm sorry, m'ija. You must embrace it. But"—he leans close to her, smiles very slightly—"I see you are already doing that, just a little, hmm?"

Tía Lucia nods.

"Would somebody please tell me what's going on?" I yell over the drumming.

"She will," he says, already dancing away. "When she's ready." He shoots her a sharp glare. "Which will be soon."

"Soon," my tía confirms. Then, before I can pester her any more, she takes my hand and drags me onto the dance floor as the drums pick up and the whole world spins into a glorious whirl of brown skin and white fabric and laughing spirits.

CHAPTER TWENTY-FOUR

CHELA'S NOT AT SCHOOL THE NEXT DAY.

The politics banter has ratcheted up to ten—it's the morning of the big vote, so of course it has—and I want none of it. It seems like a joke to everyone, even though I know that mostly it's not. We laugh because it's all we know how to do, and because somehow that's the only response that makes sense in such a mad world. So everyone's shooting quips and threats and zingers back and forth in homeroom, and laughing, sometimes yelling, and I just want to hide, disappear into the floor, or turn into fire and scream as I burst upward through the ceiling and into the sky.

Is that so much to ask?

And then I simmer down as Dr. Kobrick finally calls everyone to attention in his rickety old voice. The whispers of *bambarúto* echo on, as do the snickering smears on Tolo or Gerval, but finally everyone shuts up and Kobrick starts droning on about procedure or whatever.

And my mind runs off. Gerval wants me to bring him Chela. He said she wouldn't trust him, and he was right. But do I? No. I trust no one. But if I'm honest, I trust some less than others. And that keeps changing. Everyone's keeping something from everyone else, that's about all that's clear. Meanwhile, Chela now thinks she's a sacrifice of some kind, but she won't talk about it. And, of course, Tía Lucia has a secret. When we got home last night, she immediately jumped back into her midnight baking and wouldn't say a word about whatever it was Johnny Afrá/Elegguá was talking about. Tolo and Safiya are undoubtedly still poring over that ledger book, trying to make sense of it before tonight. Chela is who knows where—and wherever that is, I want to be there to comfort her, give her an ear to talk to and a shoulder to rest her head on.

When I sneak a glance at my phone, Vedo has texted me:

Mateo

I need to speak to Chela BEFORE the vote

Meet me behind Tolo's club with her, please

This is for her own safety. And yours

I'm sure that matters to you

I'll be waiting

For our safety, huh? Something about that doesn't feel real at all. Truth is, nothing seems real after seeing that ledger. I pored over the music book all night without so much as a clue showing up. It really does seem to just be the ramblings of a very unwell person. Mostly, I feel sad. We don't know the extent of whatever that trade was, but it doesn't matter. We're not who we thought we were, who we pretended to be, and that's something we all have to reckon with.

Vedo is at the far end of the room, looking as glum as I feel. Probably frustrated he can't complete his mission for Gerval or talk to his crush, and that both failures are one and the same. Meanwhile, here I am carrying the burden of probably being able to do both and still not knowing what to do. We're messes, both of us.

"Ayo." Tams shoves me playfully as we leave class. "Thanks for coming last night."

I shake off my doldrums and find her a smile. "I'm glad I did. It was fun."

"You all right? Don't lie."

"I mean, I'm . . ." What's the point? "I don't know what I am."

"Tell me."

So I do. We stroll down the hallway and out into the yard as I wind through the horrible revelations of the day before—the ledger with its still-uncracked code and its nasty truth that somehow, despite all the claims to the contrary, San Madrigal was tangled up with the empires we've always shunned.

Tams shakes her head as I talk, her mouth grim. We're quiet for a long time after I finish. The orange autumn sun sends shadows of maple leaves dancing across the concrete. The wind whispers sad songs about all the lies we've been told.

"I guess . . ." she finally says, then just scowls. "I guess it's better to know for sure what we've always suspected was true, anyway."

I nod. I'm shocked by her words, for sure. But they also make some sense. Still, it all breaks my heart. And there's so much we don't understand yet. "I just want to . . . blow up everything," I say, gritting my teeth. "I'm so mad."

Tams nods, eyes far away. "What's your plan?"

"Heh." I rub my eyes. Dig the tip of my sneaker into the pavement. "Find the child of Madrigal so we can raise the island ourselves and then shout from the rooftops that everything we know is a damn lie."

"Sounds about right."

Walking over to the club that night, I open my recorder app and hit Play—it's already cued up to where I want it, because I've listened to this clip so many times.

"Not that kind of weird," Gerval's voice says through my headphones. *"Things about our history that no one knows. Well, almost no one . . . A secret history."*

A secret history, huh, Gerval?

The only thing that's clear about him is that nothing he says can be trusted.

———◆———

The big screen looms over the stage at Tolo's club.

It's an impressive setup, I'll say that. Yes, Big Moses Arroyo is the baddest bouncer in town, but quiet as it's kept, he's also a mean IT guy, and a few years ago, he went ahead and modernized the entire wildly outdated, extremely fudgeable Galerano voting system. It's probably for the best that Tolo had him do it all in the wee hours of the morning when no one was paying attention, because I'm sure more than a few powers-that-be achieved their positions by miscounting raised hands or ballots tossed in a hat.

Any member of the Cabildo has to win a majority of not just their own community, but also at least one of the other two. The idea is to keep any one group from voting in someone endemically hostile to another and, hopefully, prevent the intercultural warfare that everyone's so afraid of. So, there are three circles on the huge screen—one for the Santeros, one for the Sefaradim, one for the pirates. And each seat at each table in the great hall comes with a little mechanism that lets you cast your vote. As votes come in, the circles, which are really pie charts, show the shifting balance in real time.

After the first vote, the loser can call for a revote within one week. They usually ask for exactly that much time because they'll need all of it to try to shift the narrative somehow. And if they lose that one, it's over for them. If they win, though, one more challenge can be raised, this time within only twenty-four hours, and that's it: the results of vote three are *final* final. It's rare anyone challenges and even rarer that they win the challenge.

The system is impressive, I'll give it that. But it's also terrifying now that so much rides on this election. And there's so much we still don't know. First and foremost, for me, anyway, is where the hell Chela is. Because she's not here.

The place is mostly empty when Tams and I walk in for preshow setup and sound check. (Of course there has to be music playing on vote night! And, of course, it's us who have to play it!) I'm not saying I expected Chela to just be sitting on a barstool fiddling with her phone, or perched on some pillar preparing to assassinate someone, but . . . Okay, yeah, I did. And when she's not, something sinks in me, because maybe she's gone for good, she's just had it with all of us regulars, and who could blame her? Or maybe she's dead.

"Mateo," Tams says.

"Hmm?"

"Stop frowning like that, man, come on. You're freaking me out."

"Ah. Right."

We set up in our regular spot on the creaky wooden stage, right under the skylight, and the place feels so empty. Even when people start shuffling in and the general hubbub of excitement rises, I barely feel it. I'm playing, my fingers dancing along the keys to our regular shuffle through the Galerano hit parade, boleros and praisesongs and murder ballads, but I barely hear the music.

Chela's not here, and noticeably, neither is Gerval.

Tolo came in a few minutes ago, nodded solemnly at us, made the rounds shaking hands and chatting with folks. Councilwoman Anisette Bisconte did the same, in her stiff, politico-type way that still seems to work on some people. Vedo came in with her and quickly wandered off to sit with a bunch of other teens in a far corner. Even Tía Lucia made it, along with a whole crew of Santeros; and there's Rabbi Hidalgo and his retinue.

But no Gerval. No Chela.

Suddenly, I hate this whole thing. Lives are hanging in the balance, and all anyone wants to talk about is a place hundreds of miles away that's been gone my whole life—a ghost island! *What about what's right here, in front of us?* I want to yell at the whole room, to make them see that *we're* what matters, not some sunken memory. Chela matters.

"Mateo," Tams calls sharply from her kit. "You just gonna keep soloing, or we gonna go to the chorus?"

"Arg," I growl, raising a fist to let her know we're closing out the number.

"What's up?" Tams asks as we simmer to a sudden end.

I take my ancestor's weird old music book out of my bag and set it up on the piano. "Trying something different."

I'd plunked out a few of the melodies on my keyboard at home, but they kept creeping me out and didn't really help. The only thing I noticed was that the *voz* part of each song—the part that someone's supposed to sing but doesn't have any lyrics—is just the same melody line over and over. It's just as chaotic and nonsensical as the rest, but it's the one thing that repeats in the whole book.

"We're playing a song that's a secret code?" Tams asks, and I whirl around.

"What did you just say?"

"I'm guessing it doesn't have the clave, just given what a mess those rhythms are. I can tell from over here."

Clave.

Like a shortsighted, overly focused clown, I had assumed that the word was being used in a musical sense.

But it has another meaning, too, of course. I slap my face, a little too hard. *Clave* means *key code.*

I feel like I'm going to burst. The melody is the *code* we were looking for! How did I miss that? It's literally been right in front of my face this entire time, probably the least hidden thing about the whole situation.

"You okay there, buddy?" Tams asks.

I haven't filled her in on what we discovered in those old books. I don't even know how to explain it to myself, let alone to someone else. But I'll learn how. Whatever the truth turns out to be, we need to face it. That much I know.

"Let's play," I say. That's the only way I'm going to crack this.

We do, and man, this song *sucks.*

People notice immediately. Out of the corner of my eye, I see them looking up, scowling. The music is—this is the only word for it—ugly. Sorry, great-great-great-great-grandpa or whatever. But then again, it clearly wasn't supposed to be pretty, jumping two octaves up for one note and another back down for the next. Ugly.

The notes of a scale have alphabetic names, and even though, yes, most Spanish-speaking composers use the do-re-mis instead, if I were making a secret code with music, I would start with the letters. Archibaldo Medina obviously did—that would explain why it's all just the white keys; there are no sharps or flats, which would complicate things beyond comprehension.

I keep playing, keep cringing. Keep tuning out the looks of disgust and anxiousness around me.

What if it . . . ? What if at the end of the scale, instead of starting over again after G, the alphabet kept going? So the A below middle C would be *H*; the B, *I*; and—I squint through the crunch on my poor overused brain as I play—the note I'm about to play, G, would be an *N.* Then back to the low D, making it *D.* And the B below middle C, so *I*, followed by the low A . . .

NDIA.

I hit a long chord, signaling Tams to slow it down so I can check the note that came before what I worked out. It's that same B, which makes it *I*, which makes it *INDIA*.

Wait. *India* as in *Dutch East India?*

I stand up, slamming the song to a close.

"¿Qué carajo fue eso?" someone demands, and I can't blame them.

"We cracked it," I whisper.

Tams blinks her question at me.

When I look around the room, most people are glowering back irritably, and a few have gotten up from their seats. Mostly pirates. There's Arco "El Gorro" and Simpatico. There's Tantor Batalán. I can see it all over their faces: they heard something they recognized. Worse: they're nodding at me, like I'm in on it somehow. I glance up at the stage and realize Anisette Bisconte is staring sheer murder at me.

In an instant, she wipes off that death glare and the friendly neighborhood politician mask falls into place.

What have I done?

"My fellow children of a lost island!" she calls with a weird little laugh that doesn't fit the occasion at all.

"Uh, go solo a sec," I whisper, and Tams nods, sliding into a corny jazz run on the hi-hat while I pore over my long-dead ancestor's partitur.

"Shalom, mi gente! Alafia!" It sounds so forced coming from Anisette, but we're all used to that. Pandering. I signal Tams to switch to brushes and wonder how this utterly uncharismatic woman got elected to anything in the first place, even with her dead best friend's implied endorsement. "It's a big night, huh?"

DUTCH EAST INDIA COMPANY is exactly what the first song says!

Holy crap.

Around me, people cheer on the councilwoman, others yell to get on with it. Tolo moves into position on the far end of the stage from her. He's wearing funeral blacks, a three-piece suit instead of his usual guayabera, looking like a mean young gangster lord through and through.

Where is Gerval?

Bisconte must be wondering the same thing—she shields her eyes with one hand and squints out into the crowd, frowning. Truth is, she doesn't have it in her to act this well, so Gerval being absent probably isn't part of some elaborate theatrics. At least not any that she's in on. "Well," she says, giving up with an exaggerated shrug, "even without the candidate present, we can still go on with the excitement of the night, right?"

Sure, okay seems to be the general response from the murmuring crowd.

The second song doesn't take much time to untangle now that I have the code: *LA FRUTERA*. The United Fruit Company, which every Galerano kid knows plundered Latin America with its steel grip on the banana trade for most of the twentieth century.

"As always, there will be a five-minute timer on the clock as we vote and make our cases. I'll be speaking on behalf of the Maestro until he shows up, of course, ha!"

It's all right here in front of me. Now all that's left is to connect it to the ledger.

The councilwoman raises her hand, shapes her fingers like a pistol, and screeches, "Let the voting begin!"

CHAPTER TWENTY-FIVE

In another life, another world, Tolo could've been a rapper. He probably knows it, deep down, but either way, he uses that lyrical prowess to devastating effect. It's in the way he chokes up on the mic and struts across the stage like the world is being laid to waste around him, like he's invincible, and the words fly out of his mouth in a furious torrent. He's not thinking; he barely pauses for breath, just unleashes that cannonade of words onto the room, unstoppable.

My brain is still on fire from what I just figured out, but I gotta play. And anyway, I need a moment to process the whole thing.

Tams and I know exactly what to do for this kind of verbal rampage. She breaks into a high-octane thrash beat with early '90s hip-hop inflections, and I switch to a bass-heavy, static-laced setting and chime in with syncopated hits on a crude reggaeton rhythm.

"It's a new future we lookin' at," Tolo asserts heavily, reaching the end of the stage and then turning to face the audience. "I'm not talking about forgetting the past, I'm talking about bringing it with us as we move ahead. But we can't make up easy answers just because we have nostalgia, mi gente." He pauses, lets the beat run past a measure, and then we grind to a halt, too, and Tolo yells, "We gonna raise San Madrigal, y'all!"

Tolo told me earlier he wasn't going to use what we had unless it was rock solid. Said it was too risky; such a huge revelation has to be done right. Otherwise, it could blow up in his face. I know he's right, but now that I have the other piece of the puzzle lined up, all I want to do is shout it from the rafters.

Fortunately, Tolo seems to be killing it without the help of any giant history-changing bombshells.

Cheers erupt all around.

"But we gonna do it right," Tolo insists as we kick back in behind him. "Not because some celebrity sellout insists on it for popularity!"

"Oooh!" people yell at the undeniable burn.

"Not because some washed-up politico used-car-dealer lady said it!"

"Ayyyy!"

The councilwoman, standing behind him, giggles awkwardly, trying to play along.

"And we don't need no hotels to make it work! We don't need no theme parks! Am I right?"

Behind him, the pie charts had been wavering around the fifty-fifty marks. Now Tolo's purple surges, eclipsing Gerval's yellow in all three circles.

"She says the three initiated children of the original saints have been found. So where are they? Or maybe she's too busy looking for the dude she wants to take over!"

Jeers. Love it.

Tolo passes the mic to Councilwoman Bisconte, and I *almost* feel bad for her.

"Well, young Mr. Baracasa and I agree on one thing," she snarks as Tams and I slide into a smooth jazz feel to match her tone. "It's a brand-new day. And it's Gerval who will guide us into that future, because he's ready to take action *now*! He has a plan, unlike Mr. Vague No-Plan Baracasa here! Gerval is ready to make moves *today*! Not in some indeterminate point in the future when half of us will be dead! Right?"

The room seems unsure of what they're supposed to say to that one. *When half of us are dead* isn't really a talking point that people can get excited about, even in a derisive way. A few folks cheer, but most just kind of scrunch up their faces.

There're only two minutes left. The Santeros are still firmly with Tolo, I notice, but both the pirates and Sefaradim are wavering back toward the half-and-half mark. You'd think pirates would be more wary of an established politician, but I guess she's *their* politician, so . . . go figure?

"My good people, we can do this together!" the councilwoman exclaims. "But not with this inexperienced local glad-hander leading us. We need someone with worldwide recognition to bring us into a new era of Madrigal history. And we have that in Maestro Gerval!"

The Sefaradim hover somewhere in between, and with a minute and a half on the clock, they could still swing it into a draw. But then Rabbi Hidalgo rises and calls for the wireless mic. Gone is the genial giant who invited me over for dinner the other day. This is the Rabbi Hidalgo who's a grave pillar of his community, a warrior, his face stern and drawn.

Accordingly, Tams and I pull back to a sparse vamp.

"As many of you know," the rabbi says, sounding more like he's speaking at a funeral than an election, "my nephew and I haven't spoken in years. Tolo Baracasa chose a lifestyle I neither agree with nor condone."

Onstage, Councilwoman Bisconte grins. Tolo stands perfectly still, eyes glued to his uncle.

"However," Rabbi Hidalgo goes on sullenly, "criminal or not, I believe my nephew is a good man, an honorable one. And I do not trust Maestro Gerval, who has already brought much unwanted attention to our streets, and who did not even have the respect to show up for his own vote."

Boom! Scattered yelling and arguments erupt, and the line dividing the Sefaradi circle trembles once, then swings hard for Tolo.

"Furthermore!" the rabbi yells over the rabble. "With all due respect to the councilwoman, I call on the pirates to embrace their roots and recognize their true leader, one from a lineage of pirates *and* Sefaradim, one who has done the hard work of building trust in our community his whole life!"

That seals it. As Tams and I ramp up the music's tempo to match the clock ticking away its final seconds, Tolo's votes slide just over the fifty percent line on the pirate circle, and cheers explode all around us.

It's done.

My phone vibrates with a text.

"Wait!" Councilwoman Bisconte hollers into the mic. "I call for a twenty-minute recess and then an immediate revote!"

They almost never call for immediate revotes because if someone wins twice in a row, that seals it. Usually, a revote only comes after the losing side has taken their week to change the story.

But my work is done, so I pull out my phone.

It's from Safiya: *Tolo's office. Now.*

"Bring Maza," I tell Tams, showing her the message. "Meet you there." And then, before Anisette or anyone else can reach me, I pack up the music book and make myself scarce.

———◆———

"And that's the long and short of it," I say about ten minutes later. Across the room from me, Tolo, Safiya, Tams, and Maza all stare with their mouths open.

For a moment, I'm not sure if I messed it up somehow and

they're looking at me like I'm a complete fool. I'm already rework-
ing the whole thing in my head when the silence shatters and they
leap into action.

"Whoa," Maza says. "I'm extremely geeky, and I'm blown away
by your levels of geek."

"Yeah, that was brilliant," Tolo says, launching toward the
makeshift chart I've set up with the code on it. "So the only thing
we're missing is what these letters mean, right?"

Everyone gathers around, and we just stare for about ten seconds
before Maza yelps, "Colors!" and we all step back in awe.

They're right.

Each song spells out the name of a company or government
organization that was a trading partner; each song is also a different
color. "The colors are what's matched in the ledger," Maza explains.
"*R* is *rojo*, *V* is *verde*, *A* is *azul*, *AM* is *amarillo*, yellow."

"Right!" I yell.

"Maza, aren't you always building apps and stuff?" Tolo says,
standing and moving toward me like a tank. "Can you put all this
in some graphic form that's understandable to a mere mort—"

"On it," they report, already opening a laptop.

"Safiya and Tams, run the code on the rest of the songs, and
let's see what we got."

He stands beside me and crosses his arms, face stern. "That's
great work, Mateo. Only thing I don't understand is this top line."
He points to the staff labeled *voz* that has the same weird melody
for every song.

I shake my head. "Me neither. It just says one word over and
over. A name, maybe? *V-I-Z-V-A-R-G-A-L.* I was hoping you'd have
heard of it."

"Doesn't ring a bell, no. I think I'd remember that. Safiya?"

My phone buzzes with another text.

"Not one I've ever come across," Safiya says.

It's Gerval: *Outside. Where are you?*

Tolo sighs, pulling a book down from his shelf. "Well, we can keep looking for that part. The rest is enough to get us what we need."

"Good," I say. "I'll be back."

———◆———

"Where is she?"

Maestro Grilo Juan Gerval cuts an impressive image in the lights of the alley. He's all dressed up in a shiny crimson outfit, top buttons undone just so, sleeves wide and droopy. It'd look utterly ridiculous on anyone else, but somehow he makes it work. Shimmering rings adorn his fingers, and a gold chain hangs around his neck with an antique pendant of some kind dangling off the end.

"I wouldn't know," I say, standing in the doorway, arms crossed over my chest. "Just here to say I'm not bringing her to you."

He shakes his head, eyes still on the ground, a wry smile on his face. Raises his eyebrows in mock admiration. "Oh, wow." Finally, he looks at me. "And why is that, Healer? Hmm?"

"Because I—" The words stop short because I don't know how to explain it. My fists are clenched at my sides suddenly, my whole body wound tight. I feel like all the tension that's built up from the past couple of days is rolling through me in one thick, rising wave. It's the secret history, that ledger, the terrible songs . . . the bambarúto tearing through the crowd, attacking Chela. Whatever's going on with Tía Lucia that she won't tell me about. It's everything. "You know, don't you? About all of it."

He's still smiling, which I really don't like. "So it was you who took the books. I thought Chela, maybe." He tilts his head, appraising me. "Or was it *both* of you? That'd be something."

"You haven't answered my question."

"Yes, Mateo, I know about it all. And no, I don't like it, either.

But I also know what it means. Sure, a lot of the things we thought were true are a lie, but that lie has sustained us, and it's hiding a truth that has sustained us, too."

"*Sustained us?*" I spit.

"You don't have to like it—I already said I don't—but that doesn't make it untrue. Crunch the numbers when you have a chance. It wasn't just pocket change that came out of all that trade. It's our economy, Mateo. It's how you and I even exist. Do you understand that? San Madrigal is just like every other country, and that's sad. But it's what we have to deal with."

"Right," I say. "We have to deal with it. Out in the open. We can't hide it like Anisette has been doing. We have to—" I stop, because he's just staring at me blankly, and I realize what a fool I've been for even hoping he wasn't like her. *That lie has sustained us.* "You're going to go along with it, aren't you? Hiding the whole history."

"Do you have any idea what will happen if that history gets out, Mateo? It will destroy us. That's not a guess; it's not what I think will happen; it's a fact. That truth will destroy us. We are already hanging on by barely a thread. In another generation, we might not really exist at all, just get swallowed up by the great generic masses of the United States. If this gets out, if *you* let this out, all you'll do is accelerate that. I give us a year, tops, as a people."

"But—"

"But if we raise the island . . ." His eyes are alight with everything he seems so sure of now, and he takes a step toward me, not threatening but excited. "If we raise that island, Mateo—and we will, we definitely will—and open it to the world, tell them exactly who we are, *then* we will have a national identity for real. One that *everyone* will see, recognize, and respect. Not hidden in the shadows, not a lost island of lost people—a found one! A miracle! Seen and acknowledged, we will be unkillable, invincible. *That's* what I want for us. That's what I would do anything for."

I just stare at him. I don't have a response, not one made out of words, anyway.

"I'm asking you to join me," Gerval says. "Will you?" Words I'd longed to hear for so long. Words I'd anchored all my hopes for my own future to.

Words that sound like pure garbage to me now. I narrow my eyes at him. "Not on your life, you pathetic clown."

He laughs, looking off into the distance, and I wonder if this is going to come to blows. My fists tighten, ready. Instead, Gerval sighs and says, "I guess that's the difference between you and me, Mateo. I'd do anything to save San Madrigal. And you're willing to throw it all away for a truth no one wants to know, anyway."

"Nothing based on a lie is worth fighting for," I say. "At least not without undoing the lie first." Pretty sure I read that in a book somewhere. But it doesn't matter—it's true.

"You know what? Okay!" Gerval moves toward me so fast I don't have time to dodge. He wraps a long arm around my shoulders and, propelling both of us on the sheer momentum of his frantic stride, fastwalks us back into the building and down the backstage corridor toward the event hall.

"Wait!" I yell. "Listen!"

Everything's happening so fast, I can barely keep up with his steps or his logic, but I can't slow down, either. "*You* listen!" he snaps. "You don't get to control what happens. It's not for you to decide."

He kicks open the stage door and bursts through it, still with his arm around my shoulder, then pushes us onto the stage.

The whole event hall, all of Little Madrigal, falls into a stunned silence.

"Ah, hello, mi gente!" Gerval yells into the emptiness, squeezing me tightly to him. "I was just chatting with my friend Mateo here, and he's told me so many interesting things!"

Suddenly, *the lie kills the liar* feels like much more than some old-time Santero saying—it feels like a prayer. I imagine his words becoming solid things, gridlocking against each other in his mouth and toppling down his throat; then, that lying airway clogged with them, he collapses with a whimper and a bleat.

But that's not what happens. Instead, Gerval croons triumphantly, "Shall we get this second round of voting underway?"

One face stands out in the crowd, bright eyes staring deep daggers into my own. Chela Hidalgo's.

CHAPTER TWENTY-SIX

I'M SHAKING MY HEAD NO, STARING AT CHELA'S DISBELIEVING EYES. I'm even yelling "No!" with everything in me, but nothing can be heard over Gerval's booming voice. He's grabbed one of the mics—the only one nearby, since Tolo and Anisette are down working the crowd—and he's practically yelling into it, x-ing out any protest I try to make.

"It's fitting that the once-divided Hidalgo-Baracasa clan has seen fit to close ranks yet again," Gerval booms to a rapt audience. "Because they're trying to protect someone dear to them. Family. And I understand that." He laughs sadly, shakes his head at the tragedy of it. "We can all understand that. But what we can't understand, because it wasn't shared with us, is the terrible secret that the family harbors—the secret that *girl* harbors!"

He points a finger directly at Chela, who now turns her murder-gaze onto him.

"No!" I yell. "Stop!"

But no one cares. Everyone's lost in Gerval's hypnotic bochinche.

"I know this will be hard to understand, what I'm about to say.

It'll sound like myth and fairy tale. But who are we if not a people made from myth? After all, we're gathered here tonight to decide who will guide us into a new era in which we will raise our lost island from beneath the waves. We worship rare gods made of stones and water; we hold sacred the words of our hidden texts and believe the secrets of the shells to be divine messages. We don't just under-stand myth—we *live* it! It's built into us. It's in our blood!"

It's a good speech, I'll give him that, and it only makes me hate him more.

"So you'll understand, mi gente, my good people," Gerval con-tinues, "that I'm not being facetious or fantastical when I tell you that the being who roams among us disguised as a regular mortal girl is not simply the daughter of a goddess, not an initiate to our precious santo, no . . ."

A murmur of fear and anger rises all around.

"The child is an actual creature of the darkness—Okanla, the Destroyer, incarnate!"

Everyone gasps, and Chela stands. She's wearing a stunning low-cut black gown with purple lace netting that extends over her shoulders and up her neck. I've never seen her so dressed up before. At her bat mitzvah, she'd worn some unremarkable frock-type thing. This is something else entirely.

"How?" people demand. "What does it mean?"

Something flickers through the darkness above us—a beam from the projector—and I whirl around to see grainy video moving in slo-mo across the screen. Surveillance footage. It shows the alley Gerval and I were just standing in, but in the video it's Trucks, fac-ing the street.

I turn back around, because I know what's about to happen, and hundreds of wide eyes reflect the flickering images back at me.

They've been planning this all along.

I don't know how, and I'm not totally sure who, even—Anisette

Bisconte, surely, and Gerval, among others—but whoever it was, this has been in the works for a long time now. And they've been trying to use me throughout, one way or another.

And now, if nothing else, they've created the impression that I've sided with them and passed along information.

"You see?" Gerval says, shaking his head. "My man Trucks, murdered in cold blood. No normal girl would do this. No child of God. This is a demon that walks among us."

A kind of rage I've never known before unfurls inside me.

"Isn't that right?" Gerval has them now; the whole of Little Madrigal sits in the palm of his hand, ready to hear whatever comes next. And Chela stands like a statue in the middle of it all, her glare fixed on him.

The footage cuts off, and the three voting charts return. Already the numbers have started tilting back toward Gerval.

"Yes," Chela says calmly into the silence of the room. "It's all true."

"Chela, no!" Tolo yells, shoving his way through the stunned crowd toward her. "What are you doing?"

"Stop!" she commands him. "What Gerval says is true. I haven't always known it, not really—" She shakes her head, the moment suddenly intimate, and she looks like just a regular teenager, like me. "But maybe deep down, I did. I dunno. I wasn't hiding it, though. No one else was, either. And whatever I am or am not, it has nothing to do with Tolo joining the Cabildo or raising the island."

"Oh, but it does," Gerval snarls, a prosecutor coming to the crux of his closing argument. And then, slowly, as if it breaks his heart: "Oh, but it does."

"What are you talking about, man?" someone yells.

"Okanla the Destroyer wasn't satisfied moving about in our midst disguised as a mere child—deceiving us. No. Okanla also went ahead and destroyed our island, all those years ago. On the day of her initiation the spirit became flesh, and the Destroyer was reborn. Chela is the reason we have no home! The cause of our infinite exile!"

"No!" Chela yells, but her protest is swallowed immediately by what seems like the whole room, the whole world, screaming at once.

Gerval's voice carries over all of it. "With one thing the world begins; with one thing the world ends. With that same thing, we will bring back the world we lost. And there it is—Okanla!"

Except Chela's already gone, vanished into the crowd somewhere. Tolo and Rabbi Hidalgo tear frantically after her.

"With the destruction of that one thing, our world will be reborn!" Gerval yells. "The girl is not a girl—she's a demon. And the demon must die!"

On the screen above us, hardly anyone pays attention as the voting clock ticks away its last few seconds once again. The election has gone almost entirely to Gerval in all three circles.

I can't pretend I understand the larger play at hand, or who is lying to whom. But I know I hate Gerval with everything in me. And demon or not, I'll take Chela's side over his.

I just hope it's not too late.

Tams meets my eyes from in front of the stage. Her nod is all I need to know everything is set. Over by the tech stand, Maza gets in position.

Gerval is distracted, grinning out at the chaos he's sown and reveling in his victory, so he doesn't notice me walk slowly up behind him, doesn't see it coming when I snatch the mic out of his loose grip, doesn't have time to stop me as I take a few long steps away and yell into it as loud as I can, "I call for a revote! Right now!"

CHAPTER TWENTY-SEVEN

ALL THOSE EYES.

My entire community glares back at me, and the words that had been burning to explode out of me seem to just crinkle up and turn to dust in my mouth.

This is just like the night of the fete, except now I'm onstage.

But also, it's just been a few days since then, and already my whole world is completely different. The world I knew then seems as far away as my globe-trotting parents. Another lifetime. Everything I thought I knew has been shattered. Something infinitely better and infinitely worse showed up to fill the vacancy.

And now I have called their attention to me. I chose this, despite how much I hate it. And I do hate it, the way their eyes seem to mark me, stain my skin. The way my knees tremble and all I can think about are the many ways this will go wrong.

But there's one thing, and only one thing, I hate even more than this, and that's Chela's face when she thought I'd betrayed her.

"What is this, Mateo?" Councilwoman Bisconte demands. "We

have voted! Twice already! The people have spoken. They reject the Destroyer and her dangerous family! A third vote is unprecedented."

The Destroyer. I wonder, for a moment, whether or not what Gerval said is true. Chela said it was. I'm not even sure what that means, and suddenly, I just don't care. So what if she's Okanla incarnate? It's still better than the secrets San Madrigal has been hiding all along. Okanla didn't enslave people or prop up empires for blood money.

"Look," I say, the words finally starting to come to me on the strength of all this wrath. "Listen, I—"

"Who is this kid?" a voice says, railroading right over mine. Gerval. "I'll tell you. This is the kid who decided he was better off spending his childhood traveling the world with his fancy doctor parents than being here with us!"

Each word feels like a punch in the face. I don't think the audience expected any of it, either. Everyone just sort of gapes at us for what feels like forever.

"He's not one of us," Gerval says, bringing it home. "He just learned our songs. A tourist."

Another silence. I can't make out individuals through the glare of the stage lights in my face. All I see are wide eyes and open mouths. Hundreds of them.

They hate me. I am 100 percent positive that everything Gerval just said is only giving voice to what they've all been thinking this whole time.

Tourist. That's all I am. A tourist in my own neighborhood. A man at home nowhere.

I can almost hear their accusations, feel their visions of me slide beneath my skin and become even more true as they shape me, hurl me farther and farther away from this place, from myself.

Panic rises. My whole body screams at me to run, just turn around and run.

I glance at the muttering crowd, avoiding their angry faces, trying to decide if it makes sense to try to barge through them or take the back way. Then I catch Tía Lucia's stare.

She's sitting right up front, her eyes boring into mine. *Escucha,* she mouths, like an incantation, and like an incantation, it works. All those shrieking voices inside me suddenly go quiet.

Go deeper.

I'm trying, Tía. My body still demands that I run, but I hold my ground. Close my eyes. And finally, finally, I listen.

"He played at my sister's funeral," someone says. Bertol Alahambra, I think. "He's a good kid."

"He killed it at my bar mitzvah," someone else yells. "That boy has magic hands."

"And he was just little when his parents took him traveling! That's not fair!"

Fear is a lie, Tía had said. Because it's not the whole truth.

"Beside the point," Gerval insists, but the crowd is already talking among themselves. They're talking about *me.*

"That's even more impressive, if you ask me—the kid was gone all that time and still made the effort to learn the music so he could play for us."

"Where were *you* all that time, Gerval?"

"He was jet-setting!"

"On the YouTube!"

"Hanging out with Christina Aguilera!"

"Don't drag that nice lady into this, Paka!"

"Mateo healed me the other night! ¡Hijo de Galanika!"

"Mateo is one of us!"

They see me. People I barely know and barely know me, *see* me. I'm not just a ghost. I'm not a pretender. I've been so deep in my head for so long, and all I could do was tell myself horror stories about what other people must be thinking. Lies, really.

"Lies," I say into the mic.

"Huh?" someone calls.

"This man has been *lying* to you, to all of us. Just like Anisette here."

Some people sound concerned; others mutter their disbelief. I sound like some kid making baseless accusations to save face. Easy to dismiss.

"Every pirate member of the Cabildo has been handpicked by their predecessor," I say, now coming across at least a little smart. "Going all the way back to the peace accords of 1810."

"That's not true!" someone yells. "They were voted in! Come on, kid!"

"Well, we all know the support of the sitting member basically guarantees a win," someone else points out.

Other voices rise. "Let the kid talk!"

"Why should we?"

"Shut up, everybody, damn!"

Nothing to do but let it all out. "A secret group of pirates has been collaborating with various slave traders and agents of empires all along!" I say, finally spitting out the most inflammatory part. And as I say it, the truth of it seems to wash over me. It feels like a nasty mold has been festering in me, in all of us, for so, so long. I hate it, but there's no denying how the pieces fit together. "With the very forces San Madrigal swore to defend itself from! They've been trading with and supporting slavers . . . and aiding inquisitors and conquistadors!"

Oop—people are pissed. Whether they fully believe what I'm saying or not, the very notion is a spark that ignites a flame inside them. There are yells from people horrified I would dare to make the accusation; a few can't believe this is even possible.

"I'm going to show you evidence to support what I'm saying," I assure them, praying to any god that will listen that it's true, and

Maza has had a chance to put it all together. "But first let me say this: if you think about it, we all know there's been something going on that doesn't add up. Tams and I talk about it all the time. How did we inherit the worst parts of colonialism when we were supposed to be hidden from all that for generations? We were an outlaw island, right? ¡Nunca conquistada! Why, then, do we follow their rules and patterns? I know we've all asked ourselves these questions!"

Arguments break out across the room, and for a moment, I think it's going to spill over into another brawl. I signal Maza.

"We deserve an answer!" I yell over the din. "And now we have one, because it's all spelled out in a secret ledger book that Councilwoman Bisconte—"

"Lies!" Anisette screams, making her way across the stage. "He's lying!"

And just like that, something finally goes right tonight: Maza's infographics appear on the voting screen, complete with big-fonted notes and arrows explaining the whole terrible history of secret empire trade networks on San Madrigal. I'm impressed. It's way clearer here than I'd have ever been able to explain it.

People start gathering closer; they eye the screen curiously, mutter to one another.

"These ledgers look legit," someone says. "That date there refers to the Third Maritime Convocation of Madrigal!"

Of course, everyone's a historian!

"It's true!" another voice insists. "And those shipping routes are clearly part of the slave trade!"

"Wait, wait, wait," Anisette pleads into the mic. "Just hold on, everyone! Mateo, where did you even get that stuff?"

She says it like she's talking to a little kid who stole some cookies. I'm about to answer and bring Gerval down with her when the maestro himself jumps onto the stage and takes her mic. "That's what I would like to know, too!" he booms, glaring at Anisette. "What is the meaning of this, Councilwoman? Have you been lying to us all along?"

For a couple of seconds, no one's sure what to say.

I get it. The audacity of that dishonesty really does the job of startling people into silence. I'm done being silent, though. "Don't let Gerval fool you with those lies!" I say, stepping up to the edge of the stage. "This book came from his bedroom! Where he was reading it to prepare for—"

"My bedroom?" Gerval gawks, in mock horror. "What were you doing in my bedroom, Mateo?" The mixed implication is just confusing enough to distract everyone into more chaos. I'm not even sure how to answer that, which is exactly the point.

Gerval doesn't waste time taking advantage of the mess he made. "I swear to you, brothers and sisters of Madrigal, I have no idea what this is about, but my first act as a member of the Cabildo will be to root out whatever this cancer is and destroy it! Don't believe Mateo and his demon friend! I know nothing of this! It's the first I'm hearing it! But you owe us answers, Councilwoman!"

There it is.

Gerval turns to me, lowers the mic, and mutters, with the slightest grin, "Told you not to trust anyone."

"Oh, I didn't," I say, also off-mic. Then I lift it and say, very slowly and deliberately so everyone quiets down, "Hey, Tams." I take out my phone and hand it down to her. "Can you plug this into the speaker system, then go to the recording app and play the track that's cued up?"

"Sure!" Tams says cheerfully.

"What?" Gerval demands. "What is this nonsense? Come on! This *tourist* is trying to—"

One lie, I think as the maestro's voice booms out over the speaker system. *"I've learned a lot about San Madrigal these past couple days. It's opened my eyes, the things I've discovered. Really . . . weird stuff."*

"This was a conversation the maestro and I had two days ago," I tell the crowd. "After we played that concert in the park." *One lie will bring the whole house of lies crashing down.*

"*I mean, our whole history is weird . . .*" my voice says back. Behind us, the ambient sounds of the park churn and simmer on the recording.

"*No,*" the Gerval of a couple days ago says, just as the flesh-and-blood Gerval yells, "Stop this!"

But there's no stopping it. "*Not that kind of weird. Things about our history that no one knows.*"

"Turn that off!" Gerval hollers.

"Shut up!" someone counters. "We're trying to listen."

"*Well, almost no one. There's so much more to it than they ever told us—a secret history—and . . . I'm just now seeing it all. And not just our history—our present tense, too. This. Right here and now. It's . . .*" He trails off.

"*Who's been telling you this stuff?*" I ask on the recording. "*Anisette?*"

"*Yeah, her, others. Been reading up on it, too.*"

Tams stops the recording, because now people are yelling so much no one can hear it, anyway. "Liar!" they shout. "¡Mentiroso!" "Uydurmasion!"

One yells, "¡Que sea espíritu, coño!" and I'm pretty sure this time the emphasis is on the spirits being dead. Told ya we love multiple meanings!

"So you see," I say over the clamor, "Gerval does indeed know what this is about. He's known it for days because he's in league with the councilwoman, and most important, he just lied to all of you! Right to your faces! Just like he's been lying to me! *About* me! You can't believe a word this lying-ass liar says!"

Gerval takes a step back, speechless for once. Probably trying to think of a new lie to clean this up.

I don't give him the chance. "And they're still at it!" I yell, hazarding a wild guess and praying I'm right. "Bringing outsiders into our community against our wishes! Ask them! Ask them who brought the cops into Little Madrigal on the night of the fete!"

"We had nothing to do with that!" the councilwoman hollers in such a strained voice it's clear to everyone she's full of it.

Got her.

Time to bring it home. "So maybe a goddess does walk among us," I say, choking up on the mic and taking long strides across the stage like Tolo did. "Maybe she is the Destroyer! But we Galeranos know better than anyone that we have to destroy in order to create, right? That the seed of creation lies within everything that breaks!" That was fire. Maybe I *can* do this public-speaking thing. "And even if Chela is the Destroyer, she's *our* Destroyer!"

People are actually cheering now, which I only barely register because I've gotten myself so keyed up. Tams kicks up a smooth march on the kit as more people gather round. "And as for whether or not she's responsible for the sinking of San Madrigal, well, you can take the word of a goddess, or you can take the word of a lying, sell-out politician and her fake rock star fanboy!"

Bam *bam*!

"Vote!" people are yelling, because the screen has flicked back to the three circles, all dancing wildly between purple and yellow, and time is running out. "VOTE!"

"How do you think you pathetic ingrates managed to stay afloat for all those years if not for us?" Councilwoman Bisconte yells into the mic she's finally gotten ahold of. I guess the last desperate play of the powerful is to flail at honesty. "We did what we had to do to keep us all alive! You think your little trade goods and folk songs did that? Your farmers markets and bembés? No, dammit! *We* did that! We kept you alive!"

"It's all been a lie!" someone cries. "Our whole history!"

"How dare you!"

"What gives you the right?"

"And what about the cops the other day? They beat up my grandpa!"

"That girl *murdered* Trucks!" Bisconte insists as the clock plummets to single digits behind her and all the circles swing purple. "Our beloved community member!"

"Who even was that dude?"

"I didn't know him."

"He never showed his face!"

Something stirs at the far edges of the room. A glint of light off a plastic face shield.

I see Gerval stare in that direction and nod ever so slightly.

The timer buzzes out the end of voting and a wild cheer goes up, but it's immediately interrupted by a scream. The first towering bambarúto enters the crowd swinging, carves a gruesome path of broken bones and bleeding flesh as it storms through toward the stage.

Tía Lucia is out there somewhere. And Tams. Maza.

"We're under attack!" the councilwoman yells. More screams rise up. More bambarúto emerge from the shadows. They're part of all this, woven into the fabric of that ledger book, those music notes. Our history. There are so many more of them than I thought possible. Eight, nine, ten . . . a dozen now.

Then, with words that have clearly been rehearsed time and time again in front of a mirror, Anisette declares, "In the absence of a new leader, I invoke the emergency combat powers of leadership and appoint Maestro Juan Grilo Gerval as my successor to the Cabildo, and ruler of Madrigal!"

I was wrong. So, so wrong. The last desperate play of the powerful isn't honesty, I realize, as the sounds of a dozen blood-soaked tragedies shatter the air around me.

It's just more lies.

PART
FOUR

IV.

The same way it moves you, it paralyzes you.

Change is water, seeps through the strongest frontiers.

The ocean can never be stopped.

The Holy Spirit swells and devours.

The Destroyer nods her weary head, and with a single word, ushers in
total annihilation.

With a single word, births a new world.

Madrigal.

Daybreak.

—*The Book of Beginnings and Endings*, author unknown

IV.

Así como te mueve, te paraliza.

El cambio es agua, entra aún las fronteras más fuertes.

El mar no se puede detener nunca.

El espíritu santo hincha y devora.

La Santa de Destrucción cabecea su cabeza cansada, y con una sola palabra deja entrar la aniquilación total.

Con una sola palabra, da la luz a un mundo nuevo.

Madrigal.

Amanecer.

—*El Libro de Comienzos y Finales*, autor desconocido

CHAPTER TWENTY-EIGHT

ONE WEEK HAS PASSED.

Overnight, everything changed. And then nothing changed at all. Nothing but the season, anyway. Before, it was hoodie weather. Then, sometime in the past couple of days, November showed up, and with it came puffy-jacket-over-hoodie-over-sweater weather, cruel winds whipping along streets glistening with ice.

After all those bambarúto charged in on vote night, everyone scattered into the streets, and instead of gathering like they had at other times, instead of fighting back, people just kept going, each to their own home, and there they stayed, and there, for the most part, they've been ever since. I guess without Tolo around leading the charge, the fight just seeped out of us—no one knew where he or Chela or Rabbi Hidalgo went, we just knew they weren't there.

The fear was infectious. It lanced through us, sizzled, and broke us, a static that became a shock wave. I felt it in my gut, and every wide eye and open mouth around me, my friends and neighbors just amplified it more. I found Tía Lucia and wrapped myself around her, and we made fast tracks for our place, imagining those towering demons bursting out of every shadow. Tams texted that she and Maza had made it out okay and were holing up at the Bushwick ocha house where the bembé had been held.

And that was that.

The next day, the world went on as usual, but nothing was the same: the streets remained dead. The Gerval-and-Bisconte coup did what we never thought could be done—it silenced the unflinching bochinche machine of Little Madrigal. Some stores opened, but no one lingered outside them to argue and carry on; no one posted up on park benches debating what had happened; no voices rang out from the nail salons or peluquerías.

Worst of all, the music went silent. Conjuntos stopped playing in restaurants and bars, spontaneous street fairs and rooftop rumbas ceased entirely, just like that.

No, it wasn't the cold weather. Please. We Galeranos found ourselves in this ridiculous and sometimes frigid new world and quickly decided folks would have to bundle up to keep the party going, so bundle up we did. One of my first memories is clinging to my dad's shoulders while he and my mom, both looking like big marshmallow people in their winter jackets, swung each other through the wild passes of a sultry mambo as snow fell all around a cheering crowd.

Cold can't stop festivities, no, but fear certainly can.

Fear became uncertainty became paralysis. And beneath it all, the fear stuck around, mocking us in our stillness.

A silence so deep you can taste it moves through these Brooklyn streets now; it feels something like death.

Meanwhile, Chela is somehow everywhere and nowhere at the same time. She went to ground that night and hasn't shown her face yet. And who can blame her? My impassioned defense only moved the needle just over the line for Tolo on the pirate side, and I'm sure Gerval and them are hunting her.

So she's gone ghost, but for me, she's all I see.

She's turning a corner as I walk down these skeleton streets, lighting up at the sight of me, telling me all the things that have happened since she got gone. Or, more often than not, she'll go for her blade, face wide with surprise and then darkening, just like it did the night of the vote when she saw me walk in with Gerval.

My fantasies dissolve as I strut past the corner she didn't turn, exhaling my disappointment in misty puffs and shaking my head at myself. And then I imagine her coming around the next corner, and the next.

At school, she's every brown-skinned girl with poufy hair and her back turned, and then she's not, and everything in me sinks again, even though I know, I know, she's gone for good, and probably hates me, and has every right to.

And anyway, she's a goddess or whatever. Is it possible to fall for a holy saint of destruction and chaos? Is that what I've gone and done?

I've known Chela Hidalgo my whole life, and I barely know her at all. I feel like I know things about her no one else does, that she let me in in ways she'd never let in anyone else.

And I ruined it all.

"Mateo?" Tía Lucia calls from the kitchen. "¿Ya terminaste con Elegguá?"

It's the anniversary of her initiation as a priest of Shango, the warrior king orisha of thunder, and she's put me to work. Well, she's tried to, anyway. I'm supposed to wash the little stone head Elegguá at the door—palm oil and dog hair don't mix, FYI—but instead I'm just sitting here on the floor, staring at nothing, thinking about everything.

"Ah . . . not yet."

Ever since the vote, she's no longer baking all night, but it's clear she's still going through whatever it was Johnny Afrá's Elegguá hinted at, and she still hasn't told me word one about it.

And I'm fed up, to be honest. With all of it.

"Bueno. When you finish . . . Wait." She's come into the room, and now she's staring at me with her hands on her hips and abject disappointment on her face. "Pero you haven't even started."

I look down at Elegguá, still shiny with palm oil and grimy with Farts fur, then back up at her. "I—"

She cuts me off with a shake of her head, grabs her wallet off the table. "No importa. The bodega's open, right? I need sugar and five mangos. Oh, and—"

"Tell me," I say. The words just burp out of me without permission.

She almost asks me what I'm talking about—I see the ghost of that dodge fade on her lips. Instead, she looks away.

"You have to," I say.

"No tengo que hacer nada." It comes out quietly, though, barely a whisper. And she's right, she doesn't have to do a damn thing. But she should tell me, and she knows it. I've asked many times since the bembé, but something in both of us has frayed down to the bare bone in this past week of excruciating silence and snow, and there's no more fight left. The silence of the streets has seeped into our apartment and taken over, choking us all into submission as we slept.

"Siéntate," she orders, nodding at the empty chair.

I notice Aunt Miriam hovering in the doorway of their bedroom, face sad but otherwise impossible to read.

Tía Lucia pulls a cigar out of her pack and lights it. "You know how we make fun of people who come for a reading and are worried it will say they're going to die?"

"Uh, kinda," I say, already not liking where this is going. "Go on."

"Right. ¿Por qué? Porque así no funciona. Divination doesn't work that way, m'ijo. Not really. These shells"—she pats the little sack she keeps the sacred cowrie shells in—"they tell you about the energies you walk with. Which santos stand up for you, work with you. What's happening in your spirit. Sure"—insert Galerano shrug—"sometimes that energy is death, hmm? But usually it means metaphorically speaking, eh? Como, algo que tiene que terminar. You have to dump your good-for-nothing, cheating-ass husband, or you're going to get fired from your job—but your job is terrible, anyway, so maybe you're better off. ¿Entiendes?"

"I guess." I hate this. I hate all of it. The air in the room seems to thin with every word she speaks; I take it in little gasps—soon, I will suffocate.

"And anyway, you don't really ask that kind of question—is a person going to die? It's just weird."

"But?"

She takes a drag of her cigar, rolls her eyes. "I did."

"What?"

I don't have to ask what her reading said. Already Aunt Miriam has swept over and wrapped her eerie phosphorescence around Tía Lucia, who has put her head in her hands and let out the longest, saddest sigh of all time.

"I . . ." Whatever words were gonna come out, they just fade. What do you even say? "But . . ." I try again. "Can't we . . . ? Stop!" Suddenly, I'm standing, pulse racing. Tía Lucia looks up, confused. "Stop! Stop smoking! Just . . . We can . . ."

Her wide-open face squints into a creased smile, then she breaks out laughing. "Ay, m'ijo . . ."

"Why are you laughing?" I demand, reaching for her cigar.

She swats me away. "¡Cálmate! It's not that simple, coño. Let me live what's left of my life with what pleasures I can get!"

"I . . . No," I say, shaking my head, slumping back into the chair. "When did you find out?"

"The night of the—"

"Grande Fete," I finish for her. "That's what it said in the reading. That's why you didn't come. And why you've been staying up all hours baking."

"Mmm." She nods. "It's not easy to look death in the face, Mateo. But—and I mean this—I have made peace with it. I accept it. The bembé helped. I can't explain why; it's just true. Everything felt different after that night. Pero, Mateo"—she fixes me with a sharp look—"what Baba Johnny said holds."

I had almost forgotten. And now I wish I could.

"When it happens, you won't be able to stop it. I know you can heal. Pero esto . . ." Her voice trails off, gaze distant. "This won't be something you can heal. You must stay focused."

"What am I . . . ?" I'm crying, dammit. The sobs come out in hiccups as I try to talk around them, and tears trickle down my face. "What am I supposed to do, just watch?"

"You're supposed to live your life. The best life you can live. And if my death is the fault of anyone in particular . . ." Her eyes narrow to slits, and she's actually smiling. "Destroy them and everything they love."

"I . . . I . . ." Nothing makes sense.

"Escucha. I know it's not easy to take in, believe me. So do what you have to do to deal with it, pero don't hover, por favor. I have enough of that with this one." She nods toward the bedroom, where the quiet, urgent burble of Aunt Miriam's old radio has been going nonstop all week. "No pun intended, pero it can be a lot with her. And I get it, I do. I just don't want to spend whatever time I have left in mourning for myself."

Mateo, Lucia, Aunt Miriam calls nervously. *Something's going on.*

Tía Lucia rolls her eyes. "Ay, Miriam, something is always going on! If you keep listening to that broadcast, they will keep finding things to get you riled up about, hmm!"

That broadcast is the Pirate Radio Hour, a show they livestream from Tolo's club. It used to be an actual illegal airwave they broadcasted over. (Get it? Pirate radio? Har-har.) But, you know, times change. Ever since the disaster on vote night, it has turned into the Pirate Radio Damn Near Twenty-Four Hours, and I have to admit, it's kind of comforting. They must've snuck equipment into different houses around the neighborhood, because just about any time, day or night, someone is on there, chatting about recipes, or historical tidbits, or streaming music. It does wonders for keeping us feeling like a community in the absence of big gatherings and concerts.

But now it's Safiya the Butcher's voice coming out of the tinny speakers on Tía Lucia's laptop, and she sounds tense. ". . . revealing Tolo's exact condition at this time, but please, if anyone knows a doctor or someone with medical knowledge, we need your help."

That's me. Well, I am neither, but I'm the Healer. That's what I do. The urge to run out the door and straight to the club is almost overwhelming—it's like a physical presence in my body. I can do something, and after all this time doing nothing, after the devastating truth that Tía Lucia just revealed . . . all I want is to do *something*. Even if it's not for the person I'm most worried about. As far as I know, neither the Baracasas nor Hidalgos want anything to do with me. Chela didn't return any of my texts, and eventually I just gave up. I didn't even try reaching out to Tolo or his crew, because what would be the point? They saw what they saw, and it looked how it looked. I still cringe in the depths of my soul when I think about it. Whether or not they heard about what happened after is anyone's guess. All I know is, nobody has said word one to me, and maybe that's for the best.

I'm heartbroken in more ways than I can count—too many to bother sorting out which is for what.

But.

Tolo is in some kind of trouble.

And maybe, just maybe, it's something I can actually help with.

"Did she say what ha—"

"Chh!" Miriam shushes me. "She's explaining."

". . . divulging the exact location, or, more specifically, how to get there, for obvious reasons," Safiya explains sharply. "Suffice to say, if you know, you know. The club itself is on lockdown, and no one will be coming to open the door. We assume these broadcasts are being monitored by empire pirates, so do what you have to do to stay alive, and send help. Siempre pa'lante."

A reggaeton beat drops, and this kid from school, Ems, starts spitting verses over it. My mind spins and spins as the lyrics flow past. . . .

I can't go by myself. It's clear I'll never get inside, and the streets are too dangerous for me to be standing around outside like a fool.

And I'm not bothering Chela anymore. Her silence has made it clear we're not talking right now. I just hope she's okay.

But . . . I do know someone who might know how to get in. It's a long shot, but so is everything these days.

"Tía," I call, walking back into the kitchen. "Do you have Rabbi Hidalgo's number?"

"Claro que sí, mi amor. ¿Por qué?"

———◆———

It takes some wrangling and convincing, mostly of Aunt Miriam—I think Tía Lucia's glad I'm actually doing something after moping around for so many days, just going to school and coming home. Of course she's worried, too, but that's a constant state these days.

I glance around the street—it's clear—and then for a few moments, I just stand there, shivering, even though I'm wearing, like, five layers and it's not *that* cold. Shivering because Tía Lucia told me she's going to die.

Tía Lucia is going to die.

She's never missed the mark with her readings, that's one thing. People call at all hours for consults and then later sing her praises at community meetings and bembés—*Iya Lucia helped me get over my heartbreak! Iya Lucia cured my insomnia! She helped me dump my cheating, good-for-nothing husband! She sent me to get checked and it turned out I had cancer, but they caught it*—all thanks to Iya Lucia!

But who heals the healer? Who will be there now that Death has come knocking at *our* door?

My parents are unreachable. We didn't even have our weekly Skype chat Monday, because they're in some no–Wi-Fi zone. And even if I could talk to them—what would I say?

I shake my head, try to feel my feet on the ground, the light flurry of snow spinning around me from the cloudy sky.

I don't know what to do.

About her, or this broken neighborhood, this broken world, or Chela. I have no moves to make, no idea in what direction to even point myself.

Move, Mateo. Standing here gaping won't save Tía Lucia. Apparently, nothing will. I turn toward the end of the street, where Rabbi Hidalgo texted that he'd meet me. Take a step.

Maybe he handed the phone to his daughter, and it's Chela who will walk around that corner.

She's definitely someone you could talk about loss with. Someone who can sit in silence and then speak when she has the words, not just fill the air with meaningless jibber-jabber to ward off the emptiness.

And she lost her aunt when San Madrigal went down, which I guess she may or may not be responsible for . . . who knows? Either way, she probably feels terrible about everything going on, and needs someone to talk to about it all.

Take another step, Mateo.

I do, I do, even though my head is spinning and nothing makes sense, nothing is okay. Sometimes the only move you can make is to take the next step forward, and then the next one.

I know it's ridiculous to think, in this moment, of a girl—especially one who's sure I betrayed her and may very well want me dead. Then again, if she wanted me dead, I would be.

Point is, it's just her ghost, not really her, I know, but the thought of her brings me peace. And it seemed like, before everything went bonkers, she really did care about me. Like I brought her some peace, too, somehow.

I take another step and then another, and soon I'm striding toward the corner.

Things are still terrible, but at least I can move.

Someone comes around the corner at a run.

It's not Chela, but it is her dad.

Rabbi Hidalgo sprints toward me faster than I would've thought he could move.

Behind him are three bambarúto in body armor barreling through the snow.

CHAPTER TWENTY-NINE

I'VE GOT TWO BARBELLS UNDER MY BED; I EVEN USE THEM SOME-times. I'm long and lanky, so muscles pop up any-ol'-where on me without much effort. Point is, for a music dweeb who hates gym class and often trips over himself, I can actually move pretty fast when my life's on the line.

Rabbi Hidalgo? Not so much. As he passes me, I hear him gasping for air.

The guy is as huge as his nephew, but while Tolo throws all his weight around like he's made of water, a fluid geyser of flesh and muscle all within his total control, the rabbi's stiff lumber carries him in a rocking, uneven dash that seems to threaten total collapse at any moment. Plus, he's, like, fifty or something, with gray streaks in his red beard.

After a moment of shock, I turn and take off, too, and soon I've outpaced him. But I stick close to make sure he's okay.

The bambarúto chase us down one side street after another, and we keep turning corners until they seem a safe distance away. They move awkwardly, a terrifying kind of shamble, but they don't seem to tire and I'm sure they'll catch up soon; I can already hear their stomps and the rattle of trash cans as they approach.

"Come on," I say, helping Rabbi Hidalgo back into a jog even though he's still catching his breath. "We gotta keep moving."

"Where do we even . . . ?" He shakes his head as he resumes jogging, and coughs. "There's nowhere to go."

If Little Madrigal were what it's supposed to be on any given day—teeming with life, commerce, gossip—then we could just duck into a shop or bar and either gather reinforcements or dip out the back and be on our way.

But these winter streets have been empty for a week, and almost all the stores are shuttered, the houses dark. It's not even noon yet, but with that snowy gray sky and these desolate stretches, it might as well be midnight.

Behind us, the bambarúto stride out from an alley. There's three of them, and their bodies are still in heavy armor, but now those monstrous labyrinthine heads are exposed—all horrible, gnashing teeth stretching back toward the ill-shaped masses that glisten with some kind of foul ichor.

Ugh.

Then I hear a familiar rumble from up ahead.

The train!

"To Fulton!" I yell, pulling Rabbi Hidalgo back into a run. "It's the only way!"

The station is a block and a half up. I can just make out the big green tracks that stretch like a rusty snake over our main through-way. I've made it before, sprinting at full speed as soon as I hear the growl of an approaching train. But that was on my own.

Rabbi Hidalgo is already clutching his chest and wheezing.

Behind us, the bambarúto break into a run.

I don't know if they'll follow us onto the train or not, but my gut says they're trying to keep a low profile.

Anyway, we don't have any other options.

The high whine of the brakes squeals out as we reach Fulton and hustle up the stairs to the station.

We might make it!

"I haven't been on the train in . . . a long time," Rabbi Hidalgo huffs at the first landing. "In fact, the last time was when I was here visiting family, long before the island sank. How many tokens is it?"

Then again, we might not. Tokens were phased out, like, twenty years ago.

Down below, the bambarúto have reached the stairs and are glancing around, trying to game out their next move. One shakes its head and launches toward us, retractable baton clanging against the railing as it comes.

No time.

We dash up the second flight in time to see the train grind to a halt beyond the entry turnstiles. Fortunately, Councilwoman Bisconte's biggest claim to fame—keeping cops out of Little Madrigal—has carried over into her coup and apparently includes mass transit. There's no one working in the booth.

"Wait here." I hop the turnstile, then kick open the emergency gate as the train doors slide open behind me.

An off-key *beep* sounds, which means the train's about to leave. I dash ahead of Rabbi Hidalgo, out onto the platform, and throw myself in between the doors just before they slide closed.

The bambarúto, now helmeted again, appear at the top of the stairs.

The conductor's voice comes out scratchy over the loudspeaker. "Stand clear of the closing doors!"

Rabbi Hidalgo bursts across the platform and hurtles past me onto the train, the bambarúto right on his heels. I step all the way in after him.

The doors slam shut.

The tall monsters watch from behind their face shields as the train whisks us away with a rumble and clack.

———◆———

All around us, the regular world goes about its business, that forever churn of flesh and machine that is New York City beyond our small, strange community. An old guy reads the paper. Two nurses chatter about their shift. Some tween has her headphones turned up loud enough for the whole train car to hear.

It's strange how people commute through our weird, entrenched little universe every day and have no idea of all the myths and messes it holds. Then again, I guess that's true of everywhere, huh.

I think the me from one week ago would've put his head down in his hands and sobbed, I really do. And that probably would be the right thing to do after being chased and almost killed by huge demons, only saved by the grace and timing of the MTA, which, lord knows, is not something ever to place your hopes for survival on. Seems like a good cry is in order.

But as I've watched the streets ice over and empty out, as I've seen Little Madrigal retreat inside, part of me has retreated, too. It's gone quiet, grown cold, crystallized.

I don't know what the word for it is, but it feels like a kind of death. Like an essential piece froze within me somehow, and I don't know how to thaw it out.

Then the memory of Tía Lucia's words rises in me—or her silence, really, and what it meant.

Soon, she'll be gone. Dead. She knows this. I'm not supposed to stop it, theoretically, but I'll be damned if I just stand by and watch while someone I love is killed. Not me, being who I am, with the power I have.

No.

I will find a way, somehow. I'm a healer, after all. The only one left.

The last shivering fragment inside of me—the part that would've splash-collapsed into a deluge of tears—hardens with resolve, and I turn to Rabbi Hidalgo, ready to tell him what happened, what I have to do.

Instead, I find him hunched over, face in his hands, shoulders heaving up and down in silent sobs.

"Rabbi, I . . ."

Rabbi Hidalgo has always been a pillar. I know this actually has nothing to do with it, but he's so tall and wide it just seemed like he'd never break—a walking definition of *solid*. Yet here he is, sobbing.

What happens when our elders, our spiritual leaders, are the ones who need our help?

I put my hand on his back, pat once or twice. Feel ridiculous. It's like trying to play a song I've never heard, never seen the sheet music for, just going off someone else's description of it.

"Is it . . . Chela?" I ask, then scrunch up my face at myself. That probably sounded like I'm only worried about her, my crush, my strange, impossible partner in crime, the girl/goddess who thinks I betrayed her. What a time.

To my surprise, though, Rabbi Hidalgo lifts his head and wipes a few tears away. He sniffles and says, "Ah, you really do care for her, huh, Mateo?"

My shoulders pop up to my ears, maybe defensively. "I mean, of course!"

Why is my voice suddenly high-pitched? I want to be mad that he'd even question my feelings, but Rabbi Hidalgo was there the night of the vote, too. Everyone was. He watched me walk into the room with Gerval, heard the man's lies. And then the rabbi was gone, chasing his daughter out into the streets. I never had a chance to explain.

"I didn't . . . I went to tell Gerval that I wouldn't side with him against Chela. He—"

The rabbi shakes his head, erasing my explanations with a swipe of his hand. "Tranquilo, manseviko. I know. He tried the same thing on me."

"He did?"

That's right—on the day before the vote, Chela overheard him planning to meet with Gerval.

"He wanted to meet," says the rabbi, "to convince me he was doing what was best for Chela. Thought he could play my enmity with Tolo against my own daughter somehow." He rolls his eyes, looks away. "I was going to go just to tell him off, but what good would it have done? Things were already getting explosive in the streets, and I realized there was some kind of scheme in the works." He chuckles icily. "These young pirates forget that my sister was their queen once."

Mimi Baracasa—she was on the Cabildo until the island sank and took her with it. *I'd* almost forgotten.

"Mimi may have been born into a religious Sefaradi household," the rabbi continues, "but in her heart, she was always a pirate. No one was surprised when she married Si. So, I grew up dealing with her chaos and subterfuge." A harrumphing noise comes out of him that's half grunt, half sigh. "I know these games."

"I—"

"And anyway"—he turns back to me, his dark brown face alight with sudden excitement, pride even—"I saw what you did on vote night, that speech."

"*You did?* How? I thought—"

"And all the remixes!"

"*Remixes?*"

"*And anywa-ay-ay-ay!*" Rabbi Hidalgo croons in a horrifying robotic voice. "*She's ooooour deeeeestroyer!* It's all over the internet, manseviko!" He's laughing for real now, a full-bodied, generous chortle that bubbles freely through his words. "You didn't see everybody with their phone cameras out?"

"I guess I didn't think about it." I've barely been online the past week—it's too depressing. San Madrigal social media tends to be just various cold takes and pet videos ricocheting off each other ad infinitum. Same everywhere else, I guess, except for the requisite shoddy animations of the three peaks rising over the waves with some terrible inspirational quote scrolling by on a banner. It's hell, in other words. So, I mostly just played piano and lifted my weights and stayed out of the way.

"Oh yes, Mateo. You're a viral sensation, apparently." He starts digging for his phone. "Let me see if I can show—"

"No, no!" I say, because the last thing I ever want to see in life is an autotuned version of myself making an impassioned political speech. I would be forced to jump out of this train. "Please."

Rabbi Hidalgo gets that wise-sage look, but with a glint in his eye, like he knows he's doing the most. "As an anonymous hakham from centuries ago said, 'Devarim hayotzim min halev, nikhnasim lalev.'"

He looks at me like I'm supposed to know what that means, and I stare right back, waiting him out.

Then he laughs. "It means *Words from one's own heart are able to enter the hearts of others.* And your words, manseviko, were both genuine and passionate." A very rabbinical shrug happens. "We were very moved."

I don't know what to do with my body. Compliments about music are one thing—I know they're true, so it's no big deal. Plus, I've been hearing them my whole life. But my public-speaking abilities? That's something else entirely. It doesn't even feel like it was me who was up there. It was someone else wearing my body like a suit.

Wait.

Did he say *we?*

I turn to Rabbi Hidalgo, take in his long red beard, the fluorescent train lights shining off his richly toned skin. That playful squint in his eye.

"I . . . Is she, though? I mean, have you—"

"I can't talk about it," he says, gaze focused suddenly on the long window in front of us, the rooftops speeding past. "But if I did have a way to see her, I would tell her you asked about her." He gives a genial little head tilt. "And I think it would make her smile."

I exhale. Sit back. Find myself blinking, my eyes wet. I had envisioned so many horrible things happening to her, so many ways for her to die, all of them melodramatic. Those were the visions that had taken over whenever I tried to imagine her safe.

But she *is* safe. I can picture that now. And her smile. The image busts through all the ice cages in my chest, all that faux hardness that I knew wouldn't do me any good, anyway. And then I'm the one leaning forward, my shoulders rocking, and the rabbi's huge warm hand is on my back, rubbing gently.

"Let it out, manseviko." His voice is a soft rumble over the ambient rickety drone of the train. "It's good to let it out."

"Can I . . . I know you can't say where she is, but . . . can I somehow, you know, talk to her?"

The rabbi shakes his head gravely, and I'm not sure if it's for her safety or mine. Sure, she's probably seen this horrific video of me that's unfortunately also my redemption, but . . . I doubt she's as forgiving as her father.

Whatever. She's alive and it sounds like she's okay. That's what matters.

"What's wrong with us?" I snorfle, pulling my jacket sleeve across my face.

Rabbi Hidalgo chuckles through his own tears. "Ay, it's not us. It's the world. I've . . ." He shakes his big ol' head, suddenly serious.

"I've never seen it this bad. We had some times, you know, back on the island. But it never felt like this . . . this kind of . . ." He flails for a word.

"Silence," I suggest, because it's the only one that makes sense.

"Eso."

Rabbi Hidalgo stands as the train grumbles and whines to a halt at the next station. He smiles at me sadly as I step beside him. "I'm glad you reached out, Mateo. We need your help, and it's about time you learn some of the real secrets of Little Madrigal."

CHAPTER THIRTY

IT'S EXHAUSTING, THIS MILITARY OCCUPATION OR WHATEVER IT IS.

Exhausting and humiliating and hateful. Rabbi Hidalgo and I got off the train only a few blocks from the club, but twice we had to hide and find a new route when bambarúto appeared in the streets ahead of us.

The whole time we were ducking and glancing and creeping, Tía Lucia's and Chela's faces spiraled endlessly through my mind. And then Tolo's. Rabbi Hidalgo wouldn't elaborate about what had happened to anyone, so I was left imagining worst-case scenarios while also running for my life. Fun!

"I was at that last divination before the island sank, you know," Rabbi Hidalgo says as we soft-tread through empty streets of newly fallen snow. "The one your aunt did."

I stop. Of course he'd been there—he was the head rabbi of San Madrigal, after all. I knew that, but it's still strange to imagine.

"Did she . . . ? She talked about what was going to happen?"

"In a way." He nods with a solemn grunt, and we fall back into a cautious stride, our eyes darting along every corner, fire escape, and trash bin. Bambarúto lurk behind them all, or they might as well, the way my heart keeps lurching at any flicker of shadow or gust of wind. "The letters foretold massive destruction and tragedy, yes. But they also spoke of rebirth, miracles, things that rise from the ashes. People clung to your aunt's words, her interpretation of the shells. They believed her then, and they still believe now that because she was right about the disaster, she must also be right about the possibility of somehow bringing San Madrigal back."

"Were you part of that? Trying to find the children of the original saints?"

He nods gravely. "After she got the message from the shells, your aunt did a reading on you immediately. You'd had respiratory issues since you were born, and her spirits had warned you could die at an early age. But they also indicated that initiating you to Galanika would save your life, and it did. As for Chela . . ." Rabbi Hidalgo's face hardens. "We were still looking for the person who could be the child of Okanla. I . . . I didn't let them check Chela. It was selfish, I admit. It's a . . . It's a heavy burden for a child to carry, you know . . . the Destroyer. But they all are, I suppose. Parents want to save their children from the pain of this world. It's a fool's errand. In the end, all we can do is stand beside them when the pain comes. . . ." The train rumbles over his fading voice. "If they let us."

"Si initiated her behind your back."

He looks up from his wistfulness. Sighs. "Behind all our backs."

The cut is still raw. I can imagine why.

"Any idea who the third is? The child of Madrigal?"

He shakes his head. "The three initiations were supposed to deliver us from utter destruction. . . ."

"Hrmph," I scoff. "So much for that."

"Well, we only managed two," Rabbi Hidalgo reminds me. "But we are here, are we not? Considering that an entire island sank, things could've been much, much worse. And if we hadn't been gathered at the ceremony when the storm hit, who knows what would've happened?"

"But . . . your sister."

He looks away, then back at me. "I'm not so sure it was the storm that killed her. She disappeared in the chaos, but you know, Mimi always had a hundred different ploys going at once. It seemed like there were a lot of secrets surrounding her at the end of her life—even more than usual. Si was spending most of his time here by then, setting up his syndicate, and she seemed to have drifted away from most of us. We found out later that she'd taken measures to prepare for the oncoming disaster."

"Measures?"

"She raided the synagogue's basement. *My* synagogue. Airlifted a huge stash of sacred weaponry here to Brooklyn."

"Whoa! Sacred weaponry?"

"Mmm. Along with a note saying that if anything should happen to her, the pirate's seat on the Cabildo should be filled by her best friend, Anisette."

"The councilwoman."

"I never trusted her. Then again, I never trusted my sister, either. When we survivors settled in with the Galeranos who'd already immigrated here, there was a vote, and of course it went to Bisconte. Only a fool would disregard the dying wish of a pirate queen."

"You make a good point."

We reach a corner and peer around it, ready to run at any moment.

Brownstones line the long street. Parked cars white with the first gusts of snow. Skeletal trees crack the pale sky. No bambarúto in sight, sure, but plenty of places for them to hide. Ever watchful, we start walking. "Turns out," Rabbi Hidalgo says, "the pirates really have been handpicking their successors this whole time. The vote is just theater. And you see what happens when things don't go their way."

I can't stop thinking about my tía's prediction of her own death. The same letters had fallen, she said, at the reading back when I was a baby. It foretold the collapse of the whole world, called for my initiation, Chela's. . . . "Did Chela . . . ?" I ask. "Is she really the Destroyer?"

The rabbi lets out a sigh that sounds like it was millennia in the making. "It's hard to explain, manseviko. And I don't totally understand it myself. But . . ." He stops, looks at me carefully, then says, "Yes."

For a few seconds, we just gaze at each other, bewildered by the full weight of this world, which seems to be rebirthing itself brand-new with each passing moment.

"One thing I've never understood," I say when we fall back into step. "I thought Jews were all about one God and only one God, right? Isn't that, like, the whole thing?"

Rabbi Hidalgo tips his hat at me with a wink. "Ah, but we have angels, Mateo. Angels of destruction, of creation. Disease and divination. So many angels. *Irin*, we named them—the awakened ones. Some say they are reflections of God, avatars. Some call them messengers. Whatever their names, divine beings have always lit up the space between humanity and the All-Powerful."

I smile, because that's exactly what it feels like when I think about Chela—a light. And then I suck in a sharp breath. Up ahead, five towering figures are standing in front of Tolo's club.

CHAPTER THIRTY-ONE

"Come quickly." With a firm grip, the rabbi yanks my arm first, and the rest of me follows in a startled stumble—"This way"—down one snow-dusted alley and around a corner into another.

I don't have time to check whether the bambarúto have spotted us and are giving chase or not, but I guess it doesn't matter—we'll know soon enough. In the meantime, I have to keep up with Rabbi Hidalgo's suddenly relentless stride.

We barrel around another corner, and a few mice scatter ahead of us. Fading, peeled posters on the aging brick walls announce concerts long past. The sky is a gray chasm above, and whispers of snow paint the air.

Rabbi Hidalgo stops so abruptly I almost crash into him. Somewhere not far away, heavy footsteps clomp; I can't place where. "Aquí." He opens a heavy door and slips inside. I could be wrong—the network of alleys that crisscross Little Madrigal is a world unto itself, and I don't know it as well as I should—but I think this is the back end of the block across from Tolo's, where Baba Calvo's atelier sits beside the Scuttleback Diner.

"This . . ." I enter the darkness. Rabbi Hidalgo closes the door behind me, secures it with a series of *click*s and *clack*s. "This leads to the club somehow?"

A flashlight beam flutters around, then settles on a rickety staircase leading to what looks like some kind of underground tunnel. "Down here."

I must have gasped because the rabbi's mischievous belly laugh sings out around us as we descend. "I didn't know about it, either," he says, "until my nephew and I reconciled last week."

"So wait—Tolo owns *this* building, too?"

"The building? Ha! The whole block!" Around us, wooden beams hold up the sagging ceiling. The flashlight slides along weird collages formed by crumbly brick and cement work. Pipes stretch into the darkness overhead, and impossible shadows tremble and lurk amid it all. "Turns out my brother-in-law, Si, did pretty well for himself, you know." The rabbi scowls. "Blood money, of course. That's why I had to step away from him."

"Oh?" I had figured it was something like that, but I never knew the truth of it, just the bochinche.

"Most of these pirates, they're just playing dress-up at this point. I mean, they're authentic in the traditions they honor, sure. And in the past few days, we've all learned what a sham that really is. But as far as the actual pirate life? Pirating itself? Well, Si Baracasa and his crew—Safiya, Big Moses, the rest—they were the only ones still upholding that part of things. The only *real* ones, as the kids say."

"Smuggling?"

"Drugs, guns, you name it. Territory wars. I know I shouldn't have been surprised, given where we're from, but . . . I didn't want my nephew around all that. He was so young. And Si was so determined to keep him close. Teach him the family business. At a certain point, it became clear that I was enabling the whole thing, giving tacit approval just by coming around at all. I couldn't give my blessing to it."

For a few moments, our footsteps echo up and down the dank underground corridor.

"Told young Tolo that even though I was cutting off his father, I would always be there for him no matter what. But I don't think it mattered. He was just, what, eleven at the time? When Si was killed a year later, Tolo wouldn't speak to me at the funeral, and he's barely acknowledged me since."

"Did it . . . Did it hurt?"

Rabbi Hidalgo stops, looks at me. The contours of his face and beard shine with the edges of the flashlight glare. "Every single day, my heart breaks for my sister, my brother-in-law—both of whom I loved even when we were at odds—and, most of all, my nephew, who lived on but I somehow also lost." His mouth curves upward just the slightest bit. "Until now, it seems!" And then we're on the move again, the tunnel widening as we go, and the rabbi has a little bounce in his step. "There's a lesson in that, you know? Kuando muncho escurese es para amaneser."

When things get darkest, it is only so the dawn can come.

"Certain flowers only bloom in the depths of caves," the rabbi says. "Often, it is only in dark times that strange miracles can take root, hmm?"

"Wait, are we . . . ?" I can't put my finger on what it is, some smell too subtle to name, perhaps, but everything about this now-cavernous hall reminds me of the club.

"Right beneath it, yes," Rabbi Hidalgo says. "Which means we're safe."

"But the bambarúto attacked here on the night of the vote."

"And in so doing, let it be known we are in a state of war, hmm? The empire pirates showed their hand. That was their surprise maneuver, and it gained them some amount of political power, but it also put the rest of us on notice. In this community, Tolo has the muscle, even with Bisconte and Gerval holding the Cabildo seat hostage. They've got some goons on their side, sure, but those bambarúto are the only thing giving them an edge right now. It won't last forever. They know what's in this basement."

"Wait." Around us, I can just make out an array of tall pillars reaching into the darkness above. "What's in this basement?"

Up ahead, the dim light of a lantern casts long shadows in all directions. There's another glint of laughter in the rabbi's voice when he says, "Remember I told you my sister airlifted a shipment of sacred weaponry right before the storm?"

Not columns—figures! Towering stone figures, with broad shoulders and mostly flat features. Golems! A whole army of golems.

"Ah," Tolo calls from somewhere up ahead. "The Healer! Fantastic. Just in time to watch me die!"

CHAPTER THIRTY-TWO

TOLO BARACASA LOOKS LIKE HELL.

The young gang boss sits on a folding chair amid several flickering lanterns. Despite the chill, he's sweating, and one hand presses against his chest while the other sits planted on his knee like it's holding up the rest of him. Safiya the Butcher stands beside him, frowning.

"What's wrong?" I jog over, ignoring the rows and rows of silent stone figures all around us. It's not hard—the second I laid eyes on Tolo, the world began spiraling into a crystal-clear focal point: him. Everything else—the golem army, the rabbi's sad story, even Chela and my doomed tía—slid into a blurry background realm. Only one thing matters right now: not letting Tolo die.

"I'm having a heart attack, obviously," he scoffs. Then he reconsiders his tone. "Ah, thanks for coming."

"It might *not* be a heart attack," Safiya points out, but it sounds like she doesn't believe that.

It's odd. Tolo is young and seemingly in excellent health. He must have a gym around here somewhere—clearly there's room for one!—because the guy has muscles for days and is built like a tank. Then again, from what I remember of health class and my parents' random medical conversations, when it comes to hearts, genetics can throw all that out the window.

At first, I'm not sure what to do with myself. The other times, it was obvious where to start—shattered bodies writhing in the street don't leave time for awkward standing around and asking questions. "What happened?"

He shakes his big shiny head and pulls a hand down his face, eyes squeezed shut. "I just . . . I was going over numbers with Safiya and the crew, 'bout to, you know . . . make a plan." He flinches, like the very word sent another dangerous pulse of death through him.

"Shhh," Safiya says gently. Then to me: "He just got quiet suddenly, held a hand to his chest, and started sweating. I put the word out over the Pirate Radio Hour. We were hoping you'd hear, but we didn't want to reach out directly, because they're probably monitoring the phones."

"Turns out they're watching the streets, too," Rabbi Hidalgo says.

Tolo looks up, that familiar flicker of violence in his eyes. "Oh?"

Rabbi Hidalgo waves him off. "We're fine, sobrino. You worry about you, please. The underground tunnel system came in very handy, as you've seen, so thank you for that."

System? There's so much more to Little Madrigal than I ever realized, and I always thought I knew more than the average schmo.

I kneel down in front of Tolo. "I'm going to put my hand on your chest, okay?"

"Mmm." He nods his assent, breathing, I can now see, way too fast.

"Oh, and if I hum," I tell them, placing open palms over his heart as I close my eyes, "that's normal."

"This kid," Tolo scoffs, not unkindly. His chest rises and falls quickly a few times with laughter. "No wonder Chela likes him. Weirdos, both of 'em."

She told him she likes me? I manage to keep my hands from shaking, but that whole focus thing I just mentioned? Gone. Out the window.

Did she tell him before or after she thought I betrayed her? I have so many questions, none appropriate at the moment, I know. But still I wonder: Is she the forgiving type? Can she be reasoned with? Doesn't seem like it, but then again, she's unpredictable. Deliciously unpredictable.

Stop! Concentrate!

I pull in a big breath of air and exhale it with a whispered melody. The notes pull my mind back into my body, and then, thankfully, into the inner workings of Tolo's chest.

That heart is no joke. It's not that I can see it, exactly; it's the presence of it. Each galumphing beat thunders through him, through me, through everything, like his pulse registers tiny terremotos through the fault lines of Madrigal, reaches all the lonely, uncertain souls cooped up in their apartments with their weary eyes on the empty streets. The beat is solid, unflinching, the sure stride of a warrior who stands solid while the whirlwind of battle rages around him.

No, there is nothing wrong with Tolo Baracasa's heart.

But I think I do know what is struggling.

Gently, I let my hands slide upward to the man's huge shoulders. Eyes still closed, I stand, ignore the sounds of concern and wonder coming from Rabbi Hidalgo and Safiya, ignore my stray thoughts about Chela, and focus on the melody, let it guide me.

This song is somber and stern, full of dangling whole notes, a chant that glides across the booming mountain range of Tolo's heartbeat. But as I get closer to his head, the melody falters, drops off, shambles back in a crumbling shadow of itself, cuts out completely.

"What is it?" Tolo's voice booms through my reverie. "What's wrong?"

"Quiet, man," Safiya insists. "Let the kid work."

The melody returns, resolving into a jangly, dangerous thing. It wants to shatter all constraints, a caged beast—now furious, now withdrawn. There is no rhythm to it, no logic.

I open my eyes. "You're not having a heart attack." I'm surprised by the certainty in my voice, even more surprised that no one else seems to question it. They just listen and nod. Well, Safiya and Rabbi Hidalgo nod. Tolo leans back and lets out a huge, dramatic sigh of relief.

"Oh man! Thank freaking God!" he bellows. "What the hell is it, then?"

"It's panic," I say, and immediately wish I hadn't.

Tolo leans forward, both hands on his knees now, and glares at me. *"Excuse me?"*

"I . . ." I step back, grasping for a better explanation. So much for certainty.

He stands, and look, it's rare that someone can make me feel small, not at my big height. But Tolo is a sheer wall. Even in a weakened state, it's obvious he could just walk forward and crush my very existence into dust.

Then again, I'm right. "Panic," I say again, shoring myself up. "It's okay. I mean, you're okay. I mean . . ." Rabbi Hidalgo's words from earlier return to me. "It's not us—it's the world."

Tolo stares and stares. Then he grunts. Sits. Slouches. "The kid's right," he finally says, head in hands. "This whole thing has me all jacked up inside, can't lie. We've been through war, but this is something else. It's worse. Because it's our own folks. And those things." He lets out a long, sad sigh. Looks up at me. "Panic *is* actually better than a heart attack, huh?"

I manage to smile. "Definitely. Except I'm not sure there's anything I can do for it."

"Oh, you already did," Tolo says. "I mean, I'm still panicking, don't get me wrong. I just . . . At least now I can panic about what's actually wrong instead of that *plus* a heart attack to boot." He looks at Safiya, who's already heading toward the door at the far end of the room. "Am I allowed to have coffee now that I'm not dying?"

"I'll have Big Moses put some on." She shoots him a skeptical glare as she heads into the shadows. "Gonna get another patrol out on the streets and let folks know you're okay. And for the record, *I* never thought you were dying. Not really."

"Yeah, great," Tolo says. "I'll put that in the official books."

"And thanks, Mateo," Safiya calls. Then a door slams and she's gone.

"Why don't you just turn these guys loose on 'em?" I ask, now taking the time to look at the stone figures standing throughout the basement.

"What, the golem army I inherited from a mom I barely remember?"

"They originally belonged to the San Madrigal Beit Hashem congregation," Rabbi Hidalgo points out. For a moment, I think these two are about to shatter their still-fresh peace.

Instead, they both burst out laughing, some long-lost family joke that's way over my head.

I can see the resemblance between these giants—that full-bodied chuckle, those tree-trunk arms. Tolo strolls nonchalantly among the ominous sculpture garden around us. "Lotta good these damn things do me."

"Why?" I ask.

He throws up his hands. "We can't figure out how to turn 'em on! Mom forgot to send the instruction manual."

"I was hoping, now that we're reunited," Rabbi Hidalgo says, "we could put our heads together and figure it out. But so far . . . nothing."

"Fortunately," Tolo adds with a grimace, "Gerval and them don't know that. But it's only a matter of time before they figure out we would've used 'em if we knew how."

"Those books we stole from the recording studio don't help?"

"Well, Chela—" Tolo starts to say, but a look from Rabbi Hidalgo cuts him short. "We only have access to the ledger and the music book," he amends. "And so far, all we've gotten from them are what came out on vote night—a small breakaway sect of pirates has maintained power since at least the 1810 accords. They were trading and cutting nasty deals with agents of various empires and slavers all along. Empire pirates. Seems I didn't turn out the way they hoped—they could tell I wouldn't be friendly to the cause, which is a compliment, I guess—so Bisconte had to pivot to someone more amenable to their machinations."

"Gerval," I spit.

"The other end of things," Rabbi Hidalgo says, "the spiritual stuff, is out of our hands right now, unfortunately."

I stand. "I should get back. I gotta help my tía set up for her ocha birthday party."

Tolo raises his eyebrows. "She's still celebrating, even with everything going on? Respect. We'll come through, right, Tío?"

Rabbi Hidalgo looks all teary-eyed for a moment, probably still getting used to his long-lost nephew acknowledging their bond. "Of course, of course. We must celebrate even in darkness. I'll escort young Mateo home, hmm? I think this time we'll take the tunnels most of the way."

CHAPTER THIRTY-THREE

"I HAVE TO APOLOGIZE," RABBI HIDALGO SAYS AS WE EMERGE FROM the underground darkness onto the wintery backstreets near my place.

"Huh?"

It's only been, what, a few hours I've spent with this man, and we've laughed and cried together, run for our lives *twice*, and he's told me family secrets that have probably never been revealed to an outsider before. I didn't wake up this grim morning thinking I'd make a new friend, especially not a middle-aged, red-bearded rabbi. He certainly has nothing to apologize for.

"When I saw you at the cemetery the other day and asked you a question, I was being cryptic, you know. Mysterious. It's a thing they teach us in rabbi school." He looks at me, and I realize, a moment too late, that he's made a joke and is checking to see if I'd laugh. "Bah, that's all right. They don't really, but they might as well. Rabbis love to ask deep questions that people have to answer for themselves. Usually, it's a very effective way to get someone to learn. If I tell you something, you will nod and smile and keep moving, hmm? But if I *ask* you something and you come up with the answer yourself, well, it's true in a different way, isn't it?"

"I guess so, yeah. But who knows what answer I'll come up with."

"Heh, indeed, indeed."

We've reached the corner of Fulton; it stretches on and on in either direction, empty. Shuttered shops. A thin layer of freshly fallen snow on the street. This can't go on. These businesses must be hemorrhaging money. Maybe that's the empire pirates' plan: strangle the tiny economies along with our lifeblood and culture until we're all just gasping for breath, and then fill the void with their power grab. I hate it. All of it. I don't even know how everyone decided to shut down. It was like a silent understanding passed through the neighborhood over the past few days: if our electoral voice can be snatched away so easily, then fine, we won't speak in any other way, either. No songs, no stories. No gossip on the corner, no old folks in the park. We're only hurting ourselves, really, but when you're left with no move to make except to withhold your voice, maybe that's the only thing that makes sense.

I shake away all these chaotic daydreams, glance around again, then look up at Rabbi Hidalgo. "Sorry—you were apologizing for something and being all woo-woo again, and then I got distracted."

He laughs. "Maybe you should think about becoming a rabbi."

"Ha." We fall into a cautious stride down the middle of Fulton Street—that way we could easily break to one direction or another if needed, I guess. Our footsteps crunch a whispered song in time with our strut. In this moment, the world feels like ours, even though it's anything but.

"Anyway, as I was saying . . . At the betahayim, I asked if you knew why it was called that."

"Technically, you made fun of me for thinking it was the name of the cemetery," I point out.

"Technically, my daughter did that. I just had a good laugh at your expense."

"This is the worst apology ever, just FYI."

"That's fair. Here." He pulls one hand out of his overcoat pocket and extends a fist toward me. A thin golden chain dangles through his clenched fingers.

I place my open hand under his closed one, and he drops a little pendant necklace into it. "What's this?"

"It's for you. The answer."

Two Hebrew letters, *chet* and *yod*, glimmer up at me from my palm. They spell the word *chai—life*. I look at the rabbi. "Thank you." Then I squint. "You're still being cryptic, though. You know that, right?"

He waves his hands defensively. "No, no! This is just a visual aid—I was about to explain!"

"Uh-huh." I let the chain dangle and then clasp it around my neck.

"Hey!" someone yells from behind us. We both freeze, my heart already racing, then slowly turn. "Who said you could be out and about?"

An old Mercedes idles at the top of the block. Arco "El Gorro" Kordal stands by the open driver's side door, leering at us while he slaps his palm with an aluminum baseball bat. I have no idea why they call him "the Hat"—he never wears one. But pirates love their nicknames, and Arco loves being a pirate. I can just make out someone in the passenger seat, but it's impossible to see a face.

A few feet behind the car, Vedo Bisconte stands stock-still in the snow, his expression blank. I've never trusted him, but seeing him here, my own classmate on the side of the people who brought our whole world to a standstill, makes the iciness rise back up inside me. There's something different about him (though, of course, the past week has changed all of us). That sniveling teenager with the crush on Chela is gone. Someone colder and crueler has emerged in his place.

Rabbi Hidalgo shakes his head with a scoff. "*I* said we could be out and about. The head rabbi of Little Madrigal and a member of the Cabildo, as you know. But no one needs anyone's permission to walk these streets, my friends. Now, Arco, put that bat away—you look ridiculous." He starts to turn his back to them, still chuckling to himself. "And, Vedo, get home to your mommy. Tell her she's gone too far this time."

The engine roars before Arco has even slammed the door. I feel more than see that Rabbi Hidalgo is frozen in his tracks, like he can't quite believe what's happening. I can, though. I shove him as hard as I can as the car barrels toward us. Rabbi Hidalgo stumbles onto the far sidewalk and I leap the opposite way as a *whoosh* of steel and glass hurdles past. I slam into a mailbox and glance up when I hear brakes screech. The Mercedes skids on the snow and then cuts hard in the opposite direction and plows straight into a parked SUV, crumpling both vehicles' sides.

After the horrific sounds of smashing metal and shattering glass, there's a second of stillness. I clamber to my feet—shaken and bruised, probably, but fine. Arco lurches out of the totaled Benz, bat in hand. Rabbi Hidalgo is already making his way toward them, probably to help, and Arco takes one long step and swings. It's haphazard and off-balance, but the rabbi catches it right on the side of his head and drops with just a whispered gasp.

I launch forward, propelled by fear and rage and I don't know what else, skid over the back of the Benz, and crash into Arco with all my might. He clatters to the ground, and his head cracks against the curb with a sickening wet crunch. And then there's bright red blood on the snow and Arco's not moving at all; he's just an object, perfectly still.

I'm not moving, either, but breath leaves my mouth in tiny

clouds. It seems like that's the only movement in the whole world, the tiny *shush* of my breath leaving my body in a gentle mist, rising, rising.

A soft crunching sounds, and I look up, past the sudden violence of those drastic tire tracks in the freshly fallen snow, to where Vedo has turned and is slowly walking away.

CHAPTER THIRTY-FOUR

The rabbi.

With a glance, I know he's alive. His chest rises, and his skin is still the same rich dark brown.

I don't have to check anything to know that Arco is dead. That I killed him.

I didn't mean to.

I drop to my knees beside Arco's body. He's so still. And I made him that way. With a single shove, I set off a series of tiny disasters inside him that wiped out everything he was and would be and snatched him from all those who cherished him.

And probably enshrined him in my own nightmares for all time.

No.

I refuse to go down that path. I might be the only person who can actually reverse things. So I will.

If I can, that is.

I roll him over. Bright blood still spills from the pink gash across his forehead. His eyes see nothing. His light brown skin is clammy under my fingertips.

Then I block out the world and let the melody slide in.

The curb split his skull, reached all the way to his brain, and hammered that enough to shut everything down. There are shards of bone in there, too. All that will need repair, yes, and that's where I'll begin. But there will be more beyond that. His life is another matter. That will be something new.

A lonely waltz unravels inside me; the damaged brain matter strengthens, hums, and reinvigorates as my fingers stretch along Arco's temples, through his blood-drenched hair. I feel the tissue push outward, expel each splinter of bone. Then cartilage forms across the slim chasm on his skull.

The song swells, and my open palms land on his chest.

"You will live," I say out loud to the empty street, the dead man, the falling snow. "You will live."

One-two-three, two-two-three, the waltz sizzles on within me, within him, and harmonies break down, re-form, twist, and tumble toward some ever-dissonant climax, and then all of it grinds to a halt.

Silence.

My own breath.

Silence.

The churn of the city.

Silence.

No.

Something's wrong.

It's a silence deeper than everything else. It blots out the ambient hum of the world, covers everything. Pure void.

Death. It's death I've touched upon, and it will eclipse me if I let it; that silence forms a canyon so vast, it is beyond any song, bigger than the world.

I pull back with a gasp. I'm standing before I realize it, backing away.

Arco's stopped bleeding, but he's still dead. I've still killed him.

The rabbi's chest rises and falls, steady. He's okay for the moment. But the passenger in the car . . . I glance at the wreck. He might be alive, too.

In seconds, I'm working my way through the crumpled steel where the two cars met. There's an older man in the seat; I can see his hands, now his face. Tantor Batalán, the grocer. His granddaughter Zala is a grade below me. He always makes corny jokes in the checkout line. Tonight, though, he tried to kill me. Instead, he's . . . I look closer: he's gone, too. No movement, just that impossible stillness of the dead.

Yet maybe . . .

I know this is ridiculous. I do. But I'm already pulling him out through the smashed window, laying his body on the sidewalk, ignoring the tiny fractals of glass that dig into my knees as I lean over his body and listen.

Nothing.

Nothing, and then, a tiny something . . . A faraway note, then another. Two notes is a melody, however faint.

Again.

My hands land on his shoulders, slide up to his bruised neck.

Speckles of snow land on his gray face.

I close my eyes.

Listen.

Something took flight in the crash, became a projectile. I can almost see it. The thing ricocheted off the dashboard and made a direct hit with his throat, crushing the windpipe.

I can fix that. What happens next . . . Well, that's another story.

The two notes find a third, and a new melody is born—a distant thing, but there, real. It repeats, even stronger this time.

It's all I need. Tantor Batalán's crumpled cartilage smooths out, hardens, and rises against my fingers. Air pours through what once was a closed passageway.

And then . . . silence rears up so suddenly it blots out all sense of the world around—all sight, sound, and smell—and almost knocks me over.

Death.

I remain, and the sheer void of it sends wave after wave of panic through me.

I remain.

I'm ready for it this time. I know it now. It still might overwhelm me. The tiniest flinch could send everything spiraling; the maw of the abyss grows wider.

It's just nothing and more nothing.

And then . . .

Ga-gung.

One double-tap heartbeat against my palm.

Silence.

Another *ga-gung.*

And again. Then a fourth, a fifth. Chaos organizes itself into a rhythm. Life.

I rise, watching, feel the dizzy abyss shrink as I stand.

Tantor's eyes—the eyes of my enemy, my neighbor, my patient—pop open, and he heaves forward with a gasp as I step back.

"What the—" He skitters to his feet, frantic, the grayness giving way to pink on his face. "What the devil did you do to me?"

I don't have an answer to that, so I just shake my head.

Tantor stumbles a few steps away, then turns and runs.

For a moment, I stand there, breath rising in misty clouds. A sharp tingle whispers through me, and I know without having to wonder that it is death. I have stolen this void from him, and I should probably do what Tía Lucia taught me: cleanse it off in a river or a crossroads somewhere, be rid of it.

But I can't lie—there's a strange comfort in knowing I carry death within me now. The icicles were already there. They've grown and glistened all week in sharp, unforgiving angles, and now I realize they've formed the perfect nest to embrace this new entity within, this eternal emptiness that I carry, this sweet abyss.

And maybe, just maybe, I can study it, understand it, and somehow use it to save my tía.

Or even . . . I glance over at Arco, the man I killed. The man I couldn't save.

I reach him at a run, skitter to a stop, and place my hands on his cold, dead skin, already turning paler than before, a cruel blue-gray taking over.

I can save you.

But when I reach him, I don't even feel an abyss. It's like I'm touching a fleshy rock. There's no music, no abyss to snatch. Nothing.

"Come on!" I grunt, my concentration shattered, reaching deeper and deeper with nothing to show for it. "Come on!"

"*MATEO!*" Huge tree-trunk arms wrap around me, and I know this isn't the first time the rabbi has yelled my name. "We need to go!"

He's yanking me to my feet, and the world spins in a wild drunken carousel as Arco's body is wrenched from my grasp.

Rabbi Hidalgo's strong hands grip my shoulders, and I manage to meet his glare. "You *can't* help him! And we have to go! Now!"

He's right. Maybe I could have saved Arco earlier, but now I can't, and . . . Movement at the far end of the street catches my eye.

Towering figures. Four of them. Bambarúto. They stride toward us like they have all the time in the world. Which makes them even more terrifying.

"We run," Rabbi Hidalgo urges. And we do.

———◆———

In the tunnel, the rabbi squints at me as the lump on the back of his head diminishes beneath my touch. An audacious bolero rises; I guess a prayer would've been too obvious to expect. Already, healing has become second nature to me; it was always there, waiting to take flight within.

"What happened up there?" he asks.

"You took a bat to the head," I say, hedging. "One of the guys died in the scuffle." I don't say I *killed* one of them. But it's there, the truth—it's in me. Doesn't matter. No, that's a lie. It matters more than anything. "I scared the other one off." Another lie, if only by omission. "Vedo, too." Then: "Didn't take much. Cowards." I feel both smug and ashamed, but I know very simply, very clearly, that what I've done—the taking of life and the taking of death—is not an anecdote, not a story to vomit out simply because it happened, because someone asked. No. It is a sacred thing, and I will honor it.

The rabbi is safe, that's what matters.

He regards me with uncertainty. "You saved me, didn't you?"

I do a kind of halfway nod-shrug. That much I can admit, sure. And it's true. Just not only in the way he thinks.

"Thank you, manseviko. I will not forget this."

"It's not a big deal," I say, and mean it. "You don't have to . . . It's fine. I just—I have to get back to my tía." Who I can't save, supposedly. None of this is fair. "You'll be okay getting home?"

He nods, still rubbing the back of his head. "I'll take the tunnels and be careful. See you tonight, Mateo."

And then he trudges off into the darkness, and I am alone.

CHAPTER THIRTY-FIVE

"Oh, there you are. Tolo lives in the Bronx now o ¿qué?"

"Sorry, it took so long, Tía. I . . . Things got a little complicated."

"¿Y eso? Pass me that cornmeal and put a pot on to boil, hmm? Rápido."

"He's okay. But those bambarúto creatures are out in the streets."

"Comemierdas sinverguenzas del carajo. Chop this onion. And your healing powers, mmm?"

"They're, uh, improving, yeah."

"Menos mal."

"Tía Lucia?"

"Hmm?"

"Who do you think—"

"*Chop*, I said, not . . . whatever that is you're doing."

"Tía . . ."

"You're cooking for santos, m'ijo. You can't just do whatever. Here, give me the knife. Roll this cornmeal into little bolas."

"Tía, I'm trying to— OW! Damn!"

"Language, m'ijo. The cornmeal is still hot, be careful."

"So I noticed!"

"Hrm."

"Who do you think the San Madrigal initiate is . . . or was supposed to be?"

"Ay, m'ijo, these questions. It was fifteen years ago, papito. We did the best we could, Mateo. I don't look for the shells to tell me what I want to hear. I listen to what they're saying, and then check with them to confirm what I hear. It's the same when you heal, I think. You see—or feel, maybe—what it is that is wrong. Then you check, and then you act. The shells speak in riddles, sí. Pero usually they are very clear, if you are paying attention. The shells said the island would fall. We didn't realize how soon it would happen, but the island surely did fall. They said it would rise again, that the same thing that destroyed it would raise it, hmm? And now we have to see what that means, or do what that means. No sé. Some answers are bigger than we can fathom, ¿Entiendes? Ahora aqui—revuelateme esos huevos."

"Santos eat scrambled eggs?"

"No—bueno, sí, pero this is for the French toast."

"Santos eat French toast?"

"Ay, m'ijo, have you really not been paying attention all these years? Jes, French toast is Oya's favorite food. Ahora, por favor, scramble these eggs and put some more butter in the pan and then get the bread out before I escream."

"Fine, sheesh."

"And put the coffee on."

"Do you believe Chela is really Okanla incarnate, like an actual walking living santo?"

"Sí, como no."

"Does that mean I am . . . ?"

"Hmm?"

"You know . . ."

Finally, finally, Tía Lucia stops what she's doing and looks at me. Her face has aged since I've been gone, like time has accelerated with the knowledge of what's to come. In spite of all her efforts to dye her hair that ridiculous blond, more gray is showing. Crow's feet form tiny tributaries down her cheeks. She's at home amidst this flurry of movement, and her tired eyes look somehow so sad and so alive, invigorated at the same time. She puts two fists on her hips and narrows her gaze to a squint, a slight smile painting her face.

"Do you *feel* like a sacred spirit, Mateo?"

It's the kind of question most people would ask in jest, to mock the very notion. But she means it. Chela had told me she'd somehow always known she was Okanla. That's nothing I can relate to. I'm just a kid who loves music and, sure, can magically heal people. But I'm still just a kid. I shake my head slowly.

She tips her head to one side, then the other, raises a shoulder, and lets out an extended "Buuuueno." Then she turns back to the chopping board. "Bring these plates out to the altar. We'll put down what's ready and do the rest later, hmm? Guests will be coming soon. MIRIAM! ¡VAMOS A PRESENTAR, MI AMOR!"

Farts appears in the doorway, then waddles ahead of me like an escort as I carry various dishes full of delicious spirit delicacies into the living room. I guess I'm not a demigod or whatever like Chela, an angel. I didn't really think so, but the whispered idea had been dancing tiny tantalizing circles around me for a week.

I carry an icy shard of death itself now, and that in itself makes me feel somewhat unstoppable. Recklessly so, perhaps, but these are reckless days and nights of silent warfare, so no, I won't walk unarmed again.

Tía Lucia stands in front of her shelf full of spirits, a steaming plate in each hand. "Ay, mi gente," she sighs with gusto.

Aunt Miriam floats up beside us, beams. "They look beautiful, mi vida. Just beautiful."

They do—she must've dressed the orishas while I was out. Each one has been wrapped in glittering fabric that winds upward and bursts in an elaborate flare from a metal crown on top. Fruits and wineglasses full of honey and molasses adorn them, and the whole scene looks like some luxurious Caribbean throne room.

Tía Lucia kisses the plates, then presses the edge of each to her forehead and heart while mumbling Lucumí prayers. Afterward, she hands them to me with instructions on how to arrange them on the straw mat.

"I already spoke to them," she says when we're done. "You want to salute, Mateo?"

I drop down, pick up the red-and-white maraca for Shango, Tía Lucia's main santo, and shake it.

This is when I'm supposed to pray.

I've done it a million times—well, dozens, anyway. I don't always necessarily believe in it, but it's just something we do, you know? You pray for people you love. If God or some spirit hears you, all the better. If not, no harm, no foul.

But right now, no words come out.

Instead, my mind wanders to Tía Lucia's casual acceptance of her own death. She's not mad about it, not fighting. I know it took her some time to get there, but still . . . And then Arco, that sudden blue-gray color he became, that I made him. I took a life, and while I'll be marked by it forever, he's just gone.

I feel that iciness glisten and tremble within me; what it means, I do not know.

"Ay, please don't cry at my santos, Mateo," Tía Lucia says, halfway joking.

I'm not crying, though. I'm angry, I don't know who at. And I'm lost.

Galanika's serious face glares out at me from his picture on the wall.

"Take care of my tía," I finally whisper beneath the sharp shush-ing of the maraca. "Whatever happens. And help me know what to do."

I press my forehead to the mat and stand, hug Tía Lucia, and trade cheek kisses with Aunt Miriam's chilly shroud. Then the doorbell rings and the first round of guests piles in with shrieks of excitement and even more food, and the party has begun in earnest.

⬤

The elder Madrigalerano Santeros arrive first, and they bring all kinds of delicious meats and seafood platters. They come with kisses and gossip, salutes and songs. They braved the hazardous streets to get here, and now they wonder in vivid whispers about the chilly silence that has come to rest in our little barrio, perhaps to stay, and what other curses these icy November winds will bring.

But mostly they pray. Each elder takes a turn on the mat, clang-ing a bell or shaking the maraca to accompany their words up to heaven with a sultry beat. The others touch fingers to the floor in a sign of respect, eyes closed, heads bowed. Holy Yoruba names of ancestors stream past amid exultations, gentle jokes, songs.

Then the door busts open, and Iya Lisa rolls in with a whole other crew, all in their fancy whites, carrying dessert trays wrapped in tinfoil and bags of treats. "You didn't think we'd miss this, did you, Mama Lucia?" Iya Lisa yells. She even brought Oba Nelson, a high priest and renowned diviner from the Bronx who only shows up on special occasions—he's from the Cuban branch of Santería, not the Madrigal one, and with him is a whole entourage of tough-looking priests all dressed in white. Our little apartment is suddenly so full, bursting at the seams with love and laughter, and it feels like a hot bath after so much separation and silence.

I peer out into the hallway as the parade of smiling revelers streams past. The *clank* of a cane sounds from the stairwell, and then

Tams's smiling face appears with Baba Johnny Afrá at her side. I'm so happy she's okay. We've been texting, and she knows how to take care of herself, but still . . . danger lurks everywhere these days.

She glances behind her and yells, "You comin'?" and for a second, my heart races into overdrive, imagining that Chela has joined them. But no—of course not. It's Maza, who is wearing a nice white suit and brought some kind of fried-dough treat.

"Welcome to chaos." I smirk as Tams and I hug. Johnny Afrá punches my shoulder with a playful wink, Maza and I trade a dap, and then we're all inside. The place is full of laughter and the delicious smells of many different cuisines, and of course, someone brought a conga, and someone else a guitar, and soon music swirls around us.

Tía Lucia soaks it all in with a forever smile plastered across her face. She's right at home, surrounded by the love of her people, enshrined in her seat of power. Iya Matilde belts out a high-pitched ode to Shango's prowess, mostly in Lucumí, and the whole room raises their voices to answer her call, a wild and raucous chorus.

It's only now, as I'm belting out the Shango song with everyone else at the top of my lungs—possibly butchering the pronunciation—that I realize I'm not anxious. I'm not hiding in the corner, not consumed by a hundred versions of the terrible things people are probably saying or thinking about me.

A week ago, I stood up in front of everyone in my world, and the person I once admired most tried to tear me down. And all those people—all *these* people, the ones around me now—they wouldn't let him. They've always been here, really, even when I was in my own head, even when I was imagining the worst about them and what they thought of me.

A whole new threat has arisen; there's a new truth to be reckoned with; there's so much work to be done to deal with our past and our future. But, finally, I don't feel like I'm all alone in the world.

Our voices rise and rise in the night, an absolute middle finger to the past week of crushing silence. Just when I think someone's about to pass a spirit, the door opens again and everyone goes "Oh!" Rabbi Hidalgo and Tolo walk in, arm in arm, with huge smiles and a whole gang of pirates and Sefaradim in their wake.

This time I know enough not to expect Chela to be with them, but I look for her, anyway. Now the apartment is so thick with folks it might burst, and everyone is carrying on like the snow outside isn't spiraling toward streets full of dread. Somehow we've warded off the foul stench of silence, if just for this moment.

Rabbi Hidalgo nods at the altar—which, though small, is quite an edgy statement, given his practice and status. Then Tolo shocks everyone by dropping into a full on-the-ground salute, picking up the maraca and rasping out a few shaky lines of Lucumí before wishing long life and eternal happiness to Tía Lucia. His father was a Santero, I remember—it's just that everyone focuses on the pirate stuff. He stands, embraces my tía, and turns to find all of our bewildered, wide-open faces staring back. We want answers. And action. Some sense of what we can do. I feel it move through the room, through me, that hunger.

Tolo takes a breath and looks like he's about to speak, but instead Mama Korinna hits an audacious, jangly flamenco chord on her guitar and Tolo laughs. Then, once again stunning the rowdy room into silence, he sings.

His voice sounds a thousand years old. It's a deep baritone tinged with a charred growl, and when he launches into an ancient Ladino lamentation for a lost homeland, I think we all feel it in the depths of who we are.

I had no idea the man could sing. I don't think any of us did— even Rabbi Hidalgo looks caught off guard.

I just close my eyes and let the sound and the story move through me. Then something seems to shift in the air ever so slightly. I feel the shuffle of bodies turning, hear quiet expressions of surprise beneath those dancing chords and Tolo's barbed-wire voice.

When I open my eyes, Chela Hidalgo stands in the far corner of the room, staring right at me.

CHAPTER THIRTY-SIX

CHELA ALL IN WHITE IS A REVELATION. HER BROWN SKIN SEEMS TO glow against the contours of the lace-lined blouse and flowy skirt. A single strand of reddish hair dangles down over her face, but the rest is pressed under a white headwrap that she's wound into a tight bun in the back.

"Okanla," the whole world whispers with a mix of awe and fear. Chela strolls—or maybe floats—through the crowded room as Mama Korinna keeps strumming away on that flamenco riff, and no one's really sure what to do, what's about to happen.

When she reaches Tía Lucia and all the well-dressed santos, Chela crosses her arms over her chest and lowers her head, eyes closed, at the altar. Tía Lucia just stares at her for a moment, then embraces her with whispered prayers.

Everyone watches, wide-eyed.

Chela turns to face the room. "I don't like speeches," she says with a slight, self-effacing smirk. "And my apologies to the Iyalocha for taking center stage at her celebration."

Tía Lucia waves at her to keep going.

"I know some of you gathered here aren't even technically part of the San Madrigal diaspora, but—"

"We are tonight!" someone yells—Oba Nelson, I think. And everyone laughs and agrees.

"We know what's going on," another Santero says. "These creatures you face, and the ongoing infiltration of empire pirates. Tams filled us in. And we ain't with it."

Chela smiles for real now—it's something like a sunrise—and nods in acknowledgment. "Good. Because our community is under attack from the inside, and what happens next will determine the course of our history and that of a great many others as well. Our enemy is not just a few corrupt pirates but the entire legacy of empire, conquest, slavery, and inquisition that has lurked among us all along. This is not just about Little Madrigal, or San Madrigal, or whether an island is raised or who does it—it's about the future and past, who we've been and who we choose to be now." She looks up, her dark eyes panning the room like slow searchlights. "All of us."

Murmurs of agreement—"Aché" and "Eso es"—ring out.

Chela holds up the little book we stole. "Our enemy worships a strange divinity." And my heart, which has been tapping in triple time since she appeared, suddenly sinks into my stomach. There's only one male deity of San Madrigal, and I am his only initiate. Do those pages hold his name? "They have worshiped it in hiding for more than a century. They formed an entire secret cult right beneath the skin of our society and moved quietly all along, consolidating power, forming alliances with slavers and predators and warmongers, while we celebrated our independence and sang songs of freedom."

Anger rises all around, and fear churns within me. The thought I've been having on and off all week returns: Is Galanika the secret god of these fiends? Am I the sworn adherent of my own enemy?

"We don't know the name of this demon they worship," Chela says, and I exhale ever so slightly. "And we don't know how to destroy it, how to make it bleed. Not yet. But the bambarúto that stalk our streets are its messengers, and they do bleed. They *I* will handle. And the people who brought this curse of demons to our homes— they are but flesh and blood, and flesh can be rended, blood spilled. Even kings fall."

Shouts now, the room whirled into an excited frenzy.

"Councilwoman Bisconte and Maestro Gerval are holed up with their supporters at the recording studio. Earlier today, they attacked my father and beat him unconscious—he's only still with us because we have a healer on our side." She shoots me the slightest smile as everyone turns and nods approvingly in my direction.

I want to disappear into the floor. Just let me hide and play music.

"Tomorrow morning," Chela says, snapping their attention back to her, "my cousin rolls out from his stronghold for a raid on theirs. I ask that you join us in any way you are able, so that we can rid this place of our tormentors and thrive together."

"We are with you!" someone yells.

"¡Siempre!"

Baba Johnny appears out of the crowd and stands beside Chela. "As the eldest priest in the borough," he says, nodding proudly and wrapping his hand around hers, "I can say that the Santeros of Brooklyn stand with you and the people of San Madrigal, Okanla."

Oba Nelson, the high priest, makes his way forward, his face grave. "I speak for the Bronx Santeros," he says solemnly. "We have long cherished our friendship with Iyalocha Lucia and the Galerano Santeros. Even if"—he pauses, squints at the distance—"her pasteles will never be as good as mine!" Everybody groans as Oba Nelson lets out an extended cackle. "No, no pero en serio: ¡los Santeros del Bronx estamos contigo!"

Everybody cheers.

"We can't all fight. Some of us are old, even if we don't look it." He winks, chuckling at his own joke, then gets serious again. "But others are not so old, and they are ready. The Bronx and Brooklyn Santeros stand at your side. And those who can't fight will support you in other ways. With pasteles, perhaps. You can count on us, m'ija."

Another celebratory cry goes up, then it quickly becomes excited chatter—planning, imagining, preparing. Chela looks up at her cousin; they trade a nod, and then she settles her eyes on me.

I feel like my face is on fire, but inside, it's still all icicles and the cool zephyr of death.

She moves through the crowd, exchanging cordial, one-word greetings, and then stands in front of me. "Can we talk somewhere alone?"

CHAPTER THIRTY-SEVEN

TECHNICALLY, YOU'RE NOT SUPPOSED TO GO ONTO THE ROOFTOP OF Tía Lucia's building.

There's a sign on the access door to let you know in no uncertain terms that opening it will set off fire alarms, alert cops, etc., etc.

Lies, all of them. Like, c'mon, man: this is Little Madrigal, not Manhattan. Anyway, the sign has been graffitied over time and time again by now.

I shove the big metallic handle and step out into the winter night; Chela stands beside me, and we take in the cloudy sky, the city a sparkling constellation around us.

There are so many things I want to say, to ask, but they all gridlock with each other on the way from my brain to my mouth, and none come out.

"I, um, missed you," I finally manage. It's a vast understatement. *I've been walking around with your ghost for a week,* I really mean. *Your smile is a sunrise. I am wide open to you. I am yours, Chela. I would burn down the world for you.* But I'm trying to take things step by step. "And I was worried about you."

She nods, her eyebrows knitted beneath the headwrap, mouth a tight frown.

"What is it?"

"I . . ." Chela looks up at me. "No, it's that . . ." She sighs, flails her hands around a few times. "I don't know how to do this."

"Do what?"

"Any of it," she growls, but it's the world her ferocity is pointed at, not me. Then she softens. "Sorry, I . . ."

"You gave a hell of a speech," I say. "Miss I-Hate-Giving-Speeches-But."

That at least gets a half smile out of her. "I do! And anyway . . ." She takes in a breath, and then, in the most grating, mock-autotuned voice possible, belts out, *"She's ooooour deeeeestroyer!"*

"Noooo," I groan, face in hands, but I'm laughing, and so is she now, and we're just two kids, really. Maybe one's an angel of devastation and the other a healer with a hidden shard of death, but still . . . all of it is suddenly smaller than this moment.

Our laughter fades, and for a few minutes, we just stare out at the city lights sprinkled across the darkness.

"I missed you, too, Mateo." Just a whisper, and it ends in that way that people speak when there's more to be said.

"But?"

"No buts. Just—what I didn't say downstairs, I still don't know how to say."

"Try me," I say. "I'm a good listener."

She holds up the ancient notebook. "All week, I've pored over this thing more times than I can count. A lot of it still doesn't make any damn sense to me, but . . ."

She trails off. I wait. We're facing each other, and it's a brisk night, and everything is terrible, but there's nowhere I'd rather be.

"I think something they're right about . . . is that for the island to rise, I have to die."

"*Die?*" I demand, startling even myself. "No. Absolutely not."

"Mateo, just listen. . . . I'm trying to understand it still, and yes, it's all weird translations of things, but over and over, there's the refrain of *The destruction of that which destroyed shall cause the ruins to rise*, in some form or another. And then there's the letters your aunt dropped that made them initiate us, and . . ." She shakes her head, tears suddenly spilling down her face. "I don't know. They certainly think it. That's why Gerval and Bisconte keep trying to get people to bring me to them—so they can figure it out for sure and sacrifice me to bring back San Madrigal."

"But . . . but . . ."

"You can't just argue with it because you don't want it to be true," she says before I can even try. "Maybe it's just what it is."

"Then *live*," I plead. "You're more important than the stupid island! It's a rock underwater—it's gone! We have a life here. *You* have a life here."

"They'll never stop, Mateo. It's bigger than all of us. They've been planning this for centuries, and they will never ever stop."

"Then we stop *them*. We have you on our side, and—"

"It's not just Gerval and Bisconte, it's the bambarúto, too, and whatever god these empire pirates worship. It's—"

"Galanika?" I ask before I can stop myself. "Is that who it is?"

She stares at me. Then: "I don't know. They never name him. Or it. Does it matter?"

"Of course it matters! I . . . want to know what's being done in the name of a spirit whose powers I'm using."

"Would it change what side you're on if it was?"

"No," I say. "Never. And . . . that night—"

She holds up a hand. "No need to explain. It's okay. You went to tell Gerval no. You didn't realize how devious he could be."

"I just—"

"Don't make me do the autotune again, Mateo. I saw your

speech online. I know who you are." The night seems so quiet suddenly. Everything holds perfectly still. "I know who you are," she says again.

"Who am I, Chela?"

"Mateo Matisse," she whispers through her sad smile. "Healer." Then she reaches her face up to mine and our lips touch, then our teeth—ouch—then just our lips again, and I pull her closer.

It's like coming home. For once, I let go of all thoughts about music and our churning history, and I give over to the pure bliss of Chela Hidalgo's mouth against mine.

"Mmm," she says a couple minutes later when we come up for air, still holding each other tight, panting breaths of steam up into the dark sky. "Thank you . . . for everything."

"I didn't do—"

"You saved my father."

"Ah, I just—"

"Shh."

I do what I'm told, and we look at each other, and our rising breath, and the blinking lights, and the impossible night. "I don't want you to die," I say.

"I don't want to die," she says.

"We have to find another way."

A noncommittal shrug, and then she looks at me. "Can I stay here tonight, do you think?"

"Of course."

"I don't want to be alone."

"Of course."

"But can we just stay right here for a while, and just be?"

"Of course."

And we do.

CHAPTER THIRTY-EIGHT

BACK IN THE APARTMENT, WE'RE GREETED LIKE RETURNING HEROES, thankfully without any corny winking or nudging about how we went off together.

Tía Lucia is in rare form, going back and forth with Iya Lisa about some bembé years ago with a running commentary from Oba Nelson as everyone else looks on and laughs. Baba Johnny nods his old head and enjoys the show while Tams keeps time on the clave.

You'd never know Tía Lucia's days are numbered.

Maybe they're not.

Slowly, with hugs and whispered blessings, the crowd disperses into the night, until it's just a small crew of us—Tía Lucia sitting happily beside her well-dressed santos with Aunt Miriam, Rabbi Hidalgo, and Tolo, while Tams, Maza, Chela, and I clean up and do the dishes.

"What's wrong?" Tía Lucia prods, poking Tolo. "So solemn. It's still a party, you know."

"Mmm, I was born with this face," he says, cracking a rare smile. "But also, we have a lot to think about, a lot to prepare."

In a way, it's a Cabildo meeting, I realize. Tolo may have had his title unceremoniously snatched from him by that coup, but in most people's hearts, he's the true pirate king.

Rabbi Hidalgo leans forward, elbows on his knees, and nods. "My nephew is right. We won't sully your celebration with our planning, but we must meet. And soon."

Tía Lucia shrugs. "My celebration is unsulliable. We may plan as needed. But it's not just the future we need to talk about." She nods to where Chela, Tams, and I are clearing some paper cups and plates. "These jóvenes told us something about who we really are last week. We can't pretend it didn't happen, or that it doesn't matter. We must face the ugly truth about ourselves head-on."

"Agreed," Rabbi Hidalgo says. "I've barely slept since, to tell you the truth."

Tía Lucia laughs. "What is this thing you speak of, *sleep*?"

"Heh," the rabbi chortles, but his smile is slight, sad. "The truth is what we needed, though. A tremendous gift, even if it's a painful one. And clearly, everything is at stake."

Tolo lets out a raspy sigh. "I wish I'd been more surprised. Can't say I knew all that, but I always suspected something was up. And there's still so much we don't know. Either way, you're absolutely right, Iya Lucia. Whatever happens next will hinge on how well we deal with what's been hidden all along."

Soon, the talking dwindles, and Rabbi Hidalgo and Tolo say their goodbyes. Chela tells them she's sticking around to finish the cleanup with us, and everyone hugs and then it's just the few of us, and the vibe is gentle, a meandering song, as we let the hell of this past week seep away.

This is how these events are supposed to go, but this is also the part when usually my parents would be here on cleanup duty with us, and for the first time in a while, I miss them.

How different would all this feel if I had the guidance of Mom or Dad, their ear to confide in?

Truth is, I'm not sure.

They respect all of Lucia's spirit stuff, but it's just that to them—stuff. Stuff for an academic debate, something to be considered and regarded carefully, from a distance. Rare quality for a Galerano. Must be why they fell in love.

I wonder what they would say about the past week, the bambarúto, Chela.

Chela.

I watch her laughing with Tams as they walk around picking up plastic cups and emptying ashtrays. She slipped into the bathroom earlier to change out of her nice whites for the cleanup, came out in some blue flowy pants and a halter top. I can't tell if there's actually an ethereal glow to her or that's just my own besotted brain coloring everything I see. How can she be so real and down-to-earth, and something so ancient and powerful, all at the same time?

How can I explain to her all the feelings I have? Half of it feels like some ridiculous teenage crush, half of it feels much huger, a thing outside of time.

"You all right?" Maza asks, watching me watch them. They pause their sweeping and follow my gaze.

I shake my head. "Yeah . . . I dunno. Nothing makes sense."

"We'd be bored if it did."

"I guess. I could use a little boredom these days, to be honest."

Tams dumps a seashell full of cigar ash into the trash and slides over to us with a half pirouette. "You ready to head out, mi amor?"

I snort. "Oh, it's *amor* now? All right, hot steppers!"

"It's been a week." She shrugs, looking more bashful than usual.

Maza rolls their eyes. "A week! Let's not pretend you weren't calling me *mi amor* twenty-four hours into everyone going on lock-down, okay, mi amor?"

"Wow, spicy," Chela calls from the kitchen.

"¿De qué están hablando, jóvenes?" Tía Lucia asks idly.

I wave her off. "Nada, Tía, boberías. Go back to hanging out with the santos."

"Ay, mi vida," she croons. "¡No hay nada bobo sobre el amor!"

"What did she say?" Tams asks, reaching her hand out to Maza with a single dashing eyebrow raised.

"There's nothing silly about love," Maza says, swinging their now-I-guess-girlfriend into a wild tango and then dipping her so low the metal jewelry in her hair clacks against the tile floor. "And yes, let's make tracks. Sounds like tomorrow gonna be a *day*."

Tía Lucia brings them each a plastic bag full of fruit for good luck and thanks them for coming, and Farts and I walk them to the door. Then they're gone, and Tía is already getting ready for bed and pointedly ignoring the fact that Chela's still here, which I appreciate more than words can say.

Soon the floors are mopped and the dishes done, and most of the lights are out, and it's just me and Chela standing in the dim glow of the altar candles.

Pffttttt!!

And Farts.

"Go to your mommies," I chide while Chela cackles. "¡Acuéstate, ya!"

Farts rambles off, sulking, and Chela is still laughing, and then we're face-to-face and very close together. I don't know who stepped toward who first—we just gave in to the invisible pull that's been yanking us closer and closer for the past few hours, our separateness a grating tension that wouldn't resolve until we finally touched, and so we do. The back of my hand curls inside her open palm, and she closes her fingers around mine and tugs me ever so gently.

I wrap myself around her, feel her breath match mine, and we lower ourselves onto the couch. She curls up against my chest and whispers, "Just hold me?"

"Of course," I say.

She pulls my arm around her and slowly, slowly, runs her fingertips along my jawline and neck as we both slip off into sleep.

CHAPTER THIRTY-NINE

Laughter lures the two of us from this darkest part of the myrrh forest.

We move in a slow, fluid glide through the underbrush, stirring gently against the edges of leaves and sticks, sometimes merging with each other, other times far apart, just flickering shrouds in the mangrove shadows.

Emerge at the edge of the trees, where rocks descend in an embankment to a small tide pool.

There, two brown bodies splash, yell, release howls of long pent-up love and rage and then lie out in the grass, letting the sun kiss their flesh as their limbs and then torsos find each other, tangle, become one loving, sweating, cursing masterpiece.

Shy, we retreat at first, but our curiosity pulls us back and soon they sense us. One stands, his skin glistening with the smooth afternoon glow. He walks over to us and holds out a hand, a smile stretched across his beautiful face. The other human draws near, eyes wide, blinking through his disbelief.

Side by side they face us, and then both reach out.

They know.

They don't have a language for us; we bear no names, not yet. But they know what we are, and they know what they can offer.

Between us, a tiny consultation.

We writhe with the knowledge of what this means.

We have been this for so long—centuries, in flesh-and-blood time.

We have not been flesh, held flesh, known the touching of bodies, in so long. And never with one another.

We have loved in so many ways, but never like this.

A new love.

A new language.

It calls us. Since we came to rest here, amid all this, it calls us.

Now, matching the two outstretched hands with long, trembling reaches of our own, we answer.

———•———

I wake up with the hunger of a hundred years inside me.

Chela's awake, too, and by her face, I know she saw what I did, the dream was birthed between us somehow, and it still hangs there, filling the dark room with its steaming, aching presence.

I take her face in my hands as she slides up higher on me, and though the winter howls through the empty streets outside, this moment fills us with warmth, the feeling of so much loss healed, the sense of so long alone suddenly undone, and finally, finally, we fall fully into each other and release.

———•———

"There's something different about you," she says as we lie face-to-face on the couch, breathing each other's breath, limbs a tangle.

"Is that your version of the thing guys usually say?" I make my voice all low and sleazy. *"You're not like other girls."*

She laughs, pulling herself closer to me, and it's the best feeling, the *only* feeling—making her laugh, the touch of her skin on mine. But also, I know what she means. Deep down, the ice within me gathers and bristles, bracing for what's coming next.

"No, Romeo. I mean, yes, guys say that to me plenty, but that's not what I mean."

"To be fair," I say, drawing out the moment, only prolonging the inevitable, "they're not wrong, in your case."

She rolls her eyes. "Whatever. That's not the point."

We get quiet, because she knows that there's something to be said now, something I haven't told anyone yet. Of course she can see it, even if she doesn't fully know what it is.

"Earlier today, with your dad . . ." I say. "That's not all that happened."

I tell her each moment and how it felt: my rising fear when I laid my hands on Tantor Batalán, and then the relief at finally getting at least a fleeting glance of certainty about what had to be done. I tell her about Arco. That I killed him, and I couldn't bring him back. I flinched when maybe I could've. And yes, I am changed from it, from all that and this whole week of slow-motion tragedy and silence.

When I'm done, I close my eyes because I know she's putting the pieces together, and I know what's coming next.

"Man, you're better than me," she says, and I have to laugh—that's not what I was expecting. "I probably wouldn't have even tried to save Arco. But it was my dad he knocked out," she amends, "so it's a little different."

A moment passes, and then: "So, you can defeat death, Mateo."

I shake my head. "I don't know if it would work on you, Chela. I don't . . . I don't want to try. I hate it. I hate all of it."

"I don't know what other choice we have."

I push myself up on my elbows; she rests her head on her arms, which are splayed over the back of the couch, maddeningly calm. "You could run. *We* could run. Leave and never look back. It sucks, but it's better than—"

She shakes her head. "You know that's not real for us. Well, I know it's not real for *me*. Our families, our people—they're part of who we are. We can't just cut loose like that and, what, never see them again? Never talk to them? No. And anyway, you don't think they'd be in the bull's-eye the second we're in the wind?"

My aunt already is in the bull's-eye, somehow, but I keep that to myself. And anyway, everyone is, these days. "I don't know. . . ."

"But you did it already. You stole death from some rando in the street. I'm . . . me. Of course it'll work."

"There is no *of course*, Chela. We don't even totally know what you are. Do you?"

For a second, she almost looks hurt, but then she relents. Shrugs. "I'm sure there's a lot of names for it. Doesn't really matter which you choose, does it? I'm not human, not exactly."

"Your dad says you're an angel," I say, halfway smirking.

She slides her mouth to one side, eyes narrow. "Of *course* he does. He's my dad."

"I'm resisting saying something really cheesy right now, and I want credit."

"That's not the point," she growls. "The point isn't what some humans decided to call me or whatever."

"Is it like in the dream? You saw that, right? The two guys? Is it possession?"

She shakes her head. "I saw it, but no. That was . . . temporary, whatever that was. This is . . . This is who I am. Okanla isn't living in Chela's body. Chela's body *is* Okanla's body. There isn't a place where the human ends and the spirit begins. It's one. I'm one. The only way I can describe it is . . . it's like I . . . I traveled a long way, waited a long time to get to this moment, to come fully into flesh-and-blood existence in this body. The ceremony clinched it. I'm sure they were just going through the motions of the initiation ritual. But something they did lit up the deeper spirit within me. My dad told me about this notion the old hakhams had called *ibur*—the idea that an older being's soul is embedded in a living person, and it's there to help us live our destinies. I don't know if it's that— I don't think there's a place where Chela ends and Okanla begins, we're just one. It was always true, and it became truer the night of the fete, when I took out Trucks. My awakening." She pauses, eyes distant. "But either way, maybe I, we, that union or whatever it is, was just supposed to last for these sixteen years and that's that."

"No!" I say, throwing into it all the hardheadedness I can muster.

"It's not up to you," she says, putting her forehead against mine.

"Do you remember it?" I ask. "Your ceremony? The storm?"

"Just . . . No, not really. It's like . . . the memory is behind a foggy glass door, and I can only kinda see it. I don't really understand it."

I lie back down. "Chela."

"Hmm?"

"What if I can't . . . ?"

For a long time, we just lie there wrapped in each other, our breathing synchronized, our hearts beating as one.

CHAPTER FORTY

It's still dark out when we rise and get ready.

I slip into Tía Lucia's bedroom, find her at the edge of her bed, rubbing her eyes.

"You're not coming. Get back into bed."

"Ay, pero, Mateo . . ." she starts, but I can tell I'm going to win this one.

"Lie down," I order, imperious, ridiculous. "I know you've made peace with it or whatever, but that doesn't mean you can just go running into danger all reckless."

He's right, Aunt Miriam says, floating out of the shadows. *Stay.*

"Aunt Miriam, you're on guard duty. Keep her here."

I take Tía Lucia's warm shoulders and ease her back down onto her pillow. She blinks up at me. Without makeup, she is like a whole other person; it's such a rare sight. Her features seem laid out across her face in a different pattern, and she looks disarmed somehow. "Ten cuidado," she says sternly. "Te quiero."

"I will." I kiss her forehead. "Te quiero, Tía."

I rise, blow a kiss to Aunt Miriam. "Love you, Auntie." Pat the lump nestled under the covers. "Later, Farts."

⎯⎯◆⎯⎯

The day breaks with a pale, crisp sunrise as we slide gingerly from backstreet to backstreet to Tolo's. Chela has changed into all-black everything—ripped jeans and a leather jacket over a hoodie, properly goth for once. Her hair swirls down in ringlets from under a knit hat.

"I assume you're going to tell me some plan that I'm going to hate, right?"

She smiles slyly without looking at me. "I figured we'd improvise."

"Absolutely not! How are you so cavalier about this, Chela? It's your life!"

She rolls her eyes. "It's a coping mechanism, Mateo, déjame en paz."

I exhale a groan, and we tread a few steps in silence.

"But what I figure," she says eventually, "is that I'll take down enough of those bambarúto to even things out a bit, and then give myself up, since I'm the one they really want, anyway. When they kill me or whatever, you and the crew will come in like *Pow! Shazam!* and knock some heads. After that you revive me, and—boom!— everyone's happy. The island will rise, the empire pirates can go about their merry way with their creature friends—the ones we let live, anyway—and we see what's what with the new San Madrigal. You know?"

"You really think that's how it'll go down?"

She laughs grimly. "Not at all. I just don't know any other way."

⎯⎯◆⎯⎯

We round the corner onto Fulton and stop.

The streets once again belong to us—for now, anyway. A huge

crowd has gathered outside Tolo's—way more people than were at our celebration last night. Santeros, Sefaradim, and pirates all stand at the ready in the intersection, bristling for action. I spot Tolo at the front, with Safiya at his side, and start to head that way.

"Wait," Chela says, grabbing my arm and pulling me back. She looks up at me for a few moments, and I'm content to savor the moment. "This is where we split."

"You're not—"

"This is where we split. I just want to say"—she scrunches up her nose, lets out a low growl—"be careful, Mateo. I'm personally requesting that you make it out of this alive, please. Now that I've finally found you, it would really suck if you died."

"I—"

"Shh. Just do as I ask. Everything goes more smoothly when that happens."

"Bu—" She kisses me full on the lips, and then she's gone.

Damn.

"¡Galeranos!" Tolo's cannonade voice booms out, silencing everyone. Then a cheer rises. "¡Varios amigos!" Another cheer. "¡A la lucha!"

And just like that, we're on the move, winding down Fulton like a vast, unstoppable river, and I'm making my way through the crowd.

"You ready to heal, Healer?" Safiya asks as I fall into step beside her and Tolo.

"I am." A week ago, I barely knew what that meant. Now it has become a part of me, awakened like a ghost limb that had been asleep all this time. And I can already feel the tendrils of whatever's ahead pulling at me. Certainly, there will be blood. This time I know I won't flinch, won't shrink from it.

Within me, death writhes, expands, bristles.

A mass of bodies march behind us, faces tense, fists clenched. Ready.

Right now, I feel like we could do anything; the world is at our backs.

"I don't like it," Tolo grunts as we flow along the curve of the street toward the recording studio.

I look around, then up at him. "What's wrong? The streets are empty."

"Exactly." He slows his pace, holds up a fist, and the river behind us grinds to a gradual halt.

"Big Moses has the club," Safiya says. "You left him plenty of backup. Don't get jittery on me now, Tolo."

He shakes his huge head, squints at the studio. "Not jitters. Something's wrong." He glances to either side. "*No* resistance at all? None? Not bambarúto, not human, nothing? Uh-uh. Call Moses."

"I already am," Safiya snaps. "He's not—"

Even standing a few feet away from the phone, I can hear the screaming.

"Back!" Tolo booms, already shoving his way through the crowd. "Back to the club!"

And then the street becomes a frantic dash of stomping feet, shoving bodies.

"We form up at the rear entrance!" Safiya is yelling.

A strange shimmering light unfolds out of thin air before me; no one else seems to notice.

"Jackaby, take your team through the tunnels," Safiya continues. "Bakadon, take the front! Trajón, peel off! Peel off! Side streets! Go!"

And then the world slows, grows quiet, because the shimmering light has become a figure. Bodies rush past on either side, urgent to heed the call of war, but I stand perfectly still, taking in the spirit that writhes in the air above me. Tears stream down my face. The icicles within me tighten, then shatter.

Tía Lucia.

The apartment door's been kicked in.

A thousand booming choruses of *No!* thunder through me.

This can't be real. It must be a dream. A hallucination.

But it's none of that.

The door's been kicked in, the place is a disaster: our coffee table shattered, chairs overturned, the couch—the couch I was sleeping on with Chela just a few hours ago—shredded. It's so quiet, when it should be filled with chatter and excitement, music. All I hear is a quiet *splish*ing sound from somewhere farther in. And the place is too bright. They pulled down all the curtains and blinds, the day pours in like a headache. There's nowhere to hide, no ignoring the devastation they've wreaked.

Also, there's a body on the ground.

It's definitely not Tía Lucia.

I hadn't noticed it at first—the place is such a mess, and most of the man's pale skin is buried under books and papers from a knocked-over shelf. But his boot is sticking out and, as I walk closer, there's his face, eyes wide, mouth open. I don't know who it is. A letter opener pokes out of his neck, and the floor around him is stained crimson all the way to the kitchen doorway, where Farts sits lapping it up.

She's gone, Aunt Miriam wails from the corner. She's barely there, just a flicker. *They killed her. They took her.*

"What . . . What happened?" I demand, my voice hoarse with tears.

Aunt Miriam shakes her head. *They busted through the door*, she sobs. *Demanded she come with them. She said, "You'll have to kill me," and they said they would. So she stabbed one and the other hit her on the head with his club. . . . Dragged her out.*

"Where is she?"

Doesn't matter. It's too late. She knew this was coming. It's not her you have to find, Mateo. Do what you have to do. Miriam's almost gone now. It really had been Tía Lucia keeping her here all this time. *We love you, Mateo,* both their voices say from the emptiness. *We love you.*

"I . . ." The rest comes out as a sob. I'm on the floor; broken glass digs into my knees. Glass from a picture frame. I look up. The altar is in shambles. They murdered her and destroyed her altar.

I crawl forward, choking on my own mucus and tears.

The picture of Galanika slid out of the frame when it shattered. Did they do this in his name, the name of my father spirit? It doesn't matter anymore. It's done. I still am who I am, and I'll do what I have to do, but . . . I lift the picture with a trembling hand. Galanika stares at me with that cool glare, stern and unbothered, his back straight, shoulders wide.

I turn it around—maybe there'll be an inscription on the back, or . . . I find a whole other picture.

Galanika, the same Galanika, but now a raging demon, carousing across a fiery landscape, mouth stretched wide. Death and destruction pour from his fingertips as entire nations race to escape his wrath.

Galanika.

I feel something poke my chest and pull the chai pendant out of my shirt. I'd forgotten about it—so much has happened since Rabbi Hidalgo gifted it to me.

The cemetery, *betahayim.* Beit Achayim. House of . . . That's the word on my pendant: Life. The cemetery is a house of life.

The end moves within the beginning.

One thing creates the world.

I stand, brush broken glass off my jeans. Death churns within me, ready.

One thing destroys it.

I know what I have to do.

PART
FIVE

V.

Ocean crashes on these rocky shores,

Stains crumbling facades,

Sends that salty smell through white-curtained windows into wide-open
rooms where lovers sleep.

Through the night we released these truths into our small world, each
other:

Even when war is constant, peace lives in every moment.

Each of us is a tortoise; we carry our home, and our home carries us.

That sliver of moon across the skin of your back holds all the power of a
thousand armies.

———•———

Tomorrow we awake and set fire to the world.

—*The Adventurous Night*, Zolman Armal

CHAPTER FORTY-ONE

I KNOW WHAT I HAVE TO DO, BUT I'M NOT SURE HOW TO DO IT YET, and grief keeps devouring me whole and spitting me back out every couple steps.

The sun has made an appearance, which seems absurd, because the world is still covered in snow and everything is terrible.

I round the corner onto Fulton, hoping to find someone, anyone, to hurt, to break, because maybe somehow that will release this sorrow from me. But it won't, of course, and I know that, too. Still . . .

The streets are empty, but I hear yelling, glass smashing somewhere up ahead. The tense calm has finally shattered, and I must find out where.

I pass the shuttered storefronts of Dal Pilay's instrument shop, Safiya the Butcher, Mira's Café, and a tinkling melody begins to turn shy pirouettes within me.

All I feel is rage, though—rage and a sadness so sudden and vast the only thing I can compare it to is the death that I yanked away from Tantor Batalán.

All this past week, I've wondered what it would feel like to lose

Tía Lucia. I imagined it carving a Lucia-shaped hole in my heart. Instead, it has hollowed me out entirely, shoved away everything but loss, the simple truth of knowing I'll never wake up to her making breakfast again. That's it: so simple, so huge.

And since she's been torn from me, I'll break the world.

Up ahead, people are massing around the intersection outside Tolo's. Chela will be there somewhere, and if ever I needed an angel of destruction by my side, it's now.

Except . . . she's got that plan.

I break into a run as the pieces fall together.

Chela thinks that if she gives herself up and lets them sacrifice her to bring back the island, I'll be able to show up and resurrect her.

I don't know if that's true or not—I don't know if any of it's true—but I have to stop her. I can't let her fall into their hands. No island, no *thing* is worth her dying, even if I might be able to save her. They won't take her from me. Not her, and not Tams or Maza—both of whom are probably somewhere in the fray, fighting for their lives.

"Eh, eh, eh," moans a middle-aged woman hobbling away from the crowd, clutching her arm.

I stop running and catch my breath. "I'm a healer," I say when she looks at me dubiously. It comes out without me even thinking about it. It's just true now. And so is this: "Hijo de Galanika."

She nods, allowing me to place a hand on her wounded shoulder. The tissue is already mending as her song rises in me. "What happened?"

The woman shakes her head. "Just chaos. The empire pirates set up a barricade in front of the club. I was with a group that charged them, but they flanked us somehow, and then it was just everyone for themselves and I got knocked over—I don't even know who did it! Whoa!" She gapes at me, extending her arm all the way. "Thank you!"

I'm already sprinting off toward the fight. "You're welcome! Get to safety!"

I have to find Chela before she gives herself up.

More wounded stragglers pass as I get closer. I heal the ones with obvious injuries and stash each sliver of brutality within me, preparing. And then I'm surrounded by angry shouts and clenched fists, and there's chatter about making another run at the barricade.

"Mateo! There you are!" Safiya yells, emerging from a group of Tolo's foot soldiers and various Santeros. "We've been looking all over for you! We have to get you to—"

"Over there!" someone hollers. "A runner!" And then the crowd shifts and seems to collapse sideways as folks chase down a tall, skinny guy who'd tried to dash from the barricade down a side street—probably carrying a message.

Safiya shakes her head, turns back to me. "These jackasses have been parked outside the club since the empire pirates overran it." She nods at the barricades: a pile of overturned cars, assorted trash, and a few tables from the club. From what I can make out, the crew on the other side is about three dozen strong. I recognize some folks from the community, sure, but mostly it looks like they rounded up a bunch of Manhattan-bar douches and offered them a moderate bag to start some trouble.

Meanwhile, we've got maybe half their numbers, but pound for pound, ours are fighters, and they look ready for combat. Still, it'll be messy whichever way it goes. And there's no telling how many more are inside.

"Why don't you go through the tunnels to get in?" I say, not too loudly, because they're still mostly a family secret, far as I know.

"Tolo and Chela took a team that way."

"She's still with him?" A glimmer of hope. Tolo won't let Chela give herself up easily, at least.

"Last I heard," Safiya says. "But I think they lost signal at some point. We haven't had word in a bit. Anyway, we'll go underground, too, if we have to, but whatever happens in there, it's gonna be messy, and we gotta clear these guys out of the way so they don't show up when we least want them to and turn the tide. Our eyes say the leadership has gathered on the roof of the club, so that's where we're headed, whether it's around or through. But I'd like to make things bad for them on the way, you know?"

Over by the crosswalk, some street medics from another Santero house treat a group of walking wounded—probably more casualties from when they attempted a direct charge.

I look at Safiya, feel something ferocious churn awake within me. "I say we go through."

Ten minutes later, the walking wounded are all healed and I'm strolling into the no-man's-land between the two encampments.

"Hey!" some guy yells, running up to stop me as I approach the barricade. "What're you—"

I windmill my arms once and release a world of hurt. I don't even have to make direct contact—just focus my attention and let loose. A concentrated blast of sheer pain and cartilage devastation catches the man right in the face, lays him out. Two more guys emerge from behind an overturned SUV, and I spin, unleashing as I go, flatten them both.

Tía Lucia had told me that intentionality was what mattered—in cleaning off, in spirit work. I wonder if she knew how much I would need those words right now. Well, my intention is super clear: damage, inflict it. All those injuries I just fixed are locked and loaded within me, ready to be unleashed.

"What's going on over there?" a woman calls, peering up from a table. More men rush toward me, ready to play hero and stop the intruder. But now it's too late—Safiya took advantage of their confusion and sent her people forward in a furious throng. They swarm over the barricades, and in seconds, the world around us becomes a circus of groans, thuds, smashing bottles, and breaking bones.

Up ahead, three girls I know from school are swinging bats at a tall guy in a rumpled suit, but he has a pickax, so they're trying to keep their distance. I walk through the chaos, one arm outstretched. When he sees me, I let the bristling agony of a fractured elbow sizzle from my fingertips. It's nothing anyone can see—just particles of energy moving through air—but it's a direct hit on his left eye, and boy, does he feel it. Immediately, the dude is doubled over in pain, and then one of the girls drops him with a swing of the bat and we all keep it moving.

Momentum has been on our side from the beginning, and pretty soon the empire pirates and their hired thugs are in full retreat, running in different directions, screaming over their headsets to each other for backup, etc.

And then Safiya is next to me, and we duck into a tunnel, the whole surly, triumphant battalion of Santeros, Sefaradim, pirates, and assorted randoms behind us. The passageway winds up, up, and around in a long, strange circle.

Then a familiar voice calls from the darkness ahead. "Speak or we destroy you!" Tolo demands.

"It's us, pacho," Safiya yells, laughing, arms raised. "And I've brought a friend."

Tolo emerges into the light. "Mateo?"

"Where's Chela?"

He shakes his big head. "I tried to slow her down, but . . ."

I'm already surging past him. "Where is she?"

"Whoa, whoa, whoa, papi, hold up, man!" Tolo's huge hand lands on my shoulder, but I won't be restrained. I'll find Chela. I'll end this mess once and for all. Nothing will stop me.

"Don't you want to see what she left behind for you?"

Okay, that stops me.

Safiya tells the others to hold where they are, and Tolo leads the two of us around a corner to a small open area where more of his crew awaits. "Bambarúto up ahead," he says gravely. "They already got a few of our people, even with Chela holding them off, and then . . ." Tolo looks away, face crinkled in fury, or perhaps sorrow. He shakes his head. "She swore this was the only way. Surrendered herself. Said *you*'d understand." An accusation.

"I do, a little," I admit. "But I don't agree with it. I'm . . . There's gotta be a better option."

"Well, she made me swear not to follow her. The main thrust of their forces is converging on our basement." He grimaces. "Seems they've breached the tunnels. So, I'm leading our troops down there to head them off, but you—you gotta go get Chela. That's what she told me you'd do. So, you better take this." He signals a woman named Nadia from his crew. "She said you'd need it." Nadia hands him something long and curved like a scimitar. The handle, which Tolo now holds out to me, is beaded like Chela's dagger.

"A sword?" I manage to get out, taking the weapon. The power of it thrums through me—it feels . . . alive. It's heavy, but not so much so that I can't get some good speed on it with one hand.

Tolo allows himself a slight smile. "She uses the little one for sneak attacks and whatnot. This one is for what we're in now: war." His face goes grim again. "Now go get my cousin. We'll work on clearing out the rest of these fools."

I nod and head through the crew of heavies up the ramp into the darkness, a whirlwind of pain and death swirling in one hand and the sword of a beautiful destroying angel in the other.

I think I love Chela Hidalgo.

Now I just have to make sure she doesn't die.

CHAPTER FORTY-TWO

I DON'T KNOW HOW ANY OF THIS WORKS, WHAT ANY OF THIS MEANS. The only way is forward.

My restless, terrified brain vomits up flashes of what might've, what must've, happened to Tía Lucia as I make my way through the dim tunnel. She's rising from the couch to see what the commotion is, now yelling, grappling with some strange man. Falling.

A scraping sound snaps me out of it, and then I throw myself against the wall, sword raised, because something's moving up ahead. Something tall.

Before I have time to adjust my stance or even take a breath, a bambarúto barrels out of the darkness. This one has no helmet—why should it bother?—and its spectral screaming mouth snaps shut inches from my face as I stumble backward, then swipe at it with the sword.

It's a messy swing, the result of my messy retreat, but the blade still slows and then splats to a stop, shredding the creature's hideous translucent face. The bambarúto rears with a shriek, and I hear other howls farther up the tunnel.

Great.

I pull the blade back for another swing, but this thing moves fast—faster than I thought possible—and it's on me before I can finish my windup, toppling both of us in a heap. The air leaves me, my chest crushed between this creature's bulky body armor and the ground, and then that slimy, too-many-teethed maw opens across the whole darkness, right in front of my face.

My sword hand is pinned, but I shove my left elbow into what I think is its throat, feel a chilly static where my skin meets its icky phantasmic flesh . . . and just manage to even annoy it, from what I can tell. It snaps at my face, and I barely hold it off, my forearm shoving against its neck. Then I summon up all the battering and breaks I've healed in the past hour, place my hand on the bambarúto's face, and release.

The creature rears again, stunned. My attack was enough to get it all the way off me, but . . . that much hurt would've crumpled a human. The bambarúto is already shaking off whatever weirdness it felt. Worse, two more are approaching behind it.

Human injuries don't translate to these creatures. Not enough, anyway.

Which means— I don't have time to figure out what that means, because it's charging me again. This time I'm ready, though. I catch its face with my upswing, cleaving off most of that ichorous snout, and . . . that does it. The bambarúto stops in its tracks, drops to its knees, and starts to fade.

I need the power of its demise, though! Just before it blips out of sight, with the next two enraged monsters just a few seconds from reaching me, I lean over and reach out with one hand—and feel the impossible chaos of molecules ceasing its vanishing swirl.

I am the last son of Galanika, and I will take my prize. The spinning galaxy of that felled bambarúto keeps trying to fade for good, but I hold it. Through sheer force of will, I hold it, and just as the next one races up, a void opens within me as I suck the first creature's very death from it and shove it right into the screaming face of the second bambarúto.

No hesitation.

The blast throws it back, and I spin, slicing off the third attacker's head and letting it disperse into nothingness, and then finish off the second one with a clean stab through the mouth.

And then I stand there, panting, surrounded by empty body armor. I'm covered in sweat but still alive. Up ahead, there's a glint of light that looks like daytime. I'm close.

I've meted out death and snatched it back. Delivered it again.

I take one shaky step, then another, find my stride, and then fall into a steady jog upward, upward, sword poised, hands ready— let's go.

I step onto the slim brick walkway surrounding the glass roof. Across from me, right in the center, is a concrete island. Chela is there, her head drooped. Vedo and Anisette stand on either side, holding her up by the arms. One bambarúto stands over Chela, its hand on the crown of her head. This creature is not translucent like the others—it's almost entirely flesh, with horrific spikes poking out all over its huge scaly body. And I realize the one I saw form in Tolo's basement hadn't had a chance to come into its own yet. They get so much worse. This one has long claws at the end of each spiny arm, and it's about nine feet tall, dripping with ichor, and breathing in long, hideous snarls as it grows and strengthens right before my eyes.

Behind them, Gerval looks on like a vaguely amused emperor. Another fully incarnated, huge bambarúto stands beside him, and a crowd of spectral ones wait nearby, getting ready to become flesh by feeding off Chela's powers.

I break into a run, sword raised, but the damn ghostly creatures see me coming and skitter to get between me and the concrete island. They're sloppy, though, and aren't wearing their body armor. My sword slices clean through the first one, and it's gone. I behead the second, snatch away its death to use on the third, then behead the second again. The fourth and fifth ones come at the same time, and I'm finishing them off when the fully formed one that was beside Gerval roars across the rooftop at me.

It shoves my blade away with one arm and cracks me across the face with the other. Everything is a bright light for a half second as I stumble back. More spectral bambarúto are closing in behind it, surrounding me, and I feel their icy claws scratching my arms, my neck.

I lash out with the sword, my head still thundering from the hit, and they flutter back some, but there's too many. I cut down one, another, and then I see a fully-flesh-and-blood claw swing down on me. I raise my blade to block, but it's too fast, and a sudden searing pain opens up across my face, my eye! My eye!

Then my knees hit the concrete. I hadn't realized I'd made it this far across the roof, but it barcly matters. Half my face is on fire from the bambarúto's claw. Everything around me dances with weird colors I can't make sense of. I'm bleeding from my face, and the creature is probably about to finish me off.

It can't end like this.

Escucha.

I don't know if it's really Tía's voice, her spirit, saying her favorite word, or just the memory of it.

Doesn't matter. She's right.

Go deeper.

I'm trying, Tía. I don't know how.

Escucha.

Everything's moving very fast but so slowly at the same time.

And then the world gets dead quiet, and all I hear is Chela's voice cutting through all the dampened chaos, all the pain.

She says my name.

No. That's not it.

"Galanika!" is what she says, and when I look up from my bloody heap, I see why. The shimmering bearded spirit is kneeling in front of me, and everything—the spinning sky, the horde of bambarúto, the whole world—seems to slow as our eyes meet.

Escucha.

As our eyes meet.

Go deeper.

As my eyes—one blinking, wide open, the other slashed and bleeding—lock with his: one blinking, wide open, the other scarred and milky.

"Galanika," I whisper. My name. My own name all along. I rise to a squat, bring myself face-to-face with him. Above us, the incarnated monster swings its arm back in slow motion for the killing blow. But it doesn't matter.

I know my name.

I know myself.

Galanika the ancient spirit rises, and I rise to meet him. We merge, become what we've always been, what we'd been yearning for all along, what the gravity of this broken world has tilted and slid us toward since the day of my birth, my initiation, and the fall of the island, the night of the Grande Fete: one.

Escucha.

A song opens up inside me. Galanika's song. A tune from long ago, far away. *Awaken, my Galanika.* The world spins back to speed as I swing Okanla's sword in a vicious upward arc. *The dawn approaches.* Slice through scale, muscle, tendon, bone. Black blood sprays; the bambarúto bellows, then falls.

Awaken.

Now I am awake.

Strange, trembling colors still dance across my vision, but I can see clearly enough to meet Gerval's frenzied snarl. He barrels toward me, and I launch across the rooftop to meet him, my whole body singing with this long-awaited moment: Galanika lives, incarnated and awake at last. He, I, we have waited centuries to be born into a full flesh-and-blood body, and then another sixteen years for that truth to be revealed.

And now I will not be stopped.

Awaken, my Galanika!

I swat away Gerval's flailing attack and shove my hand into his face as Tantor Batalán's death surges along my arm, out from my palm, and directly into the open mouth of the man I used to call my hero. He flies backward from the sheer force of it, eyes wide, smashes straight through the skylight, and plummets in a shimmering hail of glass.

Everything stops. The hugeness of what just happened seems to stretch like a shadow at dawn across all the fighters and creatures on the rooftop.

Who knows what stories will be told about this moment—what myths and lies and songs will spring up. I will be a hero and villain, I'm sure, but right now, none of that matters.

Right now, I know I did what I had to do.

This death feels different.

Arco's threat was a contained one. I didn't mean to kill him, and if I'd taken a different approach somehow, he might still be alive.

Gerval's murderous wrath still extends around us, even with him gone.

I barely have time to catch my breath before the other fully formed bambarúto swings at me with one claw and then clobbers me with the other when I dodge. It's standing over me, wide mouth splayed into a toothy, horrific grin, when a small brown hand explodes through it, splattering me with more black ichor. The creature shrieks and whirls around, flinging Chela, with her arm still shoved through its midsection, toward me.

"Starting to get the hang of these powers!" she says, managing a slight smile in spite of looking like hell and being covered in creature goo. "They're already coming in . . . handy."

I want to cheese with her, but I'm too busy being happy she's alive and . . . the bambarúto is wounded—mortally, I'm sure—but it's still got some fight left. Plus, the phantom ones are closing in from all sides now, and Vedo and Anisette have finally recovered and both have blades drawn, raised to kill.

I look at Chela, glowing brightly with a ferocious effervescence as she pulls her bloody hand from the creature and nods at me with a glance toward the skylight.

The only way out is down.

I run forward to meet her embrace and launch us both, along with the bleeding bambarúto, off the concrete, into the air.

Glass explodes around us, and then we're supposed to plummet— the creature will cushion our landing and then we'll collect ourselves and rejoin the fight.

But that's not what happens. As soon as the skylight shatters, the world around us vanishes. . . .

And we're surrounded by warm wind and water and the fresh smell of the ocean.

CHAPTER FORTY-THREE

WITH ONE THING THE WORLD BEGINS.

———◆———

We are not old, but we have been around a very, very long time when we begin to understand ourselves, know our own ways and rhythms.

———◆———

We are of the ocean, like all things, but we are also of heaven.

When the waves churn, we know that song; it is a part of us.

And we know the slow dance of clouds across a magnificent sky.

———◆———

Once, torn and wounded, we flitted over the foamy sea, barely alive, side by side, and fading, both fading.

This is how we remember ourselves.

This is how we become what we are.

One thing. A sanctuary.

You, creator, destroyer, bind and brandish, you wield the rocks and soil, from nothing pull the essence of this earth, and in your sparkling hands, a new world is born.

Three peaks rise over the waves.

The land formation entangles, then traps the thing that pursues us, finally binds it beneath the sea. And we are free.

Free, and we spread out side by side in the wavering tall grass of this strange new island.

Slowly, lovingly, I heal you. Restore vitality to your aching heart, run my sparkling hands along your contours to find the breaking points, the damage; soothe to a stop each hemorrhage and ache.

You watch as I close my own torn shimmering skin, and then we hold each other as countless suns set and moons rise, and this small world grows and grows around us.

One thing.

But will it hold? The demon beneath the island grows restless, tests its boundaries daily.

We surge out over the water again until we find flames rising from a boat, humans escaping in a small raft. So desperate to survive, they've forgotten that they were supposed to kill each other; their only notion is to flee. No gold can replace life.

Their skin is burnt and torn, ligaments shredded, bones broken.

Silent, invisible, I mend them.

Ablaze with light, you guide them.

Three peaks appear over the waves as they approach—our home is now theirs.

We find more people—the desperate and dangerous—the barely alive but so full of life.

We whisper our stories in songs while they sleep. They bring their own spirits, and we mingle and churn; new tapestries shift and reveal themselves in the night sky above the city that now rests in the rocky embankment of this new island.

Together we grow.

And as a tiny civilization rises, so do we.

Once, a couple offers their bodies to us to feel, just for a few hours, what it means to inhabit flesh again, and within their skin, we find a new love.

You—angel of creation, angel of destruction, shining light over a stormy sea, an unrelenting warrior at my side against that ancient giant.

Tongue made of fire.

A thousand swords, your wings.

I can't make something from nothing, not like you, but I become the light in each strum against strings, the *clack* of the clave, the wild *thump* of each drumbeat that calls to the blood, thunders through the heart, raises the spirit to dance, to heal.

Each scar a story.

———◆———

For you, I usher whole new musics into this sparkling world, new dances, new stories to call your name, to sing your praise, to try to make sense of the eternal rumba that is the way you move through me, with me, inside me.

They call this music *kama*—the dagger. Because it was named for you, burakadóra.

Through their tongues, the tongues they sing, whisper, and shout with, make love with, we gift each other names.

I sing one for you into their ears as they play songs of adoration—a word poem from the Santeros: *Heart, way. One, dream. Okan, Ala.*

One. The one that begins, the one that ends, yes.

But also my one. The one I come tumbling back to, at the end of each song.

———◆———

They come up with their own name to go with it. Madrigal—a refuge. Madrigal, the Creator.

You reconstruct an ancient bawdy love ballad into a praise hymn, slide it into their throats as they heal, and when they are in need, they call me: *Avrix mi Galanika.*

When we wander each to our battles and villainies out in the world, we call each other home, gently, fiercely:

Return to me, my love,

Through stars and burning cities,

Awake, my love. The dawn approaches.

Change is water, seeps through the strongest frontiers.

Ocean crashes on these rocky shores, stains crumbling facades, sends that salty smell through white-curtained windows into wide-open rooms where lovers sleep.

Awake and we rise.

As one, we rise, but distinct.

One thing.

———◆———

My love.

Our love.

One thing.

———◆———

A crash and the sudden warfare of a storm, as we are born and reborn.

With one thing

the world ends.

CHAPTER FORTY-FOUR

An ancient laughter echoes around us as the ocean world begins to dissolve.

Soon we will be back in that plummet, that chaos, but not yet. Not yet.

Right now, in this place between past and present, this niche within the world, outside of time, it is just us.

I take her in my arms, and she wraps hers around me.

Our bodies shake, and I don't know whether it's with laughter or sobs.

I don't have to ask if she saw it, too. She was there, has always been there, by my side, as my partner, lover, sometimes commander and other times rival, warrior twin, inspiration, teacher, student, and savior. Hers is the body my hands learned to heal on, the spirit that found mine in the void and pulled me back.

She takes my face in her hands, brings it to hers, and we pause as starlight dances all around, we pause.

"Just hold right here," she whispers. "Let me feel you in this moment."

I nod. Then, because I can't contain it. "You're both! It's been you, all along."

She smiles, a sunrise in the middle of this impossible night between worlds.

"Did you know?" I ask.

Shakes her head. "But I do now."

"It's not over. Not yet."

"I know."

"Don't leave me, Chela, Okanla, Madrigal."

"I haven't yet, have I?"

And then, with a *whoosh*, we're plummeting once again. Starlight becomes shattered glass that cascades all around us.

The bambarúto grunts and flails before it smashes through the wooden stage in Tolo's club with an explosion of snapping planks and splinters. We fall through the dust clouds and land in a tangled heap on the creature's bleeding carcass.

Chela launches herself up before I can even take in what's happening. She smashes her fist into another bambarúto, hurling it backward in a mass of suddenly hemorrhaging flesh and shrieks.

We're in the basement. The stock-still golems towering around us make it impossible to get a full glimpse of what we're up against, but I can see at least five or six fully incarnated bambarúto stomping through the shadows amid a handful of empire pirates. Yells and footsteps echo across this dark hall, the desperate scuffle of confusion.

Directly above us, the ruptured stage lets in a shaft of light from the main club, and a little farther away, another hole in the ceiling illuminates a pile of rubble.

I place my hands over the bambarúto's corpse and pull all its injuries into me as an eerie, chaotic song rises. I recognize that melody—it's the one that my ancestor scribbled over and over on the key-code partitur.

But there's no time to untangle why.

These damages will have to do, since I'm not about to bring the creature back to life.

Chela stomps on the one she just smashed and then turns to me, her face a question.

Her sword! I'd completely forgotten. My hands are empty. "I . . ."

She glares. "You, what, forgot about it?"

"I must've dropped it as we were plummeting through a few centuries of memories!"

A bambarúto charges out of the shadows. I sidestep and unleash a swath of broken bambarúbones into its back as it rushes past.

"Well, find it!" Chela yells, backstepping as five burly guys advance on her.

The bambarúto stumbles and shrieks but doesn't fall—it renews its attack with a whole new rage.

"Don't you have your little dagger thing?"

"Why would I bring a little dagger thing when I have a big fancy sword, *Mateo*?" She blocks the first guy, spins him to the ground, takes his hand, and holds it up for the others to see. Then she literally crushes it to pulp while he screams.

"Whoa!" I dodge a swipe from the bambarúto's claw. "I mean . . . doesn't seem like you need a sword that much, is all I'm saying."

"Mateo," Chela growls.

"I'll find it! I'll find it!" I duck another claw attack, then let a wave of crushed creature organs surge through my hand and into the bambarúto. It drops to its knees, and I Spartan-kick it in the face, collapsing it.

Which is all well and good, but more are closing in around me, and I don't know how many times I can hurt and heal and hurt again before the net result is just a lot of pissed-off bambarúto.

What's more, I thought Chela's whole hand-crushing thing would scare those guys away, but it just got them more furious.

Chela and I back toward each other, facing down our respective enemies, and somehow it feels like old times. I wonder fleetingly if spirits can die when they take mortal form. Then I realize things could actually be much worse for us if we *can't* die, depending on how all this goes down.

And then something long and sharp whizzes from the darkness and plunges directly into the thigh of an approaching bambarúto, and Baba Johnny Afrá's raspy laughter seems like it's coming from all around us.

"Ha!" the old Santero yells, stepping out of the shadows and pulling his cane—which I see has a steely, sharpened point—from the fallen creature. "Keep calling Death and Death will answer, hmm? Heh-heh-heh!"

"Baba Johnny!" Chela and I both yell. He whacks the writhing creature once, then again, and a stream of people pour in behind him.

Tams! Maza! Tolo and Safiya! Iya Lisa and Oba Nelson! At least ten or fifteen more! They're all armed with machetes and clubs and look ready for a fight. They surge into the ranks of empire pirates and bambarúto with a vicious battle cry.

"You didn't think we'd let you guys have *all* the fun, did you?" Tams laughs in my ear as we quickly hug and then turn back to fighting.

"I . . . Tía Lucia," I choke out, because her loss suddenly overwhelms me, burns through everything else happening.

Tams shakes her head, blinks away tears. "I heard. The empire pirates were trying to take out the whole Cabildo with some hired goons. Rabbi Hidalgo captured a couple who came for him and forced them to lead him to where they were keeping prisoners. He . . . found her body there. I'm so, so sorry, Mateo."

"I . . ." There's nothing to say. Well, there's too much to say, and no time to say it. "I have so many things to tell you."

"Then stay alive," Tams says. "So we can compare notes when this is all over. Damn."

"Less talking, more murdering people who are trying to kill us!" Bonsignore yells, whooshing past us with a sharpened lacrosse stick and smashing some random guy in the face. He collapses with a yelp, and the gym teacher pauses, suddenly stricken. "Shit. He wasn't on our side, was he?"

"Reckless," Tams says. "But no, that was one of the goons."

And then we're fighting again, swiping, blocking, dodging, backing each other up.

Chela flits in and out of various fights, crushing random body parts when the enemy least expects it.

And for a few moments, it seems like we're actually getting the upper hand, even though they have the numbers and huge creatures.

But only Chela and I can do much damage to the fully incarnated bambarúto, and even with all we have, it takes a lot to bring one down for good. Especially, as Chela reminds me more than once, without her sword. Both of us are still new to our powers.

Everyone just tries to stay out of the way, but Safiya charges one and takes a claw across her face, and then Tolo goes down trying to pull her away.

Neither one is dead, but the remaining empire pirates swarm to where they fell, and it suddenly seems like we're going to lose two of our best leaders at once.

"Break through the crowd!" Tams yells, and she and Baba Johnny charge side by side into the thick of things.

Chela and I have a trio of bambarúto cornered, but they keep slashing out and it's impossible to get a good angle to finish any off.

"I need to get to my cousin," she huffs between stabs and blocks. "And this situation won't hold."

I nod and send one of my last shards of hurt into the closest bambarúto. We break toward the swarming masses, but it's too late: the empire pirates have pulled out Tolo, bloodied but alive, and now Anisette Bisconte stands beside him with a blade to his throat.

Everything stops.

The councilwoman laughs, then sighs. "It didn't have to be this way, you know."

"Don't . . . stop . . . fighting . . ." Tolo grunts.

Anisette shoves the blade into his flesh, just enough to draw blood. "Quiet, thug."

Chela goes to rush in, but I grab her arm and whisper, "Wait."

"No, *you* wait!" Anisette snaps. Then she sags, knife still shoved up against Tolo's neck. "None of this was supposed to be this way! None of it! This fool should've died like his fool father. You two assholes should've listened to Gerval when he tried to talk to you about all this! You should've listened! He listened to me—why couldn't you listen to him?"

A thought has been building inside me. Something I can't quite put my finger on. "The bambarúto," I say into Chela's ear. "What if . . . What if it isn't your destroyer powers they are feeding off of?"

"I had everything set," Anisette complains. "Everything!"

Intentionality, Tía Lucia had said. But that can go in both directions, I figure. If they knew she had dual powers, the enemy could've used both, even if she herself didn't know. . . .

"Mateo . . ." Chela says, but it comes out as more of a snarl. It's clear her whole body is aching to bring down all her wrath on the councilwoman's head. But we both know Tolo wouldn't survive if she did. She softens. "What do you mean?"

"Here's what's going to happen," Anisette says, a little tremor in her voice, though she's obviously trying to keep her cool. "You all are going to put down your weapons, and you're going to do it now, hmm?"

"I mean . . . you are both, right?" I whisper to Chela. "Destroyer *and* creator. You've only just figured out how to destroy, but what if you—"

Chela stops me with a raised finger. Her eyes meet mine, and then we both gaze at the towering stone figure beside us.

"Hmm," Chela says.

CHAPTER FORTY-FIVE

CHELA PUTS ONE HAND AGAINST THE GOLEM, CLOSES HER EYES, and . . .

Nothing.

Crap.

She opens one eye and grimaces. Gives the statue a little kick.

"I thought for sure you—" I start.

The statue rumbles and then surges to life with a deep, sonorous growl.

Chela points at Anisette. "That one."

"Ah, but wai—" is all Anisette can get out before the magnificent stone monster barrels toward her. Tolo leaps out of the way just in time. There's a terrible crunching sound—there won't be much left of the councilwoman, I'm sure—and then the golem rises, brushes some gore off itself, and leaps into battle.

Everything explodes into motion at the same time. Bambarúto charge. Tams and Maza pull Tolo to safety, and a few of our pirates grab Safiya. Baba Johnny cackles, leaping back into the thick of it. Chela starts running from golem to golem, activating a whole army of giants around us and directing their efforts. And then the fighting rages at full tilt as pirates, Santeros, Sefaradim, and monsters clash in the shadows of this vast hall.

I'm back in the middle of the melee, side by side with Chela and Tams, beating away a surge of hired goons, when Tams says, "Destroyer and creator, huh?" and Chela nods with a slight smile. "And you." My best friend turns her wily glare to me. "Galanika."

I raise my eyebrows. "You've been watching closely, huh?"

She scoffs. "Doesn't take much. It's not like anything is subtle these days."

"Well . . ."

"One question, though." Tams prods her bat into the face of some barfly who stumbled too close, then finishes him off with a quick swipe.

"What's that?" Chela says.

"There were always three gods of the island, no? From the beginning. The three peaks, all that. So, if you're both San Madrigal and Okanla . . . And, Mateo, you're Galanika . . ."

"Uh . . ." I say, not liking where this is going one bit but not sure why.

"Who is the third spirit of San Madrigal?"

"Maybe there were just two all along," I say.

A tumble of stone answers as a tall figure rises from the dust clouds around the pile of debris a few feet away.

"Wrong," Gerval says, drawing Chela's sword and smiling with a thousand pointy teeth. "*I* am Vizvargal, the third god of Madrigal and true ruler of this broken world."

CHAPTER FORTY-SIX

All I can think about? Chela.

I know. Makes no sense, not really.

There's an evil god/demon/thing about to kill us and also, I'm some kind of god, too, and oh yeah, so is Chela. *Two*, in fact! Shoot. But most important, we're going to die. We've come all this way and for what? So I can be lovestruck when I most need to keep my head in the game?

But look—Chela stands beside me. Her shoulders rise and fall with breaths that are supposed to be keeping her calm. She's trained her whole life for this moment, with Tolo and Moses and Safiya and the crew. She's a literal angel of destruction, only just now coming to truly understand her powers, and I know one thing: she must make it out of this alive.

She already tried to give herself up once for the cause; I'm not letting it happen again.

I'm not letting anyone else die, either, dammit. I don't know how yet, but I make that silent promise to myself in the seconds of quiet we have before all hell breaks loose.

"We got the others!" Tams yells, and smashes into whatever's left of the enemy lines with Maza at her side. "You guys get whatever Gerval turned into!"

I'm glad the two of them found love during this nightmare, too. I want them to walk away safe and sound so we can all look back on this one day and smile.

"I remember!" Gerval—or *Vizvargal*, I guess—yells in a freakish, otherworldly howl.

Vizvargal is the name ol' Archibaldo transcribed into a melody over and over. That's the demon god all these empire pirates have been secretly worshiping this whole time. I watch in horror as another set of arms unfolds from his back. He takes a step out of the rubble, swinging Chela's blade to get a feel for it.

"Hey, how come *we* didn't get a second set of arms?" I hiss.

Chela shushes me.

"I remember it all now!" He moves his now-glowing red eyes between Chela and me. "The chase, the battle, your trap. It was you two who woke me up, so I should thank you. I was so confused, trying to make sense of so many things when I didn't have all the pieces."

Well, that's one thing I can relate to, although in a totally different way.

"It was vote night when I finally became awakened," he goes on. "That's when it all started coming back to me for real. Before that, it was just tantalizing dreams—hazy, impossible moments. But that night was just the beginning. I was only getting started." He directs a ferocious glare right at me. "Do you remember, Galanika?"

I have no snappy retort to that, and the truth—*I kinda do*—doesn't really seem like something you say in this situation. So, I just lean down and casually slide my hands along the broken body of the nearest bambarúto and suck in its injuries. I don't know how much good it'll do—if human wounds don't do a whole lot to these creatures, who knows what it'll take to hurt a god. But it's worth a try.

"I remember, too," Chela says, breaking into a run toward him. "I remember whupping your ass into the bottom of the ocean."

He screeches and she leaps, and suddenly I remember, too—the swirl of wind, salt water sparkling our spirit forms as we waited and then pounced, the shrill sound of the giant's scream as the trap sprang and he was sucked into the deep. I remember the way Okanla/San Madrigal pulled layer after layer of earth, rock, mountain out of the ether to pile on top of him until those three peaks rose out of the water and she was almost completely spent.

Gerval stops Chela in midair now, one hand wrapping around her neck, and I know he's going to swing that blade and end everything in a second, before I even have a chance to fight him.

Instead, she grabs his forearm with both hands and obliterates it.

"Hraaaaaaaagh!" Gerval shrieks, and blood gushes from his stump.

I thought I'd lost her forever that night over the ocean, the night she created what became San Madrigal and trapped a demon beneath its might. She was just . . . empty when it was all over. Just a flickering, almost-nothing shroud.

I didn't lose her then, and I won't lose her now.

Chela goes to finish him off, reaching for his head with both hands, but he's fast and powerful, even in agony, and he swats her away with his bleeding stump. I'm there before he can recover, though, pouring every last bit of hurt I can out of my fingertips into his writhing body.

Gerval hollers, stumbling back one step, and another. Then he bursts out laughing as his arm bubbles and regenerates itself in a hideous, festering explosion of flesh.

"You *don't* remember, I see!" Gerval jeers.

Chela's beside me, wiping blood off her lip, and we spread to either side of him, bracing for the next move.

"You were just as ignorant back then as you are now. You thought you could contain me! Ha! I am unstoppable. I can't be buried, can't be burned, can't be stopped. Can empire be stopped? Never! I am progress, commerce, the movement of brilliant minds across the globe! Do you not see that, you foolish children? You buried me for centuries, thought you could convince your people to forget me, thought you could force amnesia on them and lock me out forever with your little love songs and boleros. Ha!"

He lashes out so suddenly neither of us have time to make sense of it. He feints toward Chela and then slaps me hard across the face when I lunge for him. I skitter backward, rubbing my cheek and healing myself instantly, and fling the injury back at him. I'm shaken, though. He's too fast, and we're running out of moves.

"I have my own songs," Gerval gurgles. "And I whispered them night after night to anyone who would listen. And they did listen, you know? They were hungry for my music. I gathered my children to me, and I didn't need many. It never takes many. Just a few, a handful of devotees who will do what needs to be done. Soon I had them set up trade partnerships, and I summoned my children—the ones you call bambarúto—to inhabit the darkest crevices of your little sanctuary. And then warfare broke out, again and again and again."

He swings at Chela, and she's ready this time. She leans out of the blade's reach and then springs at him, her hands pummeling sheer devastation across his chest.

"Uh-uh-uh," Gerval chides, dancing away from her as Chela lands in a pivot and makes a grab for his sword hand. She skids toward me, and I reach out, steadying her. "They tried to suppress me forever, you know? After the great Madrigal War, the elders decided to banish all memories and mementos that bore my name and divided the spirit Madrigal into two opposite parts to keep their precious trinity intact. But my true believers kept on as they do now and will forevermore. You can't suppress this power. All that did, all that ever does, is strengthen the resolve of my children, remind them of their sacred and secret duty."

That must have been when the island elders divided Okanla and San Madrigal into two gods in the lore. Tolo said there were no written records before 1810. They probably destroyed them all to banish this powerful entity from the histories.

"I need that sword," Chela says, panting. "Otherwise . . ."

I know what she's thinking, what she wants to do. She's seen how I use my power, what I'm capable of. And I don't know how to stop her.

And then, very suddenly, it doesn't matter what either of us wants anymore. Gerval spots Tams pulling Tolo toward the door. They're only a few feet away, trying to slip past while he's distracted.

There's a glint in Gerval's bright red eyes as he spins toward them. Chela yells, "No!" and breaks into a run.

I can see everything that's about to happen. It's very simple— Gerval was never going to waste a swipe on Tolo when his real target was closing in at warp speed.

Chela knows it, too. The prophecy still echoes through her. She'll sacrifice her life to take the sword, and then she'll leave it to me to snatch her death and use it against him. I know because she turns just as she reaches Gerval, and her eyes lock with mine . . .

Then they open wide with surprise.

She didn't know how close behind her I'd be.

I lift Chela and throw her out of the way just as Gerval lunges forward with a vicious stab of the blade.

I close my eyes, turn inward. I want to feel every second of this, to memorize each beat, each breath.

The sword slams through my skin, enters my stomach, rises,

shredding through my liver, my lungs; blood seeps and spurts from organs in its wake; the blade doesn't stop until its tip punctures the bottommost chamber of my heart.

An impossible void opens across the world and begins to devour it.

I don't need my hands for this.

My own song rises. Galanika's song. It's not just one, but so, so many—hundreds of songs birthed within me over centuries as thousands of voices lifted in praise, despair, hope, uncertainty, love. As rumbas, boleros, ballads, prayers simmered through the night and greeted the dawn.

Arise.

All those sounds, all those lights. They mingle with a wailing noise—Chela's sorrowful cry behind me. They form shining threads that wind within me as the abyss of death blots out the world. The threads race down my arms and out through my fingertips.

———◆———

One.

———◆———

One thing. Life, death, love, hate. One.

———◆———

The abyss covers everything . . .

———◆———

. . . and then slips . . .

———◆———

. . . across that tiny spot of air between where I end . . .

. . . and Gerval begins.

My eyes fly open. I'm face-to-face with Gerval. He blinks at me once, mouth hanging wide open in shock, and then emptiness eclipses the light in his eyes and his head falls back.

My death—the death of a god—transferred to him. That's all it took.

One last pulse of blood shivers up his throat.

He drops to his knees. Collapses forward in a heap.

Done.

"Mateo!" Chela is all around me, her eyes searching my body. Her hands find my face and then she pulls me close. "You . . . you're . . ."

I nod, which is all I can manage while inside everything slowly slides back into place, wounds mend, blood swirls home.

"I'm alive," I finally croak.

"You . . ."

I smile. "We."

CHAPTER FORTY-SEVEN

"THERE WAS A MOMENT . . ." RABBI HIDALGO'S VOICE BOOMS ACROSS the sky, laughing and sorrowful at once, just like us. "Well, it was a few hundred years, hmm? But still, a moment—back during Muslim rule of Spain—when Jews, Muslims, and Christians lived together in some kind of harmony. We call it La Convivencia, and it probably wasn't quite as ideal as all that."

We're cleaning up, sweeping glass, helping each other stand, pouring coffee from steaming thermoses into waiting paper cups. We're trading jokes and gawking at all the damage in disbelief. We're checking hastily scribbled lists of the dead and wounded, praying our loved ones aren't on it, knowing some will be, because we love many, and so many have been hurt.

"There were still massacres, forced conversions, street battles," Rabbi Hidalgo goes on, still laughing, still heartbroken, just like us. "And yet, compared to the brutality that happened before it, and the brutality that came after, when we were murdered by the tens of thousands and banished into the wilds, well . . . it must've seemed like a kind of paradise, to some at least."

We look up at the makeshift stage where he stands, chuckle to one another, our eyes meet, we sigh and shrug and keep cleaning, keep listening.

"And then some of us landed at Madrigal, and we thought: Here, on this strange island in the Caribbean Sea, is La Convivencia, perhaps. Here it is reborn, but with a different trinity, a new harmony, and"—the rabbi's big cheeks rise, his whole face a squint, to indicate a joke is imminent—"better weather, of course!"

We groan and roll our eyes and giggle anyway, nudging one another and shaking our heads, and deep down, we're still breathless with relief that we made it through that chaos, that hell, that the bat of some empire pirate didn't shatter us, no knives found our veins and opened them. We're still here, and so we'll tolerate any amount of dad jokes from Rabbi Hidalgo.

Of course he swings immediately serious again, because the man has range. "But like so many of the stories we tell ourselves about ourselves, that one was a lie, too, even if most of us didn't know the full extent of that lie until a week ago."

Muttered agreements, sighs, anger. The long *shhhhk* of a broom pushing shattered glass over concrete. The anxious gossip of pigeons watching from the train tracks above. A shuddering sense of loss.

"La Convivencia will always be a lie," Rabbi Hidalgo declares. "And La Convivencia will always be true, will always be with us. It's not a whole society, it doesn't last centuries, it's not even one small city on a tiny doomed island. No. But we re-create it in each moment that we choose to, hmm? It is right here, right in front of me, as we clean up, heal, mourn. Most of all, as we love. It will be with us tomorrow, when we decide, together, what to do next, what this new chapter in our history will look like. When we decide to tell the truth even though it hurts like hell."

With nods and shouts of *Amen* and *Aché* and *Eso es.*

"We'll be something brand-new, going forward. And it's scary.

But I know this: we have two badass angels at our back, watching over us. They're not trapped by false histories or the lies we used to tell ourselves. They're not scared of a fight. They're warriors, they're outlaws, and they're only just beginning to discover who they really are, just like we are only just beginning to find ourselves as a people in this brand-new day. We are still just learning our name!"

We stop what we're doing.

"Let's join with these brand-new and very ancient outlaw angels of creation and destruction, and let's create a new language, a new future, together!"

We stand side by side, arm in arm, broken and confused and wary but very much alive, and ready, ever ready, for all that lies ahead.

EPILOGUE

THE OCEAN AIR SURROUNDS US, BUT THIS TIME IT'S THE REAL OCEAN, not a vision, not a spirit memory swirling up from afar.

Chela smiles at me from across the motorboat. The sun dances across her face, shines along the contours of the lapping waves. I feel it on my own skin, a gentle blessing. It's been only a few days, but we're so far from that chilly Brooklyn night now.

After I killed Gerval—Vizvargal—the remaining bambarúto didn't shrivel up or explode like monsters in movies do when the hero kills the evil final boss. They just lashed out harder in one final push and then broke for the tunnels along with whichever empire pirates hadn't been killed or captured.

Vedo got away. I'm not even sure if he was in the basement for that final battle. No one's seen him or any of the others since.

And then there were bodies to gather, wounds to heal. Funerals had to be held, long sighs released, along with tears and laughter and moments of shock. My parents came home, and there were weird, impossible explanations to make and long, strange nights trying to help them understand (they couldn't).

Tolo hooked us up with one of his smuggling boats and a crew every bit as eccentric and menacing as you'd imagine them to be. We headed south along the coast, past Florida. The weather warmed, and we swept deep into the Caribbean, laughing over songs and stories under the stars at night, trying to catch up on reading to make sense of this all during the day.

That gash down my face, it won't heal. I already knew that. But I didn't expect to find myself smiling whenever I catch myself in the mirror. It reminds me of what happened, who I am, the power that's within me. I'm still a long way from figuring out a lot of that power, but there's time.

Grief ripples through me constantly, but I know my aunts wanted me to live—to thrive—and I'm trying my best.

Chela's smile makes it a lot easier.

We pull our eyes from each other and gaze at the horizon, because it's coming. We both can feel it. We headed off from the yacht about an hour ago and let our sense guide us, that pull. It's indescribable and unmistakable. Madrigal's siren song.

I kill the motor, and we drift.

There's just ocean and sky, ocean and sky, and then something else: a dark spot emerges from the sea and then two more alongside it.

I shake my head, realize I'm crying.

Suddenly, Chela's holding my hand. "I just . . ." she says, tears streaming down her face.

"Didn't think it was real, somehow," I finish, and she nods.

The ocean, the sky, three small peaks cresting the waves . . . and then, a memory.

It's another morning, fifteen years ago. Still dark, dawn creeping at the edges of the world.

Everything was in place. After existing for so long as spirits, we would finally walk the earth as humans. Our human bodies had already been born—it wasn't a matter of taking over an existing being so much as merging with one we were already a part of. The ceremony would complete the oneness.

It would be a strange relief, like falling into ourselves. A becoming. Also, we had both been weakening over the past year, ever since our incarnated forms had been born. It was a strange kind of love moving through us now, love like fading. It would be alarming if we didn't know it just meant the dawn of a new era.

In the Santero temple on top of the far westerly peak, all the sacred implements were laid out on a mat: various jars of things, food for the spirits, feathers, a pair of scissors. The community gathered, everyone dressed all in white, excitement rising. Iya Lucia hushed the room and ushered in two nervous people, one cradling a baby.

They placed the baby on the mat in front of Iya Lucia, and she sprinkled water on him, her lips moving in a quiet prayer. The ceremony had begun.

Good.

Down the mountainside we surged, the excitement of all that was about to happen burning through us.

We will hold each other again. The thought was like a living thing between us, ferocious. *We will rebirth the world in each other's arms, flesh to flesh, a new day. It is time.*

On the middle peak, in a hidden chamber known only to pirates, a smaller ceremony had already begun.

Hooded figures gathered in the darkness, their faces barely lit by the flickering candles each one held. The ocean seemed to swell and sing as Si Baracasa began chanting, a tiny baby in his arms. She was alert, face dead serious and wary, ancient eyes gazing up into her uncle's.

"Something's happening," a hooded woman whispered to him. "I must find out." And she was gone before he could object.

This is not right. We knew it in the fullness of our beings, the strange prickling that careened suddenly through us.

We followed. Weakening, ever weakening as the moment of our incarnation drew closer, we followed.

Mimi Baracasa stood in the muted twilight, head bowed.

She felt us. She did not see us, but she knew we were there. Eyes closed, she raised one hand to the sky.

To us.

Her whole body thrummed with what this meant, what she needed. Fear rippled through her, but deeper than that, something had finally broken. A wall she had built many years before now lay in shambles.

Whatever it was that did it, she had made a decision. And she wanted—needed—us to follow.

A moment's pause, the air heavy with hints of rain and the salt of the sea.

Then Mimi Baracasa slipped silently down a rocky embankment to the base of the eastern peak. The waves crashed, sprayed foam and tiny droplets into the air; the day was only beginning to break around her as she heaved a small boulder aside and climbed into yet another hidden chamber, this one unknown even to most pirates.

Unknown even to us, and we had made this island.

We followed. We followed along a dank corridor, then upward into an open cavern. She felt us with her; it brought a tiny, fleeting warmth to her pounding heart.

A single candle lit the hall; the shadows could've gone on for miles for all we knew. Many creatures lurked in that murky darkness. We could feel them, their shrill hunger, their idle impatient twitches and rumbles. Their breath hot and heavy.

Most of these beings were not made of air and spirit matter like us. They were flesh and blood, horrific impossibilities, creatures of nightmares and cursework. Bambarúto, of course, and other things, too. Worse things.

And all of them held a singular focus: the small circle of hooded figures that Mimi Baracasa joined in the center of the cavern.

One was just a toddler; he held tight to Mimi once she found her spot. Then the chanting began: *Vizvargal*, they called in an off-kilter melody. *Vizvargal*.

Before we could react, the whole island rumbled. A pale greenish glow filled the chamber, glinting dimly off horns and beady eyes, gnashing teeth and long claws.

They're destroying the barrier. Your whispered voice seared through me. *The whole island will crumble and release the demon.*

Vizvargal, they chanted, relentless. *Vizvargal*.

Everyone will die. The truth sizzled around us, our own terrified thoughts. *Even these maniacs. And the demon will rise.*

"What have you done?" a woman's voice shrieked from the darkness. The chanting persisted. Mimi stepped back as a figure emerged, pulling down her cowl. "What the hell have you done?" Anisette Bisconte demanded. "What intruders have you summoned to this sacred place?"

"I'm done. I'm done, and I'm shutting it all down. We can't do this." Mimi stopped retreating, and the two women stood face-to-face. "I don't care what you do to me. This must end."

Anisette let out a raspy laugh. "There's no ending it, Mimi. You should know that, after all the years you've been around. This is destiny. It was always going to be this way. And the two pathetic spirits you've led here can't do anything about it."

Vizvargal, the circle continued to chant. *Vizvargal*.

Another pale green glow opened up deeper in the shadows, and the snarling cackle of an old man came trickling out. "It begins!" he shrieked. "Vizvargal rises!"

No.

It was your voice that suddenly took over the sky with a thunderclap. A drenched wind whipped through the cavern, beating against this small army of creatures and empire pirates. This was what you and I had been summoned for. To stop a terrible destiny.

"Okanla has called forth a hurricane! She's trying to push the barrier deeper and trap our lord and master!" Anisette yelled. "You did this!" She shoved Mimi into the darkness, and chaos erupted all around.

Screams and footsteps and curses, and amidst it all, a small, mis-shapen sphere of flesh dropped and rolled across the floor toward that feverish green light.

"The child!" Anisette commanded. "It must be the child!"

The toddler followed the sphere, slipping easily between the rushing bodies, his tiny feet splashing through the dark puddles.

As if pulled by an invisible thread, the ball of flesh bounced once, then again before landing in a shivering, emaciated hand reaching out from a small altar.

The boy didn't hesitate. Even as we reached out to stop him, he leaped into the lap of an ancient, shriveled old man—more corpse than living thing but still moving, those rotted eyes glancing around, jaw hanging open in an eternal silent scream.

The boy reached for the sphere. The old man held it away, laughing in a shrill, guttural howl.

Three fully formed bambarúto blocked our way, bristling at the knowledge of our presence.

Sirens howled outside the cavern as the wind picked up even more.

Water coursed through the darkness.

The corpse man relented; the child snatched the sphere of flesh and hungrily devoured it.

A hooded figure then grabbed the child, who was now scream-ing at an inhuman pitch, his tiny body contorting.

The bambarúto stepped toward the corpse man, obscuring that heinous green glow.

"Sister Anisette," the man's crinkly voice called as the bambarúto closed in around him. "You know what you must do."

"I won't fail you," Anisette Bisconte yelled over the child's shrieks. "This I swear, Maestro Medina." With a grinding thud, the bambarúto sealed the old man within their circle like a fleshy ichorous coffin. More water gushed into the cave as man, woman, and beast fled.

And for us, there was only one thing left to do.

We blitzed through the cavern, then up, up, up into the storm-torn sky.

Down below, the evacuation was already underway, and the other two ceremonies were wrapping up.

Our gazes locked.

The storm raged—your storm—and soon it would take over everything. There was nothing left of either of us—already we were sinking, then plummeting toward our human forms, our memories stripped away. . . . And you, my love, warrior of this world and the next, used your last gasp of consciousness to send a final thrust of power into the storm that was quickly devouring the world. The gigantic monster we had faced so long ago would be crushed beneath the sinking island, but its essence had slipped free.

We would have to find it and destroy it as humans, but to do that we'd have to rediscover who we were.

I held you close, our spirit forms merging one last time. Felt the familiar gentle grace of your presence inhabiting the same space as mine, that love.

And then the wind seemed to swallow us, and we were nowhere at all.

—◆—

A rumble and a splash pull me back to this world, this time.

Your head is on my shoulder; we're both crying.

"All those creatures," I whisper.

"She . . . We . . ." You smile, then finally find it—"I"—and shake your head. "Still getting used to this, who we are."

"Same," I say, laughing through tears.

"I used my essence to create the island, so its every speck of dirt holds the seed of creation."

"That's why so many spirits and monsters are able to take shape there."

You nod.

"So, when we raise it, they'll all be waiting? *He'll* be there?"

You shrug, smile a little, wipe your eyes. "You ready to take on your own great-great-whatever-great-grandfather and his hordes of monsters?"

I laugh, still crying some. "Please. I've probably been waiting for centuries to do exactly that."

"Good. Then we'll face them like this." You stretch your hand out over the water.

I do, too; our fingers entwine.

I catch your eye, and we're both smiling now, smiling uncontrollably. "Together," I whisper.

Up ahead, the three peaks of San Madrigal once again surge toward the sky.

GLOSSARY

The people of San Madrigal speak a mix of Spanish, English, Ladino, and Lucumí. Here are a few words you'll find in the pages of *Ballad & Dagger*.

Abuela Spanish. Grandmother.

Aché Cuban Spanish. The animating life force of the world. The power to make things happen. Also used as a strong affirmative, giving power to what has been said.

Así es Spanish. That's just what it is.

Así nos caemos Spanish. This is how we fall.

Bambarúto Ladino. A bogeyman said to roam the streets at night to scare children. From *pan barato* (cheap bread), the call of bakers roaming up and down the street to sell bread, their clothes blackened by the smoke from their ovens.

Bash Ladino. Boss, chief.

Bochinche Cuban Spanish. Gossip.

Burakadóra Ladino. Someone who pierces holes.

Chancla Spanish. Footwear favored by abuelas and tías; also a dangerous weapon.

Dobale Lucumí. To prostrate oneself in a traditional Lucumí salute.

Escuchar Spanish. To listen.

Fijika mia Ladino. Affectionate term for a daughter.

Kama The music of San Madrigal, from the Ladino word for dagger.

Kamero Players of kama.

Manseviko Ladino. Affectionate term for a young man.

Mariscos Spanish. Seafood.

M'ijo Spanish. My son.

Nunca vencido, nunca conquistado Spanish. Never defeated, never conquered. Official motto of San Madrigal.

Ocha Lucumí. The physical altar where the orishas are kept.

Pasteles Spanish. Delicious Cuban pastries.

Peluquería Spanish. Hair salon.

Puñeta Spanish. Puerto Rican curse word.

Sea espíritu Spanish. Be like a spirit, instructions for kameros from the old Maestro Archibaldo Coraje Medina.

Tía Spanish. Aunt.

ACKNOWLEDGMENTS

FIRST AND FOREMOST, THANK YOU TO THE GREAT, UNSTOPPABLE, and extremely generous soul Rick Riordan, who made this book possible, this dream come true. Rick, I have always admired and looked up to you from afar—both the stories you tell and the story of who you are, how you've moved in this messy world—and I'm honored beyond words to be part of this magnificent imprint. I so appreciate your input on this book and how you brought the best out of it and me.

Secondly, Stephanie Lurie, the living legend—you know this well, but let me tell the world how long I've wanted to work with you. *Ballad & Dagger* turned out to be just the right project for us to finally collaborate on, and it was definitely worth the wait! Thank you for all your insight and thoughtfulness along the way and for having my back through it all!

And many thanks to coeditor Rebecca Kuss—so happy you're on the team!

The whole crew at Hyperion has been magnificent: Guy Cunningham, Dan Kaufman, and Meredith Jones in copyediting;

Marybeth Tregarthen and Jerry Gonzalez in production; Holly Nagel, Dina Sherman, Andrew Sansone, and Kyle Wilson in marketing; Seale Ballenger in publicity; and the entire sales group. Special thanks to cover artist Irvin Rodriguez, map artist Virginia Allyn, and cover designer Phil Buchanan for bringing this world to life so stunningly!

Rabbi Devin Maimon Villareal read and evaluated *Ballad & Dagger* from a Sefaradic cultural lens and gave such thoughtful, brilliant feedback. I am so grateful for your wisdom, bigheartedness, and analysis, Rabbi, thank you! Of course, any mistakes here are very much my own.

I was also blessed with three early reads from incredible writers I admire deeply and am proud to call friends: Leigh Bardugo, Tracy Deonn, and Amerie. Their insightfulness and story-smarts really transformed this book and helped make it what it is. Thank you all!

Special shout-out to Leigh, who, after putting up with me texting her nine million variations of Saints of Ballads and Outlaws and Outlaw Dagger Angels, finally said, "What about just *Ballad & Dagger*?" And was right!!

Dr. Jorge Juan Rodríguez V was kind enough to talk through the world-building and historical aspects of the story with me very early on—a wonderful conversation that helped me make sense of it all.

Over the course of one long phone call while I walked the streets of New Orleans, Akissi Britton clarified and brought new depth to some key spiritual points in this book, hearing me out and sharing her own stories. She also provided the bulk of that stellar definition of aché—thank you, Ki!

And throughout this writing process, I turned to Brittany Williams, as I always do, whenever I needed to untangle a story knot, have a good laugh or cry, fix something that didn't make sense,

or just binge some good TV. Thank you, my love. You make my life and work better and so much fun! I love you.

Special thanks to my teacher and padrino Nelson "Poppy" Rodriguez, aka the greatest diviner in the galaxy, for his wisdom on odu and Lucumí tradition and guidance throughout!

Joanna Volpe is really a special person and agent, and she has been such a huge part of this book all along the way. I can't thank you enough for your support, your excellence, your energy, and your magic.

Thanks also to all the great folks at New Leaf, including Pouya Shahbazian, Jenniea Carter, Jordan Hill, Abigail Donoghue, and Meredith Barnes. Thank you all—no one in the business is doing it like you are.

And thanks to the most excellent hosts, Krystina Arielle and Kristin Baver!

To Tito, mi hijo, thank you for falling asleep on my chest while I got edits done. A young legend already. You came right on time for me to dedicate this book of my heart to you, my wonderful boy.

And thanks always to my whole amazing family: Brittany, Dora, Marc, Malka, Lou, Calyx, Paz, and Azul. Thanks to my godmoms Iya Lisa and Iya Ramona, and to Patrice, Emani, Darrell, Jair, April, Iyalocha Tima, and my whole Ile Omi Toki family for their support; also thanks to Baba Malik, Mama Akissi, Mama Joan, Tina, and Jud and all the wonderful folks of Ile Ase. Thanks also to Sam, Leigh, Sorahya, Akwaeke, and Lauren.

Baba Craig Ramos: We miss you and love you and carry you with us everywhere we go. Rest easy, Tío. Ibae bayen tonu.

I give thanks to all those who came before us and lit the way. I give thanks to all my ancestors; to Yemonja, Mother of Waters, whose asé I have proudly carried for more than ten years now; to gbogbo Orisha, and Olodumare.